NORTHLIGHT:
A Quiller Mission

D1098867

NORTHLIGHT:
A Quiller Mission

A STAR BOOK
published by
the Paperback Division of
W. H. ALLEN & Co. PLC

A Star Book
Published in 1986
by the Paperback Division of
W. H. Allen & Co. PLC
44 Hill Street, London W1X 8LB

First published in Great Britain by
W. H. Allen & Co. PLC, 1985

Copyright © Trevor Enterprises., 1985

Printed and bound in Great Britain by
Anchor Brendon Ltd, Tiptree, Essex

ISBN 0 352 31607 1

This book is sold subject to the condition that it
shall not, by way of trade or otherwise, be lent,
resold, hired out or otherwise circulated without
the publisher's prior consent in any form of binding
or cover other than that in which it is published and
without a similar condition including this condition
being imposed on the subsequent purchaser.

To Michalina

CONTENTS

1

RAIN

AT THE INTERSECTION from Sloane Street into Knightsbridge I put on speed when the lights changed to amber but it was a mistake because the flashing began in the mirror right away and I pulled into the curb and waited with the engine still running. I'd known the police car was behind me since I'd come through Sloane Square but I didn't think they'd make a fuss about jumping the lights on a filthy night like this; there'd been a freezing rain coming down since late afternoon and the streets were black and silver now under the lamps, with reflections across the surface and the gutters beginning to stream.

I let the window down and got out my driving licence to save time. *In my opinion, sir, you could have pulled up safely enough at the traffic lights when they changed to amber,* and so forth. It was a temptation to show him my bureau card and drive on again without having to go through all the bullshit but it's strictly against the rules if there's no actual emergency.

His face came into the window gap, with rain dripping from his cap peak.

'May I see your driving licence, please?'

I gave it to him, and he checked it.

'Thank you, Mr Gage. I just wanted to be sure who you were.' He handed it back. 'They'd like you to phone in, as soon as possible.'

Nothing to do with the lights.

'All right.' I put the licence away and got into gear. I'd

[1]

switched off the phone in the car a couple of days ago and started using the Ansafone monitor in my flat, because at this stage – three or four weeks after you're back from the last mission – they start getting fidgety.

'They said it was urgent,' the policeman said insistently, his face still in the window gap.

I knew that. I'd been mobile for the last ninety minutes and when they couldn't get through they hadn't just given up: they'd phoned the Yard and asked for an immediate all-points-bulletin by radio with my description and number plate – *Black Jensen Interceptor with cellular antenna and bunched spotlights, BBT 1872* – and a request to pick me up on sight and tell me to phone base.

I slipped the gears into neutral again and switched the phone on, because there was nothing else I could do and I knew that. We sometimes play with the idea of goofing off somewhere and not answering the phone, but it's like denying the voice of God and bringing down a whole bloody mountainside of fire and brimstone.

'You can stay here, sir, while you call in. We'll look after you.' The lights were still flashing in the mirror.

'Fair enough.'

His face vanished, and I touched out QU-1 and waited.

'Were you switched off?' a voice came.

'Yes.'

There was a short silence. He was the little shit at the operations switchboard, with enough experience to know that I'd broken the rules but not enough rank to tell me.

'Hold on,' he said.

I waited again.

'Quiller?'

'Yes.'

'We want you to make an immediate rendezvous.'

It sounded like Trench this time: cool, impersonal, the tone a shade touchy because I'd been difficult to contact.

'I can't do that.'

He said carefully: 'This is fully urgent.'

[2]

'I'm not on standby, you know that. I've got to meet someone at the airport and I'm already running late.'

'This is from Main Control,' Trench said, and left it at that.

Slight skin reaction: gooseflesh. When you've got your phone switched off and they still tell the police to pick you up and then tell you the instructions are coming direct from Main Control it's not because they can't find where you put the fruit gums.

'Why do they want me,' I asked him, 'particularly?'

'It was Mr Croder who told me to find you.'

Cold air was coming through the window, and I closed it. I don't like the cold. Through the windscreen the lights of the police car were sending an intermittent rainbow of reflections across the surface of the road, blue and white . . . *flash-flash-flash*. . .blue and bone white . . . *flash-flash-flash*. . .while my skin reacted again to the nerves. I took a slow breath to steady them.

'Is this the submarine thing?'

'I don't know,' Trench said. There'd been nothing else in the headlines for the last four days. Of course he knew. He was high in the Control echelon, with powers to brief.

'Trench,' I told him, 'I've got to meet this man at the airport. He's a sixth *dan* coming in from Tokyo and it's my personal responsibility to escort him to the *dojo*. When I've done that, I'll phone you.'

'You'll have to get someone else to meet him.'

'There's no time. The *dojo*'s south of the Thames, and they'd never reach the airport by nine-fifteen.'

'He must take a taxi, then.'

'We don't leave *this* man to get his own transport. This is Yamada.'

In a moment Trench said thinly, 'I'd rather not have to ask Mr Croder to come on the line. It shouldn't be necessary.'

The sound of the engine suddenly seemed louder and the lights in the wet street brighter. 'Listen, Trench, I'm not officially on standby and I'm not due to report back for operations until next week and you know that, so you've got a bloody nerve to put out a tracer on me and expect me to drop everything and give up the rest of the evening just because Croder's panicking all over the ops room. Tell him from me that as soon as I've met Yamada at the airport I'll–'

'Wait a minute.'

Silence again, while I tried to cool down. The Bureau is the sacred bull, and if you're in the shadow branch you're expected to make *any* sacrifice at *any* time its bloody disciples demand it of you, even unto death. But between missions you're technically allowed to unwind and lick your wounds and try to forget the frontiers and the searchlights and the cry of the dogs getting louder in the night and the thud of boots as the bastards come out of the van at the double with their guns drawn while you look for a doorway or an alley or a bit of wasteground where you can at least try zig-zagging flat out for dear life instead of just standing there with death already creeping into your body because you know that this time they won't let you go again, this time they want you badly and they're going to break you until you talk, until you scream, until you feel the slow surprise in the last remnant of conscious thought that it's happening *this* way, with the brains beaten out of the skull and the life draining out with the blood instead of the blessing of a cold clean shot from the distance to nail the spine to the dark and leave you hanging there with a shred of your honour still intact *because you didn't talk, you didn't tell them, you kept the faith.*

Faith in the sacred bull.

The Bureau.

'This is Mr Croder.'

'Good evening.'

'I realize I'm imposing on your free time, Quiller, but something rather urgent has come up.' His voice was heavy, measured and civil. 'It would really be very helpful if you could go along to No. 10 Downing Street with the greatest possible despatch. The PM is meeting some people there, and I'd like you to be present.'

I switched off the engine.

'In what capacity?'

'Quite unofficial. But I'd like you to hear what they're talking about.'

'The submarine.'

There was brief silence. 'Yes.'

The wipers had stopped when I'd switched the engine off, and I watched the rain making serpentine rivulets down the windscreen. We'd all known, of course, that the sub thing would send waves as far as London sooner or later.

'Are you offering me a mission?' I asked Croder.

'Not immediately.'

'When?'

'I'm afraid I can't tell you. There's quite a lot going on, as you can imagine, and things will need time to sort themselves out. But I really would be most grateful, Quiller, if you could do this for me.' He allowed a pause. 'As a personal favour.'

I owed the man nothing. He was chief of Main Control, the administrator, coordinator and organizer of any given number of shadow operations that might be going on at the same time. He was good at this. Before him, Strickland hadn't been: he was too wild, too ready to commit an executive to uncalculated risks, too inclined to influence the control who was actually running the mission. With Croder you felt safer; he saw us as chessmen, yes, to be pushed around; but he didn't push us blindly over the edge of the board, as Strickland had.

With Croder you could hope to live longer.

I glanced at the digital clock on the facia.

'Look,' I said, 'I'm running it close tonight. You'd have to get a police car to pick someone up at Heathrow for me and take him down to Streatham.'

'That can be arranged.'

'All right. His name is Yamada and he's coming through from Tokyo via Karachi on JAL Flight 287, ETA 9:15 at Heathrow, our time.' I didn't repeat anything because ingoing calls were automatically taped. 'I want him brought off the plane through the VIP lounge and cleared through customs and immigration without formalities. Take him to the Shotokan Karate Dojo in Gracefield Gardens, Streatham.'

If he said no, then he could send someone else along to No. 10.

'That too can be arranged.'

'You'll see to it personally?'

'Of course.'

'All right.'

I got out and walked back to the police car. 'I've got to get to Downing Street rather fast. Will you help me cut the corners?'

'Okay, sir.' The call to pick me up had come from the Yard and they must have given him my operational status. When it has to, the Bureau can request assistance from public services and get it so fast that you'll miss it if you blink. 'We'll proceed ahead of you,' he said.

By the time I got back behind the wheel and switched the engine on the police car had swung out and slowed in front of me with its lights still flashing and the siren starting up. I got into gear and we did a tight U-turn across Knightsbridge and went east with the rear end of the Interceptor waltzing a fraction as the tyres lost their grip on the wet surface and then found it again through the gears. They'd been using their radio, and before we reached Hyde Park Corner another police car had fallen in behind and was keeping station as the evening traffic slowed and pulled over to let us through.

We touched sixty in places and my nerves were settling down again. It's always like this when you catch the scent of a new mission; it's like the smell of smoke to an animal. But we don't *have* to go out again. We have to report to operations four weeks after debriefing from the last time out, but that's all: we're simply on standby again, available but not committed. And when they offer us something we can tell them we need another week or two, even another month or two, before we're ready to take on whatever they've got for us – and even then we can refuse if we don't like the look of it. It wouldn't work in any other way: it's our life on the line and we're not in the army, we're on our own once we're into the field and too far for our local control to help us.

This is the waiting time, between missions, when we've got

a chance to look back and think about what we were doing the last time around, how close we came, how lucky we were to get back at all, whether or not we had the product they'd sent us to get: documents, tapes, maps or plans or diagrams or sometimes a defector for debriefing if we can bring him across alive, whatever it is that's going to give us an edge over the potential enemy when it comes to the push. And when we look back, we don't like it. We know we came too close to mucking it up and digging ourselves an idiot's grave in the rubble of some alien city with a bullet in the back or the wreckage of a car for a tombstone or the glass splinters of the capsule still in our mouth if we had a chance to use it.

So this is when the nerves start working on us, and they know that, the people in operations. They know that if they don't handle us with kid gloves they're going to lose an agent, not out there in the field but safe at home here in London, ready at any second to take offence, to read double meanings in whatever they say to us, to flare up at the slightest thing, at a tone of voice, like tonight when that *bastard* Trench tried to throw his weight around, *I'd rather not have to ask Mr Croder to come on the line,* as if he'd been talking to a bloody trainee down from Norfolk on his first bloody mission, as if—

Slow down. This is just the waiting time, the worst time. I'd seen Bradley coming out of Clearance last week – he hadn't even got *that* far – with his face white and his hands flying all over the place for something to hang onto, some sort of spiritual lifeline, while he'd gone on shouting at them – *You'll have to get someone else for this one, God damn your eyes, you'll have to get someone else.* He'd been back only ten days from the Beirut thing and his nerves were still like a disco hall after what they'd done to him in the interrogation cell.

When you're that far gone, it's *finis*. They'll write you off the books and send you home with a final handshake, their eyes not quite meeting yours, and you'll end up pruning the roses and washing the Mini to pass the time before you can go along and pick up your pension cheque. Mother of God, don't let it ever happen to me: let them find me out there somewhere with my arms spreadeagled on a minefield and the earth still coming down and the stink of cordite on the air, not with a whimper, gentlemen, with a bang when it's got to come.

Slow. Slow down. This is the waiting time, that's all.

Take it easy. Go and see what's happening at No. 10. Then ask Croder what he's got lined up for you, because you've got to go out again *some* time, you know that.

We swung into Whitehall with the sirens still going, then slowed for the right hand turn into Downing Street, and when I pulled up at the curb I cut the ignition and looked at my spread fingers and saw they were steady, because the waiting was nearly over.

2

SPODE

'I REGARD THIS AS a deliberate act of war.'

Spode everywhere, on the marble mantlepiece and in glass cabinets in the corners of the room and along the windowsills. Spode, Turners and Chippendale, and an atmosphere of controlled shock.

'Unless the ambassador believes that in fact the submarine was actually within the twelve-mile limit.'

This was Lord Cranley, Foreign Secretary. I'd recognized him when Frome had brought me in, but only from photographs I'd seen of him. I'd never been here before, but I'd seen most of their pictures: the prime minister, US ambassador, foreign secretary, three or four members of the cabinet and the leader of the opposition. The others were aides and assistants. Frome had been here before I'd arrived: the Bureau had obviously sent him ahead on the assumption that they'd somehow get me here. He'd met me at the front door when the constable on guard had knocked, and led me to this room.

'The meeting's already begun, but in any case you won't be introduced. You're just here to listen.'

Frome was in a dark suit, his grey hair smoothed back on his narrow head, his eyes watchful, his skin dead-looking and with a sanatorium pallor; they said he'd got cancer. He hadn't spoken since he'd shown me where I was to sit; no one had spoken to him, nor even looked at him, or me.

'If the submarine was in Soviet waters,' Ambassador Morris

said deliberately, 'it was there by navigational error, or some mechanical breakdown with the steering gear or something like that.' He was a heavy man, sitting with his hands along the arms of his small fragile chair, his head lowered as if prepared to charge. It had said in one of the news reports I'd seen that he'd had a nephew on board the submarine, but that in any case his personal feeling was that if the entire Soviet fleet were to be blasted out of the oceans it would express the attitude of the United States with accuracy. 'If it was there within the twelve-mile limit, the Soviets should have warned the crew in the normal way, by dropping depth charges and sonar buoys. It could have been done, it should have been done, and it was not done.'

The PM said at once, leaning forward in her chair, 'That is why I regard it as an act of war. But unfortunately we have not only to put our own personal feelings into the background, Mr Ambassador, but to do all we can to damp down public concern to the minimum.' She leaned back again, resting a slim hand on the arm of her chair. 'It won't be easy.'

The foreign secretary looked at the ambassador. 'You don't think there's even the slightest chance of your president simply saying that unless the Soviets come across with an immediate and generous apology he'll call off the summit meeting?'

'I would like to think so. I do not, however, think so.'

'There's not the slightest chance,' someone said impatiently, 'that they'd apologize anyway. They've denied any blame and they'll go on denying it.'

'Are your people still trying to locate the submarine?'

'Yes. So are NATO investigators. But those waters are within the Arctic Circle and it's midwinter, with rough seas running.'

'Mr Ambassador, if the vessel could be found, would it be possible for divers to see whether it was an explosion on board, as the Soviets claim, or an armed attack that sent it down?'

'I think there's no question of that. But it's academic; I'm told there's almost no chance of the submarine being found, in those conditions.'

'Wouldn't the crew have signalled by radio if the ship had been in some kind of distress?'

'If they could have surfaced to do it, yes. They might not have been able to do that.'

'Do you think it was a depth charge – a warning depth charge the Soviets had in fact dropped but later decided to deny – that sank the submarine?'

Two or three of them looked at the thin man who sat with his legs crossed, tall in the chair. I put him down as Admiralty. 'It would need a great number of depth charges to sink a vessel the size of the SSN *Cetacea*. Again, the Soviets could have dropped a very great number, without coming anywhere near the target. The boat would have normally surfaced perhaps a couple of times a day to spread her antenna and signal base; in those waters, where in midwinter there's no sunlight at noon, she could have done this quite close to the Russian coast without being seen. In other words, I don't think for a moment that she was unaware of her location at any time; and if the captain had heard one depth charge going off, he would have surfaced – or changed course at once towards the open sea.'

'Can we be sure that the Soviets did in fact detect the presence of the *Cetacea* off their shores?' The PM.

'Not completely sure, ma'am.' He recrossed his long thin legs. 'But it would have been difficult for them not to. In those waters, very close to their largest naval base at Murmansk, they have underwater listening stations in a very wide array. Transonar-transducers would pick up the presence of an alien vessel easily enough, and relay the information to manned posts. Of the Soviet's six hundred or so active submarines, about four hundred are obsolescent diesel-powered boats used for patrolling the shores of the entire continent of Asia. A good few of these patrol the Barents Sea, to protect Murmansk, and they could well have picked up the noise of the *Cetacea*. They would–'

'But with all their own submarines around, how could they distinguish–'

'Every boat makes its own personal kind of noise, and a

fast nuclear-powered Los Angeles class submarine sounds vastly different from a Soviet diesel.'

'Could they have known how far off shore the submarine was?'

'You mean whether it was beyond the twelve-mile limit, ma'am?'

'Precisely.'

'They would have had a fair estimation. I wouldn't go further than that.'

'Do you think, Admiral, that the Soviets attacked and sank the submarine?'

The silence came in like a shockwave.

I watched the prime minister. She was leaning forward again, not taking her eyes off the admiral. He was studying his thin veined hands, giving himself time; but he didn't need very long. 'Yes, Madam Prime Minister, I believe they attacked and sank it.'

'Without warning?'

'We can't even guess at that. There were no survivors. Only the Soviets know.'

'Wouldn't it have been to their advantage to warn the submarine before attacking, to avoid a grave international incident?'

The admiral uncrossed his legs and got up stiffly. 'If you'll excuse me, I need to stretch a little–'

'Of course–'

'Thank you.' He took a pace or two, his hands tucked behind him. 'I would have thought, yes, that they would have warned the boat first, if they'd given themselves time to consider.'

'Do you see any parallel–' this was the US ambassador now – 'between this act and the downing of the Korean airliner?'

'Several. But the aspect common to both acts is unfortunately that we in the West haven't got full information.'

'No survivors.'

'Quite.' The admiral took another turn across the Persian carpet. 'I should point out that although we might regard the sinking of the *Cetacea* as an act of war, the Soviets might

[12]

claim with equal justification that the presence of a NATO submarine in their waters and within the proximity of their major naval base is also an act of war.'

'But they don't claim that.'

'Not at present. Their line at present is simply that they had no knowledge of the *Cetacea* until the Norwegian coastguard sighted debris drifting from the east.'

'That's typical of them,' said the Foreign Secretary, and got up too. 'If you don't mind, Madam Prime Minister—'

'We should move about, of course. This is going to be a long session, gentlemen.'

'Typically,' Cranley went on, 'they start out by denying everything in a case like this. It gives them time to think, and avoids the risk of putting their foot in their mouth. Today they're saying that the submarine must have exploded of its own accord. Tomorrow they'll start screaming that it shouldn't have been in their waters anyway.'

The PM was still in her chair, and I watched her, not getting up like most of them. I hadn't got the drift yet. I couldn't see why Britain was so involved as to call a high-level meeting in Downing Street. Or why *the Bureau* was involved.

'Wouldn't you say, Admiral Cummings, that a major incident like this, entailing the loss of more than a hundred lives and a nuclear submarine, would come under the terms of the Incidents at Sea Treaty we all signed with the Soviets in 1972?'

'Oh yes. I tried to telephone Admiral Novoselov in Moscow as soon as I heard the news of the sinking, but they told me he was unavailable. That's unusual.'

'In the case of the aircraft carrier *Kitty Hawk*,' said the US ambassador, 'our people were able to contact Novoselov immediately.'

'There's not so much in common, Mr Ambassador, with the two incidents. True, the damage to your carrier by the Soviet submarine was in the region of two million dollars; but the collision occurred in international waters in broad daylight, and was the obvious result of poor seamanship on their part.

Also there was no loss of life. In the present case we have a death toll of one hundred and five sailors on active duty and the presence of a NATO submarine in waters close to the Soviets' major naval base. With the *Kitty Hawk* there were a few red faces and the dismissal of one Soviet submarine commander. With the *Cetacea,* we already have your president's declaration of a national day of mourning throughout the United States of America.'

The PM got up at last, and took an elegant step across to the fireplace, standing with her back to it. The central heating was having a job to cope with the winter temperatures outside; from where I was sitting I could feel a cutting draught coming through a gap in the curtains.

'Let me ask you, Admiral, whether you've reached any kind of construction, in your own mind, of what actually happened in the Barents Sea four days ago. Perhaps that's not quite a fair question, but it's an important one.' In a moment she added: 'You don't have to commit yourself, of course.'

Cummings studied his hands again, and took longer this time to speak. 'I've thought about it quite a lot, Madam Prime Minister, as we all have. From my experience as an ex-submariner, and as an observer of the Soviet thought processes in East-West relations and diplomacy, I do in point of fact have a feeling – quite a strong feeling – that what really happened in the Barents Sea was that the SSN *Cetacea* was not detected by the Soviets until she was close to the twelve-mile limit, and was at once attacked by a sonar-guided torpedo – or perhaps several. And I believe that no warning was given because the Soviets were taken by surprise, and thought the submarine was within their territorial waters, offering a distinct threat.'

'You mean there was no time – as in the case of the Korean Airlines disaster – for orders to be requested from higher authority before action was taken by a local commander?'

'Quite so. I'd say that the element of surprise was inevitably involved, even of panic on the part of some young naval shore-defence officer.'

'Or simply over-zealousness? Ambition in the line of duty?'

'What we're trying to say,' the foreign secretary cut in heavily, 'is that someone blundered.'

It was gone midnight before the PM broached the real issue I'd been brought here to listen to.

'I'm glad to have had your expert opinions, gentlemen, on what is in itself a matter of grave and tragic proportions, affecting the personal lives of so many Americans, and the already critical relationship between the two great powers and their allies. But as I'm sure you've realized, what we are here to discuss is the appalling threat this incident has brought to the summit meeting that was to have taken place in less than two months from now in Vienna.'

Half an hour before we'd been moved into another room, where there were sofas and deep armchairs; a huge silver tea-tray was being cleared away, and some of the men present were holding whisky glasses. What had gone before was only the preamble to the night's work.

'The agreement by Washington and Moscow to convene the summit conference was made because of the very precariousness of the East-West relationship, and the danger it presents to world peace. And what we have to do now is to ask ourselves whether the incident in the Barents Sea – however tragic in its loss of life and however shocking in its impact on East-West relations – can be allowed to bring down our hopes for a successful summit meeting in Vienna, and our hopes that the United States and the Soviet Union can work out their differences and diminish the threat of a final and annihilating war that the whole world faces today.'

I saw the US ambassador lift his head quickly to look at her. Someone behind me reacted so sharply that the ice-cubes jingled in his glass. I looked across at the foreign secretary. His eyes were down. He'd been told what his prime minister was going to propose tonight.

'This incident is not, of course, of major concern to Great Britain, though as a loyal ally of the United States and a member of NATO we are indirectly affected.' She lifted her wrist and adjusted the thin gold bracelet: it was the first sign of nervousness she'd shown since I'd come into the room. 'We are well placed, however, in the area of international intelligence, and may be able to make ourselves useful to the United States in the immediate future, when diplomatic relations between East and West will be critically and dangerously strained. If certain information I received earlier tonight is reliable, we may shortly be in possession of absolute proof that the US submarine *Cetacea* was in fact attacked and sunk by Soviet arms.'

Tension was suddenly in the room again, and we all froze.

'My God,' someone said quietly.

I didn't look at Frome. I'd see nothing in his face if I did. *What did she mean, 'proof'?*

'The feeling of outrage among the people of the United States at this moment is so strong that there is no way the president could go to meet the Soviets in two months' time. But if we can secure irrefutable proof of their criminal act in the Barents Sea, then the United States will be in a position to demand – and with God's help extract – a full and unstinting apology from the Kremlin. And this may be the only chance we have of saving the summit conference.'

It was gone two in the morning when I left Downing Street and turned along Whitehall with the windscreen wipers on high speed to get rid of the rain. A constable with a drenched cape was guarding the only two parking spaces left outside our building and I slid into the end one and got out, just as Frome came in with his mud-caked Rover. He drove up from the country every day and never had the thing cleaned.

All he'd said to me when we'd left No. 10 was that he'd rather I didn't go home until I'd seen Croder.

We didn't talk on our way up in the lift. I didn't know how much his mind was occupied with the submarine thing and how much with the diagnosis the doctors had given him; in the flickering light he already looked like death.

He left me on the fourth floor, turning away without a word

while I went into the small cramped room where the security sergeant was sitting at his desk filing his nails. He picked up one of his phones right away and poked out a number with a nicotine-yellowed finger and waited, eyeing me with a companionable stare. I heard the line open.

'Sir? Quiller's in.' He waited again and then said 'Yes sir' and put the phone down and told me: 'He'd like you to go along for a minute. Room 7. Still raining, is it?'

'Yes.'

'Shocking, isn't it? Simply shocking.'

3

BREKHOV

'THEN WHAT THE fuck are you waiting for?'
There were only three other people in here,
sitting in the corner by the tea urn hunched over
what they were saying, as if they had to keep it a secret. My
God, if anyone could keep a secret in this bloody place they'd
have to be deaf and dumb.

'Clearance,' I said.

The Canadian sat back in his chair and I heard it creak,
or it might have been his bones. He'd been here for years
now, haunting the Caff, refusing to go, refusing to spend half
the rest of his life picking up his pension at the post office
and other half spending it on raw bourbon and cheap tarts
till they came and picked him up and dropped him into an
economy-model pinewood box and shovelled the earth over
him.

He sipped his tea. Daisy had laced it with whisky, as she
always did, strictly against the rules but of course she'd do
anything for Charlie; the last time he'd come in from a mission
she'd gone over to him with the entire stock of bountiful
motherhood remaining in the world and gathered him into it
with the passion of a Salvation Army girl who'd found a hit
and run victim in the middle of the road.

'That was a nasty one,' she'd said – I'd been there, helping
him find a chair – 'but you're all right now, dear, everything's
all right now.' She'd sat down at the rickety plastic-topped
table with him and automatically wiped a puddle of tea away

[18]

with her cloth while she stared into his face, reading his soul with those copper-dark fathomless eyes of hers until Charlie had started to laugh gently, coughing a bit at first as he always did, as the thought was borne into his mind that maybe he was all right now, maybe everything was all right. 'Go and get me some tea, you fat old whore,' he'd told her, and she'd got up and brought him some, and that was the first time she'd ever put a tot of whisky in it, and she'd been doing it ever since.

'You're getting clearance,' he asked me, 'at four o'clock in the morning?'

'Croder's phoned them. They're on their way.'

'You're going out for *Croder?*'

'Someone's got to.'

He watched me, sitting back in his chair because his vision had been going lately; you had to be at arm's length, like the newspaper. His hatchet-shaped face had gone quiet, as if he'd found something significant to think about. I didn't like that. Tonight wasn't for significant thoughts; it was for getting through as fast as I could without thinking about what I was doing. Only Croder could have got me back into the action within fifteen minutes flat: that's why they'd given him the job, I suppose.

'It's awfully good of you to come and talk to me, Quiller.'

A soft manicured hand, a brilliant smile. Tonight he'd pulled a polo sweater over his pyjama trousers: he was in the top echelon, London Control level, and sometimes slept in one of the small dormer rooms under the eaves of the building, where a hundred years ago the servant girls had slept two in a bed for warmth, nursing their chilblains.

'You found things interesting, I'm sure, at No. 10.'

'A bit too political for my taste.'

His bright smile came again, like a flicker of lightning. 'She does wax a shade rhetorical, I know. But as long as you got the background. A little brandy?'

'I'd like to get down to business, if that's all right with you.'

'At once.' The pale blue eyes glittered slightly, lighting the fixed smile. Some people said he had a face massage once a week; others said he'd come back from a tricky one as a young shadow executive and they'd had to stretch a brand new skin graft right across his face; in some lights it did have the look of a mask. 'We would very much like you to go and fetch something for us,' he said, 'from Germany, or thereabouts.' A brief smile, as an apology for being so vague. 'It's only a small package.'

He stopped right there. He wouldn't say any more until I asked questions. At this stage, before briefing and before clearance, they want you to know as little as possible in case you turn down the job.

'When?'

'Soon, I believe. I'm sorry I can't be more explicit. Within a day or two.'

'From a courier?'

'Yes.'

'Which border?' If they wanted anything from West Germany itself they'd just shove it in the diplomatic bag or put a Queen's messenger on special assignment.

'Again,' he said in his soft tone of apology, 'we're not absolutely sure. Not yet.'

'Running like hell somewhere, is he?'

He didn't smile now. He looked at me with his bright eyes losing all expression as he took me another inch towards the heart of the matter. 'They're not on to him yet. But yes, he's running hard with it.'

'With the package?'

'Yes.'

'Is he trying to get into Norway?'

He shook his head. 'No. That would be too difficult.'

'But he started from Murmansk?'

'Yes,' he said straight away, and the lightning flickered faintly in the depth of his eyes.

I didn't want this.

'I don't want this,' I told him.

'Why ever not? There's nothing very complicated.'

I turned to look through the black glass of the window,

where the rain made silver rivulets across the Houses of Parliament in the haze. 'I'm not a bloody messenger boy.'

'Oh, come.' I watched his reflection. 'You don't really think I'd encroach on your evening's leisure and ask you to spend all that time in Downing Street just to propose our using you as a messenger boy, surely?'

'It's too political,' I said.

'You're just dodging the issue.'

'I know.'

His soft laugh came. 'Now please don't equivocate.'

Wrong word. Before he'd come into the Bureau he'd been a schoolmaster, and it still showed.

'Cliff can do a job like this,' I told him. 'Or Wainwright.' I turned to face him. 'I'm ready to go out again, but not just to fetch the paper.'

'Certainly we could send Cliff, or Wainwright. But this is extremely important, as you should realize. You know what's in that package, don't you?'

'Proof.'

'Quite so.'

If certain information I received earlier tonight is reliable, we may shortly be in possession of absolute proof that the US submarine Cetacea *was in fact attacked and sunk by Soviet arms.*

'Anyone can bring that package in,' I said. 'Tuft, Malone, Flood, why on earth don't you use them?'

He watched me with the light playing in his eyes. He'd be in a towering rage by now, I knew that, because I wouldn't do what he wanted me to do. But this was as much as he'd show: just this shimmering light at the back of his eyes.

'You know, of course, that the Vienna conference may depend on whether we can bring this package across. That is why I sent – that is why I asked you to go along to Downing Street. You know we're not being specious. You know we're not just asking you to fetch and carry. We are asking you to do what you can to ensure that in four weeks' time the president of the United States and the Chairman of the Presidium of the USSR Supreme Soviet will meet in Vienna and call an armistice in the Cold War.'

'Bullshit.'

He gave a gentle sigh. 'If you're trying to test my patience, Quiller, it happens to be infinite.'

That was true. The last time out, Wainwright had smashed up three Avis cars and left an Arab contact in a doorway of the kasbah with an icepick in his brain and got himself photographed in bed with the wife of the French ambassador to Morocco *knowing bloody well* that the KGB had stuck a camera in the wall of the Hotel Palais Jamai, and Croder had debriefed him personally and given him the keys of his flat on the Croisette with a chef and maid service and instructions to get his nerves back into shape. That was patience.

'There just isn't enough to it,' I told him.

'You're so terribly egotistical.'

'Didn't anyone tell you?'

'Oh yes. But I didn't realize how much it got in your way.'

'So I go and bring this thing in and they tell the Soviets they've got proof about the sub and they'd better apologize or they'll wreck the summit and I get a pat on the back, is that it? For Christ's sake, give me something more interesting.'

'I would have thought you'd be interested in the fact that Chief of Control has decided to stay up through the early hours to do his utmost to persuade one of his elite shadow executives to take something on that has international dimensions. Since you're not, why don't you think about *him?*'

'Who?'

'The courier.'

'The courier from Murmansk?'

'Yes.'

I turned away from him again, and wished I hadn't, because he could see I was ready to think, and wanted to do it without his eyes on me.

'Who is he?'

'Brekhov.'

I thought about him, about Brekhov. I'd only worked with him once, but he'd been very good: he'd taken three days to bring me something to my hotel in Moscow from our contact at the border, but that was quick because he'd had to get through a militia road check and hole up at a blown safehouse and chance his arm with the kind of papers I wouldn't even show a bus conductor. He even got to my room without going through the lobby, using a fire escape the KGB never bothered to watch because the bottom section had been taken away and they'd put chains across.

Brekhov, a short man with sturdy legs and a big black moustache and a pair of mild brown eyes that could stare – had stared – a hundred militiamen in the face with the look of an innocent child. Brekhov, running hard now through the frozen ruts of Leningrad or Minsk or Lvov or Warsaw if he'd got across by now, with his sturdy legs working under him and never stopping, never tripping, never taking him an inch away from the course he'd set for himself through the night of a Russian winter, not literally of course – they could be flying him through or bringing him out by road in the hollowed floor of a vegetable truck – but he'd be moving as steadily as that, as doggedly, all the way from the Arctic Circle to some overheated *gasthaus* west of the wall, where he'd sit with a beer and swap code-identities and look around him before he took out the package and put it down on the table, covering it with his hand until you were ready to take it, *here it is*, what about another beer, *here it is*, it's warmer in here than up there in the north, I can tell you, *here it is*.

A good courier, Brekhov. Reliable. The best.

Croder hadn't spoken. He'd wait for me all night, but he knew now that he wouldn't have to. The bastard had got right inside me when I wasn't looking.

'I worked with him once,' I said. 'With Brekhov.'

'Did you?'

He knew bloody well I had: it was only a year ago, on the Corridor thing, when he was already Chief of Control.

'How are they sending him through?'

'We're not quite sure.'

'When will you know?' I turned around and looked at him, and he offered a faint, deprecating smile.

'I think at this point the questions ought to stop, don't you?'

I took a deep breath, slowly so that he shouldn't notice. 'Not necessarily.'

He shrugged. 'We had a signal in from Leningrad an hour ago. He was trying to get onto a plane for Potsdam, using permanent cover for the run out, a maintenance engineer for Aeroflot. We—'

'Are Signals keeping open for him?'

'Oh yes.'

'Who's at the console?'

'Fletcher.'

'Listen, has Brekhov got any backups, any relay people, anyone in the field with him?'

'No. He only ever runs alone.'

I stuck my hands in the pockets of my mac, feeling the cold now, the cold of the nerves, of the night, as the knowledge of total commitment began spreading through the organism like a drug, sending a slow awareness through the infinitely manifold receptors that things had changed, that soon it would be as it had been not too long ago, only weeks ago, when I had believed, crossing the narrow neck of water from Tangier, that they were still with me, and would never leave me until they'd done for me.

This feeling would go, soon. The cold would go. It was just a kind of shock, extended in time to lessen its impact. The organism looks after itself, if only you'll let it.

'There's a lot more,' I said, 'to this thing, isn't there, than picking up a package from a courier?'

Croder turned away and turned back and said when he'd thought it out, 'I'll put it this way. Whoever we send out to meet Brekhov, we'll be putting on continuing standby in case there's more to be done. And with this kind of background – the business of the American submarine – it would be logical to think that there will indeed be more for him to do, a very great deal more. He might not even find himself alone any longer, but the nucleus of quite a complex cell.'

'I only ever work alone. You know that.'

'The mark of the true professional is that he's flexible.'

'Damn you,' I told him, 'don't keep putting up obstacles. I want the job.'

He stood with his feet carefully together and the light playing in his eyes as he watched me, while through the glass of the window I listened to the rumbling of a late taxi turning a corner down there in the rain, and then silence, and then, I swear it, the sound of steadily running feet.

'But of course.' He went to the desk and picked up a phone and pushed three buttons and waited. Someone came on the line and he said, 'Quiller has agreed to go. Set it up, will you?'

'You know, of course,' Charlie said, stirring the whisky in his tea, 'that Croder is a non-fattening, sugar-free, artificially-flavoured turd. Don't you?'

'He's all right.'

'But he's conned you into another mission, three weeks after you got back from Tangier.'

'I let him do it.'

Charlie watched me for a bit and then drank from his cup. 'Lucky bastard.'

I wanted to leave him, but we never do, or not without a good excuse. It's been a year now since they took him off the books and he's been sitting here in the Caff ever since, talking to anyone who'll listen. He says he's waiting for them to send him out again, not on his own – he knows that's over now – but to help a spook who's messed things up so badly that they can only send someone who's totally expendable to get him out alive if he can. It could even happen, but it would only be a gesture, something to tell the widow: *we sent a man out there to help him, but things were just too difficult.*

'Go home, Charlie,' I said. 'It's gone four.'

'When the rain stops.'

He's afraid he won't be here when they need him, as a gesture, as comfort for someone's widow. That's why you can never get him to go home when there's something big running, with the main console in Signals manned twenty-four hours a day and the Chief of Control sleeping here and that unearthly sense of quiet that settles over the building in ways that a stranger wouldn't recognize, not knowing, for instance, that Daisy and the other girls don't normally put the china down as carefully as this.

'You want a drop more, love?'

'I shall be pissed.'

She took his cup away.

'I shall be pissed,' he said to me with his red eyes narrowed with fatigue, 'and then I shall go out of this fucking place and walk under a fucking taxi. But that's not my game.'

His game is to wait, if necessary forever, for them to send him out again on a last hopeless mission, so that he doesn't have to be picked up in the street or in whatever bleak one-roomed flat gives him shelter. He sits here waiting to go out, and take his own death with him to the rendezvous.

'You say it's gone four?'

'Five past,' I said.

He fiddled with his Seiko. 'Synchronize watches, gentlemen.'

Then I saw Binns coming in. He looked round and saw me and came between the tables and stood looking down with the rain still dripping off his mac.

'You're waiting for clearance, right?'

'Yes.'

'Let's go.'

I put my hand on Charlie's shoulder as I got up. 'It's nothing interesting this time. Nothing you'd even touch.'

4

RUNNING

'YOU DON'T USE a gun, do you?'
    'No.'
    'Why not?'
'None of your bloody business.'
Binns gave a faint grin and made a note: *No firearm.*
It's just that I prefer to use my hands.
   'Next of kin?'
   'None.'
He looked up again, then thought better of it and said nothing, making a note. They'd got all this stuff already in the files, but some of us go through changes in our habits or our personal lives and they want to catch things on our way through Clearance. We don't get any younger and we don't get any braver in this trade; there's a diminishing return syndrome at work, and when they take a shadow exec. through his clearance and find he's asking for additional things like a larger-calibre gun or a flak vest or extra cyanide capsules or permission to kill at discretion they'll fail his clearance and send him up to Norfolk for refresher training, and if he can't put out his usual score they'll give him an office job or retire him. Charlie isn't the only one; a lot of us go that way.
   'Bequests?'
   'The usual.'
Binns looked up. 'What's the usual?'
   You're asked to be precise, in Clearance. They want statements, because they could be your last. 'Home Safe.'

'Is that a bank?'

'How did you get so bloody ignorant, Binns?'

He twisted in his chair and prodded the computer and the screen lit up. *Shelter for Abused Wives.*

'Sorry.' He made a note. 'Current languages?'

"French, German and Russian.' I picked a splinter from the edge of his pinewood desk. Some of us pull up our chair close enough to do it, and it already looks as if the rats have been at it; we do it to leave a weird kind of signal, I suppose; or perhaps we think subconsciously that if we go on long enough we'll pick the whole bloody building down and we can all go home.

But I was feeling better now. The cold had gone, and the nerves had settled down; being committed is like that: you're in it again and there's nothing you can do about it now.

'Who's going to run me?' I asked Binns. He'd get to that part eventually, but I wanted to know now.

'Croder.'

'Personally?'

'That's right.'

'Jesus.' The Chief of Control normally ran three or four operations at the same time, if there were no paramilitary involvement. 'Is he giving me a local control in the field?'

'Not yet. You won't need one. There's just the rdv with the courier and you're back home again.'

He asked the rest of the questions and pulled a medical printout from the file and went through it with me and then scratched his chest through the gap in his shirt and slid the drawer shut and said, 'Now maybe I can go home and finish my beauty sleep.'

'It's not doing you much good. Who's on watch tonight?'

He checked the roster. 'Kinsley.'

I went through Codes and Cyphers one floor down and picked up a Box 9 grid system with short-cut phrasing and saw Watts in the room next door and conned him into giving me a journalist's cover – he's always trying to push you into off-duty aircrew identities – and then took the stairs again to the floor above and went along to the room right at the end, next to Signals, and found Kinsley sitting at his desk cleaning a gun.

'Have you got a minute?'

'Sure. Sit down. Bryce-Whitney Monitor, 1912, automatic safety-catch, they only made a couple of hundred, how much do you think?'

'I don't know.'

'Four hundred quid, isn't that fantastic?'

'If you say so.' I thought about going home to bed but they might call me at any time now and I could sleep on the flight out; besides, I wanted to know a few things.

'Are you going out again, Quiller?'

'Yes.'

'Can't leave it alone, can you?' He put the cleaning kit away and laid the gun down on the desk with exaggerated care and gave me all of his attention, his wide unsurprisable eyes noting my stubble and untidy hair and my general air, I suppose, of someone who's been up all night. 'What can I do for you?'

'Tell me about the American sub.'

'Okay. Going to meet Brekhov, are you?'

'How did you know?'

'I was talking to the Chief. He said you'd be coming in here to ask me about the sub.' He got up and stretched his arms out at right angles and flexed them backwards a couple of times and then limped across to the shelf in the corner, a short, square-bodied man with stiff black hair and a beaky nose and a national gold medal for weight lifting and a framed police record on the wall from the time when he'd been arrested for bending some railings with his bare hands outside Buckingham Palace and fined one hundred pounds for causing malicious damage to a public monument, which was twice as much as the bet he'd won for doing it; but they had to use a car jack to get the railings straight again, which was what had pleased him the most.

'Sugar?'

'No.'

He plugged in the rusty water-heater and dropped a couple

of teabags into two cups and said over his shoulder, 'What particularly interests you?'

'How they decided it must have blown up near Murmansk.'

'Ah. The way I heard it from Cheltenham was that when the Norwegian coastguards spotted the debris it was quite close inshore and drifting due west on the current. This was–'

'How far from the Russian border?'

'Damn close. Roughly north-west of Grense Jakobselv. That was at dawn on the second – last Monday – and the current was running at five knots and pretty well due west. I'd say there isn't any doubt about it, wouldn't you? D'you know that area?'

'All I know is that it's where the Iron Curtain ends in the Barents Sea.'

'Right. The Norwegians looked at their seismographs and worked out the timing of the explosion and the speed of the current and put the estimated location of the sub as due north of Murmansk, give or take a couple of kilometres, when it was hit.'

'There's no way of telling whether it was inside the twelve-mile limit at that time?'

'They're still working things out. We–'

'Who are?'

'The US Navy, Norwegian Navy and coastguards, and the NATO team. But it's pretty unlikely they'll ever get a fix in retrospect.' He unplugged the water-heater and filled the two cups and brought them over. 'Want some milk?'

'No.' I dunked the teabag up and down. 'It *was* the *Cetacea*, was it?'

'Oh, yes. There were five bodies found among the general debris that morning, and they were identified within a few hours; two of them had limbs missing and so on, but their faces were unharmed and the water's not much above freezing in that area. No question.'

'Are they still searching for the sub?'

'As a token gesture. They can't look for it inside Soviet waters and even if they could they wouldn't want to: the Americans are saying that the sub was outside the twelve-mile limit and the Soviets are saying they didn't know it was in the Barents Sea anyway. Politically, it's a kind of stand off, and both sides are trying to keep the matches away from the powder keg, because of the summit.'

'Is that why they—'

'Hang on.' The phone was ringing and he picked it up. 'Kinsley.' He listened and then put his cup down and went around behind the desk and reached for his pad and a ballpoint. 'When? Okay, see if you can get him on any direct flight with takeoff fifty minutes from now and not later than ETA 08:00 hours today.' He glanced up at me and said, 'Brekhov missed the Potsdam plane but he's on an Aeroflot to Berlin, arriving 08:15. Did you ask Clearance for a bag?'

'Yes.'

'When did you last eat?'

'I'll get something on the plane.'

'Okay.' He spoke into the phone again. 'No, not unless we have to. Try Lufthansa, then.' He pulled open a drawer and dropped the composite airline schedules onto the desk, reaching for his tea. 'There might be time to call in a chopper to take him from Battersea to Heathrow, but I'd rather find—' he broke off and listened again. 'Look, I'll do that while you tell Jones to take his bag along to the checkout room, with his clearance stuff ready for final signature, okay?' Another phone rang and he picked it up. 'Yes, sir, I've just got it from Signals and we're getting him ready now. I'll tell him.' He rang off and looked up at me again. 'Chief says good luck.'

I nodded and he began work on the airline schedules and made a note and spoke into the open phone. 'George?' He listened. *'Shit.'* His pen ran down the flight times again and he made another note, turning a page and then hearing a voice on the line. He picked up the phone again. 'What? No, this is better: there's a Lufthansa leaving at 05:45' – he checked his watch – 'in just under an hour from now. Get him on that. I know, but we can't help it. They'll have to put him on the flight deck or a cabin-crew jump seat if they have to – just make *absolutely* sure they get him on it and have his pass waiting for him at the gate, not at the counter, the gate, okay? Flight 190. We're cutting it fine so call in whatever help you need, right up to the Chief of Control if Lufthansa object to an extra bod – he can request assistance on Line 5.'

Line 5 was our NATO Intelligence connection.

He put the phone down and made a note on a new sheet of his pad. 'Okay, you'll be on Flight 190. They'll–' the ballpoint ran dry and he threw it aside and picked up another one. *'Bloody* things. They'll have your pass waiting for you at Gate 10. The rendezvous is for 09:00 in the lobby of the Hotel Sachsen, 8 Linden Platz, about thirty minutes from the airport – he obviously doesn't want to hang about. Have you seen him before?'

'Yes.'

'Okay. He'll be carrying a copy of *Pravda* upside-down. Use the code introduction for this week. There'll be an Avis car waiting for you at the airport. Any questions?'

'Have we got anyone else covering his arrival?'

'No. You're on your own.'

'That's all.'

'Okay.' He tore the sheet off the pad and gave it to me, getting up and coming round the desk. 'I'll get a police car to fall in behind you on the way to Heathrow in case you blow a tube or anything, so look out for it. We'll also tell them to watch for you at the security check and Gate 10.' He put his hand out. 'Happy landings.'

I picked up the prepacked overnight bag on the ground floor and gave them the final signature and went out through the small door at the back of the building, walking round the puddles to the car. The rain had eased off and a half moon was tugging a gap in the ragged clouds, and as I got in and started up and turned north along Whitehall the last of the queasiness along the nerves died away and left me with only the steady rhythmic sound, deep in my mind, of a man running.

5

TRAP

REVERSE THRUST, and the deceleration forces pushed us forward against the seat belts. A copy of *Stern* slid across the floor but the stewardess didn't leave her jump seat to pick it up.

'*Bitte bleiben Sie angeschnalt bis das Flugzeug vollständig stillsteht.*'

A TWA jumbo loomed across the window, its dorsal light winking in the haze. Raindrops streaked the glass: *plus ça change*, so forth.

The stewardesses were standing up, and one came over to me.

'Do you need any assistance from the airline agent, Herr Gage?'

'No, thank you.'

We rolled to a stop against the walkway and they let me off first.

'I hope you'll travel again with Lufthansa, Herr Gage.'

'I will indeed.'

They didn't know who I was, only that I was somebody unusual: there'd been a traffic jam at Heathrow and my police escort had needed twelve minutes to get me through it, and I would have missed the plane if the Bureau hadn't used its Line 5 connection to keep the flight waiting for me. I didn't like that: it had called attention.

It was 08:07 – we hadn't picked up the time the plane had been delayed – and if Brekhov had already landed, eight or nine minutes early, I could have missed him. That would be all right because the rdv was for the Hotel Sachsen and he wasn't expecting to meet me here, but I wanted to check him for any kind of routine surveillance he might pick up. Soviet nationals always come under inspection from the teams of KGB agents-in-place when they travel to the West, to make sure they meet the people they're meant to be meeting, and stay at the hotel where they're meant to be staying.

Brekhov would know that.

I went across to the Aeroflot desk and checked the screen. Flight 376 from Leningrad was due in at 08:15, on schedule. There were twenty or thirty people in the gate area and I took up my position against the far wall, sighting the exit from the walkway tunnel between two pillars for the sake of cover. It took me thirty seconds to identify all four of the KGB agents because they were spread well out, with only one of them close to the walkway. They hadn't noted me; they had seen me but not noted me. They wore felt hats and raincoats and stood with their hands by their sides, and they were good: a man in an astrakhan coat and fur hat came out of the walkway hurrying a little, and all four of them turned their heads to scan him; but when a totally stunning stewardess came through the crowd they simply went on watching the walkway. They hadn't looked at each other once, so far; they would only do that when they saw someone who looked worth their attention. I didn't like them; I don't like these agents when they're efficient.

Brekhov wasn't among the first thirty passengers coming through, and I began thinking he'd changed his appearance during the last year, or changed it for this trip, to match a difficult photograph on his papers; with a rendezvous precise as to time and place, recognition wasn't critical. It wouldn't matter if he'd shaved off his heavy moustache; I was allowing for that, watching their eyes as they came from the exit, watching their walk.

Three girls came through in sable coats, their soft-booted feet splayed and half-floating across the maroon carpeting: ballet dancers, to be greeted with small cries of pleasure from a matronly woman and two men; they were gathered into affectionate arms and led away. The agents didn't watch them; I'd seen them note, already, the welcoming party, one of whom was himself KGB.

Forty people had now come through, perhaps fifty. The first twinge came to the nerves. *I would have thought that you'd be interested in the fact that Chief of Control has decided to stay up through the early hours to do his utmost to persuade one of his elite shadow executives to take something on that has international dimensions.*

Flashlight flickered suddenly as a woman with ice-blue eyes and a perfect mouth came through, not lifting a hand to spoil the pictures the press were taking, smiling instead, not a dancer this time, and not Russian. It was Helga Aspel, the actress. Why hadn't she been among the first off the plane? She wouldn't be smiling like this when she saw her travel agent.

A man in a dark suit with velour lapels came through, his head held down and his walk too quick, *an amateur and they got him right away*, two of them closing in and asking for his papers, keeping him well back against the wall and shielding him from view with their bodies. They must have been waiting for him. One of them escorted him away while the other went back to his post by the gate desk. I felt another twinge along the nerves. If Brekhov came through and they thought there was something wrong with him there'd be nothing I could do. Nothing.

Except of course to call London. *It's no go. They got him.*

But Brekhov was a professional. He'd talk to them easily enough and say the right things and have the right answers and convince them as he'd had to convince these people before; but if there were anything wrong with his papers, if the photograph was excessively blurred or the serial numbers didn't check or there was a shift in the franking as it crossed the edges of the picture, anything like that, any slightest thing, they'd move in on him again the instant he'd cleared customs and immigration, and take him along to the Aeroflot office or the Sovietbank or the embassy and put him through full interrogation. And I wouldn't see him again. If he tried running for it or yelled for the police it would be worse: they'd drop him with a needle and grab the product and run. They've done it before: they did it with Franz Horsch on the Champs Elysées and they did it with Polinszky on London Bridge and they did it with Emil Marceau on the boat deck of the *San Cosenza* as she'd steamed out of Naples last year. They would do it if it were important enough. With Brekhov it would be important. And all I could do would be to send a signal.

It's no go. They—

But the nerves are always a little raw in the first few hours when you go out again. Brekhov was a professional. His papers would be perfect. They must be, or he wouldn't have got onto the plane.

Had he got onto the plane?

Fifty people through and I was sweating.

Sixty.

It was a full plane; I could see them still coming off as they passed the gap between the walkway and the cabin.

Six schoolboys, a thin sandy-coloured man in charge of them, his suede shoes worn and his tweed coat flapping open, 'Come on, Henderson, keep together.'

A woman leaning on the arm of the man with her, her eyes red and her dark hair over her face, the gleam of tears on her cheek, both Russians, *who were they having to leave behind?* The man looked at no one, at nothing, suffering in patience with her. The agents noted them but let them past.

Three Japanese with their smartly-cut coats buttoned, their briefcases swinging.

A young girl, unescorted, laden with souvenirs.

Brekhov.

Without his moustache but with the same eyes and the same loping walk, the floor passing steadily under his feet as if the world itself had to keep time with him. One of the KGB men was watching him, turning his head slightly as Brekhov came through the crowd at his own pace as another noted him, his eyes moving with him until he had passed the desk and I began breathing again.

They went back to watching the walkway exit and I gave Brekhov time to reach the first corner before I moved, not in his direction but towards the men's lavatory on the far side of the passageway, until I could see all four agents one by one reflected in the glass of the Lufthansa picture of the Brandenburg Gate by night. They were still watching the walkway, and I turned and followed Brekhov and saw that he was alone among the crowd, alone in terms of surveillance.

A professional, with perfect papers. Now that the tension was off the nerves I was able to recognize that Croder wouldn't have arranged things otherwise.

The traffic was moving sluggishly through the rain, the last of the morning rush hour trailing off along the Kurfürsten-damm, the smell of a bakery coming through the open window. London had ordered identical Mercedes SSL two-door saloons for us at the Avis desk, and Brekhov was four vehicles ahead of me, driving as steadily as he walked.

The rain was heavy now, coming straight down from a leaden sky, splashing in the puddles and drumming on the roof of the car. Umbrellas were everywhere along the pave-ments, and people were sheltering in doorways.

Brekhov didn't know I was behind him; we'd checked out at the Avis counter almost at the same time but I'd gone to the far end and turned away from him; he wasn't expecting me to be at the airport. There were two taxis between us and a black Porsche 944 in my driving mirror. When the chance came I overtook the first taxi: there was the risk of losing Brekhov at one of the cross-streets if the lights changed. That wouldn't be important, simply inconvenient; for the sake of good form I was trying for a perfect rendezvous, with the agent bringing the courier under protective surveillance from the time he arrived to the time he reached the meeting place.

Brekhov was also performing by the book, taking two left turns and a right before he came back to the Kurfürstendamm and shook off a dark blue BMW for practice. It was certain, then, that he didn't know I was behind him, otherwise he would have left things to me. There was nothing between us now, but he hadn't seen me before he'd gone through his diversion so I wasn't familiar. That was all right.

But the black Porsche 944 had come up again in the mirror and was still there when Brekhov turned into the Linden Platz and stopped near the entrance to the hotel. The Porsche had the same number plate: it was the one that had been behind me earlier and it hadn't driven straight here from the airport because it must have followed us through the loops Brekhov had made as an exercise. And when I got out of the car I saw the dark blue BMW slowing to a stop across the street and as I went into the hotel behind Brekhov I knew we were in a red sector.

'Hotel Sachsen, may we help you?'

'Please.' We spoke in German. 'I was to meet someone at your hotel this morning, but I've been delayed. Would you give him a message for me?'

'Certainly. Is the person staying here?'

'No. He'll be waiting for me in the lobby. He's medium height, medium build, dark hair, no hat, a light grey raincoat, and he's carrying a copy of *Pravda*.'

'One moment, sir.'

I waited.

'Yes, he's here. What is the message, please?'

'Do you speak Russian?'

'I'm afraid not.'

'Then I'll have to spell it to you.' Brekhov would possibly speak German, but this message couldn't be passed through anyone who could understand it. 'You have a pencil?'

'Yes, sir.'

I spoke in slow Russian, spelling the words out. '*God bless Queen Victoria . . . I am here . . . but you are under close KGB surveillance by four men . . . if you have the product on you, look at your watch now . . . I will follow whatever lead you make.*'

It took five minutes and the clerk had to break off twice to answer a telephone. When we'd finished I stayed where I was, pressing the contact down but keeping the phone in my hand while I watched the clerk ring off and go across to Brekhov. As he read the message slip he looked at his watch.

I put the phone down and went across to the magazine stand, moving round to the other side so that I could see the whole of the lobby. Two of the agents were stationed near the front and side doors; a third was by the lift, the fourth near the stairs. They were watching Brekhov in brief sweeping glances and in window reflection.

This wasn't very good because he was sealed in here with the product and if he tried to go anywhere they'd go with him and if he tried to get clean away they wouldn't let him. He was in a trap they weren't ready to spring yet; it could confine him to the lobby here or if he moved it could become city-wide. They could have taken him easily enough on the way here, creating a minor traffic accident to let one of them get into his car while it was stopped. They didn't want him yet. They wanted to know what he was doing here, why he'd come to Berlin. They wanted to know the people he was here to meet, and that was why I didn't approach him. He would understand that.

Correction. The Chief of Control hadn't been able to arrange this rendezvous in perfect safety. In frontier-crossing operations safety can never be guaranteed. But he'd made sure that someone with my experience and qualifications would meet Brekhov at the end of his run, in case something went wrong.

It had. The KGB had been slow in starting after Brekhov. They hadn't known about him, or known that he was on the move. But somewhere along the line they'd been alerted, and suddenly he'd become a fly seen against the vast web of their network, but not yet caught. He might not have realized this. It could have been luck. If he had realized it, he had found a gap, and got through. But they hadn't given up: the KGB network has no frontiers. They had signalled their agents in the West, here in Berlin, and the fly had touched the web, and the web had quivered. They knew about Brekhov now, in Moscow. They knew he was standing here in the lobby of the Hotel Sachsen with a copy of *Pravda* under his arm and the fear of God in his heart because he knew what I knew, that if he were under the surveillance of four KGB men he had no chance of escape. Until he made a move they'd do nothing but watch: they knew he was a courier, now, but they wanted to know more, much more: whether he was carrying any kind of product, and what it was, and who was to receive it. If he made a move to the stairs, to the street, to the lift, they'd move with him and limit his run and bring him down in the privacy of whatever room he managed to reach, whatever back street or vehicle or doorway.

If he tried to pass on the product they would see it and take it. If he brought the police here the agents would have time, ample time, a whole minute even, to use a needle or hustle him out of sight and leave him dead with his shirt torn open and the adhesive plaster ripped from his skin – because that was where the product was, not in his pockets but on his body.

He would know all this. He was a professional. He would know that the agents watching the gate at the airport had already been told he was coming through, and to let him. It had been the agents mounting surveillance in the main hall, watching the Avis counter, who had been ordered to trap him. They were here now, and they would never leave him.

Somewhere across the frontier, someone had exposed him, perhaps without meaning to. Someone had made a false move, or had talked, or been made to talk, or was missing with evidence left behind, or had gone to ground, or was still on the move. Or somewhere there was a man trying to reach Brekhov and warn him, or save him, if he could. Somewhere we had a friend.

If he were still alive.

Brekhov had seen me now, just my eyes, above the copy of the *Berliner Zeitung* I'd taken from the magazine rack. He knew where I was. He moved now, walking to the main entrance and standing there, looking at his watch, this time to protect me, to let them believe I wasn't here yet, but late.

I went over the options, putting the *Berliner Zeitung* back on the rack and taking *Vanity Fair,* turning the pages. I could call the police and say there were four KGB agents mounting guard over a Soviet national in the lobby of the Hotel Sachsen, ready to kill him if he tried to get away. My name? My address? My occupation? What gave me to believe such a thing? How could I prove that I wasn't crazy, or perpetrating a hoax?

Or I could telephone the British Embassy and ask for the chief of station, the highest-ranking MI6 officer in Berlin. He would answer very quietly, and with sympathy. *That sounds nasty, yes. But there's not a great deal we can do, you know. I mean quite frankly, this is your problem. But good luck.*

The Bureau is not popular with the legitimate secret services, because we've got privileges and prerogatives above and beyond their own franchise and they envy us. The Queen doesn't even know we exist, though the prime minister certainly does, but not officially. We are also rather dirty, and do things they are not permitted to do, even if they wanted to. They work in offices and glean their material in bars and restaurants and at diplomatic functions; we work in deep shadow, and are unknown, and leave no trace, except some-times a crumpled figure with its hand flung out, half-seen in a back alley or in the bilge of a rotting hulk or on a frosted wasteground with weeds for a wreath: the earthly remains of one of them or sometimes one of us, depending how the day has gone.

Brekhov went slowly to the door again and looked out at the rain, then at his watch, miming, coming back and glancing around him in case the man he'd come to meet had come into the lobby another way; his glance drew blank.

There were in fact no options. The only thing he could do was make a move, because they would never do it; they would if necessary bring in relief agents and wait him out, however long it took. There was no move I could make; at some stage I would have to decide whether to abandon the courier and what he carried and make my own way out, or to follow whatever lead he took and try for a last-ditch attempt to save him and secure the product. There were no rules to guide us here, no protocol for survival. As the shadow executive of the bureau running this operation I was technically in command, but a courier has one sacrosanct function: to reach the agent and deliver the goods.

In any case there was nothing I could do.

09:31.

There were some ten or fifteen people in the lobby at any given time, darting in from the rain and leaving the porters to fetch their baggage, or coming out of the lift and going to the reception desk or the coffee shop or the main entrance. They provided good mobile cover for small movements but that was all. They were useless as shields because we couldn't use them: the most sacred edict of the Bureau's creed is that we don't compromise the public. We don't steal a car, even if it's the only way we can get out alive; we don't steam open letters or bug telephones or ask anyone for help, and we don't expose ten or fifteen people to risk in a hotel lobby because there's nothing else for us to do but start chaos and take it from there.

So I knew what Brekhov would do, as soon as he'd gone over everything in his mind and thought for a moment of the girl in Leningrad or wherever she was, or maybe his mother, or a brother, people like that, before he made his decision and threw everything else to the wind and made his move. It was the only thing he could possibly try.

I felt for him. He'd come a long way. He'd signalled London and been told to start his run, and been told that it was important, vital, that he should reach the rendezvous and complete his mission. On his way here he'd been faced with risks and dodged them through the lamplit freight-yards or stared them out at the militia posts or discounted them and kept up the even measure of his pace toward his goal. And his goal was here, in the centre of a trap.

His glance passed across me again but there was nothing in his mild brown eyes, no kind of signal. His face looked paler now; his blood was draining from the surface and favouring the heart and brain and muscles; the adrenalin would be pouring into the arteries and he would be feeling that strange lightness that comes to us when we know that there might not be much longer for us now unless we are ready to do things normally beyond our powers.

The KGB men had moved only a little, a pace here or there, a pace back again, each preferring the area he'd chosen for himself, where he could get used to the angles and lines of sight and reflecting surfaces. They were in no hurry. They would sleep tonight. The day would take its direction and they would follow its measured and predestined course until night was reached, and then they would sleep.

People entered the lobby and went out. The rain filled the street with a silvered haze, curtaining the green park of the square.

Then Brekhov made his move.

6

EXIT

THE TECHNIQUE OF the gateswing turn is the European version of the bootlegger turn they use in the States: you bring the speed well down and pull the wheel over and stand on the hand brake until you're swinging at ninety degrees and then you release the brake and slam the power on and drive through the final vector. At this stage you're facing in the opposite direction and if you can do it right and do it fast enough you can be gaining ground while the hunter vehicle is still coming the other way and if you're doing it at night you can try a quick swing towards him with your head-lights full on and hope to blind him off the road.

This is what Brekhov did and I wasn't ready for it – he was swinging wild in the path of the Porsche 944 and hitting the edge of the curb and correcting with his front end pointing straight again. I caught a glimpse of his white face in the driving window as I slowed and stood on the hand brake and went into the gateswing myself, too late for anything neat but getting it half-right and bouncing a little off a fire hydrant before I could settle into the acceleration phase with the rear tyres waltzing badly over the wet surface.

The Porsche hadn't seen it coming and we lost it but the BMW had the distance it needed because it was bringing up the rear, and it simply slowed and went into a tailslide and lost usable traction until the curb kicked it straight again. It was between Brekhov and me, accelerating hard, and I tried to damp out the rear wheelspin to the point where I could close the gap and bump him with enough off-centre leverage to push him round into some kind of crash; but the road was too wet and I couldn't get close enough. I could see Brekhov still ahead, so I settled down to watch for a chance to help him.

What he had done, because it was the only thing he could possibly have done, was to try driving out of the trap.

It had gone well at first: he was a competent actor, looking at his watch again and going across to the reception desk and leaving a verbal message and then going steadily to the main entrance and down the steps to the street, pulling his collar up and loping across to his Mercedes. It had looked beautifully natural but the agents had followed suit, two of them getting into the Porsche and two into the BMW.

I took my time, because my SSL was nearer the corner of the square, which had one-way circulation. I could let them go past me before I pulled out and took up the rear, which was the only place where I could do anything. I didn't know if Brekhov would try reaching the British Embassy or a police station or somewhere crowded like a street market where the opposition couldn't use their guns without killing other people. At this moment we had the streets almost to ourselves because of the rain: a lot of the shopping traffic had pulled in somewhere to wait out the downpour, and we were now driving on dipped headlights like the few other vehicles we saw.

Brekhov was taking us eastward all the time, maybe looking for street patterns that could get him clear: narrow places with cars parked where he might be able to swing to a stop broadside across the street and get out and run clear; or loop roads with a one-way T-section where he could make a right feint and turn left and hope the hunter car would swing out of control when it tried to follow.

He knew how to drive: he was a courier. As we reached stretches of open road he veered toward the centreline and chose a late apex on the right-hand turns, losing ground on the way in but gaining speed on the way out. The BMW was keeping well up on him and I began getting worried that Brekhov would use the late-apex technique when the BMW was close because it had more power, and if it were right on the Mercedes' tail when it went into a right-hand turn it could overhaul him alongside and force him into a crash.

A lot of what we were doing was instinctive rather than planned because the wipers weren't getting the rain off the windscreens fast enough even on high speed and we couldn't see much more than a blur in front of us. The headlights of vehicles coming the other way turned the rain haze into a burst of dazzling glare and left our retinae light-shocked for seconds on end. The speedometer needle on my facia was swinging between 90 and 110 kph and I didn't like it because if we were going to get out of this one it would have to be by science and not chance, and high speed was a hazard.

They knew I was supporting Brekhov by now: I'd kept up with them too long. I hadn't seen the Porsche since we'd lost it on the gateswing turn but it didn't mean it wouldn't find us again: it was a much faster machine.

The rain hit the top of the bonnet and whipped across the screen, slowing the wiper blades before they could move it away; with both windows shut the heat of the engine was bringing a lot of warmth into the interior and I was sitting in my sweat because if Brekhov came unstuck on a turn or the rain blinded him and he hit a curb at the wrong angle or tried some kind of technique that didn't work there might not be a chance for me to get to him before the two men in the BMW dragged him out of the wreckage. They'd have guns and that would make a critical difference at close quarters.

We were in the Weissensee district now and I knew Brekhov wasn't trying to reach anywhere: he was simply trying to outrun them by pulling every trick in the bag and hoping that just one of them would work. But they were very efficient and I began wondering whether I could get close enough to the BMW to do anything useful. If they—

Porsche.

In the mirror. It had picked us up again by luck or by making a grid search with its superior speed and gaining on us along the straight stretches and through the turns. It was only a smudge in the mirror with its lights dazzling until I flicked to night vision but it couldn't be anything but the Porsche because there were no police lights flashing and no one else would close the distance on me at 100 kph in this kind of rain.

There was no point in waiting things out if I could at least reach one of them and I could reach the Porsche so I did that, sighting ahead for a clear stretch of road and then pulling to the left and hitting the brakes and bringing it right alongside before the driver could react. It was a smaller car but I didn't use my front or rear end to swing at it; I waited till he braked on the rebound and then closed in with the mid-point of the SSL's chassis locking with his offside front wing and working at it as hard as the wet surface would let me: he was steering into me now and although he didn't have the weight necessary to move the greater mass of the SSL at the mid-section he could push back hard enough to cost me a lot of friction on the front tyres.

Then his wing buckled and I was pushing directly against his front wheel and it angled over slightly, the tyre shrilling against the metal and sending a smell of burnt rubber into my compartment. Nothing very much was happening now: at close on 90 kph we were just locked together with our treads sliding across the wet road surface independently of the steering line. We were on a straight stretch but there was a curving sheen of light ahead of us reflecting from the curbside as the road turned to the left. It wouldn't do any good unless I could burst one of his tyres by insisting with every ounce of the mass I had available against him until his nearside front wheel began scraping along the curbstones and tore through the rubber.

Then I saw some kind of dark rectangle breaking up the curve ahead of us and when the wipers got the screen clear for an instant before the rain smothered it again I saw it was a side street opening to our right, and that was all I needed and the other man knew it but couldn't do anything about it because the speed was too high and he didn't have more than three or four seconds to try using his brakes and he was much too late because we were into the turn and I kept up the pressure against him until I felt the Porsche give way suddenly as its front wheel met the gap in the curb and lurched sideways. Things were very close because he was out of control now and there was suddenly no more pressure against the SSL and even though I was ready for it there wasn't a lot of time to pull out: at this speed there was too much centrifugal force to let me get away with it cleanly. The front end tried to follow the Porsche into the side street but I managed to pull over soon enough to stop hitting the corner of the curbstone; the SSL began swinging out of control and I damped things down by touching the brakes and releasing them until we found direction and steadied with the speed coming down, and as I began using the throttle again I heard the Porsche hit the corner building with the hollow sound of a bomb and then there was just the drumming of the rain on the bonnet and the roof as I drove clear.

The brake lights of the BMW flashed once and went out again: the driver had probably taken a glance behind him when he heard the crash. I was closing the distance well enough because Brekhov had slowed ahead of us through a right-angle turn. The wail of a siren was coming from somewhere now – I'd been waiting for that because you can't do this speed through the streets of Berlin for too long before a police car takes an interest. This was going to make–

Blinding headlights suddenly and I put a hand up to shield my eyes while I kept the car in a straight line but the BMW was slowing down hard and I had to brake while I tried to work out the score and there was only one answer possible: Brekhov had used the right-angle turn to do another gateswing while the hunter was still on the blind side, and it had been the Mercedes that had passed me in the opposite direction.

I got around faster than the BMW by using the curbstone as a cushion for the rear wheel, swinging the whole thing round and getting enough acceleration to keep Brekhov in sight with the BMW behind me in the mirror, but it was no go because there was a truck turning the corner and Brekhov had to swerve and then the whole thing was over, *finis*.

* * *

'Have you got the product?'

'Yes.'

There was a pause on the line.

'Why are you making contact?'

'To tell you I've got it, that's all.'

'Fair enough.'

They've got no bloody imagination.

'There was a bit of trouble,' I said.

'Ah. What happened?'

Stink of burned clothes in the close confines of the phone-box.

'They got onto him, somewhere along the line.'

'In Germany?'

'No. On the other side.'

'Tell me what happened, then.' This was Kinsley and he'd started to humour me, because in the ordinary way I wouldn't need to make contact at this stage: I'd just get the product back to London the quickest way.

'Look,' I said, 'I'll be bringing the thing over in a matter of hours. It's just a question of what plane I can get.' I listened to the police sirens coming in from all over the place. 'I didn't want you to pick up a freak signal from their network about our getting unstuck, that's all.'

'I understand.'

'They got onto him on the other side but too late to stop him crossing the frontier. They just signalled their people in Berlin to take care of things. We walked into a trap and had to drive out of it. I'm clear now.'

'Yes, I see.'

Then why don't you bloody well ask me?

I edged the door of the phone-box open a fraction to let some of the stink out. The sirens were louder suddenly. I could still see the flamelight against a white building, with the rain tinged red.

'What about Brekhov?' Kinsley asked.

'He's dead.'

Every muscle in my body slackened like a broken spring and I was leaning against the side of the box. The first need of grief is to talk about it and if you don't think we ever have time to grieve for strangers in this trade it's just that you don't understand that there aren't any strangers, really, out there on the brink.

'You're sure?'

'What?'

'You're sure he's dead?'

'Jesus Christ, d'you think I'd have left him there?'

I dropped the phone back on the hook and slumped harder against the glass panels of the box and squeezed my eyes shut and thought it wasn't going to be any good if I let a thing like this upset me when I ought to be moving on. Two hours into the mission and you're into a KGB trap and out of it again with a dead courier, big deal, a lot of jobs go like that, you should be used to it by now.

Maybe it was because I'd had to watch him go, without being able to do anything about it. He'd tried twice to correct his line when he'd swerved to avoid the truck but the roadway was too wet and he was half aquaplaning with the front end and he couldn't bring his speed down because he was trying to get the rear wheels to drive him straight. The headlights in my mirror seemed as if they were being flashed on and off and I couldn't understand why the driver of the BMW was doing that until I realized he'd made his skid-U-turn too fast and was swinging from side to side, out of control.

The truck loomed through the rain-haze and slammed past me as I saw the Mercedes reach the end of its run, hitting the corner of a red brick wall and swinging hard round and smashing against the side of the building with all four wheels off the ground and the suspension whipping as the rear tank split and caught a spark and the whole place was suddenly a sheet of flame.

I got the wheel hard over and slammed sideways into some iron railings and ricocheted with the seat-belt cutting diagonally across my ribs; then sound and movement stopped except for the hiss of the rain and I was running for the Mercedes. Most of the fuel had been hurled rearwards but there were flames all round the car and I dragged the door open to get

Brekhov out before the upholstery caught, but he was twisted sideways against the seat squab with his head at the wrong angle and I just ripped at his shirt and felt for the sticking-plaster and found it and tugged at it but couldn't break it because there were several layers round his body, so I broke a sliver of glass from the smashed driving window and used it for cutting until the small thin rectangular pack was free; then I got clear with the flames catching my clothes and the heat blinding me until I got out of range, rolling over and over in the puddles and beating at my legs till the flames were out and I started running.

There were some shots: the BMW had finished up on its side but one of the men was climbing out and using his gun. The police siren was very loud now and I broke through a hedge and kept to the cover of a row of trees until I could settle into a steady run. The shooting had stopped but I couldn't go back to the SSL: he'd be waiting for me to do that. I gave it a couple of miles before I slowed and started looking for a phone-box.

Slumped inside it, I looked down at the puddle that had formed from my soaked clothes, watching a dead match that was floating on it, until my senses got back into focus and I picked up the phone again and got the embassy.

'I was cut off from London.'

When Kinsley came on the linked radio line I just told him I'd be getting onto the first available plane.

'Do you need help of any kind?'

'No.'

A huge fire engine was thundering past as I left the phone-box, and I looked back once at the light of the flames, faint now in the distance, while in my mind the echoes of steadily running footsteps died away.

KILL

'COME IN.'

He stood aside for me.

There were six men in the room and none of them looked at me. This was Room 382 at No. 24 South Eaton Place, the office of the Chief of Political Liaison Section, the cover title for the head of the CIA station in London.

Kinsley didn't introduce me. It was the same situation as the Downing Street thing and I assumed it was the quickest way of getting strict-hush information to me: briefing would have taken much longer. I was still wearing the cheap denim slacks and polo sweater I'd bought in Berlin: my own clothes had been soaked and the trouser legs charred by the fire and I wouldn't have got near a plane before the KGB surveillance team there put two and two together. The report on the Brekhov incident would have reached their local network in a matter of minutes.

'Have a chair,' Kinsley said.

Croder was here, glancing over me with a faint light of approval in his eyes. I don't suppose he was terribly pleased that I'd let the opposition spring a trap and get the courier killed but the main thing appeared to be that the product was here in this room, presumably intact.

The US ambassador was here, brooding massively near the desk: I'd seen him at Downing Street. I didn't know who the others were but obviously one of them was the head of the

CIA over here and the two odd-looking types must be the technicians looking after the tape-deck and the sound spectrograph on the desk. They were fiddling with it while Croder talked quietly to the CIA chief and Ambassador Morrison stared at his large veined hands. I remembered he'd had a nephew on board the submarine.

'Sorry about Brekhov,' Kinsley murmured. 'Are you okay now?'

'Everything's relative.' They think you only bring back physical scars.

He watched me with his unsurprisable eyes. 'We may be sending you out again.'

Croder had warned me about that. Whoever we send out to meet Brekhov, it would be logical to think that there will indeed be more for him to do, a very great deal more.

'All right,' I told Kinsley. My eyes were still sore from the heat of the fire and my hair still smelled of smoke and I kept on seeing Brekhov with his head like that. But given enough incentive I'd feel mission-ready again.

'We're not sure yet,' Kinsley said, 'when we–' then he broke off as one of the technicians started talking.

'What we're going to hear is the actual tape recorded at the time of the incident. Then we'll listen to a tape taken from the file on routine audio-surveillance in the Murmansk area.' He wiped his thin red nose and looked at Croder.

'Very good.'

I turned my chair round the other way and leaned my arms on its back; I hadn't slept on the flight out to Berlin or the flight home and there was the whole night still heavy on me.

The man slipped the tape into the deck and set it to play. There was silence for five or six seconds and then some kind of background interference; then two voices began speaking in Russian, in between intervals of what sounded like grid hum.

I have a weak signal on No. 12.

The technician spoke in the intervals. 'That's one of their sonobuoy monitoring stations.'

And we have another signal on No. 3. Stronger.

Can you triangulate?

The background hummed.

Yes. We have a velocity of 15 knots. The position is 17–E on the east grid.

'They'll be watching these readings on a computer screen,' the technician said, and wiped his nose again. It had been freezing outside when I'd got here.

It's moving out of range on No. 12. The course is 119°.

How close is it to my No. 4 battery?

Less than half a kilometre, and closing on it.

How fast?

I don't know. Wait.

There was a long silence except for the hum.

'He's getting some trouble here. He's either picking up a stray bleep from a different sensor field, or the computer's asking for more data.'

The other technician, a man with a humped back and grey smoked glasses, said to nobody: 'We're not sure whether they've got a Magnetic Anomaly Detector.'

'If they have,' the CIA man said, 'they got it from us.' I thought it was meant to be a joke but no one laughed.

All right. All right. It's now 760 metres from your No. 4 battery. Course is now 121°, position 17–F.

It's isolated?

Yes. I have a kill ready.

Silence again.

The ambassador moved heavily to the door and went out. No one looked anywhere but at the tape-deck.

Confirm you have a kill ready.

I confirm.

Other sounds came in now, with voices in the distant background.

Keep me advised.

Something like a minute went by and there was nothing we could hear that told us anything. Croder glanced across at the CIA chief, who was sitting with his elbows on the desk and his face between his fists, stretching the skin into furrows. He was watching the tape-deck; he didn't catch Croder's glance.

I didn't know the figures involved in that area: the depth or salinity or current or the cruise speed of a torpedo.

Advise me. Did I make a hit? Did I make a hit?

The voice was excited now.

Wait.

Croder took out his cigarette-case and lit one of those black-tipped things he smoked, but he didn't look away from the tape-deck.

No. You did not make a hit.

Advise me.

Wait.

The hump-backed technician drew in his breath suddenly and turned to Croder. 'Can I have one of those?'

He lit up and turned away from the desk, so as not to watch the tape-deck.

New position: 17–G on the east grid. 540 metres from your No. 4 battery. Profile is broadside on. You have a kill.

Keep me advised.

We had to wait again. The CIA man had closed his eyes now, his fists kneading his face into a loose mask. Croder glanced towards the door and away again. The silence drew out.

Advise me. Did we make a hit? Did we make a hit?

The grid hummed. There were other sounds, vague and intermittent, and a quick beeping began. It lasted a minute, maybe more.

The hump-back had turned round to watch the tape-deck.

Confirm. You made a hit. I repeat: You made a hit.

The thin technician used his handkerchief again.

'We made modifications to this model so we could extract parameters from the speech waveform. That gives us a better speech recognition performance. What's happening is that the variable electronic filter is moving to higher and higher frequencies while the stylus is moving parallel to the axis of the drum. What we're getting from this pattern are the dimensions of time, frequency and amplification.'

The voice was almost continuous on this second tape.

No. 5 sonobuoy responding. Object at 43–A. Speed of movement constant. Approach to No. 6 sonobuoy at steady 68° with appropriate response. Transducers running in No. 1 bay.

Tape gap.

All configurations are normal. Bathythermograph average is 42°. Total east grid surveillance is now ten buoys.

Tape gap.

I'm now triangulating on S–35. It's 12–B on the east grid, course 76°. Depth now 70 metres.

'S–35 is one of their diesel subs,' the technician with the cold said. He let the tape run on for another two or three minutes and then the CIA chief asked him to shut it down. He took his face out of his hands and got up and went out of the room, coming back with the ambassador.

'So tell us,' he said to the technicians.

The hump-back prodded his cigarette out. 'All we can say for sure is that the voice on the second tape is the same as the one on the first tape that was doing the advising. He's one of their sonar operators. The other man of course was in charge of a torpedo battery.'

The CIA chief dug his hands into his pockets, putting his head back, speaking to the ceiling. 'That was the actual attack on the *Cetacea* we were listening to? The actual sinking?'

'Yes.'

'Bastards. *Bastards.*'

No one broke the silence for a while. It was a silence for the one hundred and five crew of the SSN *Cetacea*, missing on patrol.

Croder said quietly to the technicians: 'What you're saying, then, is that the voice of the man advising is genuine – a genuine naval officer working the sonar unit.'

'Right. Look at this spectrogram. Identical patterns in every single speech mode. Same man.'

'And from this we can assume,' the CIA chief said in a flat tone, 'that the tape you people just brought back from Murmansk is a genuine recording of the incident. Is that right?'

'Not quite,' Croder said. 'On the face of it, we don't really doubt that it's genuine. This is because our agent in Murmansk has been installed there as a sleeper for nearly five years, and has been sending back the most valuable material. He realized the enormous significance of this particular run of tape, and had it duplicated. He then signalled us and told us he was sending it by courier.'

I watched the two technicians for a moment. They weren't just boffins: they must have been security-screened on the highest level.

'We know, of course, that the Soviets will deny the whole thing and say that we've faked this tape ourselves. Our answer to that is that the voice on the recent tape tallies precisely with one of the voices the CIA has been recording as a routine acoustic surveillance operation for a very long time. There's a second point. If anyone – meaning, I don't doubt, the Soviets – faked this tape and deliberately allowed us to get hold of it, then we can say with absolute certainty that they had to persuade or order an actual naval officer to speak on that new tape, acting out the despatch of those torpedoes. They–'

'Why in hell would they want to do that?' Ambassador Morrison asked him.

Croder spread his hands open. His smile was almost apologetic. 'I've no wish to complicate things, Mr Ambassador. It's simply that we want to have every answer ready.'

'We're talking about Russian double think,' the CIA chief nodded.

'It's *that* convoluted?'

'Not really,' Croder said. 'What I'm saying now is that if, for example, the Soviets wished to scuttle the proposed summit conference for whatever obscure reason, they couldn't do it more simply than by faking this tape and allowing us to come by it.'

'You believe that's what they did?'

'I believe it's most unlikely. We're just covering the contingency. Most unlikely of all is the idea that a naval officer could lend himself to the deceit, however threatened or cajoled or bribed with honours and promotion.'

The ambassador watched Croder with his large head lowered and his eyes level. 'Then you believe this tape is genuine, and that it gives us irrefutable evidence that the Soviets in fact ordered the attack and sinking of the submarine. Is that correct?'

A faint apologetic smile. 'Not quite. I don't believe in the least that the Soviets – by which you mean the Soviet *authorities* – ordered the attack on the *Cetacea*. I believe that when she was discovered either close to the twelve-mile limit or actually within Soviet waters, the officer in command of No. 4 torpedo battery made the attack and sank the boat.'

'Without getting permission?'

'Yes.'

'Why?'

'For one of several understandable reasons. He's young, keen, ambitious, perhaps. What a bone to bring to the mat of his superiors! The hero of the hour, destroying in the nick of time an *American* nuclear submarine in the act of spying on the Soviets' most important naval base – the gateway to the Atlantic, bristling with the most highly secret technology.'

The ambassador went on watching him, his eyes narrowed now. I didn't know if he knew who Croder was, other than a key man in the Foreign Office. 'He didn't think there was time to get permission to do this thing?'

'Oh, he knew there was time. The boat was moving very slowly, and they were keeping track of it. We heard that.'

'Then why didn't he call up a superior officer?'

'I believe he thought they might deny him permission.' Croder spread his hands again, shrugging.

'I don't understand.'

Croder took a pace or two. 'There was once a wealthy widow who placed all her money in a phoney investment that looked highly attractive, and when she lost it all her accountant asked her why on earth she didn't consult him first. She said rather sheepishly she was pretty sure he wouldn't have let her do it.'

'My God. He was out to get that sub on his own initiative?'

'It's what we believed,' the CIA chief said reasonably, 'when the KAL plane was shot out of the sky. At first, anyway.'

Croder looked down at his shoes. 'It's what I still believe, despite a great deal of fanciful evidence to the contrary.'

The CIA chief glanced at him. 'You don't think there's any kind of connection?'

'Not in a sequential sense. I think it's a repetition of the same basic situation.'

'Okay,' Morrison said finally. 'I can report to my president, then, that the British government believes, on the evidence of this tape recording, that the *Cetacea* was attacked and sunk by a Soviet naval officer, without prior warning. Is that right?'

'Very nearly.' Croder. 'Those in the British government most able to analyse the raw intelligence data believe it, yes.'

'Bob?' The ambassador was looking at the CIA chief. 'That's your opinion too?'

'I guess it has to be.' He gave a shrug, tilting his head. 'In my field we tend to look for skeletons in all the cupboards, but in this case I think that's very simply what happened. A United States submarine was found too close to the Russian coast and they sank it. And we have the evidence on tape.'

There were five of us when we came into the street: Croder, Kinsley, the two boffins in their white lab coats and me. The political people stayed behind to go on with the meeting at a higher level, I suppose. But even if they'd left the building at the same time I think they would have been all right, unless they'd been too near the boffins as they climbed into their cars.

The blast tore the nearside door away and I didn't see anything more because I was spinning round and going down flat onto the pavement while the echo of the explosion started coming back from the houses and glass tinkled as the windows blew in. I wasn't close enough to feel anything more than the shock-wave, and as soon as the worst of the debris had come down I got onto my feet and turned round and took a look at the car. There wasn't anything we could do for the two men because they'd been inside when the thing had gone off, triggered by the ignition switch or a rocker mechanism or something like that.

I was a bit deafened but I could hear Croder asking if we were all right and Kinsley called out yes, then I went up the steps to the house to use a telephone as the last of the dead leaves came floating down in a moment of unnatural autumn.

The only clear thought in my head was that the actual target hadn't been the two boffins. It had been the tape, and now we'd have to start all over again.

'What?'

'How long have you slept?'

Kinsley was standing in the doorway looking down at me. I'd holed up in one of the soundproof cubicles where you can catch some sleep or just get away from the din outside when there's a big operation on and everyone's showing their nerves.

'An hour,' I told Kinsley.

'How are you feeling?' He looked very tight-faced, and kept prodding his fingers through his stiff black hair.

'I'm feeling all right.' I put my shoes on and got off the bunk, finding my jacket. 'Have you got something else for me?'

'Yes.'

'Where?'

'Moscow.'

'When?'

'Tonight.'

'What's happened?'

'They're on to Karasov.'

'The sleeper?'

'Yes. Someone found he'd made a copy of that tape.'

Everything became suddenly still.

'Was he blown?'

'No. He got out in time.'

'Where is he now?'

[60]

'God knows. But we've got to find him, before they do.'
'Yes, I see.'

Somewhere there was another man running.

8

FANE

'I'D SAY HE'S frightened.'

There were bits of white floating under the bridge.

'Doesn't he trust us?'

'I don't think it's a question of that.'

It could be ice, coming down-river. The air was freezing.

'You think he's been there too long?'

'As a sleeper?'

'Yes.'

'Possibly.' He stood with his hands in the pockets of his fleece-lined coat, looking down at the river.

I'd asked for Ferris but they said he was messing about in Hong Kong, helping to China watch. That didn't sound like Ferris.

I'd kicked up a stink, of course, but there wasn't enough time to make any changes: they'd put me onto the midnight flight after two hours' crammed briefing.

I didn't like their not giving me Ferris.

'What's that stuff?' Fane asked.

'I don't know. Probably ice.'

In a minute he said: 'You're not happy about me, are you?'

'I've no choice.'

'What are your objections, exactly?'

He was a shortish man, neatly dressed, with a clear white skin and perfectly regular features, the eyes level and the nose short and the mouth clear cut. There was nothing about him you could find interesting, or like, or dislike.

'I prefer working with people I know,' I said, 'that's all.' I looked up from the water to the gold domes of the Kremlin. 'With people who know me.'

'I'm told you're difficult,' Fane said. He took out a packet of cigarettes.

'Yes.'

'That won't worry me. The only thing that would worry me is your doing something stupid.' He offered me a cigarette but I shook my head.

'I've lasted a long time.'

The relationship between the shadow executive in the field and his local control is complicated. Fane was here to look after me, to do all the chores of booking me in at the hotel and seeing that I was comfortable and sniffing out the human environment – the other hotel guests, not the KGB: they were everywhere – and keeping me in touch with what London wanted me to know at this phase, communicating through the embassy. In this sense he was a kind of aide-de-camp and I could tell him if I didn't like the fact that my room exposed me too much or that I wanted a European car, not a Moscwicz, that sort of thing.

On the other hand he was primarily concerned with my safety and with the onward movement of the mission, and if London had sudden and critical orders for me they'd go through Fane. In this sense he was my superior, and could move me around the board like a knight, confronting me with the opposition and telling me which squares I'd need to cross. That's how things are ideally, at the outset of a mission. Later things can change, and you can lose touch with your local control or get cut off from communication or find yourself blown in a blinding light without a chance in hell of ever seeing him again or getting his help. It doesn't happen often; it's happened only three times to me and twice I went to ground and holed up solo while my local control finally signalled London that I was probably dead.

'By all means,' Fane said, 'tell me how you like to work. I've had a brief picture from Control, of course, but I'd like it from the horse's mouth.'

'No backups, shields or low-echelon contacts.'

'Strictly solo.'

'That's right.'

A jet was sloping down the sky beyond the gold domes, lowering into Sheremetyevo, its strobes pricking the winter dark.

'Of course,' Fane said, 'I can't guarantee anything like that.'

'I know.'

'That doesn't sound too difficult, then. You're not making demands I necessarily have to meet.'

I didn't say anything. He was being too punctilious. If there's one thing that can bog a mission down it's a bureaucrat working as local control.

'Tell me some more,' I said, 'about Karasov.'

He thought for a moment, then decided I wasn't going to let him set out the ground rules. This isn't a game: it's a trade. 'All right.' We began walking across the bridge, and I found it was impossible to tell whether he'd moved first or I had. 'As I said, he's probably frightened. Although he's been up there in Murmansk for over five years, it's been tricky for him because he's sent so much excellent stuff across. He took a lot of risks. I'd say his nerve isn't what it was any more. You know how–' he broke off with a slight shrug, which was civil of him, because the nerves of a shadow executive are just as vulnerable. Most of us go out with what they put down as mission fatigue, which can mean anything from hitting the bottle to visions of angels pissing in our beer. 'I would also say that Karasov is acutely aware of the stakes. The summit conference has been in jeopardy ever since that sub went down, and there are people who think that world peace is likewise in jeopardy, if we can't get round a table with the Russians.' He shrugged again. 'Even if Karasov hadn't decided to get out and go to ground, we'd have had to bring him in before we could tell the Soviets we've got the tape. The moment they know that, they'll go through their sonar station at Murmansk with killer dogs. I'm not *quite* sure he wasn't right to get out straight away before the trouble started.'

I watched the strobes of the jet touch the skyline of the

Palace of Congress and vanish. The chill wind blew through the railing along the bridge, moving the coat of the man standing beyond the next lamp.

'Has Karasov made any kind of rdv with us?' I asked Fane.

'Not yet.'

'When did he last signal?'

'Two days ago.'

'Saying?'

'That he'd gone to ground and would surface later.'

I turned my back to the wind. He'd been there ever since we'd come onto the bridge: the man whose coat was moving. I wondered where the other one was: they normally go in pairs.

'Is there anything,' I asked Fane, 'that seems a bit odd to you, about him getting out so fast, and on his own initiative?'

'I'd say he panicked. That's not odd, in the circumstances.'

'That's out of character.'

'With Karasov?' He turned to me. 'When did you—'

'No. With a sleeper.'

We stopped walking, and Fane stood watching me. 'What's on your mind?'

'I don't like the way we're having to wait for him to contact us. We should have given him very precise instructions on what to do when he got out, where to go and wait for us, who his contact would be, the whole thing. He should have let us look after him.'

'You want things done by the book.' Without looking away from my face he said, 'What's that chap doing all on his own?'

'Maybe they're short of staff.'

'Your papers are perfect. I suppose you know that.'

'I bloody well hope so.' The wind cut our faces. 'Is there any chance that Karasov has reached Moscow?'

'I doubt that.'

'You think he's still somewhere around Murmansk?'

'Yes. Sleepers don't normally run.'

'When people panic they'll do anything. When are you going to send me up there?'

'That's what we're waiting for. They're trying to tell us all the hotels are full.' He lit another cigarette.

'Why?' This was local briefing.

'The background is that while the Soviets are stonewalling and denying everything and the US is trying to make up its mind whether or not to accuse them outright and on presidential level, the longer they can keep the international press out of Murmansk the better. But they'll have to allow a quota, or it'll look too obvious.'

'How are you going to make sure I'm on the quota?'

'I can't. London can't. The minister here can simply say okay, get them in a crowd at a gate and let the first ten through. And we shan't know which gate.' He sounded slightly impatient: I suppose he didn't like having to admit he couldn't just wave a wand and bring the whole of the Kremlin down to show what a good little local control he was.

It occurred to me that I ought to make an effort and stop disliking him. It could be dangerous: at any next hour my life could suddenly be in his hands. But it went on nagging me, about Ferris. I didn't believe they wouldn't have called him in from Hong Kong to local-control me if they'd wanted to, and I didn't believe he wouldn't have agreed to do it, unless there was something going on that I didn't know about.

Had they asked him, and had he refused?

We're never told more than they want us to know. The less we know, the safer we are if we're caught and put under a bright light and worked over.

I thought of contacting Ferris and asking him. But how long would it take to make a phone call from Moscow to Hong Kong?

This was just nerves, the normal paranoia you've got to deal with in the first few hours in the field. I'd slept most of the day since I'd flown in; those had been my orders and I didn't complain. Lack of sleep doesn't help you at this stage; it's when the nerves need an awful lot of tender loving care.

'What happens if you can't get me on the quota?' I asked Fane.

'It'd depend on London, of course.'

'I'd have to go clandestine.'

We'd been walking again to keep the circulation going, in the other direction from the KGB man, and now Fane stopped again and looked at me with a long-suffering blink. 'Quite possibly, yes. But I don't want you to go clandestine without instructions. Please understand that.'

'I can't guarantee it.' One of his own phrases.

He humped his shoulders. 'They were perfectly right. You're difficult.'

He'd raised his voice slightly. I didn't like that. If you're going to local-control a shadow through the field you've got to keep your cool.

'How many times have you been out, Fane?'

He went on staring at me, and I wondered how far I'd have to push him before he lost his cool completely. If he did that, I'd signal London and tell them to send someone else.

'One loses count,' he said levelly. 'Doesn't one?'

He'd seen the danger and taken the heat off at once.

'How many clandestines have you run?'

'We don't keep an actual score like the shadow executives. But quite a few. And I didn't lose anyone.'

This time I made the first move and we went on walking again in the other direction, towards the hotel. I wanted to get out of this bloody wind. I hate the cold. 'Then you'll know,' I said conversationally, 'that at any given time I might *have* to go clandestine, either—'

'Yes. I know that.' He had a swinging walk, perhaps to make up for his short legs; or it could simply have been an expression of his inward anger because I was being difficult. 'And you know what I'm saying, I'm sure. I don't want you to go clandestine *unless you have to.*'

When we passed the solitary man he turned his back to us, staring down into the river. He smelled of black tobacco.

'The thing is,' I told Fane, 'you can cut a lot of corners that way.' There was a big difference between a covert and a clandestine mission, and he knew that. When you're sent out with a cover and a legend you've got to stick to it and that can slow you up: you can't go anywhere you like, you can only go where your cover takes you. Tonight I was here as a journalist for the *Monitor,* and it would be all right as long as I stuck with that cover: I could go to the press club and my embassy and the Soviet Ministry of Information, places like that, but I couldn't just wander about in the streets without an obvious destination: journalists don't rubberneck. I couldn't do any kind of surveillance if anyone interested me and I couldn't pop into a phone-box without my own KGB surveillance people noting the fact and if I stopped to talk to a Soviet citizen they'd haul me along for questioning *and it doesn't matter how perfect your papers are, you're never certain that your cover's going to hold up.* And that's when you suddenly realize it's too late to go clandestine. You can't run. As a clandestine you're a free agent, using light cover if you want to – Boris Antonov, Soviet citizen, so forth – but running free through the tunnels and the night hours and the back streets and following your own instincts, sniffing the wind for smoke.

'You can cut corners,' Fane said, 'yes.' We turned from the bridge into the Rausskaja nabareznaja towards the Bukarest, and the wind was less sharp. 'I simply want you to do it only if you have to.' He stopped and looked up at me again. 'I don't mind your being difficult, you see, if that's your character. But I don't want you to use it as a policy.'

I'd never had to spell out the parameters of a mission with my local control before. It unnerved me.

'They've never given me anyone,' I said carefully, 'who didn't turn out to be first class, even if we finished up hating each other's guts. All I ask is that you get me home alive. Even if it's the last thing you want to do.'

He went on watching me with his level eyes, perhaps not knowing whether I was being funny. 'From someone as boorish as you, I suppose that's a compliment.'

'Sorry. It must have slipped out.'

In the hotel lobby Fane picked up a message and used an outside line while I looked at a display of dolls in regional costumes and had the odd thought that there actually *were* children like this dancing somewhere on some village square to the music of a pipe band while I stood here living my lies and practising my deceits on the pretext that I was doing my bit to keep the Cold War from hotting up. Which was the real world, those children's or mine? It can only ever be the one we create, the one we have to design for ourselves to give us shelter from confusion and sustenance for our needs. I don't dance so well to a pipe band as to the tune of my own dark drummer.

Fane was coming away from the telephone.

'They've put us on the quota. We're flying to Murmansk.'

'When?'

'As soon as they've got the runways cleared up there. They've had snow.'

9

TANYA

NIGHT WAS COMING to Murmansk.

There had been no sun. This was winter.

The light was changing from steel grey to gunmetal blue, so slowly that it mesmerized. Shadows deepened as the weight of the dark came down, because the light wasn't leaving; it was simply changing, from the monotone arctic wash of the daytime, sunless and moonlike, to the trembling and fragile glow of the northern lights across the snow.

Only here, and in places along this latitude, does the coming of the night bring shadows. In its strangeness there is a certain quality of safety, if you are being watched: you can find concealment in the kaleidoscope of light and shade. And if you are watching, you can more easily detect abnormal configurations among the formal geometry of streets and buildings, such as the shape of a man's head.

Tonight I was watching. Soon I would know if I were also being watched.

The last I'd seen of Fane, an hour ago, was his short neat body with its swinging walk disappearing into the lift at the hotel. I was glad to see him go. In the days ahead I would need him, of course, perhaps desperately; but if I could make my way through this mission without his help I would like to do that.

There was something wrong about him. There was something wrong about their not giving me Ferris. I knew this without questioning how I knew, just as I knew without any question that the man at the end of the platform had missed the last train. But I didn't want to pay too much attention to there being something wrong until I knew more about *Northlight*. That was the name across the top of the board at London Control, the name for the mission. It could still be a matter of nerves, though I'd been long enough in this trade to know that your nerves will tell you things more accurately, on a primitive level where sensitivity is subconscious, than your brain, which can make up answers of its own to explain the inexplicable, rather than admit to having none.

When the next train came in, its steam clouding against the pale luminosity of the sky and its hot smell reaching me and bringing warmth, I saw the man get into a carriage and slam the door. He hadn't, then, missed the last train: it wasn't going where he wanted to go, that was all.

'My name is Tanya.'

You can't tell much over a telephone. Her voice had been low, a little husky, that was all. But there'd been caution in the tone, a note of vigilance. There'd been silences, after I'd spoken, in which she had listened a second time to what I'd said, sifting it for danger.

'Why did you want me to telephone?' I asked her.

'Because of . . .' she'd hesitated, 'the snowbirds.'

She should have brought it in straight away, the moment she'd told me her name; but perhaps some idiot at the embassy hadn't told her that; or she'd forgotten. 'Snowbirds' was the code-introduction.

'What do you want me to do?' I asked her.

'To meet me.'

'Why?' This was routine. I already knew, but I wanted her to go on talking in case there were anything wrong, anything dangerous.

'Because–' she hesitated again – 'because of the snowbirds. That is all I can say, over the telephone.'

'All right. In an hour, then.'

'Very well.' She didn't ask where. They'd told her that it was for me to make the rendezvous. She was getting things right.

'At the east railway station,' I told her. 'How far is that from where you are now?'

'Not far. Perhaps five kilometres.'

'All right. In the small waiting-room at the north end of Platform 4. Repeat that.'

When she'd finished I said: 'Tell me what you look like.'

She hesitated again. 'I am young, and not very tall. I will be wearing an old sable coat, and—'

'What colour are your eyes?' Everyone here was wearing fur; it was twenty-five degrees below freezing.

'They are dark.'

'Brown? Blue?'

'Brown.'

'All right. Don't approach anyone. I'll approach you. Wear an odd pair of gloves, that don't quite match.'

That had been an hour ago and as the train pulled out I saw the man opening a paper behind the grimy glass. He didn't glance out.

In this unearthly light the station had the aspect of an illusion. With the snow-covered roofs reflecting the sky and the shadows darker than they'd been at noon, definition was lost, and the shadows seemed more solid than the buildings themselves. Her short figure had the same sense of unreality: her shadow, moving across the open expanse of snow between the lamps, leaned and turned with a movement of its own as the light changed around it.

I let ten minutes go by after she'd walked into the little waiting-room, checking and double-checking the configurations in the environment: the line of three taxis alongside the iron railings; the black Pobeda with snow on its roof, parked facing the gates; the two men talking near the cafeteria, their breath clouding under the lamps; the group of children stamping their feet to a rhythm that was becoming a dance and leading to laughter; and the sailors over by the huge red tea-wagon. It had taken me fifteen minutes to get here from the hotel and the rest of the time I'd spent absorbing the changing patterns of movement in the whole of the area overlooking the waiting-room, and I was satisfied.

[72]

London doesn't warn you to take care when it sends you into a rendezvous. It's your responsibility to check the other party for surveillance and for traps: you're expected to go in and get out and leave no trace, but we don't look at it as a tactical regulation because if we get anything wrong it's our own skin.

'Good evening.' I stood looking down at her for a moment.

She turned quickly to face me, half-catching her breath, her bronze eyes staring into mine with something like fear. She brought her hands upwards across the front of her worn sable coat as if protecting herself, though it was probably to show me her gloves didn't match.

'I thought you weren't coming,' she said huskily.

'Sorry I'm late. It was the snow.'

'Did you–' she left it.

'Did I what?'

'Did you come in a car?'

'We're better off in here. Nobody can watch us. The car's in the open.'

She looked quickly through the small smoke-grimed window, her lips parting as if to say something. Then she looked back at me but said nothing. A shiver went through her.

'Come and sit down.' I led her across to the wooden bench. There was no heating in here; that's why I'd chosen it: so that we'd be alone. It was the best of the four or five places I'd checked out yesterday when the embassy in Moscow had prepared me for an imminent rendezvous.

'Do you know where he is?' She'd been holding the question back: it came out with a little rush, her breath clouding under the light that hung from the ceiling.

I ignored the question.

'Why did you call my embassy, Tanya?'

She took it as an accusation. 'I . . . I hoped someone there might know where he is.'

'It's perfectly all right to call us. I just want to know why you did. I mean, why us.'

She was watching my eyes intently, either not trusting what I was saying or believing there was a hidden meaning.

A lot of rdv's are like that, with strangers.

'I. . . .' She looked down, then up again. 'He said sometimes that he had "British friends".'

'In Russia?'

'He didn't say that. He just said friends.'

'So you phoned the British embassy?'

'Yes.' She darted a glance at the window again and at the glass-panelled door.

She says she's Karasov's mistress, the message had told me. It had been in read-through code with the name changed, handed to me by a small man in a duffle coat as I was getting out of the lift at the hotel, a perfect pass – I'd hardly seen his face as he'd turned away. Fane hadn't told me he was running couriers, and I didn't know how the embassy could have made contact with him: the rooms were bugged. *We suggest you meet her and see if she can be useful in any way.* The telephone number had followed.

'Have you heard from him?' I asked her, and she looked back at me from the window.

'No. That's why I'm so worried.'

I didn't know if she'd seen anyone outside, or was simply frightened. For me there wasn't much risk: I'd gone from covert to clandestine when I'd left the hotel, putting my London papers inside a door panel of the car and bringing the others – Boris Antonov, Moscow work and residence visa – because a visiting foreign journalist had no business talking to a Soviet citizen in the waiting-room of a Murmansk railway station and they'd send me out of the country at a minute's notice after the interrogation was done with. At best. If I made some kind of mistake they'd keep me here and go to work on me.

I took one of her gloved hands. 'It's all right if the militia come in here. I'm a Soviet citizen with full visa.'

She looked surprised, then relieved.

'Then what is your name?'

'You don't know it. You came in here because I was

pestering you, but I still followed. With your looks, they'd believe that.'

She glanced away with a little dipping motion of her head. 'Very well.'

'Just go with whatever I say. You're perfectly safe.' I took my hand away. 'He hasn't tried to get in touch with you, even, through friends?'

'No.' She looked suddenly desolate. 'I love him. I love him very much.'

'Are there friends he could use as a go-between?'

'No. We . . . meet very privately.' Suddenly she asked, 'Do you think he's dead?'

'No. Why?'

'Because even if they'd arrested him, he would have got a message to me.'

'How?'

Her head came down. 'I don't know. Somehow.'

'There's no reason why he should be dead. You should be hearing from him at any time.'

She seemed to know I was just trying to make it easier for her. 'Do you think he's a spy?'

'Why should he be?'

'Because he's missing from his unit, and has British friends. And there's this news about the American submarine.'

'We don't know very much about him.'

'Then why did you come to meet me, when I asked?'

'We're always interested in any Soviet citizen who contacts the embassy, in case they need our help.'

Her hands gripped mine quite hard. 'Would you give him asylum, if he asked for that?'

'Probably.'

'I love him so much, you see.'

'We understand.'

Laughter came suddenly from outside, raucous, masculine. She didn't look up; she wasn't afraid of laughter, only of eyes in the shadow of peaked caps, only of questions.

'If he makes contact with you,' she said with less despair, 'will you tell me?'

'Of course. Will you be at the same number?'

'Yes. It's my apartment.'

'What's the address?'

She gave it to me, and I wrote it down.

The laughter broke out again, and I saw the heads of three sailors passing the window, their breath steaming. I said: 'Did you go to any bars together, any cafes?'

'Sometimes.'

'Which ones?'

'It was never the same ones.'

'But you've gone there, asking if they've seen him?'

'No. I'm afraid.'

'Have the naval police questioned you?'

'No. We–'

'Has anyone?'

'You mean the KGB?'

'Why the KGB?'

She shrugged. 'That's what we always mean when we say "anyone". But nobody has questioned me. They don't know I'm his friend.'

'If anyone asks you about him, I'd like you to tell me.'

'Where will I find you?'

'At the embassy. We'd like to help him.'

Then the tears were in her eyes and creeping down her face, though she made no sound, but just looked down and let them come, and let me brush them away with my finger while we sat like that for a time, listening to the sailors laughing on the platform outside and the first rumbling of a train nearing the station.

'If they send him to a labour camp, it will kill me.'

'He'll be back.'

'I would like–' and then she was really sobbing, lowering her head so that I couldn't any longer see her face, just her fur hat as she brought her arms across the table and let her shoulders go on shaking while I put my hands over hers and waited, wondering for the first time if Karasov had even had a chance in hell of making a clear run out of Murmansk when the whole of the Soviet navy was in a state of freeze in the international limelight. He couldn't have done it in uniform; he'd gone to ground as a civilian. He'd had to; it was the only way, if he'd got clear at all.

Whatever else happens, Croder had said, *you've got to bring that man across.*

When the sobbing died away I said, 'He hasn't been in touch with you because he doesn't want you involved. That must have occurred to you.'

'Yes.' She straightened up from the table and blew her nose. She smelt of musk, and her coat had fallen open to reveal the softness of small breasts under her sweater; she was, I supposed, with her bronze eyes and that huskiness in her voice and a capacity for loving so desperately, the kind of woman who could hope to see Karasov again, if he were free.

It would be pointless to ask her about his wife, to ask if there were any chance he'd gone there for shelter. That was the last place he'd go; they'd expect him to do that, and she'd be under distant but intense surveillance day and night. If he went anywhere for help, where he knew it would be immediately granted, it would be to this woman who sat humped in the chilly waiting-room of a railway station, the only hope we had, at this moment, of finding Karasov and getting him across to the West and bringing the president of the United States and the leader of the Soviet Union to a conference table in Vienna in eight weeks' time.

'The best way you can help him, Tanya, when you see him again, is to let us know. It's perfectly true: he does have British friends, and they're very powerful.'

Then I was watching her small figure again crossing the snow the way she had come, Tanya Kiselev, leaving me with salt on my fingers and the lingering scent of musk.

10

CURFEW

'WHY HAVE YOU come here?'
        'To complain.'
        'Of what?'
'My room at the hotel was searched.'
'So?'
'I want to know why.'
He gave me a long stare.
'Why do you think we should know that?'
'Who else would search a foreign visitor's room?'
'A thief.'
I didn't answer.
'Perhaps that didn't occur to you?'
'Frankly, no.'
I had to watch my idiom.
'Then perhaps you should think again. It may have been
someone with a grudge against you.'
He wore a captain's insignia and he was young, smooth,
educated: one of the new school, not to be underestimated.
'Perhaps,' I said. My Russian was supposed to be adequate,
not fluent. I was no longer clandestine. 'But I'd like your
personal assurance that the KGB knew nothing about it.'
'You know your rights. Your famous civil rights.'
'I'm not an American.'
'You don't have civil rights, in England?'
I ignored that.
Bright lights, sticky warmth, a puddle of water near the door

where the snow had come off my shoes. KGB headquarters Murmansk was the last place I wanted to be but there hadn't been any choice: they'd searched my room while I'd been at the railway station and I couldn't just let it go: an intelligence agent would expect the odd search somewhere along the line if he became suspect, but a *bona fide* journalist wouldn't expect it and he'd be pretty sure to notice it and he'd make a bloody great fuss. I was here to protect my cover, that was all.

But I didn't like it.

'Please take a chair.'

'Thank you.'

He picked up a phone and asked for a Captain Bratchenko.

I didn't like it because it could be a trap. They'd had time enough, over an hour: they'd watched me leave the hotel and would have gone up to my room straight away. Their expertise varies: it depends how concerned they are that you shouldn't notice. This time they'd done a reasonable job – the razor was only a quarter of an inch out of place and the top drawer of the dressing-table was almost shut and my spare shoes were still touching the wall of the cupboard, that sort of thing – but it was in fact the razor that I'd used as one of the monitors and this tied in with the telephone's being five or six degrees turned away from the line from the edge of the bedside table to the mirror. They hadn't broken the hair I'd left across the medicine cabinet door in the bathroom but they'd made a mistake with the copy of *Pravda* I'd dropped on the floor by the armchair: it was turned over back upper-most. That didn't tie in with the care they'd taken generally and the thing that worried me was that they might have relied on that to get me in here, thinking I might not notice the other things.

'Bratchenko? This is Demichev, Headquarters.'

My papers were all right. I knew that. It's never a danger: the Bureau prides itself on certain things and that's one of them. The danger is always that these people are all-powerful, and they could simply take me from here to a cell with a barred door and play with me until I made a mistake, and when I made the mistake it wouldn't matter how hard the British ambassador tried to get me out: he wouldn't succeed.

You don't of course make any mistakes while you're fresh in from the street and on your toes and ready to go through with the whole thing as a technical exercise; but after a few hours of bright lights and shouting you begin to get worried and that's when you can make your first mistake and that one is going to be all they'll need because they'll seize on it and put you through the hoop until you make another one and then you're done for, *finis*.

I would very much like to have stayed in my comfortable hotel and let them think I hadn't noticed anything, but that would have been dangerous, more dangerous than coming along here and facing them on their own ground. To show them that I was prepared for a room search at any given time would be to blow my own cover.

'No, he's just making a formal complaint.' He looked up at me with a smooth swing of his head – he reminded me of the pictures I'd seen of Eichmann: a soft, delicate face with the eyes of a predator. 'Was there anything missing?'

'Missing?'

'From your room.'

'I don't think so.'

'Don't you know?'

'I didn't pay much attention. I was so annoyed that I came straight along here.'

Under the subheading *Cover* in my briefing papers someone had written a quite amusing bit about the British journalist: *He is typically polite, a degree arrogant – as befits a scion of perfidious Albion – but often tests the authority of the host country, even be it the Soviet Union, by demanding fair treatment and respect. Indignation is expected by the law enforcement, bureaucratic and secret police agencies from any British journalist placed in an annoying or embarrassing situation. The objective is to exasperate the officers of these agencies to the point of giving you what they demand, offering their apologies or simply kicking you out without pressing whatever charges may have been laid.*

'The complainant is very annoyed,' the captain said into

the telephone, and had the courtesy to keep his face straight while I heard a faint laugh from the other end. I should have liked him for that, but I didn't. He had his role to play just as I did. He'd been trained in the new school of the *Komitet Gosudarstvennoy Bezopasnosti* to show foreign visitors – especially journalists, who would be writing it up when they got home – an official image of courtesy, authority and efficiency. This didn't mean that if he found anything wrong with my papers or I made some kind of mistake he wouldn't order me into an interrogation room and get enough out of me to send me to a forced labour camp for ten years, and the fact that he'd be doing something perfectly understandable in protecting his country from the activities of an espionage agent wouldn't do anything to soften the guards' clubs or break the ice in the buckets or give me more than a bowl of watery gruel with only the roaches in it to crunch for protein.

'Please show me your papers.' He leaned forward slightly with the phone still to his ear and took them from me. I'd already shown them to the guard at the desk outside but I couldn't refuse. He studied them, taking his time.

'Clive Gage,' he said into the telephone. 'He is in Room 45 at the Hotel Leningrad.' He waited, occupying himself by gazing at my papers, turning them to the light with his eyes narrowing slightly: I think he was simply trying to frighten me, but he did it well.

Please tell me what is happening.

The prime minister had a reputation for phoning people before they could phone her.

As far as we know, ma'am, Karasov is still somewhere in Murmansk. We've now placed our agent there to bring him across the moment he makes contact. We also have a lead that should enable us to do this before very long.

That wouldn't satisfy her but she wasn't aware of the difficulty. There was only one, but it was a facer. *Karasov wouldn't make contact.*

The 'lead' was of course Tanya Kiselev. I suppose they could call her that. London knew their sleeper well enough to be sure that if he was more likely to go to anyone else for shelter, they'd know about it, and instruct me accordingly. But the longer time went on and he didn't surface, the more difficult it was going to be. A shadow executive or a cutout or a courier would break for a frontier within an hour of closing down his mission and he'd expect instant help and he'd get it – I'd brought three of them across like that, carrying one down a mountainside into Bavaria and throwing another into a meat truck on the drug route across the Isonzo Bridge and shoving a third man into a plane in Topolovgrad with a bullet still in his shoulder blade but a lot of life left in him and a photocopy schedule of the Warsaw Pact military exercise still taped round his leg. It's difficult work but it's fast and you don't have to rely on signals or changes of plan from London: you just make your run and bring him with you and there isn't time to think about frontier rifle-fire or airfield security forces or sirens in the night – you're running hard and you can only keep up the pace by going into Zen, and it works, it really works, because the instant you switch off and leave it to the alpha waves you're moving into a protection zone where you can do things that would otherwise kill you off.

But with a sleeper it's different. He's like a mole, deep underground, and when he surfaces he finds the light too bright and it frightens him and he's liable to go back and stay low for a while. In the case of Karasov the temptation to do this was greater than usual: from the moment he was reported missing, the KGB would have started a massive search – they'd already been looking for the man who'd copied the tape of the submarine kill and he was the obvious target.

The thing that worried me most was that he hadn't contacted Tanya, simply to reassure her: it was the first thing he'd be expected to do. But the answer to that could be that he *hadn't* gone back underground: he could still be on the surface somewhere, running, and running too hard to stop.

'Very well. Thank you, comrade.'

Demichev put the phone down and dropped my papers onto the desk for me to pick up and said carefully, 'I have talked to the officer who would have been in charge of any search made in your room at the hotel. He assures me that no search was in fact made. I can only assume that it was a thief, or one of the staff, or that you were perhaps mistaken after all. I wish you a pleasant stay.'

He didn't get up. I put the papers into my coat.

'All right.' I turned back, halfway to the door. 'What's your opinion, Captain? Do you think this submarine thing is going to stop the summit?'

He laughed nicely. 'You people never miss an opportunity, do you?'

'We can't stop anyone in the street and ask them, without getting them into trouble.'

He let that go. 'I think it depends a great deal on whether you go back and vilify us as usual in your popular press. We are looking for mutual understanding, you see, and without it there's very little chance of a summit meeting.'

His smile had died away and as I left the office he was simply staring at me through narrowed lids, and as I touched the door handle a *frisson* passed through my nerves because I was suddenly sure it wouldn't turn, that the door was locked. But that feeling is quite normal, when you walk out of a KGB building.

On the way to the hotel through the unearthly night glow from the sky it occurred to me that I'd missed something. I'd fallen into the occupational hazard of identifying too closely with my function: I was an intelligence agent, and expected to be caught – or at least suspected – at any given time. But I carried a journalist's papers and there was absolutely nothing to connect me with any kind of deception. If the KGB had thought there were any cause for suspicion they wouldn't just have searched my room: they would have taken me along to their headquarters and put me under a light and yelled and gone on yelling until they found something. The only reason they'd have for making a room search would be to turn something up and confront me with it later; but they didn't normally work like that: they didn't need to.

If they'd made that search they'd found nothing: my Boris Antonov papers were in the door panel of the car. But that wasn't so important. *Why would they have made it at all?*

There was no reason.

I didn't like that. The only possible answer was that they'd found something wrong with my cover, and that *frisson* I'd felt along the nerves was justified. The door handle had turned and the door had opened and I'd gone into the street by virtue of one thing alone.

They were giving me rope.

'But you can't do that!'

Her Russian was atrocious.

'I'm sorry. It's the curfew.'

'But listen, I'm an American citizen!'

'We know.'

He was in plain clothes, with the slight regulation bulge above the left hip.

'Look, if I want to go out to get some fresh air, that's what I'm going to do. Okay?'

She tried to push her way past him.

'We'd prefer you not to make trouble.'

'If you don't let me past I'm going to make so much goddamned trouble you won't even know what's happening!'

It didn't sound exactly like that, because she was using only the present tense and the Russian for *goddamned* isn't translated as *accursed*, so forth.

'It won't do any good,' I told her in English and she turned to face me with her eyes bright.

'What the hell do you know about it?'

'That it won't do any good.' I said to the KGB man in Russian: 'It's her first time here.'

'Americans,' he said with a shrug. 'Are you American too?'

'No. English.'

'There's no difference. You cause trouble. You are in Russia now, do you understand? You are on the soil of the

Soviet Union, and are expected to behave according to our laws.'

'What kind of bullshit is he giving you?' the girl asked.

'There's a curfew. The only thing you can do about it is calm down and come and have a drink.'

'D'you always let these bastards have their own way?'

'It's more comfortable.'

'Whose side are you on, for Christ's sake?'

'Come and have a drink.'

She stared at me with her head flung back and her eyes still hot. 'Did you know about this curfew?'

'No.'

'Then why are you taking it lying down?'

'Because this isn't my first time out here.'

'How d'you know it's mine?'

'It shows.'

'Christ, I don't know which one of you bastards I hate most.'

'You'd better choose, because I'm the one who's going to buy you a drink.'

'*Shit.*' She turned and walked off, then swung back to look at me. 'I guess that's not very polite.'

'It'll do.' I nodded to the KGB man and put an arm around the girl and took her into the bar. It was almost deserted. 'What would you like?'

'A Manhattan.'

She was young, though I couldn't tell which side of thirty: I'm no good at people's ages. In her blue parka and gloves she looked more like one of the jet set just off the ski slopes.

'But why are they suddenly having a curfew?'

I'd chosen a corner table with a view of the doorway. The three men at the bar were speaking English, but one was French; I could hear the accent.

'The whole place is jumpy. You should know that.'

'Why should I?'

'You're a journalist.'

'Jesus, I wish–' then she took her drink and looked down and said, 'I guess I need this.'

'Cheers.'

'What? Cheers.'

The other two were German. The Frenchman was getting tight.

'Where are you from?' I asked her. It was going to be fifteen minutes of small talk and then I was going up to my room because I wanted to do some thinking: I wanted to find out why they were giving me rope. It was like being on a pond in winter: I could hear the ice cracking.

'Boston. What about you?'

'London. My name's Clive Gage.'

'Hi. I'm Liz Benedixsen.' She put out a cold hand. 'I don't normally blow my top that way. I just got fired.'

'From your paper?'

'Right. They called me home, but I'm not going.'

'You like Murmansk in winter?'

'You mean the cold? I don't mind that. Why did you order tomato-juice?'

'I like it.'

'Oh. Ex-boozer?'

'That's right.'

'You don't look like a journalist, Clive.'

'This is a disguise.'

She had an interesting smile, it was private, confiding. 'What's your paper?'

'The *Monitor.*'

'Class.'

'A little conservative. Though not in your meaning of the word.'

'Redneck?'

'Quite. More blue-blooded.'

She laughed again.

A man had come in and was sitting at the far end of the bar and I watched him now and then but he was all right: he could have used the gold-framed mirrors to cover this corner of the room but he was sitting too far at an angle.

'Your editor hasn't called you back?' the girl asked me.

'No.'

'Most of them have gone. Didn't you notice?'

'Yes.' I hadn't. I'd thought they were out with a guide trying to rake up some local colour.

'You know why they've gone?'

'No.'

She looked around at the three men sitting at the bar and the man at the end, then back to me, her eyes concentrating, weighing me up. 'I haven't seen you around much.'

'I've been working in my room.'

She considered this. 'You know we're about the last ones left? You, me, and these guys in here? That doesn't tell you anything?'

'There's no story.'

'Well sure, that puts it simply enough. But I mean why not? The summit meeting in Vienna's in jeopardy and there has to be the most tremendous amount of secret diplomacy passing between the Kremlin and the White House over the submarine sinking and we're sitting right here in Murmansk where it happened – and there's no story?'

'But we're only here to make a gesture.'

'A what?'

'Secret diplomacy isn't for publication. All we can hope to get out of the Soviet Ministry of Information is continued denial.'

I was wrong. He *was* using a mirror.

'So what are we doing here?' Liz asked me.

'We're here to report that the city housing the Soviet Union's major naval base is full of tension tonight, that a curfew has been ordered for the protection of foreign journalists because the good citizens here resent the United States sending a submarine to spy on their most secret defence installations, and that they've been queueing up for clogs all day in a temperature of 25 degrees below.'

He was using the long narrow mirror between the end of the bar and the heavy plush curtains. He was watching me now.

'That doesn't sound like the *Monitor*.'

'The *Monitor* does what every other paper does when it has

to. It prints whatever news it can get, and what it can't get it makes up.'

She looked down at her drink for a minute while I turned slightly and worked out the angles and found that I could watch him in the other mirrors while he was using the narrow one, and tell by the angle of his head when he was watching me. Or maybe I was being paranoid just because of the room search: he could be sitting there trying to make up his mind what the chances were of getting rid of me and moving in on Liz Benedixsen, who was quite attractive and the only woman remaining among the press contingent.

'You know something, Clive?' She'd lowered her voice and was looking at me with her green eyes totally engaged. 'I believe I know why there's no story. I believe I know why most of the gang has gone home. I believe there's a major cover-up going on over the sinking of that submarine. I mean major. Like I say, involving the Kremlin and the White House, on a hotline level.'

I drank the last of the tomato-juice. It tasted of brine.

'Possibly.'

She leaned nearer me across the low table. 'You remember what Claire Sterling did with the attempt on the Pope?'

'Yes.'

'She exposed a major cover-up, right? And they still wouldn't listen. Even the CIA. Even the *New York Times*. She said that even though there was actual evidence pointing directly to Andropov there was just no way the West could come out with a public accusation, because if it did, there was no way the West could go on maintaining diplomatic relations with people who had tried to murder the Pope. And if we couldn't go on maintaining diplomatic relations with the Soviets, it would be the end of our chances for peace.' She moved her glass round and round on the black marble table, the reflection of her drink playing across her eyes. Then she looked up again. 'Are you seeing any connection, Clive?'

'You might not be far from the mark.'

He wasn't lip-reading: he looked up at the mirror only at intervals. He wasn't KGB: his suit had been made in London and he was showing a tan. For the first time the idea occurred to me that Captain Bratchenko had been speaking the truth: it hadn't been his people who'd searched my room.

'Okay,' Liz said quietly, 'the sinking of a submarine isn't so horrendous as the idea of a pope getting shot to death – which was their *intention*. Tragic as hell, with all those lives lost, sure, but nothing like as far-reaching diplomatically – *until* you consider how vital that summit meeting is for us all. And then we get the parallel, right? There's no way the American public would allow the president to talk to any country that has just wiped out all those lives without any attempt to warn them first. These bastards shot from the hip, and before they woke up to the fact they were also shooting the summit conference right out of the water.'

I had begun listening.

'That's quite interesting.'

'I hope that's a good old British understatement, Clive, because I find the idea so goddamned interesting myself that when my editor cabled saying I had to go home like all the others I told him he could go screw himself.' She finished her drink.

I had begun listening because the work of a shadow executive is normally close-focus. Some of the missions they give us in London carry international background but we don't have to think about it; sometimes we don't even know about it. For our own sakes we're told only as much as we need to get through the mission and secure the objective and bring it home, whatever it is, a man or a document or an article like the one I'd taken from Brekhov. But there were things I didn't like about *Northlight*. Ferris had refused to local-control me; Fane was shut in and uncommunicative, and I didn't think he'd be able to give me the kind of support I'd need if I had to go to ground in a safehouse or start a fast run for the frontier; someone had searched my room and it could be the man sitting at the end of the bar watching me in the mirror; and above all, the sleeper hadn't made contact as he should have done.

It wasn't that these things made it difficult for me; it was that they didn't make an articulate pattern. The mission was out of focus and I couldn't see where I was going. I didn't trust Fane and I didn't trust Croder and I needed more information and I knew they wouldn't give it to me if I asked them, and there was no one else – unless this American journalist knew more about the background than I'd learned in No. 10 Downing Street or Eaton Place and could put it into focus for me.

'He's cut off my expenses, of course.'

She was moving her empty glass round and round, and I signalled to the barman.

'Have you got enough to keep going on?'

'If I sleep in the goddamned snow.'

She looked close to tears of anger.

'You think you're sitting on an exclusive,' I said.

'I think I'm sitting on a goddamned powder keg.'

When the man came I asked for the same again.

'The *Monitor* isn't mean,' I told her.

'What?' She'd been thinking of something else. Her green eyes watched me steadily.

'I'll pick up the tab for you here, if it'll help you get your story.'

'Look, I'm not bumming, Clive. I'll get by. I just mentioned it, you know?' She looked down again. 'The thing is, there's another parallel with this submarine story. Right?'

'Korean Airlines Flight 007.'

She swung her head up. 'Right. I believe some trigger-happy jerk in the Russian navy just went and let go with his torpedoes at the submarine before he asked anyone's okay.'

'It's one of the theories.'

'I believe it's the right one, Clive. And I'm not just guessing.' She looked at the other people at the bar again before she went on, lowering her voice. 'There's someone I know, in Moscow. An American. He–' she stopped and looked at me. 'Look, this is my story, okay?'

'Don't tell me anything you don't want me to send in.'

She thought about that, watching me steadily. 'I don't think you're like that.'

'You might be wrong.'

'No. I don't think I'm wrong. Let's put it this way. If I can get anything big, it goes in to my paper first. Then yours. Okay?'

'I thought you said you were fired.'

'Honey chil', when I send them *this* one they're going to put me back on the payroll so fast it'll look like sleight of hand. Where did this come from?' She looked down at her drink.

'The man brought it.'

'I didn't even notice. Okay, Clive, it's going to hit my page first, before yours. Is it a deal?'

'All right.'

'Okay. Like I said, there's someone I know, in Moscow. I can't tell you who he is because he'd scalp me. But he's got a theory too, and if he's right it puts him way ahead of the game. He thinks some guy in that naval base duped a tape of the action when that sub got sunk, and now he's holed up somewhere in this city with half the KGB hunting for him. Now if we could talk to *him* . . . that would be quite a story, wouldn't you say?'

11

CYANIDE

'WHERE ARE YOU speaking from?'
　　　　'The post office.'
　　　　'Which one?'
'In Obolenskij prospekt.'
I counted the seconds of silence. Four.
'What do you need?'
'There's something wrong.'
'In what way?'
I listened carefully to his voice.

If it had been Ferris local-controlling me it would have been easier. I didn't know Fane well enough to know what the sound of his voice was like in the field. He didn't sound tense, but that might not mean anything: he could have reserves of nerve fibre that I didn't know about.

The thing was, I'd done some work on the room-search thing and the only reason for the KGB to do that was because Fane had been blown, and had talked, and if that had happened he could be speaking to me now with a gun at his head.

'Are you clear,' I asked him, 'at your end?'

Three seconds. I tried to remember the conversation we'd had on the bridge in Moscow, and whether he'd always paused like this.

'In what way?'
'Bugs.'
'Perfectly clear. I told you this number was all right.'

'I know.'

'What's happened?'

I'd decreased the risk as far as I could. This was a post office but it wasn't in Obolenskij prospekt: it was in Bockova ulica, and if anyone else were on the line and sent out a van they'd draw blank at the other place.

'My room was searched.'

A long pause but I'd expected that.

'Tell me about it.'

I just said I'd complained and the KGB had denied everything.

'How did they treat you?'

'They were civil.'

'I mean did they . . . ask any awkward questions?'

'No.'

The silence drew out, but I wasn't worried now. I'd been listening hard enough to have picked anything up, anything wrong. He was thinking, that was all.

'Your set-up is *absolutely* all right.'

He meant my cover.

'If you say so.'

'There is just *no* way they could have got anywhere near you. I know this.'

'So what's your answer?'

'You've been protected,' he said, ignoring my question, 'all the way from London through Moscow and into your hotel here. I've been in constant signals, and Croder is handling you with the most extreme care. You're absolutely sure, of course?'

'That my room was searched?'

'Yes.'

'Oh, come on, Fane.'

'Just making sure. It's so extraordinary. Have you any ideas?'

'I thought they might have got onto me and decided for some reason to give me rope.'

'I would have known.'

'How?'

'This is the most sensitive assignment I've ever been given, and Croder himself is running it. If anything had started to go wrong – in terms of Galina – we would have known at once.'

Galina Borisovna was spook terminology for the KGB.

'All right,' I said.

'What about you? Have you got any ideas?'

'Only one. There's a journalist at the hotel, a French-Swiss by his accent. He's been taking an interest in me.'

Another pause. 'What sort?'

'He's watching me now.'

The strange, saffron light of dusk was seeping through the grimy windows. It was three o'clock: the nights were long here.

'Is he in the post office?'

'No. He stopped short when I came in. He'll be outside waiting for me.'

'Does he know you've seen him?'

'No.'

I was facing the main doors and already knew the answer to what Fane would ask me next.

'Can you go out the back way?'

'No.' It would mean going past the counter and through the sorting room.

'You say he's a journalist. You mean that's his cover?'

'Yes.'

'How do you know that?'

'I know a spook when I see one.' He'd only made one mistake on the way here through the streets from the hotel: he'd hurried a little when I'd walked round a corner and slowed, looking back. It hadn't been easy for him, over the snow. Figures stood out.

'Do you know his name?'

Fane's tone had become almost casual now, and I recognized for the first time that the more the pressure came on the quieter he got. That was good: there was more to him than I'd thought. But I didn't like this new situation. It had unnerved me to the point of thinking that Fane might have been blown.

'Yes. Rinker.'

'How do you know?'

'I got a look at the reservation book.' He asked a lot of questions, never taking me for granted.

'What does he look like?'

'Short, compact, maybe thirty-five, in training, works out with weights, or it's some form of martial art. He–'

'Eyes?'

'Brown. Dark hair smoothed back. Good tailor. Why?'

'I thought I might recognize him as some kind of opposition tool. So what are you going to do?'

I thought about it. 'Do you have any instructions?'

'Not really, but I'll get some if you like.'

'If I blow him, he'll only bring other people in. That's all right at the moment but when Karasov makes contact I'll want to be free to move.'

A long pause. There was a very faint voice on the line and it occurred to me that he was blocking the mouthpiece and talking to someone else; but it sounded like Russian. I couldn't be sure.

'Fane?'

'I was thinking.'

'All right.'

'Is he worrying you?'

'He'd worry me less if he stopped searching my room.'

'You think it was him?'

'If it wasn't Galina.'

A heavy man came through the doors and banged the snow off his boots.

'See what you can find out,' Fane said, 'and let me know.'

'I can't find much out unless I blow him.'

While Fane was thinking again the heavy man came over and stood stolidly in front of me, flipping a two-kopeck coin. This was the only telephone in the place.

'Don't blow him,' Fane said. 'That would complicate things, as you say. Just see what he does.'

'All right.'

I rang off and went to the doors and out into the yellow twilight and the scent of wood smoke. Fane had sounded so very certain that the KGB hadn't caught my vibrations, and this tied in with the denial they'd made at their headquarters; but Fane could be wrong and they could be lying. I didn't feel comfortable yet: there were too many things going wrong with this mission and I couldn't trust anyone. Or maybe it was the strange light here: at noon it was either dark with snow clouds or shimmering with the first ripples of the aurora flowing from the northern ice cap. Nothing seemed acceptable; everything seemed suspect in some way.

I don't like the cold. I felt cold now, under the thick fleece-lined coat and the astrakhan hat. I was shivering with it.

He wasn't where I'd left him. He was in a doorway of the next block, barely an outline in the shadows, and I took the same route back to the hotel, never looking behind me but sighting him twice in reflections as we passed windows, climbing snow drifts and crunching through scabs of ice along the gutters while a snow plough followed us, lumbering down the middle of the deserted road and sending up clouds of diesel gas. The staff at the hotel were complaining bitterly about the traffic conditions, and the city's sanitation commissioner was being criticized in the local paper for not doing his job. Before we reached the hotel I saw a whole party of skiers gliding down the street, overtaking a tractor hauling a bus out of a drift.

I stopped once or twice to watch, and again saw Rinker's silhouette in the window of a workers' outfitting shop before I went on. He held back at the last corner and I quickened my pace through the lobby and got to the first floor balcony in time to see him come in through the doors.

This is a time for understanding.

You many wonder why we appear so truculent, and so suspicious, and so seemingly unready to sit at a conference table with the peoples of the West. It is perhaps because our Motherland has seen so much suffering at the hands of the peoples of the West, by France, when only our will to resist and wear down the forces of Napoleon saved us from defeat, and by Germany, when that same will, together with our own greater force of arms, turned back the forces of Hitler. But the cost was high. We lost twenty million of our young sons in the Second World War alone.

We ask you, today, to think of that.

It had been slipped under my door.

We ask you to try to understand why we appear so 'paranoiac', as you call us. Perhaps we are, especially to the people of the United States, who have never known the setting foot of one single enemy on their shores, who have never known the meaning of rape, massacre and the burning down of whole cities across their sacred land, as we have.

The follies and mistakes recorded in the history of the American nation are often said to be due – and in all truth are due – to the fact that it is a 'young' nation, and this we understand. But we would like it also to be understood that our Soviet nation too is young, in terms of the years since the yoke of Csarist oppression and injustice was thrown aside. In those brief years we too have made great progress, from the inception of a just, orderly and fulfilled society to the placing of the first human being into space.

It was on white paper with a red border and a small hammer and sickle in the corner, nothing else. It wasn't one of those quaint, pidgin-English pamphlets that get Xeroxed for discreet circulation at embassy cocktail parties to get a cheap laugh.

We understand that since Mr Carter relinquished the presidency of the United States it has been felt necessary to increase the production of armaments and bring America to equality with the Soviet Union in military strength. But we do not understand why President Reagan continues to vilify our nation and its leaders by verbal abuse. We would ask that we are accepted as a strong, young and successful society emerging from the shadows of oppression into the light of a common understanding with the rest of the world – if the rest of the world is ready to hear our voice. Only if we are seen as a fellow nation, with worth to offer the world, with goods to trade, with ideas to exchange and with the future to share on an

*equal footing, can it also be seen that we are ready, yes and again
yes, to go to the conference tables and join with others in drawing
the world back from the abyss of war and mutual annihilation that
lies in our path.*

*There are follies and mistakes, too, in our own short history as
an emerging nation, but we ask that they be seen as such, and not
as 'evil' and aggressiveness. It is simply that we are fearful, as
America is fearful, of war and rumours of war. Today we stand
equal in terms of military strength, as powerful enemies. We are
prepared, if others are prepared, to ensure that tomorrow we stand
as powerful neighbours, and later, even, as powerful friends.*

*Meanwhile we say to you these words that you do not believe we
mean, but which we mean in all truth and from the bottom of our
hearts.*

Peace be with you.

'Bullshit?'

Liz Benedixsen dug for another meatball with her fork.

'They don't think so.'

'The Soviets don't think so?'

She had drawn her chestnut hair back and fixed it with a
ribbon, and it left her face unframed, stark in the cold light,
her cheekbones casting shadows. It didn't give her the mien
of a sculpting; she looked somehow more alive, more defined.

'I don't think we're talking about the Soviets,' I told her.
'They didn't write this stuff.'

'Who did?'

'Some kind of human activist group.'

'You mean underground?'

'Yes. They'd get arrested for pushing pacifism under
people's doors.'

He was sitting at the other side of the room: he'd come in
soon after I had. Liz had already been here and had invited
me to join her. The curfew hour was for nine o'clock, in fifty
minutes from now. Before then, I was going to take a trudge
through the snow, and if he followed, lose him, and then see
what he'd do, where he'd go.

'But it doesn't sound—' she waved her fork in the air — 'subversive. Wouldn't the Russian people agree with the main content? Peace?'

If he came back to the hotel I'd leave it at that. But if he went to telephone someone and report losing me, then I'd at least know they had a net to throw over me.

'Certainly the Russian people would agree with it. But they can't tell their government to lay down their arms, any more than the Americans can.'

'I suppose I'm just a crummy idealist.'

'Don't lose it. It's our only hope.'

I felt her eyes on me for a while. 'What else do you do, Clive, apart from journalism?'

'Eat and sleep.'

'You don't look like a journalist. You look like an actor. You know, the face crumpled in a good cause, the eyes experienced. You're quite attractive to women, did you know that?'

'It takes all sorts.'

'And there's this look of—' she waved her fork again, and dropped a blob of beef onto the cloth. 'Shit.' She speared it impatiently. 'A look of privacy. Guardedness. You look like a man with past tragedies under the skin, and scars that won't ever quite heal.'

'That really is the most appalling journalism.'

'And you're a creep.'

I would need to leave here in fifteen minutes, to do what I wanted to do and beat the curfew. Most of all I wanted to come back to the hotel before he did and see if he were worried enough about losing me to stay out after nine o'clock to make his report. And then I wanted to see how the KGB men in the lobby handled him when he came in late. That would tell me a lot. This was what Fane had meant when he'd told me to find out about Rinker: it was routine but informative.

'Are you divorced?'

'That's right.'

'For whoring around?'

'What else is there?'

She laughed suddenly, with that rather private, confiding laugh she had, and I found myself thinking about her for a moment instead of about Rinker, but only for a moment because this wasn't the time for any diversions. Once I was out there in the street I could find myself in a red sector: it was dark now, with snow clouds lying across the city, and the moment I manoeuvred him into losing track of me he could call others in and bring the net down, and it would be too late to do anything. They'd done that to me in Berlin and Seoul and Hong Kong and I'd got out from under, but it had been close. Among the back alleys of this trade I'd used up my nine lives long ago, and every new risk was a step closer to death.

She was watching me with her green eyes narrowed.

'Did I blow it, Clive?'

'In what way?'

I had five minutes.

'Trying to get under your skin.'

'As long as it amuses you.'

'How about a drink, when we've finished here?'

'I've got to work for half an hour. Say nine-thirty?'

'Okay.'

I saw her into the bar before I got my coat from the cloakroom attendant and shrugged into it and went across to the main entrance. If anything went wrong, how would she put it? *I know I was fired but I've got something that could develop into a story. One of the journalists here was found dead in the snow last night, and they believe he was murdered. If you'll hire me back on the payroll again you can have the follow-up.*

Epitaphs vary: some are shorter than others.

When I went out through the main doors it was exactly 8:45. I saw a plain van with steel grilles at the windows parked at an angle against the snow bank that had been piled up by the ploughs earlier in the day, and when I heard movement behind me I didn't look round until I reached the first corner, letting my foot slip into a snow rut and falling down so that I could look behind me as I got onto my feet again, but I needn't have bothered to make it look natural because they were too busy outside the hotel, and I walked back slowly, getting a rough idea of what was happening.

It looked as though Rinker had followed me down the steps at about the same time as I'd reached the corner. His coat was still only half on because the two KGB men from the lobby had moved in on him and two more had come across from the van to help. It was a typical street snatch: they hadn't wanted to do it inside the hotel. It looked as if Rinker was trying to fight them off, which wasn't very bright for a professional spook, but when I got closer I saw what he was really doing, and they weren't in time to stop him. One of them tried to catch him as he fell, but he went down like a dead weight with his arms flung out across the snow and his skin already turning blue from the cyanide as he stared up at me and saw no one.

12

INCENSE

'WERE YOU SEEN coming in here?'
'Not by any professionals.'
We kneeled together, our heads bowed.
'He's made contact,' Fane said.
My nerves tautened, then rebounded and went slack.
'We haven't got much time.' His hand dug into his coat.

I'd thought it would never happen, but now it was here with us, a cold fact, and the mission was suddenly swinging into a new phase, the most difficult, the most dangerous. We had access to the objective and now it was possible, achievable, after that first long run without real direction, four deaths in five days as we'd circled blindly in the dark with nothing to do but wait. Now the waiting was over. The sleeper had wakened.

I would remember the Church of Saint Peter for a long time, and the way we had kneeled together on the cold marble while the others chanted around us, mostly women – white hair and black shawls and worn mottled furs, boots caked with snow – and one old man alone but not far from us, weeping as he prayed, perhaps for peace through the days whose number was growing small for him now in the chill of these deathly winters.

I would remember the scent of wood smoke and incense, and the prismatic light flowing from the coloured glass windows above the dais where the priest stood, a white-bearded man of immense height, a brass ikon jangling on a chain from his neck as he moved in incantation. I would only know later why I would remember this time and this place so well, as a haven for the spirit that I would soon want desperately, and in vain, to return to.

'Take this,' Fane said. 'It's your train coupon.'

I put it away. 'Where to?'

'He's in Kandalaksha, two hundred and twenty kilometres south of Murmansk, on the shore of the White Sea.'

'*What the hell is he doing there?*'

'He was trying to reach Leningrad and catch the Red Arrow to Moscow.'

'Why *Moscow?*'

'I think he just panicked and wanted to run.'

Karasov had surfaced and we had access to the objective and on the board in London where the red lamp had been glowing since I'd accepted the mission there were hieroglyphs going up: *Northlight* was now proceeding as planned, but I felt sudden anger because panic's got no place in deep operations and Karasov had made things more difficult for us all.

'What condition is he in?'

'He sounded frightened, on the phone. Badly frightened. You'll have to handle him with care.' He shifted on his knees. 'Tell me about Rinker. Are you absolutely certain it was a capsule?' I'd reported to Fane first thing this morning from the post office, but we'd been cut off; the snow was causing havoc to the telephone lines.

'Yes. I was there when it happened.' I'd seen capsules used before, when Hideo Matsuda thought he was blown when he came through London airport and saw me waiting for him, and when Clifton had lost his nerve in the run out from Beirut. In the Caff they're called blue babies but it's not very funny.

'So he was making sure the KGB didn't interrogate him,' Fane said. 'He was following instructions.'

'Yes. A real pro.'

He'd know what I meant. Rinker hadn't been operating alone: he was with a cell and it was highly disciplined. Only the really professional networks can demand of an agent that he gives his life rather than information.

'Have you any clues?' Fane's tone below the chanting of the faithful was very quiet, very controlled, and I knew by now that this was characteristic and consistent with the pressure that had come down on him. We'd assumed that our only opposition to getting Karasov across the frontier would be the KGB, and that was bad enough; but we knew now that some other network was putting its agents into the field. Rinker would be replaced – *would already have been replaced.*

That was why Fane had asked me if anyone had seen me come in here. The KGB wasn't alert to us. Some other organization was.

'No,' I told him. 'No clues at all.' That was his job, not mine: it was for local control to find out if the field had been breached. 'All I know is that he was Swiss-French with an address in Geneva, but that doesn't mean much: he could be working for any one of a dozen masters and on any level, from secret service to terrorist group.'

The priest began leading a canticle, and we all stood up.

'He wasn't CIA,' Fane said. 'They're very keen to get our reports but they wouldn't put surveillance on you: that's been agreed in London.'

I took a prayer-book from the ledge and opened it. 'I want instructions. If you think they've sent in a replacement it might not be possible to get on that train.'

He gave one of his pauses. 'You've *got* to reach Karasov and get him out. That's paramount. So if anyone gets in your way. . . .'

'You'll have to spell it for me, Fane.'

London is very touchy about taking life, unless the executive's own is endangered.

'If anyone other than the KGB gets in your way, you must get him out of it by whatever means are available, including terminal.'

'Understood.'

He began briefing me, while the singing filled the cavernous stonework of the church, his voice a monotonous undertone as if he were reciting a psalm of his own faith. 'Your train leaves at eight tomorrow morning. It's the earliest available but you'll be quicker than going by road. Don't check out of the hotel: the lobby is under KGB surveillance, as you know. I'll try to get a courier to pick up your things before the staff reports your absence. Have you got a spare key to the room?'

I gave it him.

'I'll try to get someone to take your car down to Kandalaksha if the roads are still open, so that you'll have transport if you need it. I can't guarantee that: he might not get through. Your rendezvous is at noon tomorrow in the main post office. It isn't with Karasov: he's sending a contact.'

'Why?'

'I told you. He's badly frightened. The contact will be wearing smoked glasses with the left lens cracked, and using a white stick. You'll ask him where you can find imported cigarettes, and he'll tell you that those things are only fit for women. He'll take you to Karasov.' His breath clouded against the prayer-book. 'Karasov told me he changed his identity when he left his unit at Severomorsk, and got someone to do him some new papers. They might be sloppy: you'd better check them over. I'm doing everything I can to get some good ones for him in Moscow, but it'll take time and we'll need a courier to fly them in by hand. Then I've got to send them from here to Kandalaksha. Your own clandestine papers are absolutely foolproof for the whole of the peninsular region, but if Karasov's look unreliable, hold him underground until I can get the new ones to you. Questions?'

'I'll need a bag.'

'Leave the car unlocked tonight outside the hotel. The bag will be put into a rear seat-well, packed for five days.' This time he paused so long that I half-turned to look at him. 'I hope you won't need that amount of time,' he said. 'Control wants the objective over the frontier just as soon as you can get him there.'

His nerves had begun showing, and I noted it. It might not have happened to him before. It had happened to me only twice: at the moment we had access to the objective an unknown network had sent its agents into the field to surveille my travel patterns, and this time the reason was the same. The Rinker cell was hunting for Karasov and trying to use me as a tracker dog. It wasn't going to make things any easier: Karasov himself had lost his nerve and would need dragging like a dead weight to the frontier.

'Questions?' asked Fane again.

'Put a capsule in the bag, will you?'

His eyes moved slightly towards me. 'Didn't you draw one in London?'

'Yes.' I left it at that.

In a moment he said: 'Very well. It'll be inside the head of the electric shaver.'

When the service was over he moved away from me, and I gave him time, hanging back until half the people had shuffled to the massive doors; then I began moving, going out of the candlelight into a night so black that the sky was like a shroud thrown across the city.

She had rings of dark pigment around her nipples, and a way of moving like a swimmer, long-legged and flowing.

'Then I lost my folks, when I was quite young. They were in a car and there was a drunk. By the time I could sleep the whole night through and not wake up crying I was into the cults from coast to coast. A lot of the kids I got to know had lost their parents, except that they were still alive, you know? Then there was this bad cocaine trip and I woke up in a clinic tied to the bed with restraints and everything – but somehow they pulled me out of it. Not too many can survive that amount of coke.'

She was huddled against me like a child, no longer a lover, and in the glow from a street light I saw a tear glistening below her dark lashes.

'And then – oh God, this is going to sound so corny – after two pointless marriages I realized I wanted to spend my life with something much more than a man. I wanted to marry a *cause*. It sounds more like California than Boston, Massachusetts, doesn't it? But that was the way it was.' She lifted herself onto one elbow so that she could look down at me. 'I kind of found myself standing back and seeing the whole human race caught up in lunacy – war and the fear of war and the threat of war, hot wars, cold wars, wars to end wars, you name it, it comes in all flavours. I saw high school kids on TV saying they didn't feel there was any future any more because they weren't quite sure they could go on waking up and not see a mushroom cloud through the window one day. And finally I discovered – out of anger, I guess – a sense of direction, a conviction there was something I had to do. And I've been doing it ever since, Clive, in my own way, hurling myself at the barricades while everyone else is busy making a detour and maybe getting home sooner. But the barricades are still there, and until I can bring them down, I don't believe–'

'What are they, your barricades?'

'Lies. I don't mean the ones we all tell ourselves and other people, I mean the big ones, the world-class international lies that talk peace and mean war. Like the ones we were all told about the attempted assassination of the Pope, and like the ones we were told about the Korean airliner. Like the ones we're being told right now about the sinking of the *Cetacea*.'

'Which ones are they?'

'There's no direct lie, except that the Soviets say they didn't have anything to do with it. There's a cover-up going on, and that's lying by default. Do you really think we, the people, ever really get to know what goes on behind the scenes? Are we meant to believe there's no quiet diplomacy going on right now between the White House and the Kremlin? Do you believe–' she broke off and gazed at me for a moment and then let her breath out in a quick soft laugh. 'Jesus, Clive, I guess this isn't your night. After a glorious fuck like that you find you're in bed with a poor man's Joan of Arc.' She lowered her body over mine, and I felt the tears dropping one by one on my bare shoulder, while the soft laughter went on. 'You know when people say they don't know whether to laugh or cry?'

'It's a revelation,' I said.

[107]

'A what?' She leaned away and watched me again, her eyes liquid in the glow from the street, the colour of green chartreuse.

'I'm not often close to anyone who lets their feelings go.'

'I know. You're a lone wolf type. But that's what you want. Right?'

'It's what I've got.' She was beginning to stir questions in me that I'd spent all my life refusing to ask, since the day I had looked down from the window at the broken body of the schoolboy on the flagstones a long way below, while a master hurried from the cloisters with his black gown flapping in the winter wind, to see what had happened: the day when I was suddenly old enough to understand that I had a choice. I could either do what that other boy had done, or I could spend the rest of my life outside society, where it was safe.

'The kind of loneliness I feel,' she said, 'is different.'

I hadn't thrown him, of course. But I knew why he'd done it.

'What kind is that?'

'I get so involved in this idealistic crusade of mine that I don't notice anything else going on. It's like, you know, you're acting on a stage someplace and pulling out all the stops, giving a performance that's going to go down in history, and suddenly you look up and see there's nobody out there, all the seats are empty and the whole place is dark.'

'Yes, that must be lonely.'

'But that's about me again. What about you, Clive? You really enjoy the lone wolf bit?'

I could see, beyond the curve of her naked shoulder, white flakes drifting across the aureole of a street lamp, whirling slowly in the wind.

'I expect I do.'

If there were more snow, the courier might not get the car through to Kandalaksha. It might even hold up the train.

'You expect you do?' She was watching me again. I'd put my wrist watch on the heavy darkwood table by the bed, and could see its figures. It was gone midnight, and I would need to leave here at three, in case of snow on the road to the station.

'Yes,' I told her, and pulled her gently down against me, my hands moving along her body from the warmth of her hair to her long swimmer's thighs, the thought in my mind, as it comes always to us when we've just received briefing in the field, that Liz Benedixsen might be the last woman I would ever have known. 'I'm going to let you get some sleep,' I told her.

'You don't have to go.'

It wasn't easy to leave her. With the slow drifting down of the snow from the dark sky there was a sense of foreboding. *Post coitus*, so forth.

I got into my clothes and took my watch from the table, leaning down to kiss her for the last time. When I reached the door she was sitting up in the bed with her arms round her knees, watching me, her eyes the only colour in the shadows.

'Take care,' she said.

13

MIRRORS

THE CONDITIONS WERE unpropitious.

Snow was still falling but less heavily, and on the northern horizon a crack of light shimmered, thrust between the dark earth and the dark sky like a bright sword blade.

The conditions were unpropitious for detecting surveillance.

The light was blinding if you looked at it directly. It was the edge of the sun's reflection on distant cloud banks, flooding across the polar ice cap. If you looked away it vanished. It was too distant to reach into the darkness here, where only the gooseneck lamps of the railway station kept back the night. Dawn would be hours yet.

The conditions were unpropitious for detecting surveillance, it would be reported, if anything of this would ever be reported in the file on *Northlight.*

It's one of those stuffy phrases coined by the bureaucrats upstairs, hunched at their desks with a drip on their nose and frayed cuffs and patched elbows, their chilblained feet squeezed into their cracked patent-leather shoes and a mug of cold tea beside them as they scratch the epitaph across the file in longhand, like vultures picking at the bones of a dead mission.

They thumb through their mildewed copies of *Roget's Thesaurus* for euphemisms designed to give stark truths a burial more decent than the facts will allow. By reporting that the conditions were unpropitious for detecting surveillance they mean that the executive in the field checked and rechecked and couldn't see anyone but there must have been someone there because they got to him just the same and tripped his run and slammed him into an interrogation cell or waited until he was right in the middle of the piazza and then put him in the crosshairs and dropped him like a dead duck or set up the road-block on the far side of a blind curve and pulled him out of the wreckage while it was still burning.

There are other phrases.

He endeavoured to evade termination. That one's easy enough: the poor bastard broke a door down and took the stairs and got to the top floor but they'd been waiting for that and he went through the window because they'd opened fire and there was nothing he could lose but this time he wasn't lucky because there was only a glass canopy below to break the fall and it wasn't enough, *finis*.

They are the phrases we sometimes find in our minds, like official notices pasted on a wall, when a wheel comes off and we're suddenly on the brink. It would be amusing, I suppose, if we weren't so bloody frightened at the time.

The reason why the conditions were unpropitious this morning was mainly the snow. I'd got out of the hotel through the kitchens and the rear service door to avoid the KGB men in the lobby: the curfew was still on for foreigners and in any case I wanted to gain time and get as far as I could on the way to Kandalaksha before the chambermaids reported the man in 203 was missing. I'd gone clandestine now and there shouldn't be anything to connect the English journalist from the Leningrad Hotel and the Soviet engineer in the train except facial characteristics, which didn't amount to much considering the photographs. But you don't take chances.

The car started all right but the snowfall had piled up around it and I had to put it into gear and get the wheels spinning and then climb out and heave it across the ruts and get in again before it took off on its own. The main streets were still under ploughing and they'd thrown sand down but the traffic was chaotic: the early shift at the dockyards was at five o'clock and buses were taking to the side streets as an alternative to jamming up in lines at the main intersections and sometimes backing into the ploughed streets again because they couldn't get through the drifts.

In the three miles to the station I saw one car three or four times and a KGB van had followed me half the distance before peeling off, but it wasn't possible to detect any consistent surveillance operation going on: quite a few private cars were making detours and coming back again like the buses because they couldn't get through. A man – a dozen men – could have followed me on foot over the whole distance, and I wouldn't have been able to pick them out among the others along the pavements. The conditions, so forth.

It wasn't much easier on the platform here. There was too much cover: corners, doorways, shadows. Sailors were tramping along the edge of the platform, some of them dropping onto the rails and hopping from sleeper to sleeper, making a game of it to keep warm until an official waved a flag and yelled at them. There were two KGB men on routine observation duty near the booking office, keeping to the small area that gave them a good panoramic view of the platform. Two others were across the lines, watching their own territory; I didn't know whether this was the normal scene for Murmansk, but there would have been more of them in the streets and public places since Karasov had been posted as missing.

Across from where I was standing was the little waiting-room at the end of platform 4 where I'd met Tanya Kiselev. I'd phoned her from the post office on my way back from the church. She'd picked up the phone on the second ring.

'He's alive and safe,' I told her.

There was a sudden breath on the line and then she said, 'Where is he?'

'Not far. I'll tell him you were worried.'

'Yes. Please tell him I–' It sounded as if she was crying, or just trying not to. 'But where is he, please? I want to see him.'

'That wouldn't be wise.'

'I want to be near him, don't you understand?'

'Of course. But if anyone questions you, the less you know about him the better.'

'I wouldn't tell anyone, ever.'

'For his sake, it's better. I'll ask him to phone you.' Then I'd just rung off because she would have gone on being insistent and it would only have wasted time. At least she didn't have to go on thinking he might be dead.

A green light had begun winking beyond the end of the platform and the public address speakers came on, announcing the departure of the train in five minutes. They were running it close because the locomotive was only just rolling in from the yards. I began another slow search of the environment, noting changes and new elements, walking to the end of the platform to check the shadows and coming back, passing the man with the shapeless leather bag who'd come from the booking office five minutes ago, and the other man who'd arrived earlier, no bag, but a briefcase under his arm. So far they'd avoided looking in each other's direction but that could mean nothing: I simply noted it. But they interested me more than the KGB. The people I was looking for – and the people who might at this moment be looking for me – would belong to the Rinker cell.

They'd put me under specific and close-focused surveillance and Rinker's death wouldn't have given them any reason to call off their operation: if a professional agent with instructions to use a capsule to protect his network had been given the job of surveilling me then it was important to them – it was *that* important. They had the same objective as the Bureau had: the sleeper, Karasov. And since Rinker's death I'd remained at the hotel for another six hours – ample time for his cell to replace him with a fully covert operator.

He could be the Lithuanian with the shapeless leather bag or the man with the briefcase or any one of the people who were inside the booking office or one of the waiting-rooms, and even if I could check all of them there'd be nothing to tell me who they were. I'd made three attempts to flush any surveillance since I'd got here, going into the main waiting-room and out through the emergency exit at the rear, moving into the deep shadow alongside the freight office and taking a turn round the building, going into the subway between the platforms and waiting for ten minutes on the far side of the station, but no one had followed, no one had provided any kind of image with partial cover concealment.

I'd drawn blank but it didn't mean they weren't simply sure of me, sure that I'd board the train. Once on the train it would be too late to do anything and in the normal way you don't let that happen: you don't move into a confined environment like a train or an aeroplane without making absolutely certain you're clean, and above all – *above all* – you don't start out to keep a rendezvous with a key contact until you're certain you won't expose him. But today we were going to throw the book away and take the risks as they came. *Control wants the objective over the frontier just as soon as you can get him there.*

So when I went aboard the train I looked for a compartment at the end of a carriage in the "soft-seat" second class section and chose a place alongside the corridor. Nobody else came in before the train started; at this hour there weren't many people in spite of the fact that the roads were snowed under. I suppose that only a bloody fool would want to travel anywhere inside the Arctic Circle in midwinter and I was one of them.

They'd done their best to clean the windows but there were streaks of grime on the glass. Beyond the lights of the signal box I could see flares burning, silhouetting the huge shapes of the tractors and snow ploughs trying to clear the main road from the city, with a line of trucks crawling in their wake.

'Your coupon, comrade.'

I gave it to him and he clipped it.

We were getting up a fair speed: a train this size with a plough scoop on the front would go through a mountain. The sky was clearing in the east, the thin crack of light broadening and spreading an expanse of flat slate-grey across the sky in the wake of the snow clouds – the false dawn of an Arctic day. I turned my face away from it; on this trip I'd have preferred the dark.

'KGB.'

I showed him my papers while his colleague stood in the corridor. I'd seen them get into the train earlier, and presumably there'd be more. They were looking for Karasov.

'What's taking you to Kandalaksha?'

'There's a job going at the steel foundry.'

'You've got no work in Murmansk?' He was looking at me with that expressionless stare that will turn your blood cold if you can't trust papers or if you're carrying product or if you're not sure you can get through the act without his finding something to pick on, something to develop into a full-scale interrogation. These weren't the papers I'd shown at their headquarters; these hadn't been tested yet.

'Yes,' I told him. 'But the pay's better at the foundry – they can't get engineers of my grade.'

He studied the papers again under the yellow light from the ceiling bulbs. 'You didn't care for Moscow?'

He'd noted my Muscovite accent. 'Anyone who can find a job in that place has got a cousin in the Komitet.' A bit risky because it carried a hint of corruption, but it was also a compliment, flattering his authority.

His eyes glanced up from the papers and stared into mine for three seconds: I measured the time for something to do, to take my mind off the trickle of cold that had started along the spine. It's not the thought of what they'll do to you later that chills the blood. It's the thought of getting trapped, of feeling the sudden shock as the thing closes on you with a single wrong word, cutting you off from the world you knew a minute ago where you ate and slept and moved freely along your way through the labyrinth, and shutting you into the new world of black vans and doors and bars and keys and dangerous questions, dangerous answers, and finally the bright light and the brute force and the long journey through the long nights until they're forced to go beyond the point when they can get anything out of you, when the aminazin or the sulfazin or the reserpine has blunted the intellect and destroyed the emotions and wiped out the memory and left them with nothing but a husk to throw onto the trash heap where once there had been a man.

'What about your family?'

'They'll follow me, if I can get the job.'

He was taking more trouble than usual, listening for that single wrong word, looking for it on my papers, matching what I was saying with what he was reading. The other man was watching me the whole time; I could see him in my peripheral vision. The trickle along my spine grew colder.

The greatest weapon in the initial interrogation is persistence. This hadn't been written by those snivelling bureaucrats upstairs: it was in the manual they give us on refresher courses in Norfolk – *Techniques in Interrogation.* This is the reverse of the coin, though we don't do much of it ourselves; it's to teach us what to expect and how to deal with it.

Even the steadiest subject will eventually yield to persistence, and there is a sound psychological basis for this. The subject's psyche has already been disturbed by the approach of the potential interrogator, who is often in uniform and armed. It is necessary only to develop that initial disturbance in the subject's psyche to reach a point where he will begin to doubt his chances of surviving the interrogative process without giving something away. This further alarms him on a multi-conscious level, and he may begin to exhibit subtle speech defects: hesitation, slight stuttering, the inadvertent elision of speech components and so on.

'If you find work in Kandalaksha, can you be sure your wife will be as successful?'

'She's a nurse.'

Nurses were in demand everywhere: the pay was insulting.

'What about your two children?' He was looking the whole time at my papers now, and this was also in the Norfolk manual.

To gaze steadily at the subject will intimidate him if he has anything to conceal, but this can be taken to a new phase where one can remove that gaze and study the subject's passport or visa or appropriate document without allowing the eyes to move from left to right as if reading. This gives the clear impression that one has discovered something suspicious during the interrogation and that one is therefore concealing this fact by the removal of the direct gaze and adopting an attitude of exceptionally careful listening.

'The kids will have to go to a new school,' I said. 'We can't let them dictate where we live, can we?'

He went on gazing at my papers. 'When did you move to apartment 68 in the East Park Building?'

'Apartment 58. Last July. Did they put down the wrong apartment number?'

He didn't answer specifically, but held the papers obliquely to the light, and I began feeling less worried. He'd thrown in a routine trap and I'd avoided it and left him with the impression that I didn't recognize it as a trap at all. The apartment number on the papers was in fact 58 and if I hadn't pointed out his mistake it would have meant I hadn't even read them. He'd got out of it by tilting them to the light to suggest he'd misread the number.

A trap like that can send you all the way to the Gulag if you don't recognize it.

'When did you board this train?'

'As soon as it stopped.'

'Did you see anyone else getting on?'

'I didn't notice anyone particularly. All I wanted was to get in here before my balls froze off.'

He gave the papers back to me with that typical gesture they all use to show who's in charge, half dropping them and making you catch them. It's rather endearing: there's comfort in the familiar. But the sweat was still gathering on me as I folded the papers and put them away.

'Did you notice anyone hurrying to board the train?'

'Not particularly.'

'Anyone who seemed unusual?'

I gave the impression of considering the question.

'I can't say that.' I wondered if he were actually going to describe Karasov. They must be getting desperate by now: it was four days since he'd gone to ground.

'If you notice anything unusual on the train, I want you to report it at once. Anyone who looks anxious, who looks as if he's trying to hide something. You understand?'

'Of course. Where shall I find you?'

'We shan't leave this carriage. Or you can tell the attendant.'

Karasov was a Latvian, with a facial resemblance to a northern European or an American. That was why the KGB man had taken so much interest in me.

'I'll keep my eyes open,' I said.

He nodded and went back into the corridor.

It was another half an hour before I knew they'd got me. Not the KGB. The Rinker cell. They were here and they were on to me and there was nothing I could do to reach the objective or keep *Northlight* running or save myself. Nothing.

14

GUN

GROMYKO WARNS: WE ARE REACHING THE POINT OF NO RETURN.

Picture of Gromyko, one finger held up, face blank as usual.

It was the only story on the front page of *Pravda* and the headline was twice as big as usual.

Let it be stated once again. The obstinacy on the part of the Western Powers to admit to the fact that the United States of America committed what was tantamount to an act of war, in sending an armed nuclear submarine into Soviet waters, is now offering a threat to world peace of a magnitude that has never before faced mankind.

In times of normal diplomatic relations the affair of the US Cetacea would have brought the two great powers to a situation of precipitate crisis. When it is considered that the Vienna meeting was agreed upon in order to alleviate a crisis in diplomatic relations that already existed before this irresponsible and dangerous act was undertaken, it will be seen even by the least intelligent of America's allies that only a miracle can now save the Vienna summit meeting, and the world from final and irrevocable disaster.

One of them was the man with the shapeless leather bag.

Until this is clearly understood by the intransigent West, the world must remain poised on the edge of an abyss in whose depths lies the grave of civilization as we know it today.

The other was the man with the briefcase, but he wasn't watching me now. I was holding the newspaper to cover the whole of my face except when I turned the pages. Then I checked his image.

It had taken me half an hour to realize what was happening because they were working in shifts, one at a time, and using the interior window glass of the compartments and the windows across the corridor to give them a double mirror effect.

Only a miracle can now save the Vienna summit meeting, so forth. Dear Comrade Gromyko, have a little patience, for Christ's sake. Miracles take a little longer, you know that.

But I wasn't, in fact, feeling terribly confident now of pulling one off. What we must never allow to happen had happened, on pressure from Control. Although I could understand the cause of that pressure – the front page of *Pravda* had spelt it out clearly enough – the fact remained that the executive in the field had been forced to move into a red sector without being sure he was clean in terms of surveillance and was on his way to a critical rendezvous and taking with him two components of a formidable opposition cell.

There was also a third man.

I didn't have time to worry about the third man because the other two had me in a surveillance pincer movement, but one thing about him was interesting. He wasn't working with the other two. *He wasn't with the Rinker cell at all.*

I knew this because I'd become aware of him earlier, soon after the train had started off, and I'd mapped his rather elaborate movement patterns: when I'd gone along to the restaurant car for the paper he'd sought immediate cover and didn't show up again until I was back in my compartment, when he'd used another passenger as a shield as he'd come past to check on me. It wasn't that he was inefficient: it was all he could do in this kind of closed environment with only a narrow corridor as the terrain. He was under an added strain, and I'd noted this soon after he'd surfaced.

He not only knew I was under surveillance by the Rinker people. He had to keep it from them, as well as from me, that I was his target too.

In the normal way I would have been *extremely* interested

in the fact that a second opposition network had sent an agent into the field but he was already out of the running because the Rinker cell was on to me and they wouldn't let me go and if I tried to lead them anywhere except directly to Karasov they'd close in and trap me and put me under a light and work on me until I betrayed my objective and blew the mission to bits.

There wasn't any question about this in my mind as I watched the image in the double mirrors, the face of the man who was sitting three compartments along from me with his head tilted back against the quilted upholstery and his eyes apparently closed. His cell was professional and they'd already lost a man and they'd moved in again as if nothing had happened. They wanted Karasov as badly as I did, as London did. *Somewhere else a mission control had sent his people into the field with instructions to find our sleeper.*

I began reviewing the environment, but there was nothing here that you wouldn't find in most long-distance trains across the vast expanse of Soviet Russia: doors, windows, brass rails, glass-shaded lamps and upholstered seats, leather straps and racks of netting for small baggage, the emergency chain running through the compartment, glazed posters proclaiming work targets and industrial scenes, a woman in a head scarf, a man in a worker's cap. There wasn't anything that would make a weapon useful enough to offer *decisive* advantage in a close encounter, nothing better than my own hands; and if I finally made up my mind to draw the opposition into my own immediate vicinity and make a last-ditch attempt at dealing with them and eliminating the threat to *Northlight* I wouldn't be able to do it without alerting the KGB.

The only choice I had was to close down the mission and leave the field and try to survive.

He'd taken over his shift ten minutes ago, and although he was watching my reflection from between his half-closed eyelids his attention would be less acute than when he'd changed places with his partner. Static surveillance is fatiguing; on the move there is the physical stimulus offered by the need to keep the target in sight and not lose him, but to sit in a rocking train with your head against the cushions and your eyes half-closed is wearying and even mesmeric: the mind plays tricks, and that man in the mirrors wouldn't be absolutely certain that when I moved, it wasn't in his imagination. He would react, by moving himself.

If he didn't, it would be easier, for me.

I got up and kept his mirrored image in sight and made to turn to my left out of the compartment but his head moved and I abandoned the first choice and turned right instead, initiating the more dangerous play and walking past him along the corridor with my head turned away to look through the windows, not because I could hope to conceal my identity at this late stage but because it was the natural thing to do. The scene out there was eerie; there was no true daylight yet but the edge of the snow cloud was drawing away from the northeast and leaving a shimmering luminosity across the face of the hills, and from the huddle of buildings in the valley there was smoke rising from fires that in the winter here would never go out. The light was so strange in its quality that it could be either dawn or dusk or even full moon; in this region I was already finding that the only temporal constant was provided by my own biological clock.

He didn't turn his head as I walked past his compartment; in reflection he could follow me with his eyes as far as the end of the carriage and he'd only get up and take a stroll if I went further than that.

The panel on the toilet door read *Unoccupied* and I went in and shut the door and locked it and got my heavy coat off because the window was small and I wasn't certain I could squeeze through it. They were larger in the compartments but if I'd left my seat and opened the window he would have heard it and been along here very fast. I'd checked this toilet as soon as I'd got onto the train because it was the only place where I could break any kind of surveillance and make an escape if I had to. The air outside was below freezing and the window frame was shrunk to a loose fit and slid upwards when I pulled on the strap.

The cold air hit my face and I squeezed my eyes half-shut

as I looked out. The speed of the train was somewhere in the region of sixty kph and the terrain alongside the track was black rock under a light snow covering: we'd been running due south and the wind was easterly and the drifts had formed on the other side where I couldn't jump without being seen. At this speed and with those rocks below me it was going to be sudden death but I couldn't see any choice because they'd hold off until I got out at Kandalaksha but from that point they'd expect me to lead them straight to the objective and if I started trying to lose them they'd close in right away: they couldn't afford that, and they wouldn't give me more than an hour or two before they shut the trap and took me to their safehouse and went to work. If I didn't lead them to Karasov they'd have to force me to tell them where he was. I didn't know, but the rendezvous was in my mind and they might salvage that.

I put my head half out of the window and looked south, the way we were running, but the wind was so cold that my eyes blurred at once and I was blinded. Looking below and behind I could still see nothing but rocks: there was no embankment to roll down, no deep snow to break my fall. But we'd passed through Olenegorsk and there'd be no other stop until Kandalaksha in forty minutes' time and if I didn't get out now I'd be moving into a strictly shut-ended situation.

Rocks, and light snow, and rocks, and now a stretch of flat ground with scrubland beyond it and immediately below me the dizzying comb-tooth sequence of the sleepers. There'd be some kind of chance to make a rolling *aikido* fall with my coat on but without it I didn't expect much hope of getting away with less than a smashed skull.

But there was a compromise between staying in the trap and doing a suicide drop and I pushed my shoulders through the window and twisted round and got a hand-hold on the half-inch gutter valance and hung on with my left hand and reached inside for my coat. I'd left it in a bundle across the tiny marbled handbasin and it caught on one of the taps but I freed it by whip action and pulled it through the window. The running board was three feet below me and I felt for it, swinging in the slipstream with the cold hitting my body and going through to the bone before I found the board and put my weight on one foot and dropped and grabbed for the windowsill and steadied, getting my balance.

The idea was to hang on like this until we were running across better ground but there was no guarantee: these rocks were lethal but in this terrain I couldn't hope for more than flat ground frozen iron-hard under the snow and if I jumped wrong and landed badly I could pitch under the wheels.

It was difficult even to see what was below me because at this speed the ground was blurred, and in any case it was no go because a sound came and I looked upwards into the barrel of his gun.

They were really very good.

But he was nervous. He hadn't left me in the toilet for more than a couple of minutes before he checked on me from the next window along.

It was the next window *forward* of the toilet and he'd chosen it so that he could look back without the slipstream in his face. His gun was perfectly steady and his eyes were narrowed, sighting along the barrel. He was the Lithuanian with the shapeless leather bag.

'Come back,' he said in Russian. His voice carried well above the roaring of the wheels.

I looked down and away from him to clear my eyes. I didn't need time to think; there was no decision-making to be done. We were both professionals and we understood that, and the situation was simple enough. He'd taken away the only chance I'd had – the hope of dropping and rolling on flat ground and getting away with it. If I dropped now the last sound I would hear would be the shot. He'd only need one: it was a magnum he was holding, a man-stopper.

His chances of saving his own mission weren't very good now because he couldn't afford to let me get away: if I got away I might survive and reach Karasov and take him to a frontier. The Rinker cell could no longer use me as a tracker dog to lead them to Karasov: I was blown. But if this man had to shoot me dead there would still be a small chance for him and for his mission. He would expect my network to replace me, just as his own had replaced Rinker. He would then hope to pick up the tracks of my replacement and follow him to the objective.

So there was nothing to stop him putting a shot through my spine if I let go and dropped.

'*Come back into the train.*'

He'd got the bloody thing cocked.

The acrid stink of the locomotive up there ahead was in my lungs and I began shallow breathing. The valance was sharp under my fingers and I didn't know how long I could hold on: the whole of my body was numbed by the blast of the slipstream and I began wondering if it would have been any good trying to squeeze through the window with my coat still on, and when you begin wondering things like that when you should be planning your next move it's time you—

'*Three,*' he said, and held up three fingers.

His voice brought me back to full consciousness: I'd been slipping into alpha waves because the cold was clamped round my skull and shrinking the carotid arteries below the jawline. I would have to do something, or –

You've got to do something.

Yes, bloody little organism starting to panic.

If you don't do something we'll get killed and I don't want to die.

For Christ's sake shuddup.

Panic. Panic's the real killer when all's said and done.

'*One,*' I heard the Lithuanian calling out.

A rush of clear thought came and I realized he wouldn't be joking because he didn't have a lot of time to spare: if those KGB people came past the compartment he'd have to shoot them if he could before they got to their guns because that would be professional: he still had a mission running and his instructions would be to do *anything* necessary to protect it and see it through, and even though the major Western services try not to do the kind of thing I did to that KGB colonel in Moscow when the car was being smashed up they sometimes have to take things to a conclusion if there's no other way, just as the KGB sometimes knock some spook off his perch in Paris or London or Bonn if they're running a tricky operation and he's making things difficult.

This man would take on the KGB but he'd much rather not: he'd rather get me back in the train and pistol-whip me or use a syringe and shove me under the seat until he could get me off at Kandalaksha.

'*Two.*'

I was worried about my coat. It was still draped half across the windowsill of the toilet and I was so cold now that it was the only thing I could think of by simple association, thirst, drink, so forth. I thought of something terribly funny to say – *Do you mind if I fetch my coat?*

Not funny, no. *You've got to do something, I don't want to die.*

Shuddup you snivelling little bastard.

Then a spark came flying back from the engine and stung my face and I came out of the alpha waves and thought *oh Jesus Christ this is going to be it.*

'*Three.*'

I squinted upwards and saw the gun and remembered what was happening and moved my feet along the running board and brought my hands level and then moved my feet again and saw from the corner of my eye the coat fall from the window but there was nothing I could do about that.

'*Faster*,' the Lithuanian called.

The whole thing was rocking badly now – the train felt as if it were running across the bare sleepers instead of the rails because I wasn't much more than a frozen carcass and normal consciousness kept slipping into zen as the mind tried to save the organism by relaxing and going blank and letting the body fight its way out of trouble if it could.

'*Faster!*'

Bastard thought I was a fucking miracle worker.

He had the door open and he was crouching on his haunches, because even he'd got enough sense to know that if I were going to climb back into this train I'd need some help. You can't expect anyone to hang on and go on hanging on with the shimmering light and the scent of roses, till you can't—

Wake up.

What? Yes. Nearly lost it all.

Dangerous, this is very dangerous, we—

I don't want to die.

Shuddup.

'*Come on*,' he said, and I took another look upwards with the air-rush tearing at my eyes and the stink of the coal-smoke bitter-sweet in my lungs. He still had the gun on me but his knee was hooked against the edge of the doorway to keep him stable and he was reaching down with his free hand. I thought of taking hold of it but couldn't manage that: it would be too personal, like a handshake, too intimate within the context of kill or be killed. It would pay him to take my hand and pull me to safety but it would also pay him later to shoot aminazin or sulfazin into my veins and blow the last vestige of sanity out of my skull.

You're no friend of mine.

'*Take my hand.*'

Not bloody likely, you've probably got the pox.

He was reaching down but I wouldn't cooperate so he got fed up and took hold of my jacket and I let him get the top part of my body across the doorway with my face against the floor and the smell of linoleum and ancient tobacco stains in my nostrils and then I dragged back enough of my consciousness to work things out because we couldn't go on like this, it was bloody humiliating.

I could feel the relative warmth of the compartment against my head and shoulders and it brought back a feeling of life, a small flame that began flickering through the veins and the nervous system and working on this half-stiffened carcass and bringing some kind of rational thought back into the mind. I began noting things: the bulk of the Lithuanian still crouched on his haunches; the trembling of the floor as the train rocked on its way through the snows; the uncertain light from the bulbs in the ceiling as they blinked to a faulty contact; the ring of steel pressed against my temple and the smell of gun oil.

'*Make an effort,*' he said.

Rather formal, that. He could have said come on you bastard I haven't got all day, or something equally rude. He was quite educated, quite a gentleman, but frankly, you know, when someone's digging your grave for you it doesn't make any difference if he's a gentleman or an absolute shit.

'*You know what this is?*' The ring of steel pressed harder.

'Gun.'

I suppose he was testing me to see how far gone I was.

'Get a grip on that seat,' he said.

I could see the edge of it from where I was lying with my face still against the floor. I reached up and got a hold with my fingers below the cushion and realized that full consciousness was back in my head now and my body was losing its numbness in the warmth of the compartment. I didn't know how much time had gone by since I'd dropped from the window but it was probably a good three or four minutes. That was important, because this man was in a hurry to get me phased out in some way and shoved under the seat. Or he might rely on the gun and order me to sit beside him with the thing against my ribs and make some kind of plausible conversation when people went past along the corridor, we've had a rotten grain crop again, you know what that means, we'll have to buy it from those bloody Americans.

I got it half right and that was dangerous because it left the gun flat against the side of my head and if he pulled the trigger he'd probably blow my shoulder off but at least I'd made a start and he hadn't been ready for it – I'd swung my arm up in a sweeping forearm block and that had paralysed his arm and got the muzzle of the gun away from my temple but there was a lot to do yet if I wanted to survive and I wasn't at all certain I could muster enough strength out of a half-frozen body. He wasn't saying anything, wasn't trying to warn me. I suppose he was enough of a pro to know there wouldn't be any point in talking: the situation wasn't very complex and he knew I understood that unless I could do something effective I'd either finish up with my head blown off or he'd pitch me out of the train and deal with things that way.

We were in a lock at the moment, like two wrestlers. He was a strong man and he was above me and he had the gun but the face of my *sensei* had come into my mind and his image was floating there as he lent me his spirit, his *ki*, so that I was able to stop thinking about what had to be done and concentrate instead on how to do it, which moves to make, which muscle groups to call into action, which angles and surfaces and hand-holds would be best for me if I could find them and use them. There was for instance the strap of the window touching the fingers of my left hand, and I thought about it, picturing the inside of the compartment until I could identify the strap and decide whether it would help me.

My arm was still across his throat and his neck was arched back with his head against the door-hinge but I couldn't increase the pressure enough to block his windpipe because he knew where the danger was: the throat is the primary killing area at close quarters for three very good reasons and he knew what they were. I couldn't increase the pressure there but I had to maintain it because he was waiting for me to slacken off and lose the initiative and then he would move his right hand and fix on the target again and squeeze his index finger and send a 200–grain hollow-point projectile into my skull and through the soft grey convolutions of my brain at 1500 feet per second and I didn't want him to do that.

He'd shut the inside door of the compartment after him when he'd come in here and when the train hit the tunnel it slammed a gust of stinking air across us and blocked the eardrums as the tumult of the wheels built up against the tunnel wall and produced a long sustained roaring that shut down a certain degree of consciousness while the brain tried to accept what was going on and reassure the emotions.

For the moment I couldn't do anything but keep him where he was and it wouldn't be long before muscle fatigue set in and he made a move and caught me by surprise and finished me off so I began trying to work something out, using the tactile data that was available. He had a choice, of course, and we both understood what it was: if he couldn't put a bullet somewhere conclusive he would have to push me bodily off the train; and as I thought about it I became gradually aware that the tactile information coming in confirmed it. He'd started to ease the pressure of the gun against my head and transfer it to my left arm. If he could break my arm or paralyse it at the median or the radial nerve it would release my fingers from the edge of the seat and I would fall backwards through the open doorway and he'd have time to put the bullet in to make sure.

I began putting pressure the other way to see if I were right and I was: he reacted at once, increasing his own. It was like a silent conversation going on, not terribly civil but perfectly articulate; we were equally experienced at clinging to life and there wasn't likely to be anything more than luck involved when we reached the conclusion; meanwhile our two heads were within twelve inches of each other and inside them there was going on this telepathic dialogue, so explicit that each of us had started anticipating the other's next move.

The train was still in the tunnel and I was shallow-breathing again because the compartment was thick with smoke and my eyes were streaming the whole time. The muscles in my right forearm were beginning to feel the fatigue of keeping up a constant pressure and when I took it off and clawed for his eyes we both shifted to the shock of the sudden movement and I felt the gun swinging across my temple and waited for the noise and found my right arm free and smashed the elbow against his face but missed and grazed his head and felt the whole of my weight falling backwards until I found one of his eyes with my fingers and used a gouge and sent him hard against the seat as he tried to stop me. I thought he was screaming but it was the locomotive – the sound came shrilling along the tunnel like a cry of pain.

No go. I'd relieved the strain on my arm but we were locked again and the gun was pressed against my face with the barrel pointing downwards along my body and it was only a matter of time before he fired and waited for blood loss and pushed me out of the train.

He began hurrying now and I knew why. If he could shoot me and push me out while we were still in the tunnel he'd bring off a certain kill: it wouldn't matter if the shot didn't do anything lethal because when I went down I'd hit the wall and bounce back under the wheels and that would be final. He was hurrying by millimetres and I felt it and gave it some thought and realized that he wanted to make sure of a useful shot before he pulled the trigger: it was no good just putting it into my leg because you can go on working for quite a long time unless there's an artery hit and even then you can try for an overkill before the blood loss starts weakening the organism.

So I began hurrying too and pulled my arm from his neck and formed a half-fist and went for the windpipe but he was ready for any kind of move and blocked me and then there was a rushing of foetid air and the eardrums opened as the train ran clear of the tunnel and I lost my balance and clawed for a grip on anything I could find but it was no go and I went pitching down to the track.

15

OBJECTIVE

'Look at this! And they expect me to keep to a schedule!'

The huge windscreen wiper grated across the glass.

'Three snow ploughs, in fifty kilometres. It's a joke!'

We hit a drift and he dragged us clear again.

'They should try it themselves some time!"

He tugged the gearshift, double-declutching, and the engine roared. Ahead of us the sky was black with snow clouds.

'Don't they make allowances for the conditions?' I asked him.

'Allowances?' He turned his huge bearded face to me, his eyes rolling. 'They wouldn't make allowances if the engine dropped out and the wheels fell off and the exhaust pipe got stuck up a polar bear's arse! They think this is summer! *They're whoresons!*'

He kicked the throttle with a massive boot and put the truck into a slide to avoid a stranded tractor. A man in a fur cap waved to him for help, and he stuck his face out of the window. '*Fuck your luck, comrade!*'

I shifted my weight on the worn seat to ease the bruises.

'Have you got enough petrol to get you to Kandalaksha?'

'If those constipated imbeciles have got the road clear, yes.'

It was a big Sovtransavto truck with a Leningrad licence and a TIR plate at the rear. It smelled as if it were carrying some kind of fertilizer, or perhaps it was the driver, but I didn't mind, he was my friend, my good friend. He'd been crawling in low gear through a mess of stranded vehicles a few miles back and I'd climbed into the cab without asking first and told him my car was broken down with a cracked cylinder block.

The coat was a good fit and most of the numbness had gone from my legs. The bruises were on my right shoulder and forearm where they'd hit the rocks alongside the track. The Lithuanian had been underneath me when we'd dropped because my weight had torn his one hand-hold away and he couldn't save himself.

'That's my wife!' the truck driver called above the drumming of the engine. He pointed at the coloured photograph stuck to the facia panel, of a girl with enormous breasts in a bikini.

'Very nice too,' I said.

'Don't I wish!' he yelled and gave a bellowing laugh.

I hadn't intended, in any case, to leave the train without the Lithuanian. I think he tried to bring the gun into some kind of aim on the way down through the freezing windrush but I knew he'd do that so I found his arm and twisted it and the only shot he managed to fire was wild. He was dead as soon as his head impacted on the rocks: I saw that much when I crawled back from where the momentum had thrown me. There wasn't any blood on the coat so I pulled him out of it and put it on as the last of the train rolled past and left a funereal quiet among the snows.

I searched his pockets for what I could find, leaving the wad of notes and taking the wallet to go through: his papers might tell me something about his cell and if they were forged I'd know, and if they were genuine they might be usable. In this trade you always pick a corpse: the dead can sometimes save the living.

I knocked the eight remaining rounds out of the chamber and scattered them and threw the gun across the tracks and into the deep drifts on the other side and then rolled him into a gully and threw snow over him until he was covered. One hand rose into sight again and I caught my breath and felt my scalp tighten as I stared down; it was the way he'd finished up, that was all, rolling deeper between the rocks so that his arm had moved upwards through the snow. I pushed it down again and started walking to the highway.

'*This* one's my wife, really!'

Next to the picture of Lenin was a faded sepia photograph of a strong young woman perched on a milk churn with a chicken struggling in her arms, her smile seductive except for a missing tooth. 'She's a good woman, a good cook. Feeds me like a fucking commissar!'

The road was clear most of the way to Kandalaksha and I asked him to drop me as close as he was going to the main post office. The time was 10:47.

'No. I covered him with snow.'

Fane gave one of his pauses on the line. 'What about the other man?"

'As far as I know he's still on the train.'

'As far as you know?'

'It didn't stop. No one pulled the cord. But he might have jumped off when he saw we'd both gone.'

'It's possible, then, that he could have caught up with you along the road, by getting a lift too?'

'Yes. But call it a thousand-to-one shot.' I checked the time again: it had taken me nearly an hour to get through to Murmansk. 'There was a third man on the train,' I told him. 'He was surveilling me.' There was some crackling on the line. 'Are we clear on this call?'

'What? I'm clear at this end. Are you in a hotel?'

'Post office.'

We both listened, but I couldn't detect a bug. It didn't mean there wasn't one because they're not always detectable, but there'd been heavy snow across the telephone lines between here and Murmansk and some of the poles were down.

"If you're in a post office,' Fane said, 'then we're clear. Was the third man in the Rinker cell?'

"No. He was working his peep independently.'

A brief pause. "I'm not too surprised. With an international background this big we can expect almost any group to crawl out of the woodwork.'

In a moment I said quietly, 'Fane, he wasn't one of Croder's people, was he?'

I'd tried to sound casual but it didn't quite come off. My hands were shaking now and I couldn't stop them: that man under the snow was the fifth one to die since *Northlight* had started running and I'd been with him and just because he was working for the other side and just because he'd been trying to blow my brains out it didn't mean I wasn't going to get the shakes a couple of hours afterwards – we see a lot of it in this trade but we don't exactly enjoy it, we don't exactly *revel* in it, we're not bloody *machines*, you know—

'Croder's people?' I heard Fane asking.

'*Oh come on for Christ's sake* – was he a shield or a backup or some kind of support, you know what I'm talking about.'

I was sweating badly because it wasn't only that man's death on my mind and the way his hand had come out of the snow like that as if he were asking for help, it was my own death too, the one that had nearly happened, because he'd only needed to force that gun round half an inch until it was against my head and I wouldn't have been standing here in this overheated fucking post office reporting the status of the mission to a local control I didn't like and didn't trust and didn't—

"Croder never told me he was sending anyone to support you,' Fane said. 'He–'

'That doesn't mean a bloody thing. He wouldn't necessarily tell you what he was doing if he decided to send out a pack of bloody amateurs to get in my way.'

Watch it, you're losing your cool and he won't like that, he'll signal London and tell them this one's losing his nerve, better have a replacement standing by. He's not Ferris. He doesn't understand.

'I very much doubt,' the voice picked its way carefully along the line, 'that Main Control would put secondary agents into the field without first informing me. It would endanger my executive and the whole mission.'

I waited a minute and took a breath before I spoke. 'All right. I accept that.'

'Thank you.'

He had a point in any case. When some kind of international crisis breaks between East and West they both set up priority missions to defuse the powder keg and stop it blowing the whole thing apart, and it does in fact bring a lot of low-calibre grey-area intelligence outfits out of the woodwork to look for anything they can pick up and trade. They don't amount to much more than mobile listening-posts, *I've just got hold of some rather interesting stuff on troop movements along the Chinese border, old boy, do you think your people would like me to get in touch?* That sort of thing, but you can never be certain they won't tap a line or get wind of a courier run and then they'll try to throw shadows across your operation in the hope of picking up something they can trade with any legitimate network who'll buy it.

The line had gone silent. Fane was leaving me on the hook, waiting for me to say something, expecting me to behave like a model executive in the field.

Standing here in my dead man's coat.

'Have you any instructions?'

'No.' His tone was conversational, offering a copybook example of how mine should sound. 'Will you be able to make the rendezvous?'

'Yes. He came in a minute ago.'

'Have you paroled and countersigned?'

'Not yet.' The man was going across to the end of the main counter, sweeping the ground in front of him with his white stick. No one had followed him in.

'As soon as you locate Karasov,' Fane said carefully, 'I'd like you to signal again.'

'Understood.'

I put the phone back onto the hook and watched the contact for a moment. He was a small man in a moth-eaten fur coat, hollow-cheeked from hunger or some kind of wasting disease, waiting at the counter with his head slightly lifted in the listening attitude that blind men have. The left lens of his dark glasses was cracked. The time on the round mahogany-framed clock on the wall was a minute past noon. I waited until he'd been served and moved across to him on my way to the door.

'Can you tell me where I can buy American cigarettes?'

His head tilted towards me. 'Those things are only fit for women.'

I shrugged and turned away and went ahead of him through the door, walking as far as the first corner and then crossing the street and using the window of a bathhouse to keep the post office in sight. He came out and turned along the pavement with his stick poking at the crusts of snow, and after a moment I began following.

'I wouldn't do that,' Volodarskiy said.

After the brightness of the snow outside it was semi-dark in here and the dog's fangs gleamed from the shadows. I brought my feet back underneath the bench.

"He knows you're a friend,' Volodarskiy said as he spooned his *kashta* from the bowl, 'but you're still unfamiliar to him, and he knows also that sometimes a new friend will turn.' His sharp eyes glanced up at me and his face took on something like a smile. I think he was a man to smile into the face of death itself, and I think he had done that more than once. 'He's a noble enough creature, as you can see. His ancestors hunted bear in this region a hundred years ago. He could kill a bear now, bring it down without assistance, but he wouldn't eat from it.'

As my retinae adjusted to the light from the stove and the lantern I saw the dog more clearly. It looked like a Doberman pinscher but was larger, some kind of breed native to the north here; it had the long canine teeth of the dogs that patrol a sensitive security area, the kind that I would meet again, probably, if I had to breach the frontier without papers.

'Where was it trained?'

'I trained it myself.' It was said with pride. 'One day I'm going to use him for some work I have in mind.' He looked at his stew when he said that, not at me.

Karasov said nothing, had said nothing since the contact had brought me in here. He ate his *kashta* with no appetite. He was a very frightened man.

'He would not eat the meat from a bear,' Volodarskiy said in a slightly sing-song tone, 'because I am the provider of his meat. To that extent, he is tamed. But if I slipped on the ice one day and died of exposure, then he would eat me, or enough of me to end his hunger, because I am the provider of his meat, and it would be logical. But he would wait until I was really dead before he started forward. All dogs, and most humans, are of course carrion eaters.'

I came to one of the gristly lumps in the stew and avoided it, then thought again. I needed the protein.

'Would it attack me, with you here?'

Volodarskiy tilted his head, a habit he'd formed in his occasional role as a blind man. 'Probably not. But he is very sensitive. I trained him to attack anything he feels would bring me harm, even without my orders. I did that because there may come a time when I'm unable to give him those orders.' He glanced at me in the lantern-light and his rather unnerving smile came again. 'He feels he knows, you see, better than I do when it comes to my welfare and anything that threatens it. He's an extension of my body, so what hurts me would hurt him.' He looked down at the dog. 'He's not really intelligent, in the sense we mean it. But he's intuitive, and of course deadly.'

Karasov ate his stew in silence. There were strong vibrations in here, and I'd caught one of them as soon as I'd arrived: the contempt Volodarskiy had for Karasov, for his terror.

It had taken more than an hour to get here because the drifts had blocked some of the narrow streets leading out of the town, and the contact had made a show of bumping into things now and then when there were people about. I'd followed at a distance, making short detours to dissimulate the travel pattern and check for surveillance. I had to make certain we were clean because the executive was nearing the objective and Chief of Control was sitting there in the operations room in London watching the lights over the signals board and studying the blown-up relief map they would have prepared for him as soon as Fane had reported that I was moving into Kandalaksha.

There are three main phases of any given mission on foreign soil: when you get access and when you reach the objective and when you bring the objective or the product back across the border, and things get more difficult as the mission progresses, and if I picked up the slightest hint of any surveillance at this critical stage I would break off and leave the contact to go on alone until I'd gone to cover and closed in on the opposition and wiped them out before they could tag him to the objective and blow the whole mission out of the ground or even *worse* than that, because if the KGB or the Rinker cell or anyone else reached Karasov first they'd put him under the light and prime the needle and get everything out of him, everything in his head, his local contacts and Moscow communications and courier routes and operations history, the whole ultra-sensitive scenario reaching as far as London and sending reverberations right across the network from Hong Kong to Washington. Karasov had been an important sleeper for five years in a Soviet naval base bristling with secret installations and if he got blown before I could pull him out of here it would shut down a dozen files and open up a dozen top-level enquiries that would drop hand-bearer memos on the desk of the prime minister and CIA liaison, and as I crunched over the packed snow under the black winter trees in the tracks of the contact I made certain – absolutely certain – that we were alone and clean and unsurveilled, and later I would repeat that, I would report that I had made certain – absolutely certain.

Near the end of the journey we'd crossed the surface of a frozen stream and worked our way through a knoll of black and leafless tress that stood petrified under the leaden midday sky. It was half-cabin, half-cave that the contact led me to, with walls of rock and rusting iron sheets and stitched hides from cattle buried in the snows of past winters here. Inside, in the gloom where only the one lantern burned and the stove glowed red in the shadows, I had found the objective for *Northlight*, Viktor Karasov.

He was eating his stew with the motions of a man condemned, his hands listless. Bigger than Volodarskiy, he was more brooding, his nicotine-brown eyes sliding away when I glanced at him. I think he believed I'd come here to bring his end in some way, to make a pretence of getting him through the gauntlet of the KGB and leave him dangling across the electrified fence of the frontier riddled like a colander. This was another of the vibrations I was getting: his guilt seemed as bad as his fear – he'd gone to ground without warning us and he'd stayed there and then tried to run for Moscow when he couldn't stand the fear that the KGB were slowly closing in on him while he crouched there in his bolt hole doing nothing. It wouldn't have been here, I knew that. The moment he'd signalled our network he'd been told to move and cover his tracks and make contact with Volodarskiy and leave the rest to him. We never go near the quarry if he's holed up without reporting his location first: you can go in and try reaching an agent who's trapped or been turned or has lost his nerve or his sanity and you can die in there with him – it happened to Travis in Berlin and it happened to Baker in Singapore and it happened to Powys in Tangier and we didn't get the feedback in time to realize what was going on until someone had got back to London and told us what it had been like for Powys and then thrown himself under a bus.

The dog turned its head and a sound began in its throat, a low menacing vibration as if someone here in the shadows had plucked a cello string. Volodarskiy watched the dog, pausing with his spoon halfway to his mouth, and I noticed that half-smile glittering at the back of his eyes. I'd never been near a man with so much rage in him, with so much readiness to confront death in whatever form it came for him.

I could have been wrong but these were my thoughts about him. So much in this place was tacit, unspoken.

Karasov took no notice of the dog. He was wrapped in his fear.

'Is there someone outside?' Volodarskiy asked the dog.

The low snarling went on.

'Not many come this way,' Volodarskiy told me softly. 'I am not popular. That is of course by intent.' One of the most extraordinary things about him was that he had the accent of an educated Muscovite. 'They do not like my dog either. We're well off, he and I.'

The dog stopped snarling and turned its head away from the door. Fane, I thought, had done well, finding a place like this for Karasov the sleeper, and a man like this to guard him. My worry now was how to get him to the frontier: there was no courage in him, and we'd need that.

Our host made coffee for us, black, Ukrainian, steeped in a porcelain filter, its surface gold with bubbles in the lantern-light. It was how I'd begun thinking of him, as our host; there was a formality about the man in total contrast to his life as a cave-dweller. He hadn't been brought down by circumstance to this smoky hovel; he'd come here to the end of the earth and to find his shelter.

I got Karasov to show me his papers, and our host turned the wick of the lantern higher for me without a word exchanged. The identity card was worn right across the surface instead of just around the edges, and one corner of the photograph was raised, because it had obviously been stuck on in a hurry. There were two typographical errors and there'd been two machines used, one original and the other a forger's.

'How much did you pay?' I asked Karasov.

'Six hundred rubles.'

I dropped the papers into the open front of the stove. The higher the price the worse they are: these had been put together for him in one of those little backstreet basements you can find all over Europe, all over the world, and I would say that a high percentage of the agents that have been blown or shot since the invention of the printing press were carrying papers like these.

'They were the best I could get,' Karasov said, shock in his voice as he watched his papers burning.

'That was because you were in a hurry.' I wanted to say other things but held them back because I didn't want to embarrass him in front of Volodarskiy. 'If you'd ever shown those to a KGB man you'd have been shot.'

'What shall I do now?'

He talked like a bloody child. God knew how I was going to get him as far as the frontier – he wasn't like Brekhov, I couldn't run with him, I'd have to drag him there.

You knew this, Croder, you knew he was a broken reed, you bastard, you knew nobody else would take on this bloody job.

The dog turned its head to watch me, the vibrations of my rage touching its nerves. I stared back at it in awe. *What if it had thought my rage was against its master?*

'He is sensitive,' nodded Volodarskiy and I turned to see that half-smile in his eyes. 'You should be careful of your thoughts. You should think only good things, charitable things.' He laughed now, giving a short sharp sound in his throat like a muted bark, and I felt my skin crawling.

'Look,' I said, 'hasn't it got somewhere to sleep, a kennel or something?' I hate dogs.

Volodarskiy laughed again and took the thing back into the shadows, and I heard a chain clinking. 'It is not his fault, you know. We haven't had a man here with so much tension in him. It makes him nervous.'

'It makes *him* nervous? Jesus Christ!'

He laughed again and went back through a curtain of hanging cattle-hides, leaving me alone with the sleeper.

'All right, Karasov, give me the picture.'

It took an hour, maybe more: he'd been in Murmansk five years and had a lot of contacts – not many friends but contacts, couriers, Latvian underground dissidents, Estonian counter-revolutionaries with clandestine printing presses, Lithuanians with nationalistic pride and vengeance simmering in them, the kind of people a good professional sleeper would take an interest in without committing himself, useful people, dangerous people, three of them with enough material on them to make it worth our while to get them to London if we could.

'Why did you leave Murmansk?'

'I was scared.'

'Were they close?'

'I thought so.'

'How close?'

He didn't answer. It would mean telling me how close they needed to get to make him scared and that was exactly what I wanted to know but he wasn't going to tell me: there was some kind of pride left in him and since the meal and the hot sharp stimulus of the coffee he'd come out of his shell a bit. I wanted to know how close they needed to get to make him scared because it would tell me how much work I would have to do to spring him from Russia, how much or how little I could rely on him if a wheel came off. He knew this but his fear was still keeping him halfway in his shell.

'Have you had many brushes with the KGB?'

'No. I'm a careful man.' He spoke in a low whisper, in the way one would speak in the presence of someone dead, and I wondered what it was that had died, or been killed, on his run out from cover. Perhaps it was the man he'd been, the one I would never know. His fear was as deep as that, as crippling; it had changed his personality. I think I might have left him there in that smoking cave, walked away from him into the snow and left him nursing his terror until Volodarskiy had thrown him out. I think I would have signalled Fane and told him there was nothing to bring home to London, just a wrecked psyche.

But it wasn't as simple as that. If he'd done nothing for the last five years except duplicate that one tape he'd have earned his keep and we'd have owed it to him to pull him out and see him safely home. But the tape had been blown apart and he was all we had left now, the living evidence of the death of the *Cetacea*, and even if I couldn't get him across the border

I'd have to keep him out of the hands of the KGB, find a haven for him and a new identity and a new life.

Or silence him, of course. They might ask me to do that.

'You think they got close to you? The KGB?'

'No. Not close. I know how to use cover.' There was that shred of pride in him again, waving like a ragged banner.

'Then why are you frightened, Karasov?'

Wrong move – he went back into his shell, looking down, not answering, sitting near the stove with his big hands clasped and his wet brown eyes staring at the things he wouldn't speak of.

What were they?

'Then is it someone else?' I asked him.

He looked up. 'Someone else?'

'Other than the KGB.'

I saw his eyes change but he looked down again quickly. 'Perhaps.'

A log tumbled in the stove, sending out a spark, I brushed it off my coat and from the shadows the chain clinked and I thought Jesus Christ can't I even move my hand?

Nerves not terribly good, you're perfectly right, but apart from that bloody dog I wasn't having a very nice day because I'd had to kill one man just to get here and God knew how I was going to drag this poor wretch to the frontier without having to kill a lot more or winding up in the minefield with my hands a hundred yards apart and this poor bastard here – the objective, the *objective* – blown out of his bloody shell forever, surely it doesn't take a *lot* of understanding.

All right, there was more than that.

Much more.

'Who?' I asked him.

'I don't know.'

'Have you ever heard of a man named Rinker?'

He looked up. 'No.'

'Has anyone tried to get at you?'

'I've had – ' he shrugged with his hands – 'suspicions, you know. People watching. Cars following. That sort of thing.'

I didn't believe him. I did *not* believe him. If the Rinker cell had got onto him he'd have been dead by now or full of aminazin. They would have devoted as much energy to pulling him in as they'd devoted to me, in fact a bloody sight more because their only interest in me was that I could lead them to the objective and he *was* the objective.

Or he could of course be so frightened of getting caught by the KGB that he was ashamed of it and making up ghost stories to explain it away: when the nerve goes it takes everything else with it.

I was pushing him too hard. He wasn't going to tell me anything unless I could get him relaxed and then creep up on him with the right questions.

'The thing is,' I said quietly, 'to get you home."

His wet brown eyes were turned on me again, this time for longer. 'That's all I want, yes. That's all I want.'

'Of course. It's what I'm here for.' I got up and stretched my legs, keeping away from the corner. 'Has our friend got any kind of transport?'

'What?'

'Car? Has he got a car?'

'No.'

'Then we'll have to hang on here for a bit. My control's getting one through to us as soon as the roads are clearer.' I got the Lithuanian's papers out of my pocket and looked at the photograph and looked at Karasov and read the description but nothing matched; even if we could get the picture changed there was nothing we could do about the measurements: Karasov was five inches taller and looked heavier. 'How much do you weigh?'

'Seventy-one kilos.'

'Have you got any kind of scar across your left shoulder?'

'No.'

I dropped these papers too into the stove and watched the flames. Fane was going to get some good ones for him and until they were in my hands and we had a car to drive we couldn't make a move, but at least it would give me time to coax him out of his shell and find what was frightening him like this.

There was something I was missing or something I didn't know and would have to know before I could get rid of the feeling that there was more, much more, to the routine mission Control had given me, of taking a blown sleeper across.

'We're getting you some effective papers,' I told him. 'Then we can move. Once you're out of Russia you can start making a new life for yourself.'

'Yes.' His eyes hung on me like a grateful dog's.

There'd be people he'd miss, I supposed. His wife. His mistress. 'I phoned Tanya,' I said, 'to let her know you were all right. She was worried.'

'Tanya?'

'Your girlfriend.'

'I don't know anyone called Tanya.'

16

BRIEFING

ONE OF THE sailors threw his cards down onto the table and got up and hauled another man off his chair and pushed him into the door and the hinges broke and the door swung down with the man on top of it. A bottle hit the floor by his head with a crash and I put my hand up to protect my eyes from flying splinters of glass.

'*Cheating son of a whore!*'

The sailor began kicking the man on the floor and some other people stopped him and dragged him away to the bar.

'What's that?' Fane asked me.

'Chap arguing.'

'Where are you speaking from?'

'A workers' club.' It was nearer than the post office.

The man on the floor began crawling outside, leaving a trail of blood. Two or three of his friends went out to help him.

'Debrief,' Fane told me.

'I've located the objective.' We couldn't afford to mention his name; even on an unbugged line there could be an operator with a sharp ear, and Karasov was being hunted throughout Western Russia. 'He's lost his nerve, as you suspected. Volodarskiy is first class, for your information. Also for your information, the woman Tanya Kiselev is either a KGB swallow or she's with the Rinker cell or some other opposition group.'

I waited. It was a long pause. 'How do you know?'

'The objective denies any knowledge of her, and there'd be no point in his lying.'

'Did he mention his wife?'

'No. But he knows I'm getting him out of the country and if he sees her again it'll be in the West. There was nothing to stop him admitting he had a mistress: I wasn't likely to tell anyone.'

Another pause. 'Have you been in touch with her since your first meeting in Murmansk?'

'Yes. I phoned her to say he was safe and well.'

'You didn't say where he was?'

'Not really. He's the objective.'

'Did she ask where he was?'

'Of course.'

There was silence for another few seconds. 'It's not going to be an easy run for you.'

'Croder wouldn't have sent me otherwise.'

Glass smashed again at the far end of the room where the bar was. I couldn't see what was happening because the place was thick with tobacco smoke. I think they were having trouble with the sailor. The other man hadn't come back. There was a freezing draught coming in and two men were trying to put the door back but the hinges had been torn right out of the moulding.

'I'll signal London,' Fane said on the line. He meant about Tanya.

'Don't let anyone go near her.'

'Of course not.'

She had to go on thinking she hadn't been blown.

'I've got some transport for you,' Fane said. 'It's a black Moscwicz pickup truck loaded with grain. Where do you want it left?'

'Is it available now?'

'Yes.'

'Have it left outside the public reading room behind the main post office. There's a car park there. What's the number?'

He read it to me and I memorized it. 'I'll also need some papers for the objective. His were no good: I burned them.'

'There are some new ones on the way from Moscow by plane tonight. Unless there's any kind of hitch the courier will arrive in Kandalaksha on the 11:15 train tomorrow morning, snow conditions permitting.'

'Where do I make contact?'

'Immediately below the iron footbridge across the freight-yard at the station. There's only one bridge and one freight-yard. The rendezvous is for 11:30. If the train is delayed you'll rendezvous again at twelve noon and every hour after that, on the hour.'

'Parole?'

'He'll ask you if you're waiting for the geese. You'll tell him they were sent yesterday on the market train.'

'Roger.'

They were taking the sailor out now, singing drunk. Two other men had found a carpet from somewhere and were nailing one end across the top of the door to keep the draught out.

'As soon as you've got the papers,' Fane said, 'drive to Severomorsk, just north of Murmansk on the Kola River, the east bank. I'm going to try getting you both out by ship.'

I felt sudden hope. Fane was working more efficiently than I'd expected: he'd already found some transport and was getting the papers through and working on a plan to ship us out. There was no reason for the KGB to stop us on the drive north, and the Rinker cell hadn't picked up my scent. It looked as if we were actually going to be taking the objective to the West. End of mission, so forth.

'What's my cover story?'

'I'll leave that to you.'

There was a thousand-to-one chance the two KGB men who'd questioned me on the train might now be helping in the search for Karasov along the roads, so I would say that I couldn't get the job I'd hoped for at the foundry and I was earning a few rubles carting the grain to a chicken farm in the north.

'All right.'

'Do you need anything else?'

'No. Will you be in touch with the courier before tomorrow morning?'

'Yes.'

'Synchronize watches.'

'15:21.'

'That's right."

There was a short silence, then Fane said, 'Good luck.'

'Thank you.'

I hung up the receiver and pulled the carpet aside and went out under the dark afternoon sky, and heard the faint distant singing of the drunk.

'I don't see how we can get through,' Karasov said.

I'd been expecting this. He'd hardly slept during the night: he'd woken me a dozen times, turning on the straw mattress alongside mine.

Volodarskiy spat, turning away. I already knew his contempt for Karasov's lack of courage.

'Everything is arranged,' I told Karasov. 'We're going to make a short run to the coast, and there's a ship waiting.' I turned to the heavy screen of cowhides and pulled it aside, and heard the dog voice, low in its throat. The dog too had been awake in the night, disturbed by something outside.

'I would rather wait for a time,' Karasov told me, standing there with his hands hanging by his sides and his head down. 'In another week they will have stopped hunting for me.'

Volodarskiy came back from the shadows, his eyes as bright as the dog's.

'*Out!*' he said.

Karasov flinched. 'You don't understand my position. They–'

'But I understand mine, my friend. If they find you here I shall spend the rest of my life breaking stones. *Out!*'

The dog voiced again, sensing the menace in its master's tone. Karasov flinched again but didn't move.

'It'll take me a few minutes to start the truck,' I told him. 'Once it's going, I'm driving north. If you want to come with me you haven't got long to make up your mind.' I went out into the snow. If he didn't get the point I would have to come back and drag him to the truck and if necessary all the way to the Kola River. Not terribly propitious, you might say, not precisely a joy-ride, but theirs not to question why, theirs but to do or die, so forth.

The barn was a hundred yards from the cave and I'd run the black pickup truck inside it last evening, going in backwards and leaving it to one side where the earth floor sloped towards the entrance. If the battery couldn't turn the engine after the night's cold we had a chance of a push start. As I crunched through the snow I listened for Karasov but so far he hadn't left the cave. There wouldn't be any problem getting him out of there: Volodarskiy would give the appropriate word and the dog would do the rest. The problems would come later unless I could shake him out of his blue funk.

It was just ten o'clock and the early light was seeping across the sky from the east above the black skeletal trees. It was thirty minutes' drive to the rail yards and I was leaving an hour to check out the environment before we kept the rendezvous. As I went into the barn I looked back and saw Karasov trudging through the snow, a hunched, bulky figure with its head down. There were no doors on the barn: it was a huge ruin of a building, its rotting timbers holding up as if by virtue of the dogged endurance that had brought it through so many winters here. It faced west, towards the cave, and the shadows were still deep. Odd shapes reared against the walls, of wrecked machinery and crates and implements and things unknown. Cattle, I supposed, must have sheltered here once, and even died in here, frozen on their feet.

I got behind the wheel of the truck just as Karasov reached the entrance of the barn and stood there for a moment looking in, his shoulders hunched and his mittened hands hanging by his sides.

'Don't come near,' I told him through the open window of the truck.

'What?'

'Keep away. Go back to the cave.'

I was sitting perfectly still.

'Why?'

I tried to pitch my voice loud enough for him to hear me, and no more.

'Karasov, I want you to go back to the cave. Tell him I sent you.'

My scalp had lifted and I could feel the gooseflesh creeping along my arms. It was just the smell, really: there was nothing to see or hear.

'Go back?' Karasov called out.

'Yes. Wait there for me.'

He went on staring for a long time, trying to think why I'd changed my mind; then he turned away and his figure grew smaller across the snow. I didn't move until he'd reached the cave. Then I moved very carefully.

17

TOY

THE SMELL WASN'T strong, but it was unmistakable.

The truck wasn't familiar to me – I'd only driven it three miles and in any case there were electric wires and plastic and brass fittings under the dashboard that would add their own subtle odours to the general smell of this particular machine: they weren't much different from the electric wires and the plastic and the brass terminals that I knew had been put in here more recently, during the night, perhaps when the dog had voiced, sensing something outside.

It was the smell of death that I had recognized when I'd climbed behind the wheel. It's not always the same: it can come from gun oil, geraniums, smoke, new rope and a hundred other things that in the harmlessness of their natural context can go unnoticed. But I was starting the final run out with the objective for the mission and my senses were fine-tuned and alert for any conceivable threat to the organism. It wasn't the smell of the bomb itself that had warned me. My instinct had triggered cognizance of enormous danger and in the instant I became afraid, and what I had recognized was the smell of my own fear as it sprang from the skin.

Metal banged and sent echoes through the hollow shell of the barn and my scalp rose again and the sweat came so fast that it trickled against me under my clothes. The relative warmth of the new day had expanded the corrugated iron sheets of the building where they overlapped, and a bolt had moved, that was all.

There was a lot of incoming data and some immediate decisions would have to be made because if that thing had a timing device on it that had started ticking to the movement when I'd got into the truck it could detonate at any next second and I ought to get out now and get out fast. But—

Yes, we've got to get out before—

Shuddup.

But it wasn't likely they'd done that. They would only have put that kind of mechanism in here if they'd wanted to make sure that Karasov and I would blow ourselves up in the barn before we started off, and that didn't make any sense – it would be all the same to them if we did it five miles along the road, or fifty. If they'd wanted to keep things quiet they wouldn't have chosen explosives: they would have used a telescopic lens and waited for us to come out of Volodarskiy's cave and dropped us quietly into the snow. Or they would simply have tipped off the KGB and run us into a road-block and left it at that.

It was probably wired to the ignition.

That was a problem because I wanted to use this truck and get us both out of here without wasting any more time: there was a ship waiting for us in Severomorsk and if we missed it there might not be any other way for Fane to get us out before the KGB finally picked us up in their dragnet for Karasov.

Correction: they hadn't simply tipped off the KGB and run us into a road-block and left it at that *because they hadn't wanted to.*

They wanted us dead, out of it, *finis.* They didn't want the KGB to put us under the light and drain the information out of us.

Why not?

What did we know?

The metal roof strained again and my left eyelid began flickering. There were a lot of things to be worked out but I didn't know which ones could wait and which ones had such a direct bearing on this immediate point in time that it could make the difference between driving the truck out of here or going through the roof with it.

Something had gone wrong. The Rinker cell had so many people in the field that they could afford to watch the traffic coming in on the main road from Murmansk and as soon as they knew I'd left the train they'd done that, they'd watched for me. Or they'd picked me up since then and thrown a distant-surveillance net round the periphery of my travel patterns and kept me in sight with field glasses.

But they couldn't know about this morning's rendezvous in the freight-yards. I would have to get Karasov there and get his papers and drive north if I could. We had to get out of Kandalaksha. They were too close.

Pale light came through the open end of the barn, costing me too much visual purple in the retinae: the cab of the truck was almost dark. I didn't know that if I could see better in here I wouldn't actually see an extra wire creeping below the dashboard or the glint of a terminal.

Time for decision-making. I didn't think they'd put a clock on the thing or a rocker mechanism or a remote-control receiver or a heat sensor because it wouldn't matter when it blew up and a rocker would detonate at the first corner and a remote control would mean they were still in the immediate environment and waiting to transmit and I knew they weren't in the immediate environment because they couldn't afford to be: otherwise they would have simply come here in the night and finished off the lot of us including Volodarskiy and the dog. A heat sensor would delay detonation until the engine had warmed up but that involved a time element again and it wasn't of any interest to them.

I believed they would have done it the simplest way and linked it with the ignition switch.

But when I moved I moved slowly.

It could be anything: C3, C4, Cyclonite, TNT, picric acid, gelignite, dynamite, Tetryl, Amatol, any one of a dozen sensitive chemicals. In this region they wouldn't have found the more sophisticated materials and they'd probably used something out of any army ordnance store but I couldn't count on that.

I got down from the cab and stood on the earth floor and let the sweat trickle down my flanks and waited until my scalp loosened again before I moved to the front of the truck and stood still again, looking at the bonnet lever. When they rig a bang in the electrical circuitry of the vehicle they don't like you to disconnect a battery lead and today they might have placed auxiliary contacts on the bonnet levers or the hinges so it was a little while before I decided that they wouldn't have made things more complicated for themselves than they needed to.

They too were working their mission within the hostile and all-powerful environment of the KGB and all they had wanted to do was to wipe Karasov out and do it by stealth, setting it up and moving away and leaving it to the device itself to finish the business. They could do that by wiring the ignition switch and there would be no real need to provide backup circuits or contacts so I moved the bonnet lever and waited again until the nerves came down from screaming pitch and I got my breathing rhythm back to normal. Then I went round the front of the truck and pulled the other lever and lifted the bonnet.

Filthy engine. Everything was covered with an antique film of dried mud and oil stains and husks of grain, and I got the torch out of the tool compartment and used it, looking for any disturbance in the grime. Something bright flashed under the beam of the torch and I spun away and hit the snow outside as the whole barn blew apart and a roaring filled the sky and I lay there with my body against the snow and the nerves came off their high and the barn came back into one piece again and the roaring stopped and I thought *Jesus Christ if I can't do better than this. . . .*

The snow cold under me, my face against it, my breath melting its crystals as the lungs went on pumping in the aftermath of unholy terror, pick yourself up, yes, get on with things.

When I was ready I got up and went back to the truck and

found the wrench and disconnected the battery and stood for a minute with my eyes shut, just taking a break, it wasn't over yet because the thing could have its own battery but we might have come a little further away from blowing *Northlight* across the Kola River.

'What's wrong?'

I jerked round and looked at him.

Volodarskiy.

No dog. I think if he'd brought his dog I'd have killed it.

'Someone was here in the night.'

He watched me, noting, quite obviously, quite obviously noting, damn his eyes, the sweat on my face.

'How do you know?'

'They put a bomb on board this thing.'

'How do you know?' he asked again.

'In the same way in which you would have known, Volodarskiy, if you had come here first,' using my most polished academic syntax and my best Muscovite-intellectual accent, except for the last bit, 'and it would have scared the shit out of you too.'

His black eyes glittered with amusement. 'Conceivably. Where is the bomb?'

'I haven't found it yet.'

He looked at the filthy engine. 'Are you an expert?'

'I'm finding out. If your barn is still standing an hour from now you'll know I'm an expert.'

'Perhaps I can help.'

'Yes. You can go back and look after Karasov.'

'I would rather stay here,' he said softly, 'and fiddle with the toy you think they've sent you.'

'I know you would. You can't keep away, Volodarskiy, can you?'

'From what?'

'The brink.'

His eyes glittered again. 'That is a way of putting it, I suppose.'

'You're like me.'

'I think so, yes.'

'But if I get it wrong, and this thing goes up, I want you to look after Karasov. I want you to contact my local control and tell him what's happened and ask him how he's going to get the objective out. Until he can do something I want you to keep that man with you and see that no one gets to him. He's the *objective*, Volodarskiy. The *objective*.'

His eyes moved around the barn while he thought about this, then he looked down and shrugged. 'I will do what you say, my friend; I know how important your mission is. But do what you can to find that little toy of yours and make it safe. I have no wish to keep that craven wretch in my house for longer than I have to. He's not fit company for my dog.'

'He's burnt out,' I said, 'that's all.'

'And so am I. But there is heat there yet.' He came to stand close to me. 'I was fifteen years in the labour camps, but that was not so bad. When I came home they told me that my wife had been arrested for circulating subversive material – she was a poet, and she wrote of freedom.' His breath clouded on the cold air and his eyes never left my face. 'She refused to give away her friends, her collaborators, and so they beat her, and she died. The KGB men who killed her had received promotion and been transferred. But I have found one of them, and when I find the other, I have some work to do. So has my dog.' He turned away. 'He is hungry, and so am I.'

I watched him moving back to his cave across the snow.

It took me another forty minutes to find it because they can rig this kind of thing in a dozen ways and just because you've disconnected the battery it doesn't mean you won't detonate it if you move too fast or press too hard or touch the wrong terminal, the wrong wire, the wrong connection.

It was lying under the front floorboards. I hadn't been able to see it from underneath the truck: I'd had to go in from the top, prying the floorboards upwards a centimetre at a time and shining the torch beam through the widening gap. I first saw the bomb when the floorboard was still raised only two or three centimetres and I stopped moving at once.

It would depend on how good the man was at his job. He could have used any one of a dozen initiators – chemical, electrical, mechanical, acoustic, vibratory, magnetic – or he could have used a combination initiator to produce detonation whatever I did, so I got a spanner and took the driving mirror off its bracket and slipped it through the gap in the floorboards and used the torch again.

These things are never pleasant to look at, simply because you know what they will do if you disturb them. This one had the squat shape of a giant slug and the stillness of a rattlesnake. Its potential for monstrous havoc gave it, in my mind, a kind of life: the brain refused to believe that this degree of power could be contained in such a small object. What I was looking at was something that could produce an air-blast pressure of a million pounds per square inch and a temperature of four thousand degrees centigrade and a fragmentation velocity of twenty thousand feet per second and it would do this if I made a single wrong move. The infinitely complex system of intelligence inside my skull was within two feet of the source of cataclysmic obliteration, and the forebrain was working out the options while the primitive stem kept the hairs on my arms lifted and the pressure in the arteries raised and the heart's rhythm racing.

But there were no real options. The objective had to be taken across and that was what I was here for and it wasn't the time to weigh values – Karasov's life against mine, the ruthless demands of the mission against the executive's personal survival. I was here because the brink was here and if I'd wanted anything different then I could have walked out of that bloody building in Whitehall long ago and told them to stuff it, get off my back, leave me alone. But they knew what I wanted and they'd put it on the map and set my feet in its direction and told me how far it was and now I was there. On the brink.

You can't keep away, Volodarskiy, can you? You're like me.

I think so, yes.

There's one born every minute.

Time check. 10:53. I'd been here almost an hour and the train from Murmansk was due in at the station in thirty-seven minutes and there wouldn't be a lot of time to check the environment of the freight-yards but if we delayed the rendezvous until 13:00 hours we'd risk exposure and I didn't want to do that, I wanted to get Karasov out before they came for him again.

I moved the mirror in the gap, angling it and sliding it from one end to the other, lighting the underside of the floorboards with the torch. There were no contacts and I pulled the boards higher and took another look. The bomb was the size of a small brick and preserrated with a shrapnel sleeve. The end terminal carried the wire to the junction box underneath the dashboard and the side terminal connected with earth through the chassis: they'd scraped an area clean and used grip tape, a decent enough job. But I didn't like the flat back lever on the underside of the pack and as I turned it a couple of degrees for a better look I realized it was a grasshopper switch and knew that all I had to do was pick up the main pack to send the truck through the roof of the barn, so I worked on the terminals first and freed the pack from the wires and then picked it up slowly, inching my fingers underneath to keep the switch flat to the body.

There was no sound of ticking. A timing device would have been visually evident; all we'd got here was two and a half pounds of TNT and provision for electrical initiation from an outside source and a liquid chemical in a glass tube to detonate internally by percussion: I could see the end of the tube recessed into the main pack and when I tilted it I could see the bubble.

Think. Consider binding the lever with some string and then putting the bomb onto the curved bonnet of the truck and starting the engine and walking away and letting the vibration shake the thing off and send the barn up. It had worked in Berlin and it would work now. The Rinker people weren't likely to come here and poke among the wreckage to make sure there were bodies in it: they'd hear the bang and assume that what had been designed to happen had happened, simply because the human mind prefers to believe in success rather than failure. And even if they came as far as the barn they wouldn't have much time to poke about in the wreckage before Volodarskiy told Fido to tear their throats out.

But it wouldn't work, in the long run. It would mean getting to a phone and asking Fane to organize some more transport for us and that could take days and I didn't know how long Karasov could hold out before his nerves tipped him over the edge and he went stark raving bonkers, which wouldn't please London at all. There was something on that man's mind that wasn't letting him sleep, wasn't letting him believe that I could get him out, something that was frightening him so badly that it could blow him out of his skull before I could get him to the West.

This thing in my hand wasn't ticking, but Karasov was.

Get him out. Get him out *now*.

There was some string holding some empty sacks together in the corner of the barn and I cut off a length but it was rotten with age so I raked in the tool compartment of the truck and found some electric cable and used that, winding it round the grasshopper switch and putting the bomb on the floor under the front seat on the driver's side and chocking it with a bit of wood from the littered floor of the barn so that it couldn't roll about; a thing like that could come in handy. Then I connected the battery lead and started the engine and left it running to warm up while I fetched Karasov.

He was coming out of the cave when I got there. They'd heard the engine start.

'So you found your toy,' Volodarskiy said.

'Yes.' I sensed that he hadn't told Karasov what kind of toy it was: it would have pushed him right over the edge.

'Then I wish you a good journey.'

'Thank you.' I looked at Karasov. 'We're going.'

He moved his head slowly, like a punch-drunk, and stared at me in the cold light of the morning, and all I could see in his eyes was the knowledge of death. As I led him across the snow to the barn it occurred to me that his mind, at the brink of hysteria, might be open to the dark voices of premonition that I could not hear.

18

RENDEZVOUS

THE HUGE IRON scoop slammed down and black gas rose.

'*Back!*' a man shouted, waving, and I reversed the truck again.

The snow plough moved forward another ten yards, its diesel roaring under full throttle as it lifted another ton of snow and swung it clear of the road. The exhaust gas drifted past us like a smoke screen and I felt safe for a moment, because they would have known by now that the barn hadn't gone up and they might be short of time and bring a gun in. It wasn't certain they'd do that. You've got to take calculated risks.

The man waved us forward again, standing back this time to let us through the gap: they were clearing the intersection, routing us through a detour.

Karasov sat beside me, leaning his head back against the seat and gazing through the windscreen with his eyes narrowed. He had the look of a man in a tumbril on his way to the guillotine. slack with despair.

'Was it a bomb?' he had asked me a little time ago. 'A bomb he was talking about, when he spoke of a 'toy'?'

'Yes.' He might as well know.

'How did you find it?'

'Bit of luck.'

I didn't tell him it was still here under the driving-seat. He would have got out and walked.

We ground along in first gear, shunting between a coal truck and a beaten-up Zhiguli van.

I didn't think they'd bring a gun in because they could have done that before: they could have dropped us as we'd come out of the cave. There were plenty of other ways, quieter ways, less public. But it was a calculated risk and every time we shunted to a halt I felt my head settling instinctively onto the top of the spine and my shoulders rising into the primeval startle attitude, because this was when they'd steady the aim and fire, when we were stationary. They would have to shoot twice or use two guns unless it was only Karasov they'd been trying to kill in the barn, expecting him to climb into the truck with me before I started the engine. My death could have been planned as incidental but that wasn't certain either: the Rinker cell could have reasons for taking me down, putting me out of their way.

The windscreen was filthy but I hadn't wiped it clean before we'd started off; we wouldn't be hitting up any kind of speed and it gave us a degree – just a degree – of safety: they'd have to judge where our heads were if they meant to station a gun somewhere in front of us along the road.

'Then they'll try again,' Karasov said suddenly. I didn't realize he'd been all that time thinking it out; there were a thousand things on his mind, I knew that. But I didn't know what they were.

'Not necessarily.' We halted again, and my head settled.

'Of course they will. When they know the bomb didn't kill us, they'll try again.'

'They wouldn't have let us get this far, don't worry.'

He didn't say anything to that, but put a hand into the pocket of his dark woollen coat and held something out to me. I glanced down and saw a cassette tape.

'Take it,' he said.

I put it into my pocket. 'What is it?'

'The second tape.'

We were stuck again by another snow plough and I turned off the engine so that I could hear better: not only his words but the tone. He was going to talk now. He was going to tell me why he was so deathly afraid. The sleeper had waked, now he would talk.

A second tape?

I didn't turn my head to look at him. It was already in my mind that what he would say to me would be in the form of a confessional. I'd sensed an element of guilt in this man before.

'What's on it, Karasov?'

'It's a duplicate of the one you took to London.'

I remembered the debris pattering down in Eaton Place after the two boffins had climbed into their car.

It had been for nothing, then. There was another tape.

A man's face was at the window suddenly and I looked at it through the glass. He was saying something. His breath steamed as he waved his hand, shouting now. I wound the window down. He wasn't an agent; he was a farmer, his face weathered into a grizzled brick-red mask and his eyes sunk into their sockets, rheumy with the cold.

'I'm out of petrol! Can you spare me a drop, comrade?'

I could feel Karasov's fear beside me. He was going to be like this all the way to the railway station, all the way to the coast.

''I'm almost out myself,' I told the man. 'That's why I've switched off the engine.'

He threw up his arms and trudged forward through the snow to talk to the driver in the truck. I wound the window up and asked Karasov, 'Why did you take a duplicate?'

It was a long time before he answered. 'For the others.'

The man's voice came back to us as he shouted to the driver in front. Somewhere on the road ahead I could see the shape of another mechanical scoop clearing the snow. I gave Karasov time, but he wanted me to drag it out of him like a priest in the confession box. Guilt never comes out in a hurry.

'What others?'

'The Chinese.'

It was like a bullet coming through the windscreen. I hadn't been ready for it.

'Go on,' I told him. He wanted goading.

'I–' and that was all for another minute. I didn't prompt him again, because he'd hear fury in my voice and that would frighten him off altogether. He wouldn't know that the fury wasn't against him but against myself, against Fane, against Croder. *None of us had known and we should have known.* We should have known that an international incident big enough to threaten the summit conference would inevitably involve triangle diplomacy and the China card.

'I – I've been giving product to them for a long time now,' Karasov said.

Mother of God.

'How long?

I felt him jerk in fear as his head swung to look at me. He'd heard it: the fury. I would have to do better than this but by Jesus Christ I was sitting here in a stinking farm truck with our run to the coast blocked off by snow and the objective for the mission sitting beside me and telling me he'd been working for both major intelligence networks, East and West, *for a long time,* eight days into *Northlight* and already five on the deathroll and a live bomb under my legs and someone out there putting the windscreen into the crosshairs or signalling ahead of us to get a trap set or coming up from behind us like the man who was out of petrol and there was *nothing* I could do about it until I could get this *bastard* to the frontier and take him to London and leave him there to spill his guts all over Croder's debriefing desk and *then* I was going to ask questions, an awful lot of questions about the man running our Murmansk cell and why the hell he'd let his sleeper go on working for London and Peking without checking on his product and his couriers and his contacts and his communications because *somewhere* he could have been caught, could have been seen slipping a package into a furtive hand in the shadows of a crowded bar or on a bus or in a brothel or wherever they'd set up their drop, *somewhere* they could have tapped a line or checked a crossed signal or questioned the travel patterns or stood close to a talker, catching a hint of smoke on the air, a whiff of something burning.

'What?'

'Years,' he was saying. 'Years.'

I didn't answer him until I'd got control again. Keep cool, yes, absolutely, nothing to get into a tis-was over, just sitting here thinking I'm working exclusively in the Soviet zone and all the time there's a Chinese cracker rigged to go off, love from Peking, bit of a joke really, something funny happened to me on my way to Murmansk, this one's going to kill you.

That, too, yes.

'Have you been giving them *everything?*'

He waited until I'd dragged the gears in: we'd started moving again. 'Not everything. Only the stuff they'd be interested in.'

'*Only the stuff they'd buy?*' Rather rude, that, yes, but I wasn't really in the mood for good manners.

'They were only interested in naval matters,' he said with an attempt at dignity, 'affecting the security of their own coastline.'

'And how precisely did the sinking of the SSN *Cetacea* affect the Chinese coastline?'

He didn't answer, and I realized he didn't even need to. Of course it was nothing to do with the Chinese coastline: it was to do with the summit conference in Vienna.

'*Keep over this side!*' someone was yelling, and I wound the window down for a better view and slowed the truck. Two men with shovels were out there levering a rusty Volkswagen clear of the ruts. I turned my front wheels and got the rear chains working at the surface and nudged the VW onto the cleared surface with its tyres slewing across the sand. It pulled his offside wing off but he was out of trouble now. One of the road gang picked up the wing and threw it across the snow.

'*Keep going! Keep your wheels moving!*'

The VW sent a cloud of exhaust gas into the air and I shut the window. 'Karasov,' I said, 'have you got a gun on you?'

He looked at me sulkily. 'No.'

He could be lying: his eyes hadn't given anything away. It occurred to me that he might have brought a gun along to use on someone or on himself.

'*Are you taking me into a trap?*'

Because anything was possible now. A few minutes ago he'd been a blown sleeper dependent on me to get him across but now he could be anything, any kind of Judas working for London, Moscow and Peking, raking in pounds sterling, rubles and yen while he kept the product coming and reported to the KGB through a backstairs courier. Maybe all that frightened him was the idea of sitting next to someone who was going to see the bits of glass coming at him first and then the flat-nosed slug as it moved into the target just above the eyes.

'A trap?' He shook his head. 'Listen, I'm not as bad as that.' And suddenly he was crying, and I shut up for a while and let him get it done with. It was the strain, I suppose, and the feeling that he was letting everyone down – because they're like that, some of them, the mercenaries, the people who'll work for anyone who'll pay them, two at a time, three at a time, paying off the mortgage on their little place in Hampstead and looking for a bigger one, bribing the black market commissar in the back streets of Leningrad to put him higher on the list for a nice little Moscwicz, shifting a bank account from Paris to Cannes and commuting by Caravelle from wife to mistress and back, compared with which my good friend Karasov was doing rather less well for himself, stuck in a truck in the Arctic Circle in winter time and snuffling over his sins into a filthy handkerchief.

Snow exploded against the windscreen and Karasov shouted something as his head rocked back against the seat squab. Fright, that was all. The big scoop out there had swung across the line of traffic and lost half a ton of snow in the process. I stopped the truck and got out and stood on the running board and kicked the snow off the bonnet and if they'd wanted to squeeze the hairspring at this precise moment they could have blown my head off. The other drivers were rechristening the man in the scoop, *clumsy prick, whoreson, pox-ridden idiot,* so forth, not at all popular.

'*Get moving! Come on, get moving!*'

I botched the gears in through their worn shafts and we

went forward again, shunting into the truck ahead and sliding into the clearway and getting some speed up. No trap, then, according to Karasov's behaviour: I'd been overestimating things – whatever he'd been doing and whoever he'd been busy working for he was still a burnt-out case.

'If you've got a gun on you, Karasov, I don't want you to use it. Do you understand?' He didn't answer. 'We may run into a road check between here and the coast and I don't want you to pull a gun on anyone. *Do you understand?*'

He flinched again and a hand disappeared and he brought out a Soviet military JK–3. I took it from him and checked the safety-catch and shoved the thing under the seat.

'Who are they using? Who are the Chinese using?'

'They're being serviced through Zurich.'

The Rinker cell. Rinker had been a Swiss. But they'd used local agents: the two men on the train, one of them a Latvian. I didn't know about the third man, the other man: he'd looked European.

So Peking was worried about Washington and Moscow getting round a table in Vienna next month and they'd seized a chance in a lifetime: if they could get hold of a tape or Karasov himself and hit the American news media with the message that the Soviets had indeed sunk the *Cetacea* with a hundred and five lives on board they could scuttle the summit conference and leave that on the bottom too.

'So why didn't you sell them the tape?' He didn't answer. 'Wasn't the money good enough?'

The truck ahead of us was putting on more speed and I took up the slack; we were making nearly forty kph over sanded ruts. There was a lot of honking behind us in the distance; I supposed the farmer's vehicle was blocking the road because he still couldn't find any petrol.

'They wanted me to go in front of journalists, in Moscow.'

'Didn't they know you'd done a tape for them?'

'Yes. They knew.'

'Then why – *come on Karasov I want some fucking information.*'

'They knew I had a tape but they said they wanted me to be there too at the broadcast.'

'What was their price?'

'A million US dollars.'

I looked at him. 'So why didn't you take it?'

'I knew then how serious things were. There was some talk at the naval base about the summit conference having gone down with the submarine, that kind of thing. So I told my contact the tape had–'

'Your contact for Peking?'

'Yes. I told him the tape had been accidentally wiped out when I'd passed through one of the power-station rooms. They said they still wanted me to make a broadcast, and for the same money. They also said that if I wouldn't do it, they'd blow me to the KGB.'

'That was when you got out?'

'Yes.'

'I still don't understand why you turned them down.'

He leaned towards me and a light came into his wet brown eyes. 'I was making a little on the side, don't you see, I was selling a few things to the Chinese from time to time because it wasn't doing London any harm, it wasn't anything I was keeping back from your people, it was simply a matter of duplication, don't you understand, I wasn't doubling, I was only augmenting my income. *London came first with me.* I'm not a man completely without loyalty, I didn't do anything that isn't done among – among–' he waved a gloved hand – 'among business people all over the world, but when I saw how serious things were, with the summit in jeopardy and the headlines talking about it every day, I backed out of my commitment with the Chinese and went to ground.'

'You turned down a million American dollars?'

'Yes. Do you think money is everything? Do you–'

'You got frightened, that was all, it got too big for you.'

He gave a kind of sob and I kicked the throttle and started a slide and smashed the sidelight off an abandoned trailer with the rear of the truck and got control again, slowed again, it wasn't for me to judge the poor bastard, what the hell did I know about the things I'd do if the pressure got too much or a deal got too hot to handle, I wasn't this man and I hadn't faced what he had faced, I wasn't my brother's keeper, nor his judge.

'I would've done the same, Karasov. I would've got frightened.'

I don't think he heard me. He was a man of conscience, I suppose, and what he was trying desperately to rescue from the ashes was some kind of pride.

'Slow down! There's a detour! Slow down!'

More men waving, and a truck overturned and half-smothered under a snow drift, someone sitting by a fire he'd made from some oily rag, warming his hands while the black smoke rose like a dead vine from the ground to the winter sky.

We turned left, all of us, a dozen vehicles in front of me and a lot more behind, and I saw a railway signal poking up from the horizon: we were less than a mile distant now from the station and the freight-yards were this side.

11:47.

There wasn't going to be time to check out the environment: we were going to run in cold to the rendezvous and I couldn't do that with the objective for the mission on board. But the only option was to leave him somewhere safe while I went on and kept the noon appointment: this would leave him alive and available to London if anything came unstuck at my end, but it wasn't certain that Fane could ever find him again before he died of exposure or went trudging into the nearest KGB headquarters looking for a martyr's grave or waited for the next train and lay down on the sleepers with his neck on a rail – there was no knowing what he'd do.

We could find a side turning and hole up under a drift until noon plus fifteen and then go in and check the environment but that would mean delaying the rendezvous until 13:00 hours and the longer we hung around Kandalaksha the bigger the risk we ran of drawing the opposition against us. There was no real reason for the KGB to be watching the freight-yards specifically: this was just paranoia on my part, a reluctance to take a calculated risk in broad daylight. The aura of this man's fear was reaching me, touching the nerves.

Make a decision.

A snow-clearing gang was filing along the railway lines towards a group of men hacking at frozen points with pickaxes. The truck directly in front of me was turning to the left, taking the ramp down to the main section and leaving me at the fork.

Make a decision.

If the train had been on time and the courier had got through without any trouble he'd be waiting under natural cover now for the noon rendezvous with the papers for Karasov, and the minute we had them we could head north and hope for clear roads and a final run in to the coast. We could be there in a few hours, before nightfall at mid-afternoon. By tomorrow morning we could be in Norway, in the West. And London by evening.

Make—

'Karasov, listen carefully. We're going to make a rendezvous in a few minutes from now with a courier who'll have papers for you, good ones, reliable enough to get us to the frontier. I don't want you to do anything. Do you understand? I want you to sit there and look like the upholstery, keep your mouth shut and keep your hands on your lap. Do you understand?'

He was watching me with his craven eyes, his bulk in the big coat cowering in the corner between the seat and the door.

'What will happen if the KGB are watching the station?'

'We're not going near the station. We're going into the freight-yards. The KGB won't be there. The rendezvous has been arranged by my own local control and he's extremely efficient. We can have absolute faith in him. You understand?'

He was the only danger. It would only need a couple of railway workers to pass anywhere near the rendezvous zone and Karasov would take off on his own and we'd never find him again. It was like taking the cat to the vet.

'If you think it is safe,' he said. His face was losing its colour and his eyes were dying another of the thousand deaths he'd been through since his nerve had gone.

'There'll be no trouble. Just leave everything to me.'

In a moment he said, 'Very well,' and looked away.

I swung the truck down the ramp and into the freight-yards

and saw the footbridge, a frieze of black iron girders running across the pale sky. The time was 11:59. We jolted across frozen ruts with the chains crunching through clinkers where the snow had been cleared by the work gangs. There was a man standing under the end stanchion of the bridge, the tip of his cigarette making the only point of colour in this desolate place.

'The courier,' I told Karasov.

He was waiting this side of the freight sheds, immediately under the bridge. There was a train standing on the other side, with a fat woman swabbing the windows with a brush and a steaming bucket. There was no one else here.

It was noon when I stopped the truck exactly under the bridge and the man dropped his cigarette and began making his way across the ruts towards us. The black van came from behind the train at the same moment, moving in very fast and spilling men with their hands at their holsters.

KGB.

* * *

19

FINIS

I HAVE NEVER BEEN SO cold.
You think you have been cold? Not like this.
Not like this.
This is the cold of the dead, when the blood itself is cold.
When the heart itself is cold.
This is the chill of death.

The cold was the worst.

I thought about it, recognizing it as something that I must try to stop, then realizing that there was nothing I could do to stop it. If I tried to stop it I would meet death of a different kind.

The cold was the worst.

No. The dark was the worst.

It was the darkness of not existing, bringing with it the knowledge that you have arrived somewhere unfamiliar, not where it is dark but where there has never been light. Death, yes, the regions of death far beyond any knowing.

The dark was the worst.

No. The noise was the worst.

It was the noise of infinite destruction, the never-ending tumult of holocaust, bringing the irreversible death of silence, the death of peace. I knew now that there would always be this thunderous noise, this all-extinguishing darkness, this killing cold.

Spark.

I was curled in the foetal position on one side, lodged between metal beams and plates. A rivet was against my head and I moved a little, for comfort.

Comfort? You must be joking.

Another spark and in the total darkness it brought light enough to throw a reflection on the rail immediately below me, on the shining rail, so that there seemed to be two sparks. My eyes seized on it, my soul drank from it: there was light, just for this little time. All had not been extinguished, then.

Don't fall asleep.

No. That would be unwise.

Keep awake. If you don't keep awake you'll fall.

Yes. I'll fall down there onto the–

Wake up. Wake up or you'll–

What? Yes – wake up, I'm waking up now, I'm – *oh my Christ–*

Grab it, grab that beam, *come on.*

Close. That was rather close.

I sat up now with my back to the big iron plate that spanned the chassis, pulling my legs up and trying not to think of what would have happened to them, to my legs, if I'd dropped onto the rails, under the wheels.

The stink of the locomotive raked at my throat and I shut down most of my breathing. Another spark flew and I took warmth from it into my mind. Not much, true, not much. But when you're as cold as this, a spark is like the sun.

I would have to stay like this now, sitting up. There wasn't much room, about as much as a bicycle saddle to perch on with my feet resting on a three-inch ledge, one of the big I-section girders that ran the length of the carriage. I would have to keep awake now.

Unidentified body found on railway lines, severely mutilated.

Then on to the sports news.

It wasn't fatigue. It was delayed shock. But all that was over now. *Northlight* was finished. The objective, Viktor Pavlovich

Karasov, was a dead man. The sleeper had waked but was now sleeping again, his fears at rest forever.

The sixth death for *Northlight*, and the worst.

Karasov's death was the worst.

Mission unsuccessful.

We try not to think about it. In the ranks of the shadow executives – God, you can't call them ranks, that's ridiculous – we're more like rats in the wainscoting, scuttling our random way through the tunnels of unknown territory in the earthy dark, the nerves galvanized and the ears tuned to catch the distant song of the deathbringer as he comes on his way to meet us – in the wainscoting, then, in the tunnels if you will, we try not to think about one of those snivelling little clerks in the records room picking up his pen and writing it down in the space provided, neatly in the space provided, *Mission unsuccessful.*

We would do anything rather than see it written down, to avoid the knowledge, as we lie angled across some rubbish dump listening to the sirens, waiting for the headlights, fumbling at last for the capsule and trying to find our mouth, the knowledge that it will later be written down, our failure spelled out letter by letter in that crabby hand, for others to see.

Not everyone, of course. The records are classified. And there's a gentleman's agreement that along those creaking and half-lit corridors our secret shall forever be sacrosanct, that we shall all of us conspire to protect what rags of pride may still be left in the bosom of a failed brother-rat.

Did Thompson get back?

Oh yes. Came in last night.

What sort of condition?

Bit done up.

What happened? He'd only just gone out.

Called off, I believe. They scratched it.

Change of plan?

That's right. Are you coming along for some tea?

And we sit in the Caff for longer than usual, wanting company but not to talk about anything significant, just not wanting to be alone with the creeping nightmare thoughts that one day this could happen to us. Because our pride is pretty well all we've got. None of us do it for the money. Do you know the kind of money we get paid? Then you know what I'm talking about. We do it from vanity, from the arrogant and overweening urge to prove that we can go out there and take anything on and get away with it and bring back the product. So the worst thing that can happen to us is failure.

Northlight: finis.

The train thundered through the night.

Dark had come down an hour ago at three in the afternoon. Black snow clouds, driving in from the north, had thrown shadow across the freight-yards, blotting out the light from the polar cap. Images weren't too clear, but of course we could recognize the van all right and the men running with their hands on their guns.

'*Did you know about this?*'

He didn't answer.

I still couldn't trust him, at the last. This was a trap and I think he could have known about it, could have made some kind of sordid pact with the KGB to lead me into them and then do what they wanted of him. I'd asked him before: '*Are you taking me into a trap?*' And soon afterwards he'd asked me: '*What will happen if the KGB are watching the station?*'

But there wasn't much time to think about that now. I'd got the objective for the mission with me and my local control had got an escape route set up and the one thing I was not going to do was sit here and shut down *Northlight* and let them put our sleeper under the thumbscrews and blow our Murmansk network out of the ground so I got the toy from the floor under my legs and made a rough estimate of the weight and the range and the force needed to land it where it would give us a flamescreen and swung it through the open window, but the tip of the lever caught the frame and sent the thing spinning and slowed it down and it fell too close and the whole truck came up and smashed down on its side so we couldn't get away in it after all.

In the twilight the blast was blinding and the shockwave

brought debris up from the ground and hurled it across the truck and for a couple of seconds I stayed where I was, sprawled across the clinkers with snow against my face and stones still ringing on the girders of the footbridge and pattering down. I heard Karasov screaming but I couldn't see where he was: he'd been thrown clear of the truck and was somewhere in the snow that had drifted against the bank. Then the first shot came and I got up and began running because at least one of them was still alive and had a gun and there was no point in staying put. I didn't know why he was firing but I supposed it was because Karasov was on his feet and running too.

There was a lot of smoke drifting across the ground by now and I went for the freight office and dropped behind it, crawling for a while and finding new cover behind sand-bins alongside the train. It wasn't until I was under the train that I saw what was happening over there: Karasov was running for the ramp leading to the road above and he tripped and fell and that was when the last shot went into him. He didn't get up.

You know when a record's playing and a fuse blows and the record-player slows down and stops? That was how *Northlight* ended, in my mind, as I crouched under the train with blood seeping into my shoe from the gash in my leg and the flash of the explosion still bright on the retinae whenever I blinked, that was how the mission wound down, like a slowing record, the rhythm broken and the music dying to a medley of strange moans before the silence came and I closed my eyes and watched the bright flare of the explosion again until that too died away and left the dark.

After a long time, perhaps a few seconds, I heard a man shouting in the distance of the freight-yards – *'You bloody fool!'*

I opened my eyes. From this distance I couldn't see clearly what was going on at the bottom of the ramp. I could see one of them tugging at Karasov, pulling him over onto his back, but I couldn't see whether he was dead or not. I didn't need to.

'You bloody fool!'

It was a scream of rage, and that was how I knew that Karasov was dead. It was the senior KGB officer yelling at the man whose shot had gone in. They would have had strict orders to take Karasov alive. The man who had shot him had made a mistake, that was all: he'd tried to stop his run by firing at the legs, but after the explosion it wouldn't have been easy to achieve any kind of accuracy.

It had taken me an hour to crawl half the length of the train, because a lot of people were running across the freight-yards from the station to see what had happened, and I had to wait for a chance to crawl over the sleepers between one carriage and the next before I could climb again and swing my way along the framework. I'd assumed they'd search for me under the train because it was the nearest effective cover and I wanted to make as much distance as I could before the search began; but nobody came. I think they were too worried about Karasov, about his death, to take much notice of anything else. As the agent running with him I'd been incidental. Karasov was the man they'd been hunting for the past seven days and now they'd found him and their mission too was over.

I sat with my eyes closed against the foetid turbulence. The air blew in a freezing gale from the front of the train and the wheels broke it up into gusts and eddies, sending sparks and chips of stone flying, one of them cutting my face and drawing blood, not a good thing because a mark like that can give you away when the hunt's up, it won't matter how good your papers are.

But I didn't think there was going to be any hunt for me now; Karasov had been the shared objective for both missions: the Bureau and the KGB had both wanted him, and wanted him alive. Now he was dead, and it was over. The KGB would show a mild interest in finding the agent who had been operating against them on their own soil and who had flushed Karasov under their own guns, but it would be mainly out of frustration, out of spite. They would feel a bit better if they could put me against a wall or send me to break stones in the penitentiaries for the rest of my life, but that was all: they wouldn't mount a dragnet as they'd done for Karasov.

And even if they did, they'd draw blank. They might find my body, but there'd be no identification that would tell them I was an agent. Because this was the way it was going to be, I knew that now. My body would be found along the railway, churned by that spinning steel below me and torn later by whatever beasts of prey could find me first and use me for sustenance, gorging their fill amid the winter's frozen dearth.

That would be all right. The idea of piecemeal extinction under the busy claw and beak has never troubled me; I would be there to share the celebration of ongoing life as my blood and sinew passed into different creaturehood, sustaining the ecology. The show must go on, so forth. Better that than be shovelled up by a sanitation squad and strapped into a cardboard box and dropped into the ground by an indifferent and very minor civil servant for the worms to feed on. I can't stand those bloody things.

But it isn't all right. You can't–

Shuddup.

You can't just give up. I don't want to die. I don't–

Are you sure of that? Are you quite sure?

You've got to hold on. Wake up and hold on.

Wheels thundering below.

You've got to get your senses back, or–

In this cold? In *this* cold?

Sparks flew up and a stone skinned my skull.

Wake up. Wake up.

The huge shape of the train swung me through the dark.

Yes, wake up, I suppose. But this cold was–

You'll pass out if you don't wake up.

I thought yes that's probably true but when I moved one hand I lost my balance and my foot slipped off the beam and *oh my God they're so murderous they're like a mincer they'll drag me under and flay me alive and spew me out like a red rag–*

Hanging on. I was hanging on. Awake now and hanging on with the fingers of one hand while my body swung above the void of dizzying movement below me, one foot still lodged on

[180]

the edge of the metal beam and the other hanging down, the ankle burning from the onslaught of flying gravel. My fingers were slipping because the metal was smooth and covered with a film of oily soot, and as they went on sliding I could feel the edge of a rivet, round and smooth, its shape changing under the tactile recognition of my fingertips and changing so fast that I knew that to hang here like this wouldn't be enough. I would have to swing my leg up and get the foot lodged alongside the other one so that I wasn't swinging in the void – but to do that would put extra strain on my fingers and they were already on fire with fatigue.

There wasn't, in the end, much choice. My senses were numbed now by the freezing air-rush and my lungs dragged at smoke; the thundering of the great steel wheels was dying away as my eardrums failed at last to register vibrations, and I closed my eyes and saw nothing different, only the dark, until a little while later my fingers reached the edge of the metal beam and came away and I began falling.

20

SHUTDOWN

'FIFTY ROSES, yes.'

'What colour, sir?'

'I don't mind. Red. No, not red. Anything but red.'

She stared at me. 'Not red. Of course.'

Colour of blood.

'And the address, sir?'

'Hotel Les Jardins, Paris.'

She wrote it down. 'And they are for Miss Moira Cavendish, is that right?'

'Yes. But not fifty. Not fifty roses.'

'Not fifty?' She began staring at me again.

'No. One rose.'

But of course she wouldn't understand. I'd long ago worked it out that fifty roses would be too many. Too vulgar.

'Keep still,' she said.

I always got them to write it down very carefully when I was being cleared. All my savings to the abused wives thing, and a rose for Moira.

'He's coming round,' she said. For some reason she was speaking in Russian.

'Only one rose, sir?'

'Oh Christ, you'll never understand.'

Pain burned through me like a lava tide.

'Get Dr Novikova.'

But what about the roses?

'Aren't I dead, then?'

Her pale face looked more surprised than ever.

'What did you say?'

Watch it. I'd spoken in English.

In Russian I asked her: 'What kind of condition am I in?'

I didn't ask her where I was. By the smell of the ether this wasn't a bloody flower shop.

Another woman was standing over me now, dark and greasy-looking with her stained linen coat bursting at the buttons, a stethoscope round her neck.

'How do you feel?' she asked me with monumental disinterest.

'Fucking awful.'

She gave a bellowing laugh, full of silver teeth, and poked me in the ribs. It was enough to make me pass right out, and things looked different when I came to again. They'd moved me into a ward that smelled of stewed cabbage and human sweat. The ether had been more pleasant.

'What time is it?'

'Can't you see the clock?'

I craned my neck and noticed the pain was quite a bit less than before. I felt better in terms of morale, too, and decided that if the good Dr Novikova came along and tried to poke me in the ribs again I'd have her finger off.

A lot of questions were clamouring for answers inside the skull, rolling around like dice. Then it was light again and they brought me soup. I bent the handle of the aluminium spoon more or less straight and thought: *Who blew the rendezvous?*

Nobody here could tell me that, but I kept watching the doors at each end of the ward because at any given time a couple of men in plain clothes could walk in here and *they* would be able to tell me who blew the rendezvous, if they wanted to.

Karasov?

It would explain the aura of doom about him: he'd looked like a man on his way to the guillotine. But he hadn't known they'd shoot him. He hadn't known I would throw the toy.

And he'd tried to run clear: he hadn't just picked himself up and let them take him.

Not Karasov.

'You want some more?'

A slut with the eyes of an angel, pulling a lock of hair as wet as seaweed away from her brow.

'No thank you.'

I let her take the bowl away. There wasn't anything else I had to ask them: I'd wanted to know the usual things, which town was this, where had they found me, what day was it, so forth. They'd found me between the railway lines in Murmansk station early yesterday morning, unconscious from exposure: the train had pulled in late the previous evening. So I must have grabbed something when I'd started falling and saved myself, though I didn't remember anything about it. The organism, when left alone, when left to invoke the powers of zen, can do surprising things.

Volodarskiy?

No. Without any question: no. I knew that man. I'd known him in the first five minutes. Deadly, yes, but not to his friends, not to his guests.

'Do you know what they've done? They've taken my bloody leg off!'

He leaned over and spat on the floor.

'Are you sure?'

He turned his head and looked at me with that slow stare of appraisal we save for the mad. 'Don't you know,' he said with a throat filled with rage, 'when you've got one leg or two? Can't you *count?*'

'Sometimes we get strange ideas,' I said, 'in hospitals.' But in this region he was probably right: frostbite or gangrene set in quickly.

Phantom limb. My breath blocked in my throat and the ward rocked until I shut my eyes, one hand going down under the sheet, reaching down lower and lower and then at last from side to side until I was sitting up, feeling my feet. Then I began breathing again. That poor bastard was wrong: you can't always tell. You've got to count.

I lay back and stared at the ceiling, where the husks of last summer's flies still dangled from deserted webs. It could only have been the courier, the one who came in on the train from Murmansk with the papers for Karasov. He'd been a double operator and Fane hadn't known.

He would have to know. He would also have to know that he could go home now and tell them the show was over. I'd have to get out too: he would see to that. But it wasn't urgent: I was in no hurry to present myself for debriefing at Croder's desk.

'I want to use a phone,' I told the angel-eyed slut when she came past my bed.

'There isn't one. Not for patients.'

'Where are my things?'

'Things?'

'Possessions.'

She got the point and brought the stout cardboard box with the metal fastener and waited while I fished inside it and found a ten-ruble note.

'You'll have to wait,' she said, 'till the coast's clear.'

'Soon as you can.'

The ward started rocking again half an hour later, but not as badly as it had before when I'd gone along to the loo. The girl went with me, running a gauntlet of whistles from those patients whose libido had survived gross injury, amputation, concussion and the stink of Lysol and cabbage stew.

As we reached the telephone against the wall she said, 'Are you a Party member?'

'No.'

'If anyone asks what you're doing at the phone, tell them you're a Party member.' She draped her lock of seaweed higher across her brow and pouted her little egg-sized breasts at me under her soiled white coat, turning away with her eyes lingering seductively. You don't earn much in Murmansk, nursing.

I took the phone off its hook and asked for the number.

A man was leaning against the wall between the telephone and the door of the ward, thin as a skeleton and bearded like the Ancient Mariner, his bones shaking so hard that I could hear the brushing of his hospital gown against his legs. In the yellow light from the one bulb hanging from a hook in the ceiling his eyes glinted as he stared at me, and I looked away.

The number began ringing.

Good form, I supposed, should be observed when I spoke to Fane and told him what had happened. He was my local control and in a way this would constitute an interim debriefing.

The rendezvous was blown. The mission is now shut down. The objective is dead.

He would light a cigarette, slowly, before he answered. Then he would ask, because London would ask him, who blew the rendezvous and how did the objective his death.

It could only have been the courier. The objective was shot down by the KGB, in error, as he was trying to run clear.

The phone went on ringing.

I began counting.

He would ask me where I was now.

I'm in No. 2 General Maritime Hospital in Murmansk.

He would ask–

Twelve rings. Thirteen.

He would ask me what I needed, and if I were in good enough shape for him to get me through the frontier.

I need a safehouse first. They'll be discharging me any time now.

Sixteen. Seventeen.

The hairs were lifting at the nape of my neck. The number I was calling was the number where Fane had said I would always find him in this city. Always. For the executive in the field, sometimes hard pressed, sometimes hunted, sometimes dying, the telephone number of his local control is his lifeline. For as long as I remained in the field, Fane would man that line or leave someone with total trust to take over from him in shifts.

Twenty. Twenty-one.

The skeleton with the frosted beard was still staring at me in the yellow light, one of his knees knocking rhythmically against the wall, his thin shadow behind him, waiting to follow him to the grave. He seemed to be listening, but might not be, or if he was, there might not be anything left inside his bone-white head to understand.

Did he know, even, what a telephone was?

Twenty-five. Twenty-six.

Did he know there was a shadow behind me too, coming closer one step at a time, one step closer as the telephone went on ringing?

Fane had shut down.

The trickle began at the top of my spine, the familiar visitation of terror that comes when we know it's certain that we are done for. I'd known that much already when I'd asked for a telephone, and I'd managed to contain the idea by concentrating on the practical considerations of who could have blown the rendezvous and how I would get home. But this measured, insistent ringing on the line brought confirmation. No one was there. The ringing was going on in an empty room, echoing against the blank glass of a window, its vibrations disturbing the motes of dust that had begun settling since the door had closed and the footsteps had died away.

'There is no answer,' the operator said, and the line went dead.

The executive in the field had been abandoned.

The man's knee knocked against the wall like a nail going into a coffin. *Can't you go back to bed for Christ's sake? Is that all you can find to do?*

Steady.

'Have you finished, lovey?'

I looked at her. I'd seen her somewhere before.

'What?'

'You'll get caught if we're not careful.'

The nurse, yes. Her big eyes frightened.

'I will?'

That would be terrible, to be told off by some fat cow for breaking the rules here.

I put the receiver back on its hook. Fane had already got the news, that was all. He thought I was dead, so he'd shut everything down.

Executive deceased.

Not an unreasonable assumption, actually, and not a bad guess at the future if I had to get home alone.

'You feeling all right, lovey?' She wiped my forehead with her dirty towel.

This was at ten in the morning.

I tried three times to reach the British embassy in Moscow during the day, finally getting a connection and speaking to one of the DI6 cypher clerks in Russian and telling him that my friend in Murmansk wasn't answering his phone and that I was worried about him because he hadn't been well lately.

The clerk wasn't in too much of a hurry to get the point: the Bureau doesn't post staff in any of the embassies because our network isn't meant to exist, so we're given courtesy access to DI6 stations abroad with certain signalling facilities and they do this simply because the prime minister tells them to do it, and it makes them sulky.

'Your friend?'

'This is Boris Antonov speaking.' It was the standard name for any accredited Bureau agent operating anywhere in Soviet Russia with privileges of requesting assistance. In Paris I would introduce myself as Jacques Lafayette, in Bonn as Karl Heidl, in Rome as Julio Napoli – they were the names in the secret files in those embassies and this simple-minded bastard should know that, and he should know that the designation "friend" meant one thing and one thing only: the agent's local control in the field.

'Can you spell it out for me?' he asked oafishly.

Little Pleshakovna – I knew her name now – was hanging around near the doors to the ward, keeping watch. She didn't understand that I couldn't care less about getting a lecture from the comrade matron but that I would care a very great deal if she stopped me using this telephone.

'No,' I told the cypher clerk, 'I can't spell anything out for you. Get Mr Spencer on the line.' Spencer was the code name for the DI6 chief of station in all embassies.

'I'm afraid he's out to lunch.'

'Then get his best friend.'

'I'm sorry, I don't–'

'Listen, this is a 909 call and if you don't do what I want you to do extremely fast you'll hear direct from little mother.'

There was a brief silence.

'Okay, just a tick.'

He was getting the idea. The 909 designation had replaced the original BL565 Extension 9 call a year ago but it meant the same thing: it amounted to an inter-intelligence services hotline and the little mother he'd be hearing from was the prime minister.

'Hello?'

'Is that Mr Spencer?'

'No. But perhaps I can help you.'

'I may not have long so you'd better take this down.' Pleshakovna was making urgent signs to me from the entrance of the ward. 'This is Boris Antonov and my friend in Murmansk isn't answering the telephone. I'm extremely worried about him, so if you see anything of him please tell him I shall phone him again as often as I can.' I waited while he repeated the salient information as he wrote it down. He was a senior spook and knew immediately what I was talking about.

'Where can I phone you back?'

The little white-coated Pleshakovna was hurrying up to me and glancing over her shoulder. *'You've got to put that phone down, citizen! She's coming!'*

It wouldn't have mattered but I was going to have to use the telephone again and if I blew it now it could make things much more difficult later.

'You can't phone me back. Please do everything you can.'

I put the receiver back on the hook and came away as the little slut grabbed my arm and pulled me against her. I leaned on her for support as the matron came through from the ward, a Hero of the Soviet Union medal dangling on her massive chest.

'Is this patient all right?'

'He's overdone it a bit, comrade Matron. He–'
'Then get him back into his bed, you stupid little bitch!'
This was at two o'clock in the afternoon.

Snow was falling again: in the ward we could see it through the tall grimy window panes, the flakes catching the light and then dying away into the dark. Night had come down four hours ago, soon after three o'clock.

'With only one leg, things won't be so easy.'
He'd already started whining.
'You'll look like a hero.'

I watched the snowflakes, aware of a creeping sense of limbo. The record had wound down through final discord, leaving silence. I was a man lying in a hospital bed, numbed still from exposure and extensively bruised – I'm quoting from my chart – with nothing to do except console or show contempt for the man in the bed next to me, as I felt inclined, nothing to do except watch the mesmerizing drift of the snowflakes whirled by the wind into the light and whirled away again out of sight.

By the tone of the senior man on the line I was sure that he'd try to raise Fane for me and tell him to stand by his telephone again; but there was no guarantee. I didn't know at what time Fane had got the news of the ambushed rendezvous or how long it had been before he decided to shut down his base and leave me to whatever fate had overtaken me. All he would know was that if I were dead there was nothing he could do for me, and that if I were still alive I would do everything I could to reach the capsule in time if I were caught and had to protect the Bureau.

'When can I use the telephone?'
'That depends.'

This wasn't my little waif: she'd finished her shift. This was a beefy Estonian woman, her arms folded across the bulwark of her breasts in a posture of impregnability, her dark eyes glinting with the secret exultation of power.

I got a ten-ruble note from my box of effects, rolling it and keeping my hand over it on the blanket. A gesture had to be made to propriety: the state was coming down heavily on corruption these days, driving it deeper underground.

'I'd like to make a phone call,' I told her, 'as soon as possible.'

'What's so urgent, then, citizen?'

'I'm worried about a friend of mine. He hasn't phoned to ask about me, and he knows I'm here.'

She stood over the bed, her eyes aswim with avarice. 'Perhaps you're less popular than you imagined, citizen. Perhaps she knows you're in no condition to get it up any more.' A faint wheezing came from the little fleshy mouth and the eyes narrowed to slits. She was laughing at my attempt to deceive her: a "friend" could only be a woman, and a woman wanted only one thing.

I put a second ten-ruble note with the first. 'Actually it's a male friend. He's a Party member, and it's his duty to find out if I need any assistance.'

Her eyes changed instantly, darkening. She had a problem now: if she took the twenty rubles, I might report it. This could be a trap I was setting for her – it was being done all the time.

'It's just that I don't want to get into trouble, citizen. You're not meant to use the telephone, you know that.'

'Of course. That's why I need your help. You have the authority to assist me in the interests of the state. Look at it that way, comrade.'

Her bright eyes were drawn to my closed hand for an instant. 'If I let you use the telephone, then, that will be my reason. I'll be assisting the business of the state, as any good citizen is expected to do. Is that what you mean?'

'Yes. That should be its own reward. But I'm of the old school, comrade, and I've always thought there's only one reward that's really worth anything.' I opened my hand.

It was another half an hour before she reported the coast was clear. A new matron had taken over the night shift, and I assumed that five of the twenty rubles would have been sacrificed to oil the wheels.

I unhooked the black bakelite receiver and asked for the number and waited.

Two rings.

An orderly came past with a trolley, swerving every now and then because the woman shuffling beside it was holding the man who lay there, his face moon-white and his eyes clenched shut, a blue-veined hand exposed at the edge of the sheet, clutching a small ikon. Tears trickled on the frail parchment face, but they were not his – they were the woman's, falling on him as she leaned over the trolley. I didn't think he would cry again; she had to have tears enough for both.

'I can't push on, citizen,' the orderly said irritably, 'if you won't get out of the way.'

Four rings.

I was counting from habit. There were a lot of reasons why the embassy might not have been able to raise Fane – the lines could be down between here and Moscow under the weight of the snow; Fane could be on his way to Leningrad by now to catch a plane for London; Croder could have signalled him with a change of plan.

Six rings.

The trolley banged through the doors of the ward, leaving the sickly smell of gangrene in the corridor.

'Hello?'

Flicker along the nerves. Fane's voice.

'This is Boris Antonov.'

Short silence. 'I see.'

I didn't quite know what to make of his tone but I didn't care. Contact had been re-established and my lifeline held strong again. Then relief brought its natural reaction: anger.

'Where the hell were you?'

In a moment he said: 'I received bad news.'

I thought vaguely that it was civil of him to put it like that. He was the type of director who considered any executive expendable, and on the slightest excuse.

Or did he mean some other kind of bad news?

'What did they tell you?'

[192]

'That you'd been killed.'

'I'm not surprised. The rendezvous was a trap.'

A longer pause. 'Where are you now?'

I told him. I also told him that a hostile agency – probably directed from Peking – had put a bomb on the truck. I told him the rendezvous in the freight-yards had been blown. I told him that the objective was dead.

Then I waited.

He would be reaching for his sharkskin cigarette-case now and pulling out a flat Egyptian cigarette, lighting it with care, his poker player's eyes gazing quietly at nothing while he absorbed my information.

A Chukchi woman, slant-eyed, blubbery, with skin like candlewax, came heavy-footed from the ward and pulled a pair of crutches from the pile leaning in the corner, dropping one of them with a noise that brought a cry from someone along the line of beds.

'*Peking?*'

'According to the objective. He was selling product to them too.'

'I see.' A cool man, Fane: he could absorb entire horror stories without even flinching. 'How was he killed?'

'They shot him down in error, while he was trying to get clear.'

'Are you sure?'

'I was there.'

'He didn't have anything on him?'

'No. I'd already burned the papers he was carrying.'

There was a question he hadn't asked yet.

'*You clumsy bitch!*' a man was shouting from just inside the ward. The Chukchi girl was having trouble with the crutches: every time she stacked them back against the wall they fell down again with a noise like the roof coming in.

'What is that?' Fane asked.

'Someone dropping crutches. Have you got a safehouse lined up for me?'

In a moment he said slowly, 'There's a place you can try.'

[193]

'They'll be throwing me out of here any time now. I want to hole up for a day or two before I start the trip home.'

'I see. What sort of condition are you in?'

'I'm not ready for any games yet. I'll need a day or two.'

"Games" was our word for anything demanding, like running a frontier under gunfire or wrecking a checkpoint. He still hadn't asked how the rendezvous had been blown. It worried me.

After a while he said: 'All right. I don't know yet how I'm going to get you across, but we'll work something out.'

'You didn't expect you'd have to, did you?'

A very long pause.

'No.' I thought he wasn't going to say anything more, but his voice came back on the line. 'You can go to Apartment 12 in the Old Harbour complex. It's on the north-east corner of Lenin Prospekt and Vernadskogo Street. Are your papers intact?'

'Yes.'

'Knock at the door and you'll be let in. Do you want that again?'

'No.' I repeated the address and instructions. 'Then I want a meeting with you.'

'Of course. That too will be arranged in good time.'

I wished he didn't sound quite so unshakably cool about all this. I'd called him up and told him the objective was dead and *Northlight* shut down and it should have rattled him badly: he wasn't going to get an awful lot of bouquets from Chief of Control for letting it happen. This too worried me.

Nerves, that was all. Did I want a local director in the field who panicked every time a wheel came off?

The last thing I said to him was: 'If I phone your number again I'll expect an answer. I want to go home. You're not going to leave me to die in this bloody country.'

'Of course not.'

It went on snowing all night and by morning the ploughs were rumbling past the hospital and traffic had come to a standstill.

She gave me her address, little Pleshakovna, as I walked out of the ward, writing it on a dirty scrap of paper and thrusting it into my hand. 'I'm always home in the evening, after I get off here.' Her starved face creased into a seductive smile, leaving the desperation staring naked from her eyes as a guffaw sounded from one of the men in the row of beds.

I put the scrap of paper into my pocket and slipped her a fifty-ruble note, more than she'd earn under the brutish loins of a dozen visitors. What would I put it down as on my expense sheet for those arthritic hell-hags in Accounts to quibble over? Child maintenance? They'd go straight into terminal palsy.

I walked out onto the pavement, picking my way across greying drifts of snow and through patches of sand and clinker, feeling – as I had felt before – like a soldier groping his way home from a battlefield where the cries of the dying had faded, leaving only the scratching of a pen across the documents of surrender. I wasn't quite sure if I could ever pick up the step again, or even hear the drummer.

They were breaking ice in the harbour when I reached there, dim figures moving in the haze of the drifting snow, hauling on ropes as a barge nosed along the quayside, sending miniature ice floes ringing out discordant music as they jostled together on the dark water. The Old Harbour complex loomed on the other side like a mausoleum, and I picked my way towards it over the iron bridge. There was no point in trying to check out the environment before I closed in on the safe-house: the intersection at Lenin Prospekt and Vernadskogo Street was deserted except for an abandoned truck with its belt of snow scoops hanging from a broken pulley. Any-one waiting here for me would by now look like a snow-man, invisible under camouflage, and if a watcher had been posted at one of these hundred dark windows I wouldn't see him either. I had been given the address of a safehouse over an untapped line by my local control and that should be enough: I wasn't expected to question it. The executive in the field needed shelter, and it was a responsibility of the highest priority in London to see that he got it. This was why, when I climbed the stairs to Apartment 12 and the door was opened to me, my mind lurched instantly into a state of shock.

21

WHO?

'CAN YOU TURN over?'
    The room swung and I was looking upwards into
her sea-green eyes.

'It feels good,' I said.

'Sure. I had some training once. But Jesus, it's a wonder
you're still alive.'

The smell of the Tiger Balm was sharp, pulling me out of
my lethargy for a while until I slipped back. More than
anything I wanted to sleep, because here it was so quiet after
the hospital.

'Does that hurt?'

'Don't worry.' The light from the cheap table lamp
shadowed her cheekbones and the curve of her pensive mouth.

'You didn't look surprised,' she said after a while, 'when I
opened the door.'

That gave me comfort: the shock hadn't shown.

'I already knew you were CIA.'

She stopped massaging and looked down at me with her
eyes narrowed. 'How?'

'You didn't behave like a journalist when the KGB stopped
you leaving the hotel. And your friend in Moscow couldn't
have known there was a duplicate tape and a man running
with it unless he was in the Company.'

She considered this, and then began massaging slowly
again. 'So I guess you're kind of pissed off about the whole

thing. Your case officer warned us that you prefer working alone.'

'It makes things less difficult for other people.'

'That figures. Who else needs to drag themselves around black and blue all over?' She took one foot and eased a knee-joint, carefully folding my leg. 'Does that feel okay?'

'Everything in life is relative.'

'I mean really. Is it damaged?'

'No. I walked two miles from the hospital.'

'Okay. Just relax again.'

'Liz,' I said, 'who else knows you're here?'

'Only my own case officer.'

'He's your friend in Moscow?'

'Right.'

'Does he know I'm here too?'

Her hands stopped sliding across the bruises again. 'Gee, Clive, I don't know. He just told me to get here and wait for further instructions. He didn't say you were coming. Is it important?'

'No.'

What had shocked me when she'd opened the door wasn't that I'd been sent to a safehouse run by the CIA but that Fane hadn't told me. If *Northlight* hadn't shut down on me I would have signalled London through the embassy in Moscow and our line through Cheltenham and told Croder to get Fane out of Russia and send me a local control who knew how to keep his executive informed. When you set up a safehouse you do it with the knowledge that it can make the difference between the life and death of a hard-run ferret and you don't tell anyone – *anyone at all* – where it is, not even a friendly service. It's not a matter of trust; it's a matter of *total* security. We can trust someone with our lives but we can't know for certain that they won't hit a trap and go pitching into an interrogation cell before they can reach a capsule to stop themselves blowing the safehouse out of the ground and the ferret with it.

A safehouse is sacrosanct.

The slow pain of the bruises was seeping into my head,

into my mind and burning there, becoming anger. Fane was going to get me killed at this rate: the mission was dead and buried in Karasov's grave but I still had a chance of reaching home if I had a local control experienced enough to get me there.

Fane wasn't.

Or had he established liaison with the CIA on instructions from London?

No. Croder was a crack professional. He was a bastard and he would drive you into the ground but he wouldn't throw you to the dogs unless by the nature of the mission you became expendable. He wouldn't blow your safehouse the minute he'd set it up for you.

'Does that feel okay?'

'Yes.'

My eyes were almost closed, and I watched the outline of her head against the pool of light on the ceiling, the swing of her chestnut hair and the shadowed face where her eyes were set like liquid jade.

'Stop me if it hurts.'

'It's fine.'

Her hands slowed, their pressure sliding across the pain and giving it recognition, making it acceptable instead of something I wanted to hide.

'It doesn't bother you,' Liz asked reflectively, 'to come out of the cold and have your wounds licked by a mere woman?'

Only half of what she said got through to me: I was thinking about Fane. I supposed she was a feminist.

'Where else would a man go, but to the earth mother?'

She gave her soft, private laugh. 'I can't see why the hell anyone would divorce a man like you.'

'Her psychiatrist assured me she wasn't in her right mind at the time.'

She laughed again and her hands stopped moving as she lowered her head and put her face against mine for a moment; her hair lay across my eyes and I closed them and let the lethargy well over me in a warm tide, forgetting Fane, forgetting how very unlikely it was that I would ever leave this alien

[199]

and snowbound city alive, and giving myself instead to the peace of the winter solstice the earth mother had brought me.

'Sleep,' she whispered, 'if you want to.'

The phone rang just before nine o'clock in the evening and Liz answered it.

'It's for you, Clive.'

'It's been difficult,' Fane's voice came on the line, 'to find a secure location for the rendezvous.'

'As long as it's better than the last one.'

Short pause. 'Quite so.'

'I can't come to your hotel,' I told him. The chip of gravel that had flown up from the track had left a scar across my face, the last thing I wanted: Petr Stepanovich Lein, the engineer checked by the KGB on the Murmansk-Kandalaksha train, had been missing when it had arrived in Kandalaksha and a dead man had been found later near the track; a bomb had killed an unknown number of KGB officers in the freight-yards and a wanted fugitive had been shot down; later the engineer Petr Lein had been picked up unconscious on the rail track in Murmansk and taken to the General Maritime Hospital for treatment. Those were good enough leads to raise a hunt as soon as they put the pieces together and the latest information they'd have would be from the hospital. *Oh yes, and there's one other thing – we treated him for a face wound on the left side.*

'No,' Fane said, 'don't come to the hotel. It's too far from where you are now and most of the roads are blocked.' I watched the snow still falling across the black grimed glass of the window. 'There's a warehouse half a mile from the apartment complex along the harbour road. One storey, steel construction, the number 19 painted on a board above the main doors, which are exactly opposite a weigh station with its harbourside window broken and boarded up. I shall be there in one hour, at ten o'clock.'

I thought about it. 'Are there lamps there?'

'Not near the doors.'

'What about harbour security? What about militia patrols?'

Short silence. 'When did you last go outside?'

'I got here yesterday evening.'

'The snow hasn't stopped since long before then. This city is dead. So far they've managed to keep two of the runways clear at the airport but the roads are blocked solid. The last militiaman I saw was dozing over a coke stove in the middle of the Kulinin-Terechovo crossroads. You'll see what I mean when you go outside.'

A *frisson* passed through my nerves. I was beginning to feel the squeamishness of the burrowing animal for the light of day. It was night out there but there would be lights in places and I didn't want to pass under them.

But I had to see Fane.

'All right. Ten o'clock.'

We synchronized watches and I rang off.

Place stank of fish.

There'd been lights along the harbour road and I'd had to walk under them because the only alternative was to clamber across man-high snow drifts.

'Is this safe?'

'I told you, the city is dead.'

Bad choice of words. The bruises, I suppose: pain all over, total reluctance to move, to *have* to move, to have to move *fast* if anything happened, if anyone came here.

'Have you got a gun on you?' I asked Fane.

'Why?'

'I want to know.'

I always want to know if people near me are carrying weapons but my reasons are different. With Karasov it had been because I wanted a quiet run to the rendezvous and no fuss when we got there. With Fane it was because I would know what to do if anyone came here and we had to react. I would let him draw fire and get clear if I could.

'Yes,' he said.

'All right. I just wanted to know.'

'Try and calm down.'

I bit off the first thing I thought of saying and watched him light one of his bloody cigarettes with a gold Dupont – *Jesus*, this man was *unreal* – and blow out smoke that went drifting across the oblong of pale blue light coming through one of the high narrow windows from a lamp outside. If you stood facing the light the rest of the place was dark but if you stood with your back to it you could make out some of the environment: crates of dried fish, two trolleys, a loading gantry rearing like a gibbet. I stood with my back to the light and made Fane move to face it.

Freezing in here.

'Do you want debriefing?' he asked me.

'What for? We've shut down. Leave it for London.'

My eyes were accommodating after the lamps outside and I could see the expression of long-suffering patience on his face. 'All the same, I'd like to hear about Karasov.'

'I told you.' My breath clouded in the light, as substantial as the smoke from his cigarette. 'He was selling product to Peking as well as to us.' I brought the cassette out of my pocket and gave it to him. 'This is the duped tape.'

He glanced at the labels and put it away. 'It could still be of some use. Did he confess quite freely?'

'You could say that. I didn't use any pressure – I hadn't any idea what he'd been doing.'

Fane looked away. 'No one did. This was why he didn't ask us for help the moment he went to ground, I imagine.'

'He was bargaining with Peking through their Rinker cell.'

'Yes.' Ash fell from his cigarette.

Something was wrong.

A ship's foghorn sounded a long way off and it sent a flicker along the nerves. I watched Fane. He hadn't even noticed. He was standing perfectly still, looking at the dirt floor of the warehouse, not actually seeing it. It was as if I weren't there.

There'd been something wrong with this mission from the very beginning and I still didn't know what it was and it frightened me because I wanted to stay alive and get clear of this bloody country and it might not even be important to them, to London, to Fane, to help me, to do this last thing for me, to bring at least one thing home from *Northlight*, if only a bruised and defeated executive.

Perhaps he was having to get used to the fact that I was here at all: he'd thought I was dead. That was why the phone had gone on ringing when I'd tried to call him. Not his fault: it's routine. When the executive's compromised beyond saving, his control has to close down the whole cell – bases, the safehouse, courier lines, cyphers, contacts, cutouts, every facility in the system that the executive might have given away under interrogation. Fane would have done that, and started for Moscow or Leningrad to get on a plane for London; then he'd heard from the embassy that I was still in the field.

That would have pleased him, until I'd told him the objective was dead. I suppose it was a bit of a nuisance having to get me home, bit of a chore.

He was looking up at me now, still not saying anything, watching me in silence. And then, because of the light in his eyes, because of the angle of his head or because of a thousand infinitesimal impressions that were streaming into my consciousness – then, because of all these things *and most of all because he hadn't asked me that one specific question over the telephone,* I knew suddenly what was wrong, I swear to God I knew, even before he spoke.

'Fane. Who blew the rendezvous?'

A slight catch of his breath.

'I did.'

22

TIGER

'*D*ON'T,' HE SAID.
       I suppose I'd moved.
       He hadn't gone for his gun – I wouldn't have given him time. He'd just taken a step back.

'Don't do anything precipitate.'

He watched me steadily with his expressionless eyes.

My neck pulsed: I could feel it. The carotid artery on the left side was palpable as the pressure went up, as the rage came.

'You've got guts,' I said.

He shrugged slightly. 'You had to know some time.'

'You could have waited until there were other people around to protect you.' I studied his face with its smooth white skin and its perfectly regular features, its short nose and straight mouth, seeing it for an instant as it would have looked if I'd actually decided to turn it into a mess.

'Save me the melodrama,' he said thinly.

The voice of sanity: It's one of the things, in point of fact, that the director in the field is expected to do for his executive when a fuse blows or a wheel comes off. Keep the poor bastard sane.

But he wasn't doing it very well because I moved again and only just managed to stop short *and if you think it was lack of control you don't know what it's like when you're carrying some half-dead objective to the frontier and a courier-rendezvous blows up in your face and takes the whole of the mission with it and you*

*find out it was your own local control who set it up, you think I'm
a bloody robot or something?*

Besides, that wasn't all he'd done.

'Be careful,' he said. 'I'm your only hope of survival. Don't
make things difficult for yourself.'

It wasn't all he'd done.

'Fane, did you have that thing put in the truck?'

He looked down, looked up again.

'Yes.'

I turned away and walked through the pale blue light and
saw my shadow moving across the dirt floor, rippling over the
debris as if I were walking under water, so there you are you
see, I knew there'd been something wrong with this mission
from the moment when they told me Ferris had refused it,
and I should have known better than to let that bastard Croder
set me up and set me running again – he almost got me killed
the last time he ran me, in Moscow, I tell you that man *simply
does not care* what he does to his executives providing they
bring back the product.

Stink of fish in here.

He was still standing perfectly still, watching me. From this
distance he could have shot me dead and I suppose that was
why I'd turned and walked away from him: I wanted to know
the future and this was the only way to find out, Russian
roulette, yes, but that's part of our trade, we're used to it.

'Does that make you feel better?' he asked me.

Fane is quite bright. Don't underestimate him.

'You'd have probably missed.' I walked slowly back to him.

'No,' he said.

'You missed with that fucking bomb.'

He lifted an eyebrow. 'I wish you wouldn't take it quite so
personally, Quiller.'

'Just natural reflex. It'll pass.'

I forget exactly which page it's on in the book, the dark
blue one, the first one they make us read, *Structure of Employ-
ment*, but I remember what it says, we all do. *It should be borne
in mind at all times during Briefing and Clearance that you are
considered to be expendable, and that at any given moment during*

the course of a mission it may be decided that in order to protect security or to accomplish the objective, your freedom, welfare or even life may be forfeit.

They lose quite a few of their recruits when they throw them that particular book in Norfolk – you can feel the draught. But there are substantial compensations to widows and so on, and some people feel it can't ever happen to them, while others get some kind of neurotic kick: the brink isn't enough, they like a sword over their heads as well.

'What went wrong?' Fane asked.

I stared at him. 'You don't know?'

'I mean with the bomb.'

'Oh. It's not the first time I've been near one.'

'You mean you sensed it?'

'Does it matter?'

'Yes. If that man didn't set things up properly, Croder will want to know.' The man I'd seen on the train.

'He did a good job.'

Fane had the grace to glance down. 'It was the only way I could arrange matters. London made a deal with the Kremlin from the start.'

'Before I was briefed and cleared?'

'Yes.'

'Bloody Croder for you.'

Fane looked up again. 'You know the system.'

Life may be forfeit, so forth. 'It doesn't mean I have to like Croder. What was the deal?'

'We don't need to go into that now.'

I stood close to him. 'This time *I* want to know.'

He shrugged, dropping his cigarette-end and putting his foot on it. 'Both sides needed the summit, urgently. The Soviets knew that the American public wouldn't allow the president to meet them in Vienna, after they'd sunk the *Cetacea*, so a cover-up was agreed on. It was the only way they could protect the summit, and the only way the US would go ahead with it: by demanding vital concessions in the resulting talks as a form of penalization for sinking the sub. But there was a risk.'

'Karasov.'

'Yes. The Soviets knew we'd listened to the tape, but that was destroyed now. Karasov was still alive, and might talk to the world media, a living witness to the Soviet's guilt. Again, the American people wouldn't let the president go to Vienna.'

Sound. Very slight sound.

'The Soviets didn't know where to find Karasov. He was our own sleeper. So it was agreed that the moment we had him in our hands we would let them know, and let them despatch him.'

'Kill him.'

In a moment: 'Yes.'

The snow on the roof, stressing it, making the slight sound. Rationalize.

But I turned my head to the left. The right ear feeds aural input to the left hemisphere for logical analysis and I wanted to know more about the sound, and if it meant danger.

'He was, after all, a Russian,' Fane said. 'And a traitor.'

'And trusted us.'

He shrugged.

'Trusted us with his life.'

He gave a sigh. '*Northlight* was set up to protect world peace.'

'So a few dead espions along the way don't count.'

'Of course not.'

'All right,' I said, 'I'll buy that.'

'Jolly good show.'

Tiger.

'But why did you want me out of the way?'

He lit another cigarette and blew out smoke. 'It wasn't quite like that.'

Tiger, tiger, burning bright, in the warehouse of the night.

'What was it like, then?'

'We had to–'

Not a very big tiger but I put up an arm block as it sprang for me and bounced off and hit the floor with its ears back and its claws out and a sound of total menace going on in its throat like a distant police siren; I was quite impressed.

'Pussy, you old bastard, stop that noise.'

What surprised me most was that Fane had his gun out. Local directors aren't normally so nervous.

'I think you're over-reacting,' I told him, and he put it away. The cat hadn't actually meant to attack me – they don't do that, it's not their nature. It had wanted to reach the fish crates and I was in the way. You can't always tell what's going on in their minds but I suppose it thought we were in here to open up the crates and there'd be a chance of nefarious pillage – the thing was near death from starvation, the winter and everything, and the locals in this region wouldn't keep these things for pets, they'd prefer them deep fried.

'We had to flush Karasov,' Fane went on, 'and hand him over to the Soviets. They said they'd finish him off. That was the deal.'

'But you didn't trust them.'

'Of course not. Before they killed him they would have put him under implemented interrogation and got everything out of him – our Murmansk network and all that goes with it.'

Fifteen agents, according to the background briefing I'd had in London. Fifteen agents and their communication channels and cover construction and courier lines and cypher modes: a major intelligence coup, not to be contemplated. I could see their point.

The poor little bastard was clawing at the fish crates, well not *little*, for God's sake, it was the size of a wolf, but there was no flesh on it, just fur and bones.

'Why didn't you put Karasov in the crosshairs?'

'It had to look like an *accident*,' Fane said. 'We had to flush him, but we couldn't kill him.'

'You could have said it was the Rinker cell.'

'The what?'

'The Chinese.'

'But we couldn't have proved it. There was only one way we could really convince them.' He looked down again, concentrating on his cigarette.

'By blowing me up with him.'

'Yes.'

'Who–' but I left it at that. It didn't matter who'd thought of it, who'd given the final instructions, probably Croder but it could have been someone even higher than he was in the Bureau because even in our trade we don't regard the death of a shadow executive as a family joke and Croder would have needed the sanction of a special committee. *Bloody vultures, who did they think they were, to put a man's neck on the block, to write his death certificate while he was still alive, while he was–*

Steady, lad, steady. They were the Bureau.

'You'll never do it that way, Pussy, don't be such a bloody twit.' I went over and smashed my boot down across the fish crates, breaking a wire, smashing it down again and bringing splinters away while the cat shrank back with its ears flattened and its eyes huge in the gloom and that low wail in its throat as I brought my boot down again – 'Don't you swear at me, you old bastard, or I won't get your supper–' down again and ripping the whole side of the crate away as the fish came tumbling out – 'Go on then, *bon appetit* and all that.'

I swung around to face Fane – 'So what the hell was that rendezvous all about, the one in the freight-yards, what was the KGB doing there right on time if we were both meant to be hanging from the roof of that fucking barn with our guts hanging out – *come on Fane I want to know*.'

He drew in some smoke. 'That was just window-dressing. We told them you'd be there to meet the courier.'

'What do you mean, for Christ's sake?'

'It was to cover the contingency of your getting caught and interrogated. You would have admitted the rendezvous, even though you weren't going to keep it.'

Only Croder could be so meticulous.

'What about Tanya?'

'The KGB wanted you monitored. We agreed.'

'She was KGB?'

'Yes.'

'What if I'd shown my hand?'

He shrugged. 'I asked them about that. They said you were too experienced.'

'Why didn't you tell me who she was?'

'We couldn't. We would have had to tell you the whole set-up.'

'What was she for, then?'

'The Soviets assumed that when you found Karasov you'd let her know, and let her know where he was. Then they could have gone in for him.'

'I called her, Fane.' I went close to him. 'I told her we'd found him.'

He watched me carefully. 'We thought you'd do that, yes. But we knew you wouldn't say where.'

'How can Croder take that kind of risk?'

'There was no risk. You wouldn't have given away the objective. I asked you, on the phone, remember? And that's what you said.'

'One day Croder's going to go so close to the fire that he'll blow the whole of the Bureau through the roof.'

'I doubt that.' He shrugged as I turned away. 'And it's a compliment to you, after all. He was relying on your experience. On your . . . dependability.'

'A compliment? From Croder?'

'He thinks rather highly of you, Quiller.'

'He ordered my *death*.' But that wasn't what I hated him for. I hated him for his diabolical cold-blooded cunning, his ability to sit inside my brain as I went through the mission he'd set up for me, to know precisely the things I would do, could be relied upon to do, and the things I would not do, could be relied upon not to do, until finally he manoeuvred me into the position when I would complete the mission for him and turn on the ignition of that truck and ensure his success.

He is the only man I can loathe for his excellence.

'Put that behind you now,' Fane said, and lit another cigarette. The cat jerked his head up at the flash of the lighter, then went on gorging himself. 'It's turned out well for you: your death is no longer necessary.'

'Well that's a bit of luck.'

'Yes, as a matter of fact. We flushed the objective, as we agreed to do, and he is now dead, and by accident. And since they caused it themselves they can hardly say we arranged it, can they?'

I turned again and walked through the pale blue light, and my shadow flowed like a shroud across the earthen floor. The rage was over now and I felt the chill of stale sweat on me and the iron cold of this place, its metal buried under the new snows. 'So *Northlight* was a success.'

'Not quite,' he said.

I turned to face him. 'You've just said so. The mission was to flush Karasov and get him killed before they could put him under a light, and that's what happened.'

He was standing very still, the smoke from his cigarette drifting to the edge of the light and then forming tendrils that climbed in the updraught towards the roof. I waited for him to answer, but he was silent.

'You mean you still have to get me out?'

'It's not quite that, either.'

I didn't move.

'Then why–' but I stopped short. There are questions you should never ask, and perhaps this was one of them. But it circled inside my head.

Why had he brought me here?

He watched me steadily. The distance between us was ten or twelve feet, and I noted this subconsciously before I knew why it might suddenly have become important.

'Have you got an escape route for me?'

My voice sent an echo from the high metal roof.

'No.'

The cat dragged another fish from the smashed crate and crouched over it, tearing at it.

'Why not?'

'There hasn't been time.'

Ten or twelve feet was too far. He'd whipped that gun out very fast indeed when the cat had scared him just now. I could never reach him across this distance if he wanted to do it again.

Is that what he'd brought me here for?

What other reason could he have?

I was still expendable. My freedom, my welfare and my life could still be forfeit, if it would pay Croder, if it would in some way follow the convolutions of this mission to an effective goal.

But these were logical arguments and they didn't have a lot to do with my thinking, with my being suddenly afraid: it was the cold in this place, the deathly cold, and the pale unearthly light and the silhouette of the gantry with its gallows shape and the way Fane was standing there so still and so silent and above all the terrible understanding that since they'd already written me off in their minds it might be convenient, less expensive, less complicated for them to leave me here in this dead city under the snow.

Skin crawling at the nape of my neck.

'So why did you bring me here?'

23

TEAPARTY

'THE CIRCUS, YES. I remember the circus. The clowns.'

The hot coals shimmered between us.

'When was that?' I asked her.

The ancient face was so lined that her smile was almost lost in it, but it touched her rheumy eyes, lighting them. 'Oh, a long time ago, comrade. A very long time ago.'

I took another chestnut and bit into it, feeling the urge to eat as the cat had eaten, the urge to survive. I suppose, if I'd wanted to go totally mad, I could have somehow got old Pussy across the frontier to London and put him in front of the fire, and fed him, and fattened him, and given him the right shots for distemper, turning him into a pet, a Kensington kitty, just for sentiment's sake because we'd once soldiered together in the winter of Murmansk. But that would only be a way of killing him, of bringing him a slow death among the bowls of warm gold top milk and the cushions and the hearthrugs, never again to know the fierce demented joy of seeing those fish come bursting out of that smashed crate and ravaging them, heady with rapture, scattering tails, scales and bones in that frenzied celebration of life renewed.

'You are from Moscow, comrade?'

'Yes.'

'The clowns were the best of all.' She took the poker in her withered hand and stirred the coals, and I tried to see her as she'd been then, wriggling on a board bench under the big spread of canvas, shrill with laughter as the men in their baggy trousers tumbled across the sawdust sixty years ago, seventy. 'I married one of them. One of the clowns.' Her head was going down, until I could only see the bone-yellow forehead below the black shawl. 'It is true what they say. Behind the make-up there is always sadness. And they do not live long.'

'But they live longer than others, old mother, in our memories. To bring laughter is to light the soul.'

She wasn't listening. She could span time more easily than I could, and she wasn't with me any more. I left her like that, crouched over her brazier in the midst of the new snows.

Then I rang Croder.

'You've got a bloody nerve.'

It had taken three hours to make the connection, going through the embassy in Moscow and then Cheltenham, using the 909 hotline route.

'I'm sure you're aware of the situation.'

His voice came through a lot of background slush but we didn't have to listen for bugs: I'd found this hotel at the end of a street half lost under the snow, with abandoned trucks and rubbish bins making humped white shapes under the lamps. The concierge had gone back to his desk and was asleep again.

'Yes,' I told Croder, 'I'm aware that since I'm still alive you're asking me to go on working for you.'

I couldn't catch what he said because of the slush.

'What?'

'For us all.'

Typical of him. Team spirit, so forth, mustn't let the side down.

'You'll have to find someone else.'

'Things are too urgent for that.'

It was the phrase Fane had used; I suppose he'd picked it up from Croder. They'd been in signals just before I'd gone to the warehouse.

'I brought you here,' Fane had said, 'to tell you I've just heard from London.' The smoke from his cigarette curled from his mouth. 'Something rather interesting has come up.' I didn't ask him what it was. It didn't look, after all, as if he'd brought me here to put a slug into my skull and shove me under the snow. 'The Soviet naval officer, Kirill Zhigalin, who torpedoed the American submarine, was arrested for exceeding his duties. Last night he escaped his escort and disappeared.'

Zhigalin.

That was his name? I'd only heard his voice.

Advise me.

New position: 17–G on the east grid. You have a kill.

Keep me advised.

Did we make a hit? Did we make a hit?

Confirm. You made a hit. I repeat: you made a hit.

Lieutenant Kirill Zhigalin.

A third man running.

Fane watched me.

I said: 'That's your problem.'

'Hardly a problem. It gives us a splendid chance of forcing concessions from the Soviets in Vienna. Karasov is dead, but if we could take Zhigalin across, London would be terribly pleased.'

'Fuck London.'

He dropped his cigarette butt with care and put his foot on it. 'I understand your feelings, of course. But you should try to see our point of view. If we can–'

'No.'

He shrugged slightly. 'There would be a definite advantage for you if you agreed to–'

'No.'

He inclined his head. 'Mr Croder would appreciate it if you'd at least signal him and hear what he's got to–'

'No.'

I turned and walked out of the place. And then, because my mind had started to work out all the possibilities, the alternatives, the opportunities, and perhaps because the ancient mother's voice had calmed me with its tales of circuses and clowns while the smoky tang of the chestnuts had reminded me of life renewed, my mood had changed, and I had looked for a small hotel where I could telephone.

'The fact that things are urgent,' I told Croder, 'doesn't concern me.'

'Then why did you signal?'

'To make a deal, if there's one available.'

The cubicle stank of cabbage and the dank vestiges of tobacco, and I inched the folding door open, watching the concierge. If he woke up he'd catch the sound of a foreign tongue, but there was nothing he could do about it. If he wanted to tip off the militia that a foreigner had come to the hotel to make a telephone call I'd be miles from here before they could take any kind of action: they'd have to get here on foot.

'What sort of deal?' Croder asked cautiously.

'I'll take Zhigalin across for you, if you'll set it up. But not with Fane directing me.'

The slush came in again, and faint voices, one of them speaking in Estonian.

'Why not?'

'I want someone I can trust.'

'He was simply following my instructions.'

'I know. I want someone who'll refuse your instructions if it becomes expedient again to kill me.'

Just the slush again. He hadn't liked that. Croder is a great lover of euphemism: eliminated, despatched, so forth. He likes his truths sanitized.

'That won't occur.'

'Things can change. Look, if I'm wasting your time, let me know.'

'On the contrary. But you can't hope to bring Zhigalin across without local control, or even get across without him for that matter.'

'I know. But I don't want Fane.'

'There's no one else I could send there, even if there were enough time. And Fane knows the area. He's extremely–'

'I want Ferris.'

The line was pretty bad, and he might not have heard properly. 'Say again?'

'I want Ferris.'

Quite a long pause. 'He's in Tokyo.'

'Then fly him out.'

'There isn't time.' He waited for me to answer that, but I didn't. I'd told him what I wanted and there was nothing I needed to add. 'It would be very helpful,' Croder went on at last, 'if you would consider the enormous gravity of the world situation. It is, after all, the reason for your mission.'

'I haven't had time to read the papers.'

'Negotiations,' he said slowly, 'have now broken down between Moscow and Washington. The United Kingdom is the last link between the super-powers, and yesterday Lord Cranley flew to Moscow in an aircraft of the Queen's Flight to attempt a last-ditch agreement with the Soviets to freeze the present status of affairs and keep diplomatic relations open until a solution can be found to this crisis. He may not succeed. When I sent you out there, your mission was urgent. Its success, in my informed opinion, is now the only remaining chance of saving the Vienna conference and preventing a cataclysmic severance of East-West relations. Zhigalin is the ace in our hand, and only you can get him for us.'

I'd been listening to his tone, and even over the long-distance line it was unmistakable. It had the despair of a hushed voice in a graveyard. I didn't know how bad things had got. But it didn't change anything: there was still only one way out.

'I understand what you're saying, Croder. And I'll get Zhigalin for you – if you'll get me Ferris.'

'But can't you see–'

'*It's the only way.* Are you listening? *The only way.*'

'But the logistics–'

'I'll spell them out for you. There's been heavy snow here but Fane said they've managed to keep a couple of runways open at the airport. It's the only way in from Leningrad: the overland routes are blocked. If it starts snowing again they'll even have to shut down air traffic. *Do you understand?*

In a moment: 'Yes. But–'

'If you work fast enough you can get Ferris here within twenty-four hours. If you get him here I'll do what I can to bring Zhigalin across. But not unless.'

'You don't realize–'

'Not unless. Ferris or nothing.'

I hung up the receiver.

The next day it was still dark at noon. The sun wouldn't show on the east horizon for another month, and today there were black snow clouds hanging across the city.

I'd given the concierge a fifty-ruble note.

'There's more,' I said, 'but you won't get it if you do anything stupid.' His faded eyes had gazed at me, seeing visions of stolen sable, chamois bags of diamonds, a crate or two of American cigarettes if it was a thin week. This was a major seaport.

'You'll find me reliable, comrade.'

This morning I'd got him to light the brass geyser in the only bathroom and fill the bath with hot water so that I could soak my bruises, but the smell of gas got me out before the water had cooled.

At noon Fane came.

'How long did it take you to get here?'

'Most of the morning.' He kicked the snow off his boots.

'I've talked to Croder.'

He looked up sharply. 'Have you?'

'All I want to know at this stage is where to find Zhigalin.'

He lit a cigarette. 'Are you going to take him across?'

'It depends.'

'Depends on what?'

'If they can get Ferris out here.'

'To direct you?'

'Yes.'

He looked down. 'He's very good.'

'I know.'

'Did Mr Croder agree?'

'No. I just left him with the choice.'

Fane went over to the small cracked window but all he could see was his reflection; it was like night outside. 'Ferris is somewhere in the Far East, I believe.'

'That's right.'

'We have to assume he's directing someone there.'

'Yes.'

He turned back to face me. 'It's a pretty thin chance.'

'That's Croder's problem. I don't mind whether it comes down heads or tails.'

It was a lie and he probably knew that.

The bulb in the ceiling flickered, and we waited. Power cables were breaking all over the city as the permafrost shifted under the weight of the snow and brought poles down. 'There has not been a winter like it,' the concierge had told me. 'Not in my lifetime.' He'd stared through the glass doors as if at his first Christmas morning.

'I think you should assume,' Fane said in a moment, 'that they won't be able to get Ferris here in time to do any good.'

'That's up to them. If they can't, I'm resigning the mission. That means they'll have to fly someone else out here to replace me, and that could take just as long as to send Ferris.'

'You've given them quite a problem.'

'That's a shame.'

He might have known what was in my mind and he might not. I didn't particularly care. The thing was that Croder had his hands full in London trying to set up the mechanics that would give the West an edge over the Soviets in Vienna. He wouldn't have time to get me across on my own, now that Zhigalin had become his new objective. He'd leave me to find my way home alone and the chances of doing that were lethally thin. That was why I'd offered Croder a deal: Zhigalin was my only ticket home.

'I understand your reasons for asking for Ferris to replace me, of course. But to impose a delay at this very critical stage is at the least dangerous, for you and everyone else. I know this area and I've got all my courier lines and communications still intact. Ferris would have to–'

'You're wasting your time. I've got absolutely no guarantee that the deal you made with the KGB isn't still exposing me to risk. I don't know that the minute you leave here you won't call them up and tell them where I am. I–'

'They believe you're dead.'

'How do you know?'

'I told them.'

'I don't know if you're lying, Fane. I don't know how complex *Northlight* still is, or whether you might not get instructions at any time to wipe me out.'

He shrugged. 'I can only give you my word.'

'*What the hell is that worth?*'

The cheap tin frame of the picture of Lenin on the wall vibrated to the pitch of my voice and I lowered it. 'On the face of it you want me to meet Zhigalin and get him across the frontier and that sounds simple enough, but on the face of it you wanted me to meet Karasov and get him across the frontier and what actually happened was that you were sitting here in Murmansk with your fingers in your ears while I was getting into that truck in Kandalaksha and *that* is why I can't take your word for anything now.'

He looked down, and it occurred to me that he wasn't in point of fact as cold-blooded as a toad and that he hadn't exactly thrown a party when London had told him to dig a grave for me in Soviet Russia but it didn't make any difference: he'd followed instructions before and he'd do it again.

'I'm simply warning you,' he said in a moment, 'that you could be driving yourself into a dead end. If London decides it's quicker to send out a replacement for you instead of a replacement for me, we shall be too busy to get you across the border, and you've got a pretty accurate idea of your chances of getting across on your own.'

'I have.'

He was silent for a time. He knew the score but he thought there was still a chance of keeping me in the mission without changing my director. There wasn't. Maybe there were other things I could have done if there were time to think about them. There wasn't. This kind of red sector was totally new to me: the local security forces were the primary danger and if a KGB man asked for my papers he could check them with the information that the computers had been spilling out for their all-points bulletin for the past twenty-four hours and come up with the Petr Stepanovich Lein who'd been found half-dead and taken to the General Maritime Hospital and that would be enough to make them take me along to their headquarters, and that would be that because my cover was light: it hadn't been designed to protect me under interrogation.

The secondary danger was still there in the background. Rinker had got on to me at the hotel and he'd taken a capsule to protect his cell but it hadn't kept them off: they'd been there on the train to Kandalaksha because they wanted Karasov and wanted him desperately. Now they would want Zhigalin. They were running a very sophisticated cell and they had a vital objective: to scuttle the summit conference in Vienna and widen the rift between Moscow and Washington. They would have effective communications in this city and they would know by now that Zhigalin was on the run and they'd expect me to lead them to him just as I'd been expected to lead them to Karasov. Nothing had changed.

Nothing had changed except that I was in a red sector I'd never experienced before. The primary and secondary and the whole range of hazards are common to most missions and you've got to deal with them in whatever way you can but you've always got your director in the field to support you and give you couriers if you need them and give you rendezvous if you need them and keep you in signals with London hour by hour and day by day, and if a fuse blows and you go pitching into a shut-ended situation and there's nothing at last between you and Lubyanka or the Gulag or an unmarked grave then you can still hope that your director can do something before it's too late.

Not now. My only chance now was Ferris.

'We'd better assume,' Fane said evenly, 'that you'll decide

to complete your mission and take Zhigalin across whatever the circumstances. In which case I need to brief you.'

'All right.' It made sense. If they sent Ferris out here I'd want to be ready for him.

'I suppose we can't get any heating in this place, can we?'

I think I remember laughing when he said that. It was so human, from such an inhuman man. He didn't think he'd said anything funny; he looked rather offended.

I said, 'In *this* hotel?' He should have tried hanging underneath that bloody train all night. 'The old man would bring us some tea if you like.'

He shook his head. 'I'd rather keep a low profile.' He lit another cigarette and studied the glowing tip, perhaps taking warmth from it in his mind. 'We have it from our contacts here in the Murmansk cell that Captain Zhigalin was put under close arrest in the naval barracks about an hour after the top brass learned that the *Cetacea* had been torpedoed and had gone down with all hands. It was probably a panic move. It was quite obvious that the summit conference was suddenly in grave jeopardy unless they could bind and gag the man responsible. From the reports I've received, Zhigalin was at first bewildered and then outraged. He told someone he expected a military honour for protecting the security of his country's most important naval base, not summary arrest and humiliation. This ties in with the dossier I was able to look at: Zhigalin is young for his rank and has received rapid promotion. He's said to be a staunch patriot, a fervent ideologist in terms of Marxist-Leninism and a dedicated officer.'

'The type to break.'

'Yes. We think he broke.'

'You think it's genuine.'

'From the reports. They're all we have to go on. I can't see any other reason for him to have escaped.'

'Unless it was arranged.'

He lifted an eyebrow. 'With what in mind?'

'So that they could've had an excuse to shoot him down on the run. The Soviet navy isn't a rag-tag pack of pirates – they can't simply drop a full captain into a hole and lose him. He'll have a family, he'll have friends. There'd be an enquiry, and they wouldn't want that. They want a total blackout on the sinking of the *Cetacea*.'

'There'd be an enquiry if he were shot dead.'

'Nothing like as big. His escape would imply guilt, and his family wouldn't want any questions asked.'

'I think he'd have been shot by now,' Fane said reflectively, 'if that's what they meant to do. He escaped soon after ten o'clock last night when they were transferring him from his cell to the medical block for a routine examination. If he were dead by now, we would have heard. I'm in very close touch.'

He was standing outside the door with a tray in his hands when I jerked it open.

'Some tea, comrade.' He was bent almost double under the weight of the tray: it was solid brass and the teapot was copper, the real thing, none of your plastic pissware in romantic Russia. 'I thought you might like some tea.'

I'd heard a stair creak only ten or fifteen seconds before I'd pulled the door open; he hadn't been standing outside for very long but that didn't mean he hadn't been going to. We've got all kinds of exotic cover in this trade from hotshot international journalist to butterfly collector but in local situations you don't need more than a tea tray.

'Come in,' I told him.

His faded eyes were taking in the room and resting now on Fane, but Fane had turned his back and was looking out of the window. He wouldn't say anything: the less they see of your face the better, and the less they hear of your voice.

'Unfortunately, comrades, we have trouble with the boiler room. It is often so. Tea will warm you, however.' He lowered the tray onto the split mahogany dressing-table, the strain in his arms setting a tea-cup rattling.

'Good of you,' I said.

He straightened up, turning his weathered face to me. 'I try to be of service, comrade.' On his way to the door his head swung slightly but not enough to afford him a direct look at Fane's back. He knew the delicate intricacies of the situation; a fifty-ruble note gets you more than a tray of tea:

it gets you privacy so inviolate that you can have a visitor in your room without any questions asked. But he couldn't resist turning his head just that fraction. Who was the man standing there at the window? A dealer in sables and gems? A magician who could move your name to the top of the waiting list for a little Volga saloon, an official with one life in the corridors of Party power and another in the dockside labyrinths of international crime?

'This is dangerous,' Fane said when the concierge had gone.

'Yes, but the risk is calculated. Milk and sugar?'

'No.'

The cord round the handle of the huge copper pot was coming unwound and I got one of the thin grey towels from the washstand. 'You'll be out of this soon,' I told Fane, 'don't worry.' It's easy for the directors: they keep their foreign cover.

'That will depend on Mr Croder.' He took his tea and sniffed the steam that rose thickly in the chill of the room. 'On whether he can get Ferris.'

'He'll have to.' I picked a strand of sacking out of the coarse brown sugar and put some into my tea, adding some milk. 'This is rather cosy. Quite Tunbridge Wells.'

'You really do have a weird sense of humour.'

'Takes all sorts. You worried?'

'That man.'

I sipped some tea; it was scalding, and half the chill went out of the room. 'A calculated risk is one that you have to forget you've taken, once you've taken it. If that man is going to bring the KGB here he'll have called them by now and there's nothing we can do about it.' The directors are never happy when they have to leave the security of their grand hotels and hobnob it with the ferrets out in the field. 'How did you get on to the Zhigalin escape?'

'He contacted the embassy.'

'The US embassy?'

'No. Ours.'

'Ours? Why?'

We were briefing again. Fane said: 'It seems he's ready to turn his back on the mother country and take his revenge by offering himself to the West. But he said he was afraid that if he put himself directly into the hands of the Americans they'd lynch him on sight.'

'Did he actually say that?'

'Not directly to me. I got the gist of this through the DI6 chief of station. But it's accurate thinking on his part: he'll need a lot of protection from the Company if he gets to America.'

'Does Zhigalin speak English?'

'Very little. A few naval phrases he's picked up on the ship's radio bands.'

'Where is he now?'

'He refused to say. He's to phone me as soon as he can find somewhere safe to hole up.'

'Then he'll ask for a rendezvous?'

'Yes.'

'Give me everything you've got, then.' If Zhigalin phoned the hotel and Fane wasn't there, we might lose him. The longer he stayed on the run the bigger the risk of his getting caught or shot.

Fane pulled a folded sheet of paper out and turned it to catch the light. 'Zhigalin is five foot nine, stocky, dark brown hair, brown eyes, clean-shaven, a scar below his left ear. He's wearing a merchant seaman's clothes – dark blue sweater and coat, dark blue trousers. That's his provisional cover, as–'

'He hasn't got new papers?'

'No.'

'Is he trying to get any?'

'No. He's leaving it all to us.' I poured him some more tea. 'That doesn't worry me,' he said. 'I wouldn't expect a dedicated naval officer to know what he's expected to do when he's suddenly the subject of a manhunt. I'd say his mind is in a state of some turmoil at the moment.'

'What are the chances of his thinking twice and giving himself up?'

'We don't know. But DI6 treated his call with extreme

caution. They didn't promise him anything, except to respond to any further contact he might make.'

'This isn't a KGB trap?'

'It can't be. They're dependent on our cooperation.'

'Still?'

He looked up from his tea rather quickly. 'No.'

'So tell me the score now, Fane. Whether I believe you or not is my business.'

He looked offended. 'I really wish you—'

'*You weren't there.* You didn't get into that truck and sit within an inch of getting your guts plastered all over the roof of the barn.'

In a moment he said: 'Very well. The situation with Karasov was that although he was a Soviet national he was working for the West. The Soviets knew that the only thing he could do, once he'd deserted his unit, would be contact us and request transit out of Russia and asylum. They therefore came to us with a deal and we agreed to it. They could have hunted Karasov for weeks or even months without finding him, but we could find him very easily: as soon as he made contact with us.'

The light from the yellow bulb in the ceiling was reflected upwards from the surface of his tea, and played across his eyes; they were looking down, not at me. As I listened, I had to catch the import and tone of every word, and decide, now or some time later, whether he was telling me the truth or setting a trap for me as he'd done before. 'The situation with Zhigalin,' he went on, 'is different. He too is a Soviet national but he has no ties with the West. They won't expect him to make contact with us, and so they won't suggest another deal. We shall deny strongly any report that we are involved with him. They'll hunt him themselves, and are doing so now, and vigorously. That makes it infinitely more difficult for us to take him across. For you, perhaps—' he looked up – 'to take him across.'

I turned away, going to the window. There were lights out there now, breaking the near darkness of midday. I could hear the ringing of shovels as work gangs moved along the street.

'All right,' I told Fane. 'But the rest of it is the same as before. Zhigalin is now the objective for the mission. We want him. The Soviets want him. The Chinese want him.'

'The only difference,' Fane said from behind me, 'is that we want to take him across.'

'Yes.' I turned to face him again as he went to the dressing-table and squeezed his cigarette butt into the ashtray. 'That's the only difference. This time, when I rendezvous with the objective, you might not have plans to blow us both into Kingdom Come.' I went over to him, bringing out the small steel cylinder from the pocket of my coat and unscrewing the end, dropping the capsule into the ashtray. 'But if I find out you're following any new instructions to endanger me, I'll go straight into the nearest KGB headquarters and blow London. Tell Croder that.'

24

VIOLIN

'AND THEN THEY wait till it's been snowing for twenty-four hours before they call us out. Is that intelligent?'

'What would you expect of the civic leaders in this place? They spend all day round the stove playing dominoes!'

'Or in the whore-house.'

'That too!'

'Which is not inappropriate, if you think of it, since they're a pack of whoresons!'

Much laughter.

My shovel hit on stone and sent a shockwave up my arm.

'What are you, comrade, a volunteer?'

'Yes.'

'More fool you.' He spat.

A navy transport went past, mud dripping from its dark green paintwork, and jeers went up from the work gang. Jeers came back from the bus. We were left choking on diesel gas with our legs soaked again from the slush-wave.

When I next looked at my watch it was midnight. It was eleven hours since Fane had left the hotel and I'd been back three times to see if there'd been a telephone message. In between I'd worked at the snow with the volunteer gangs, taking a break for a bowl of potato soup at the Red Dawn cafe, hunched by the steamy window in a soaked coat, sure now that Croder wouldn't do it, or couldn't do it, couldn't locate Ferris or persuade him to take over from Fane and local-control me for *Northlight*.

'Volunteers are all very well, comrade, very patriotic, but what have they done with the taxes we pay? We let them bleed us white and then do the snow-clearing ourselves!'

'Mind my foot with that bloody shovel, that's all I ask.'

After eleven hours of waiting for news I was certain that Croder would leave Ferris in Tokyo and crash-brief one of the shadow executives on standby and put him on a plane in London – one of the Soviet specialists, Hopkins or Bone or Reilly – with instructions to report to Fane in the field. I'd signalled Croder to let him know I was outraged, that was all, to make demands he couldn't hope to meet, simply as a way of easing my injured pride. He had known that.

Another bus crawled past, its wheels spinning on slush and its windows opaque with steam; an open truck followed it, packed with volunteer workers.

'*Come on home, you bloody lunatics! It's gone midnight!*'

Gravel drummed under the mudguards, thrown up by the tyres.

Fane had put it perfectly well. Tokyo was seven thousand miles from here, twenty-four hours by air even if Ferris had boarded a plane the moment London had signalled him, even if he could get instant connections in Calcutta or Karachi or Tehran and an instant connection in Leningrad. And he'd need high-level Overseas Trade Commission cover to get him through Leningrad to Murmansk: that too was true.

I pushed the shovel under the snow and swung it upwards across the side of the truck, feeling ready now to go back to the hotel again after twelve hours' more or less constant exercise. In that freezing garret I'd have gone crazy listening for the phone to ring in the hall below, and my muscles would have lost their tone.

'Come on, comrade!'

'What?'

'Room for one more!'

Men waving from the truck. I slung my shovel into the bin with the others and climbed onto the running board, hanging on as we lurched through the slush, the mudguards scraping between the snow drifts that loomed under the flickering lamps.

On the other hand Croder might not find anyone available, anyone with my degree of experience. Reilly had come back from the Budapest thing two weeks ago looking like death and Bone was in Norfolk pounding his way through a refresher course in unarmed combat. I didn't know where Hopkins was, but he'd left Bureau-DI6 relations in a mess at the end of his last mission in Rome and Croder would think twice before he sent him out again.

It could conceivably be that the only competent agent available for Murmansk was already there now, jolting his way back to his hotel with ice forming in his boots and the chill of a different climate forming along his nerves because there might, yet again, not be a message.

The concierge was asleep behind his desk when I got there, and shone a torch on me through the glass door before he'd open it up.

'You are asked to ring this number, comrade.' He unfolded a scrap of dirty paper. 'They called an hour ago, but I didn't know where to find you.'

Fane answered.

'They can't locate Ferris. My instructions are to ask you whether you are willing to continue the mission under my local direction.'

Water seeped from my boots across the worn parquet floor, reflecting the light from the cracked white globe above the doors. An engine rumbled outside as a truck spun its wheels, sending gravel hammering against the wall like machine-gun fire.

Fane was waiting.

I didn't trust him.

The concierge was sitting behind his desk with a newspaper, turning the pages as he waited for me to speak again into the telephone. How many English words did he know, apart from *football* and *chewing-gum* and *rock 'n' roll*?

I didn't trust Fane and I didn't trust Croder. Croder would instruct my local control to set up a trap for me if it suited

Northlight, if it would protect the infinitely delicate machinery of East-West relations at this crucial time, if one lone man's death could make safer the lives of millions. And my local control would follow the instructions, as he'd done before.

I will risk death in the labyrinthine tunnels of a given mission, ferreting my way through the dark and through the dangers, alert for the footfall, for the shadow, for the glint of steel that must be seen in time and dealt with, dog eat dog, for this is the way, the only way to the objective: this is my trade and this is how I ply it. I always know, when I leave the open streets of public life and slip into the alleyways of private peril, that this time it may lead me to that last dead end, that this time there may be a rose for Moira.

But I won't let my own controls plot my destruction, however vital the issue, however great the gain. I reserve the right, gentlemen, to face my deathbringer in my own good time.

'Are you there?'

Fane.

'Tell Croder no. Tell him I'm resigning the mission.'

It was the first time I'd shut the trap for myself.

Quite a breakthrough. Something new every day.

No regrets.

Master of my own fate, so forth. If I can't parry the knife in time I'll take it into the heart, not in the back.

Bullshit. Bravado.

You're cut off from London.

Aye, there's the rub.

Cut off from London, yes, the lifeline snaking away across a white-capped sea, or any other bloody metaphor you can think of.

Militia.

I bent over the map, concentrating on the frontier. It didn't give much idea of what I would find there, if I ever reached it.

Two militiamen. They'd come through the doors a minute

ago and were standing still, looking around. Routine. What did they expect to find in a public library, an English spy or something?

I concentrated on the map, leaving the two still figures at the periphery of my vision, where only movement was registered. I had my papers on me but they could be dangerous now, fatal. It would depend on what connection they'd made in their minds between the dead Lithuanian they'd found alongside the railway lines and the explosion in the freight-yards in Kandalaksha and the engineer Petr Lein, who'd been found by the railway in Murmansk and taken to the hospital. The man with the scarred face.

Had Fane told the KGB my cover?

When they'd made that famous deal of theirs, had London instructed my local control to reveal my cover: Petr Lein? So that everything should look above board? That was possible. It was possible that the two KGB officers who'd checked me out on the train had known who I was, that I was working partly for them, for their sacred motherland, by arrangement with Mr Croder. In which case my papers could now be lethal. It had been all right before that thing had blown one or two of their men to bits in the freight-yards but things were different now and if Petr Lein got picked up by a patrol he could find his name on their all-points bulletin sheet: *finis*.

They hadn't moved.

The scale was 1:250,000, the biggest I could find. Elevations and sea depth in metres, civil and military aerodromes marked, roads, railways, navigable canals. The area covered was from the junction of the Soviet, Finnish and Norwegian borders in the south to the Barents Sea in the north. The Soviet-Norwegian border was the northernmost leg of the Iron Curtain, ending in the sea.

Somewhere along this line I would have to cross into Norway.

Without London?

Movement along the periphery. They were going out. I lifted my head half an inch and saw them more clearly. One of them was looking back. Not at me, at the girl with the footballs under her sweater, ah, sweet affirmation of life, comrades, what would we do without it.

Finnmark on one side, Murmanskaya on the other. It looked easy enough on the map but the map didn't specify the number of watchtowers and floodlights and war-trained dogs and mines and trip-wires and peak-capped sharpshooters frustrated with boredom of guard duty and eager for relief, bang bang and you're dead, my good friend, you shouldn't have told Chief of Control where to get off, he doesn't like it.

No regrets.

The nearest part of the frontier to Murmansk: 110 km. The nearest town to the frontier: Pechenga, 11 km. Airports at Pechenga and Koshka-Yavr, with another one at Salmiyarvi, further west, much further west, too far from here with the roads in this condition. And in any case there was no chance of getting into an aeroplane without London's help.

It's easy for the local directors because they carry permanent cover and they don't have to go clandestine. It's possible for a shadow executive to reach his objective and get it across the border or hand it to his control or a courier and leave the host country – a charming term, yes – just as he came in with his cover still intact and his papers acceptable for franking, but it's rare. During the course of the mission things can get very sticky and he'll have to go clandestine and assume a host-country cover and operate just this side of the capsule unless he's lucky. Even if a wheel doesn't come off somewhere it's not often he can avoid going clandestine: I was working under the cover of a journalist but that was restrictive: a foreign journalist can't suddenly take off for Kandalaksha on his own and that's what I'd had to do because that's where the objective was.

The man opposite me at the worn teakwood table was nursing his chilblains under black wool mittens, running a finger down the columns of print, his one eye steady, his cracked lips moving as his finger stopped and he read the paragraph and then moved on, not an old man but a man beyond his years, his cheeks cavernous and ears shrivelled by unending winters, red as raw bacon. What was he looking for, with his eye and his finger? An apartment? A second-hand chair? A job?

Not for a hole in the frontier.

A railway line ran from Murmansk into Pechenga. That might be still open. The roads would be impossible. But once in Pechenga?

The sea.

A boat.

Without London?

In the ordinary way if your main control is good and knows how to pull strings internationally, how to handle DI6 in the overseas missions, how to use Interpol for special information, and if your director in the field is also good, and knows how to get papers forged and couriers briefed and safehouses set up and protected, you stand a fair chance of getting home, sometimes a bit shot up or with your nerves like a disco hall but getting home. Otherwise we wouldn't let them send us out, we're not in the kamikaze club for God's sake. We like to know there's a chance.

But that's with London behind you.

Different now.

A feeling of being dwarfed suddenly by the immensity of this foreign land with its regiments of men with black boots and peaked caps and holstered guns, their eyes restless as they looked for inconsistencies in the social environment, for someone hurrying or turning away or giving unsatisfactory answers to a doorman's questions – *he offered me fifty rubles, comrades, but of course I refused, being suspicious of such a thing* – and most of all for not being in possession of correct papers: that was where the greatest danger lay – at the checkpoints, the road-blocks, the frontier posts. *You are from Murmansk, citizen? Then what are you doing in Pechenga?*

A feeling of having, yes, committed suicide, or at least of having set the scene, tying the rope aloft and fetching the chair, and out of vanity, being too proud to go on marching to London's bloody tune. My chances were no better now: they were worse; the only difference was that when the time

[234]

came I would at least go decently, mown down by enemy action, not sullied by traitor's knife.

He turned the page of the newspaper, the man opposite me at the table, his lips moving again as his chilblained finger stopped at a line of print. A second-hand stove to keep back the deathly cold of his cramped apartment? A coat with more weight to it than this moth-eaten thing he was wearing? His finger moved on.

It has been known for an executive to be trapped on this side of the Curtain and never get out. Thompson is in Moscow somewhere according to rumour in the Caff, and Pick is said to be in one of the labour camps. Another man, Cosgreave, is said to be living on the shore of the Black Sea with a woman from Tashkent, having decided that the risks of trying to get across on his own weren't worth taking: there's life, after all, in Soviet Russia. Those are the ones we know about, or at least talk about, creating legends to lend a little colour to those dreary corridors. There are others, but we won't discuss them, though I knew personally a high-echelon and very effective shadow who now works for the Fourth Department of the KGB.

And there are those known to have died here, caught in the heat of a counter-operation or running for the border or finishing off a mission the only way they can. Webster, Finnimore, Clay.

Requiescat in pace.

'Have you by any chance, comrade, a violin for sale?'

His one eye watched me with the light of hope in it.

A violin, with fingers like these?

'I'm sorry.'

'Never mind. I had mine stolen, and it's my living, that's all.'

'That was bad luck, comrade.'

I walked out of the public library and turned to the right, conscious that my feet were taking a definite direction, if only back to the hotel to fetch my overnight bag and pay the concierge for his silence. After that I would take the first step towards the frontier and see how far the animal cunning of the organism would get me.

I'd left some spare gloves and a train timetable at the safehouse but I couldn't go back there now. Liz had been sent there to monitor my operation for the Company and Fane would have made contact with them: there was no point now in her staying on. Even if she were still there the place could be a deathtrap for me if she were blown; she wouldn't be utmost-security trained for light cover and she hadn't gone clandestine because her Russian wasn't good enough.

Where else would a man go but to the earth mother?

Not now.

Between the library and the hotel I saw three street-checks going on in the distance: four or five militiamen stopping every pedestrian and at one intersection a whole group of men with shovels on their way to the snow-clearing zones. The search for Captain Kirill Zhigalin, Soviet Navy, was being intensified.

Two militiamen were patrolling the street where the hotel stood and I had to make a detour and keep them surveilled until it was safe to go on. Question: if it was like this between the Murmansk public library and the Aurora Hotel, what would it be like between here and the frontier?

I kicked snow from my boots against the brickwork at the top of the steps and pushed the glass door open.

'You are asked to telephone this number again, comrade.'

He held out the scrap of dirty paper.

Fane answered after three rings. 'They've located Ferris,' he said. 'He's on his way.'

25

CHECKPOINT

I WAS GETTING USED to the thing.

Most of the time I carried it across my shoulder, and I was taking more care with it now when I passed people on the pavements.

'Watch that shovel, you stupid whoreson!'

And a happy Christmas to you too, comrade. But he was perfectly right: I'd slipped on the slush and nearly clouted him with the edge of the blade.

In the last two days there'd been three more signals from Fane. The first was to the effect that Ferris had confirmed by a radio message from the flight deck of a British Airways plane that he was prepared to local-direct me and that he needed all facilities made available to him. London would have already begun work on that, the moment Ferris had agreed to switch his operations. I didn't know who was going out to replace him in Tokyo but I hoped for the sake of the shadow there that it wouldn't be Fane.

The second signal reported that Ferris had landed in Karachi and had received Telexed briefing material from our consulate there, sent from London through Government Communications Headquarters in Cheltenham.

The third signal had been to the effect that Ferris had raised questions concerning the courier who had purportedly been sent to rendezvous with me in the freight-yards in Kandalaksha at the time when the KGB had moved in. *Had they arrested the courier following the explosion and had they interrogated him and if so how much did he know of the executive's operations in Murmansk?* That was a good question and I'd asked Fane for the answer. He said the courier hadn't been seen since the explosion and might in fact have been arrested and put under intensive interrogation. The last part of the question was therefore important. Perhaps crucial.

In the two days before the fourth signal came I had time to surveille the environment and try to find out how to move across the city without running into a checkpoint or a militia patrol. By the end of the second day I'd begun to see that it was impossible. The KGB had relied on taking Karasov and putting him under interrogation as soon as we'd flushed him for them but he was dead, and their one last chance of allowing the Kremlin to send the President of the Presidium to Vienna without making critical concessions to the West was to find Captain Zhigalin and obtain his absolute silence with a bullet through the brain. Even though they had no idea that at this moment a British Secret Service agent was flying in to Murmansk to direct an operation specifically designed to get Zhigalin over the frontier they were throwing a security net across the city to make certain that if he emerged from ground they would seize him and that if he remained there they would eventually find him and drag him out.

If they had known that he had already contacted a Western embassy and requested transit across the frontier and subsequent asylum and that his request was being given immediate and active response they would have called out military reserves to augment their efforts to find him. If Ferris actually found it possible to put me into contact with Zhigalin and arrange and somehow protect a rendezvous it was my opinion at this time that it would be impossible for him to move us as far as the frontier, let alone across it, simply because the search for Zhigalin would extend and intensify towards that frontier on the assumption that he would try to reach it. We would be going into increasing KGB and militia activity at every hour and we had no papers that could get us through any checkpoint.

It's possible to represent any given mission schematically

on graph paper and these days it's put through the computers before the monitors at the board over the mission control desk are allowed to make any report or recommend any decision, and at this stage my operation in Murmansk would look like a V configuration narrowing to a point in the direction of the future, since the more effort we made towards achieving our goal the more risk there would be of exposing the operation, be it given that the environment was at the same time being brought under increasing KGB surveillance.

This was my view, as the shadow executive in the field, of the status of *Northlight* at noon of January 18th, and it was reported in essence to London by Fane, the outgoing local director.

Nothing would appear on the operations board in that anonymous building in Whitehall to show that in point of fact the focus of the mission was at this moment a man lurching over the snow drifts of Murmansk with a shovel across his shoulder.

At 20:00 hours the telephone rang in the lobby of the hotel and the concierge fetched me to take the line. It was the last time I ever spoke to Fane. He reported that Ferris was due to land at Murmansk airport from Leningrad and that I was to meet him there as soon as I could. The precise rendezvous was arranged for 22:00 hours without further alternatives Ferris would wait for me if he reached there first.

Checkpoint.

It was two blocks ahead of me at the intersection of Lenin Prospekt and North Harbour Street. They were setting them up everywhere now and at shorter intervals, bringing in the militia from their barracks and substations in dark green vans and posting them at strategic locations. The moment they began spilling out of the van they called on anyone in the street to halt and show his papers.

I turned into a side street and climbed the virgin drifts that the ploughs and work gangs hadn't had time to deal with. Half an hour ago I'd seen a checkpoint being set up four blocks away to the west and from my observations during the past two days I'd noted that the average period of checkpoint left operating was one hour, depending on the importance of the street traffic.

Light snow had started falling again but most of the main streets were clear now except for ruts of frozen slush and gravel. In the side street where I was moving the lamps had gone out, and in the faint light from the aurora that was seeping through thin cloud banks the snow had a bluish tinge like an overcoloured Christmas card. My shovel was over one shoulder, part of my identity. The militia were checking the snow-clearing gangs as well as other pedestrians but it gave me a slight edge: they were to an unknown degree less likely to shout at a distant figure if he looked like a volunteer worker than if he lacked an instantly identifiable image. It was now 21:00 hours and I'd been moving for thirty minutes towards the airport, doubling on my tracks and making detours to avoid the main intersections where the checkpoints were set up. I didn't know whether I could reach the rdv on time in these conditions but that wasn't important because Ferris would wait for me. The real question was whether I could reach it at all.

I was now operating in the uneasy twilight zone between clandestine and the final security status they haven't actually got a name for: on the board it would simply show the symbol of a crooked cross to denote that the executive was operating in hazard. But that might not be accurate. I'd gone from covert to clandestine when I'd shed my identity as Clive Gage, journalist, and adopted the identity of Petr Lein, engineer, and if I now pushed those papers among the tea-leaves and tin cans and fish-heads of the nearest rubbish dump I would technically be operating in hazard: without papers and without any chance of surviving if a single militiaman checked me in the street. It had happened in Warsaw: I'd turned a corner and walked straight into a routine police patrol and they'd asked for my papers and I hadn't got any and they'd put me into a cell and started work.

What I didn't know, as I climbed the drifts and lurched through the freezing ruts of this city's streets, was whether the papers I carried would get me through or trap me. I didn't know whether they had made the connection yet between the dead Lithuanian and the freight-yards bombing and the man who'd been taken to the General Maritime Hospital. They could still be sifting through the routine reports and questioning the last of the passengers on that train and watching the computer screens as they punched the data in. Two things were certain: they were doing that now and they were inevitably making progress. It was like a slow-burn fuse that would at any hour, any minute reach the papers I carried in my pocket and blow my operation the instant I fell foul of a random check and had to show them.

There was only one thing more dangerous: not to show them at all. It was a matter of time, and in the diminishing time frame available to me I had to reach the rendezvous before one of the computers threw the name of Petr Lein on the screen and the KGB operator flashed an immediate all-points bulletin to have me picked up.

Checkpoint.

I turned into a side street and saw two militiamen on routine patrol coming in this direction at a distance of a hundred metres and there was no cover except for a sandbin half-submerged under a snow drift so I turned back and waited for the shout but it didn't come, though I might not have heard it because one of the civic transport trucks was getting up speed along the main street and I started running – *Halt!* but only in my mind – *Halt, that man!* but only in the nerves as I slung the shovel high and one of the men caught it and gave me a hand as I clambered onto the truck and hung jack-knifed across the side until they hauled me aboard.

'One more for the cattle-yards!'

'Run out of snow, comrade?'

Packed, yes, like cattle in the open truck with the slipstream cutting our faces as it got up speed again with the gears jerking and a shovel clanging against the back of the cab.

'Is this a work party?'

'No, comrade, we're off to a bloody circus!'

In the last two days I'd seen that the checkpoint militiamen had let some of the trucks through if they were on their way to a clearing site but it wasn't a hundred per cent predictable and the situation now was strictly Russian roulette because the work truck ahead of us was being waved through the intersection but it didn't mean they wouldn't stop this one – they could be checking them alternately to keep the traffic moving.

'Which gang are you with, comrade?'

'Number 5,' I told him.

'Five's been sent home. This is the night shift.'

Slowing towards the intersection.

'I'm volunteering.'

'Glutton for bloody punishment!'

'No,' I said, 'it's just that I've got a nagging wife.'

Raucous laughter and the whiff of alcohol in the air-rush: for the past two days the snow-clearing gangs had been sent to the workers' canteens for free soup and a vodka ration.

Speeding up again with the green-lit batons waving us through and the eyes under the peaked caps checking us without much interest and the hope now, the definite hope that within another half an hour they could change the signals data on the board for *Northlight* to read *Rendezvous made*.

'From Moscow?' a man asked me.

'Yes.' We had the same accent.

They were letting the truck ahead of us through the next intersection, the illuminated batons waving. In the far distance I could see the lights of the airport control tower.

Is Mr Croder there?

He went home.

Call him up for me. Our chap's made the rendezvous.

Much rejoicing because our first objective had been killed

and the executive was operating in hazard and his local control had been changed at his own request and that had shaken the network because it's like switching partners on a trapeze but soon there would be much rejoicing, yes, and the monitors at the signals board would make some fresh tea.

'You like it in Murmansk?'

'Not in winter.'

He laughed briefly. 'No, but the sea air's pleasant, after the Moscow smog. I'm a lawyer.' He reached inside his coat and brought out a card. 'If you ever need assistance, let me know.'

The truck was slowing again. The one ahead of us had turned left along Lenin Prospekt. There weren't any green-lit batons this time: they were red.

'All right,' I said, and put the card in my pocket. 'I'm an engineer. Lein, Petr Stepanovich.'

Slowing hard now as the red batons began waving and spreading out as the militiamen moved across the road. The truck's brakes locked and the tyres slid across the slush, no rejoicing, no you won't have to call Mr Croder, the brakes coming off and the tyres finding grip but we were still slowing. I do, as a matter of fact, need your assistance, comrade, but I doubt if this is a matter you can do much to help me with, the brakes coming on again and sending us into the piled snow at the roadside, the rear of the truck clouting a sandbin with a scream of tearing metal.

'Bloody militia check again! Haven't those whoresons got nothing else to do?'

Grinding to a halt now at the intersection as we lurched into each other and grabbed for support, a shovel clanging down and the diesel exhaust gas clouding across our faces.

'*Security check! Get your papers ready!*'

Floodlights came on, freezing the truck in a white glare, making us shield our eyes.

'*One at a time, come on!*'

The gas was sickening and we stood choking in it until the driver switched off the engine and there was silence except for the thud of our boots as we dropped one by one on to the roadway.

'*Your papers.*'

26

FERRIS

IT WAS A high-impact crash but not totally head-on because the main instrument panel was almost intact although the deceleration forces had wrenched it away from the left side holding bolts and smashed most of the dials. One wing sloped downwards from the main cabin, sheared off at the root; the other was missing altogether.

Smell of burning, and something else, like a stale oven, and I connected this with the soft charred shreds stuck to the instrument panel; in the faint light it looked like the remains of a scalp.

Small bells ringing, rather prettily.

I didn't know how long this thing had been here or whether they'd hauled it out of the way of the air traffic or whether it had finished up here smothered in fire foam, choosing its own grave-site where it could rest until the salvage crews came to settle on it like vultures and pluck it apart for what they could find. It wasn't pleasant in here because of the smell and the cold but I thought Fane had done well: as a rendezvous location it was as good as we'd get; it was a half-mile from the main runways and difficult to reach over the snow and unless we showed a light or made a noise nobody would come here.

The only light filtering in through the sooty glass of the windows was from the control tower and the occasional sweep of headlights as the Navy bulldozers turned across and across the perimeter roads, shovelling the snow into the waiting trucks. The little warning bells rang automatically when the bulldozers reversed.

A short-range commercial Aeroflot Yak–40 had landed five minutes ago with its centre engine reversing thrust as it slid past the lights of the terminal and left the scent of burnt kerosene seeping into the wreck where I sat waiting. It should be in from Leningrad.

I'd thought that the heat from my body was misting on the window where I sat but when I wiped my sleeve across the glass nothing changed. When I'd reached here twenty minutes ago the runway lights in the far distance had been clear; now they were shining through some kind of haze, perhaps sea fog from the north. Now that the sound of the Yakovlev had died away it was quiet in here, and I could hear metal creaking along the main wing as it contracted in the night's increasing cold. I could also hear faint screaming, and believed at first that a wind was rising and fluting through the gaps in the wreckage; but there was no wind outside: the tiny pennant drooping from the airspeed Pitot tube at the wingtip was perfectly still. It was just that my nerves were ultra-sensitive at this stage of the mission, taking the organism close to the zone where the psyche was picking up extrasensory vibrations from what we call the past.

Lights moved from the main terminal along the highway that had been kept clear by constant ploughing, allowing traffic to shuttle from the town and back, most of it dark blue Navy transports and coal-trucks piled with snow. Beyond them the red beacon of a radio mast winked rhythmically, then it vanished as a dark shape passed close to the window and the screams were loud suddenly as the nerves froze because I hadn't expected him to get here so soon and he'd made no sound over the snow.

Ferris.

I hadn't recognized him because he'd passed close against the window, but it couldn't be anyone else; no one would come here alone: the militia and the airport security guards always patrolled in pairs.

He moved the lever down and pulled open the emergency

door just aft of the flight deck and my scalp shrank as I watched the faint flood of light that came in. But if it wasn't Ferris there wouldn't be any problem: I was crouching now within arm's length of the door and the necessary imagery had started in my mind, going through the most effective moves at the calculated height and distance of a drawn gun.

Then he was suddenly there, pulling himself through the doorway and sending his shadow flitting across the smashed bulkhead on the other side. I could recognize his profile now.

'Greetings,' I said softly.

He stopped moving and his head turned, the right lens of his glasses catching the light and reflecting it across his temple, so that he looked like a thin, deformed monster with one huge eye.

'Sorry I'm late.'

He closed the door as quietly as he could, though the movement sent a metal spar twanging; then he lowered himself on to the jump seat opposite me, putting his briefcase down and settling it neatly in that awful prissy way he had of doing everything.

He sat gazing at me in the faint light, a thin pale owl with bits of straw-coloured hair sticking out below his fur hat like broken feathers, his gloved hands resting on his knees. This was the man who'd sat on the stairs in the Hong Kong snake-shop with a gun on his lap while those bloody things had writhed among the smashed glass jars on the floor and the assassin had brought more and more pressure to bear on my throat, the man who had taken a neat step out of his way on the pavement in Barcelona to crush a cockroach under his shoe while he'd told me this was precisely what London would do to me if I didn't take on the Sinkiang thing, the man who had seen me closer to the brink than any other control in the field and who had twice pulled me back from it, the *only* man I could trust to see me through the rest of the mission if there were still the ghost of a chance left to finish it.

'Not easy,' he said, 'this one, is it?'

'*Do you know what they did to me?*'

'Never mind that.'

I tried to let myself go limp and half managed it, furious because I'd shown him what he'd got on his hands: the makings of a burnt-out case who was ready to sell the Bureau down the river the instant it tried another trick – *I'll go straight into the nearest KGB headquarters and blow London.*

Had Fane told him I'd said that?

'I just felt a bit annoyed,' I told him much more quietly, 'that's all.'

'I'm not surprised.'

Then I asked him. I hadn't meant to: I'd told myself again and again on my way here that there was one question I wouldn't ask Ferris because it would embarrass him, but it came out in a kind of soft explosion that I couldn't stop.

'Why did you refuse this mission?'

He didn't look down. Fane would have looked down. That was the difference.

'I detected a faint smell of fish.' He went on watching me, his expression lost behind the reflection across his glasses.

'Is that all?'

'Croder was running it, and there was the most monumental flap going on. Too noisy, for my liking.'

'Did you know–' and I should have stopped right there and perhaps tried to, but again I couldn't do it. 'Did you know I was down for termination?'

'No. But I thought it could happen. I'd caught a whiff of the deal they were making.'

'Then why–' but this time I managed to stop, because Ferris had the ability to make you go on talking until you gave yourself away and I was damned if I were going to let him do it now. He'd told me enough. I'd been answered.

'You know perfectly well why,' he said rather sharply. 'If I'd warned you about it, would you have taken any notice?'

'Perhaps.'

'Bullshit.'

'True.'

'Perfectly true. You would have seen it as the ultimate challenge to your resourcefulness and you would have gone headlong into the mission with your blood up and you would have probably got yourself killed off before they'd even had time to light the signals board.'

I don't know how I manage to like a man who keeps a blueprint of my soul hung on his wall.

'It was far better,' he said, 'to let you go into *Northlight* with your talent for survival uncompromised. Don't ever say I haven't got your best interests at heart.'

'You really are a bastard, Ferris.'

'You shouldn't ask stupid questions.'

Absolutely right, yes. That's why I'd asked London for him. Ferris has been more absolutely right about everything to do with controlling the executive in the field than any local director I've ever worked with.

'A long way to bring you,' I said.

'From Tokyo?'

'Yes.'

'It was a bit important. Have you seen any news lately?'

'I've been rather busy.'

He watched me steadily for a moment. 'Don't underestimate things, Quiller. They've got far beyond the level of normal international diplomacy: that broke down, days ago. It's always the last thing that happens, isn't it, before a war? The talking stops, and they get out the guns.'

Cold crept along my spine.

'Jesus Christ. . . . It's as bad as that?'

'It's as bad as that. And you know I wouldn't try to give you any bullshit, especially at this late stage. It's your life on the line, I understand that.' He turned his head and watched the window for a moment, and when he spoke again his voice was quieter. 'It's all our lives, actually.'

I pulled in a slow breath.

'Unless I can take him across. Zhigalin.'

'Precisely.' He looked back at me in the strange half-light.

'What are the chances, Ferris?'

'I'm not sure there are any.'

Ferris has never deceived me.

'Then we'll have to make some.'

'Yes.'

'The snow's blocked the roads, from here to the frontier. I assume you know that.'

He looked through the small grimed window again. 'Yes. We shan't try to get you out by road. Even if we could get you both to the frontier, it wouldn't work. That snow's a killer.'

He was thinking of the rifles. Snow is the perfect background for a running target: they wouldn't miss.

'How much briefing did you get, Ferris?'

'I've been in signals for hours, but you'd better fill me in on the local scene. It's not good, I imagine.'

'No. They're looking for Zhigalin.'

'Of course. Checkpoints everywhere?'

'Yes. I had to go through one on the way here: I was on a truck and they stopped it.'

He became very still. 'You showed your papers?'

'Yes.'

'Well *that's* good news.'

'It can't last. I had to kill a man on a train and they'll have found him by now. Then there was the bang in Kandalaksha – did Fane tell you?'

'Yes. He met my plane.'

'So they'll connect me with the man who was taken to the hospital, as soon as the computers have spewed out the coincidences. I daren't go through another checkpoint.'

He thought about that. 'Did they match your papers with any kind of all-points bulletin?'

'No. They were using tape recorders, to speed things up.'

'Pretty intensive.'

'Yes. In the last two days I've seen fifty checkpoints putting half the population of Murmansk through the sieve. If they don't get me next time they'll get Zhigalin.'

'Oh,' Ferris said, 'he's safe for the moment.'

'He's made contact again?'

'Yes.'

'Where is he?'

'Not far. We're looking after him.'

'*That* was fast.'

'There isn't a lot of time.'

A diesel engine gunned up outside as a bulldozer started reversing. Ferris turned to the window again.

'Pretty bells,' he said. 'Rather like Christmas, with the snow and everything.' He was half in profile, his glasses no longer hiding his eyes. They were watchful.

'Are we all right?' I asked him.

He gave a sigh and turned back to me. 'Tell me about the Chinese. The Rinker cell as you call it.'

'They've lost me.'

'Are you sure?'

'They didn't show up in Kandalaksha after I'd killed one of them on the train.'

'But we're not expecting them to "show up" until we bring Zhigalin to the surface. Are we?'

I didn't like this.

'You think they're still active?'

'Yes.'

'Why?'

'For one thing, I would say that the Chinese would go to very great lengths to secure Zhigalin. Once they'd persuaded him to give a press conference they could wreck the last of our chances for a summit meeting in Vienna, and that would give them a priceless advantage.' He looked through the window again. 'For another thing, and rather more immediately, I think they're watching us now.'

The whole of the fuselage began drumming and I felt the vibration through the metal seat. Light swept across Ferris as the plane lifted from the runway, leaving the sound of its jets echoing across the airport like the booming of a thunderstorm. A loose chip of glass in one of the smashed instruments set up a tinkling vibrato.

'Where?'

'Among the trees.'

'Which trees? Which direction?'

'Forward of the plane—'

'This plane?'

'Yes.'

'How far away?'

'A couple of hundred yards. I–'

'One man?'

'I'm not sure. All I could see were the field-glasses.'

'Two lenses? Are you sure there were two?'

In a moment he said: 'Good question.'

'You're not sure?'

'I could have been mistaken.'

'It could have been just one lens.'

'Yes.'

'A telescopic lens.'

'Yes.'

The drumming eased off, and the chip of glass stopped tinkling. It seemed quieter because of it, quieter than before, and colder, even colder than before, the kind of cold that shrinks the scalp and crawls on the skin.

'I was opening the door,' Ferris said, 'when I saw him. The only way to warn you was to come aboard, as if I hadn't seen anything.'

'Civil of you.'

He could have turned back and left me here waiting. The director in the field is almost never at risk: he's too valuable to the opposition as a human constant; his job is to keep in contact with the executive, to keep the lifeline intact, to be instantly available if something goes wrong. Half the time when the executive goes to ground and the opposition lose track of him they can find him again by throwing a surveillance net across the local director's environment, physically and electronically, and there's nothing we can do about that because the alternative is to send the shadow in alone and he wouldn't last more than a couple of days in the field without support and communications: it'd be like throwing a man off a ship in mid-ocean.

'Does he know you saw him?'

Assume one man. One sniper with a long-distance rifle. It would be dangerous to assume anything else.

'I don't think so.'

'Why not? You were looking straight at him.'

'At a distance of a couple of hundred yards. And I didn't stop moving.'

'It looked as if you were just making a last check before you came in here.'

'Yes.'

He was slowly pulling off his gloves.

'It can't be the KGB,' I told him.

'No.'

They wouldn't work like that. This was their territory, what London so graciously calls the host country. The KGB don't need to set up a sniper to pick off a spook: they'll just send a van in and drag him on board and if he gets clear then they'll send in a hundred men, cover a whole city with checkpoints as they were doing now. You don't in any case get very rapid promotion in the KGB for hauling a dead spook into head-quarters without giving anyone a chance to put him under the light and pick everything out of his head.

'Then it can only be the Rinker cell.'

'As far as my briefing tells me,' Ferris said, 'they're the only active people in the field.'

Three lights, red, green and white, crossed the oblong of the window as the plane climbed into the circuit. They vanished quite suddenly into the fog layer. It was getting worse, creeping in from the sea.

'I couldn't be absolutely sure,' I said, 'when I came here.'

'Of course not.' He said it at once and with emphasis.

I always know when I'm being followed. No one had followed me here to the rendezvous. They'd used chain surveillance, and at a distance: two or three of them taking up positions at strategic points and using field-glasses – they'd be totally undetectable. If they'd used more people than that, they would have been some of the men with shovels among the work gangs: again, undetectable. It wasn't important any more to question how they'd got a fix on me at the hotel. It could have been the courier in Kandalaksha turned by the Rinker cell to work for them under duress or a bugged line or the hotel porter or simply efficient field work. What was important now was how to leave this hulk alive and if that were possible then how to lose them before I went to meet Zhigalin.

Ferris took a card out of his pocket and passed it to me, a regulation issue made of wide-grain wood fibres treated with magnesium and designed to burn in less than one second or dissolve into pulp in water. On it was an address in Murmansk.

'Your safehouse,' he said, 'though you may not need it for more than a few hours; it depends on what my people can arrange for you. The phone number is mine, though I may have to move in with you until we can secure Zhigalin. If you lose contact with me you can still call that number and they'll put you in direct touch with the chief of station in Moscow.' He stared through the window again. He couldn't see the man with the lens from this angle; he wanted to be ready if anybody came past the window from that direction: there would be one or two seconds' warning before they opened the door.

I put the card into my wallet.

'If someone else answers the phone when I call that number, do I speak English or Russian?'

'It doesn't matter. They're fluent in both.'

'Is it strictly secure?' Briefing terminology for bug-proof.

'Yes.'

'I don't think Fane's line was.'

Ferris turned from the window to gaze at me. 'Possibly not. Mine is. You're safe with it in *any* eventuality.' He paused to give it emphasis. 'If there's no answer, it just means they've had to abandon.'

'They'd cut the phone?'

He looked faintly shocked. 'No. Blow it up.'

'Sorry.'

'You really have been slumming it, haven't you?'

This was why I'd demanded Ferris from London. He's not only highly experienced in handling a shadow but he's also technically faultless. Most people would cut a phone line and leave it at that if they had to clear out, but a line can be joined together again and you can call up and blow the whole of the mission if you don't know they've done that. Ferris had rigged a bang.

'Any briefing?' I was getting impatient now. I wanted to know what was going to happen when I went through that doorway, whether I was going to get my brains blown all over the place or whether I could go back through the snow and find a cafe and sit with a bowl of soup by the steamy windows and let everything else wait while I celebrated life as the warmth reached my stomach.

It happens often during a mission but you never quite get used to it. It's the feeling that comes to you when you know you've moved into a close-focus red sector that can prove terminal, when you can't go back and you can't stay where you are and you can't move forward without risking the absolute totality of all that your life has meant until this point in time. The feeling is like hunger but less physical, more ethereal, almost mystical, because you're close to the final answer and it might not be what you hope.

'No further briefing,' Ferris said, and put on his gloves and looked at his watch. '22:14?'

I checked my own and had to set it back half a minute. It doesn't ever matter what the time is by your own watch or by the local clocks: the time is what your local control says it is, because everything depends on him.

Without my gloves on the cold was already numbing my hands; as soon as I'd reset my watch I put them on again but the cold didn't go; it was everywhere in my body now, in my bones, because I would have to go out there first. One field director could run a dozen missions, a dozen executives: he was normally an older man with infinitely wider experience and infinitely greater responsibility to the Bureau; he would always get home safely because his papers were unimpeachable, unless he ran foul of a strike or a trap that was set for the man he was running.

So I got up first, pulling my gloves tighter and stepping past Ferris to the door as the wrecked fuselage creaked to the shifting of my weight.

The man out there would be cold too, crouching against the trunk of a tree and unable to move, impatient, as I was, but for a different reason: he'd want to get it done with successfully, get it over and report back to base while the blood still seeped from the body and the whiff of cordite tainted the stillness and the arm lay outstretched with the hand reaching for what now it could never hold.

'Probably just field-glasses,' I heard Ferris say as I pushed open the door.

'Yes.' I stepped down onto the snow.

27

DEADLINE

THE FIRST TIME I telephoned Ferris was at noon on the next day.

He answered himself and at the second ring.

'It's difficult,' I told him.

One of my feet was bleeding.

'How difficult?'

She didn't go back to her desk as the man had done at the last hotel: she went out of the lobby and left me alone in the phone-box, an immense woman, immense.

'They simply won't let me go,' I told Ferris.

I'd been trying to shake them off the whole morning but the militia checkpoints were all over the place and that made it impossible to use the normal routine for getting clear of surveillance because the risk of running into a checkpoint or a two-man patrol was now appalling and the Rinker cell knew that: they had me in what amounted to a mobile trap.

'You'll have to keep trying,' Ferris said. 'I'll have a deadline for you any time now and it'll be close.'

Sweat was clammy on me: I'd been scrambling through those bloody streets and into buildings and out again and onto buses and off again and all they'd done was switch stations with their field-glasses and keep me comfortably in sight.

'How close?' I asked Ferris. I don't like close deadlines, they can be murderous.

'Some time today.' He didn't like saying that. He knew what I was up against.

'In daylight?' (If you could say that: it was already like dusk.)

'If it can be done. If not, as soon after nightfall as we can do it.'

I didn't need to ask him what the deadline was for: it was for making contact with the objective, Zhigalin. Ferris wouldn't set it up until he knew he could get us both out: we were running right into the final phase of the mission but the whole bloody place was a bright red sector and I didn't know what the chances were of throwing off the Rinker cell. Until I could do that, I couldn't go to meet Zhigalin. He was their main target: the moment I was with him they'd close right in and shut the trap and throw me onto a scrap heap and take him underground.

There were five of them. I'd seen four of them at one time and when I'd gone round a corner and into an apartment block and out through the fire escape on the second floor I'd seen the fifth there waiting for me *as if he'd known my next move* and when I'd got clear of his surveillance zone I'd run right into one of the others at a distance of fifty yards, close enough to recognize him if I saw him again. That was when I'd cut my foot on something buried in the snow, the blade of a shovel or something.

The blood seeped into my boot.

'They're extremely good,' I told Ferris.

'They must be.' He meant if I hadn't been able to get clear of them by now; I'd been working at it the whole morning.

I'd had my bowl of soup last night. Sat there with it, savouring the warmth in some stinking little railway cafe while a drunk had told me all about his bitch of a wife and the way she looked down on him because she'd landed a job in the post office as a sorting clerk. *Now she's in government service she thinks she's running the bloody Politburo,* leaning over the table with his face stuck into mine and one black-nailed hand so close to my bowl of soup that he kept getting drops on it and once or twice raised it to his mouth and licked it, *three times a week I have to get my own supper, the bitch, the satanic bloody stuckup strumpet,* but I listened to every word because I loved the man, because Ferris was right last night, it had just been a pair of field-glasses under the trees and my brains hadn't gone all over the place when I'd stepped down onto the snow – life is sweet, my friend, and never sweeter than when you believe it's no longer yours for the living, so why don't you, I asked the poor bastard – he was a huge man – just pick her up and sit her down on a red-hot samovar and don't take her off again till she promises to get your supper?

Soup in my stomach, blood in my shoe. And never sweeter, so forth, because any time now they were going to drive me so hard that I'd end up making a mistake and go pitching straight into a checkpoint, *finis*.

But they knew the danger of that. They were extremely efficient. They knew that if they drove me too hard they could lose me to the KGB and lose Zhigalin too because I was the only way in to him. I'd never been in this kind of situation before when the very people who'd trapped me were doing all they could to protect me from the host-country security services: one of them had actually given a little signal when he'd seen I was going to run into a KGB patrol on the far side of a work gang: *he'd actually warned me.*

But the rope was shortening. Ferris couldn't keep Zhigalin underground forever. The Rinker team couldn't keep on running me through the streets like this forever. One of two things was going to happen: they would unintentionally run me slap into a checkpoint or they'd close right in and pick me up and take me somewhere with thick walls and turn up the stereo and ask me where they could find my local control and get him to lead them to Zhigalin with a gun at his back, and that would be all right because I couldn't tell them where Ferris was but they'd still have to risk leaving me on the floor in a mess with the stereo still blaring away. But it would be their last chance and they knew that. They would only come for me if there was no other way.

'Can you give me any kind of picture?' I asked Ferris.

He wouldn't want to do that at this stage. At this stage there was the risk of getting caught and grilled.

'All right,' Ferris said. 'We've got Zhigalin safe for a few hours, but not much longer than that. The moment you can make contact with him we can get you both out, but that depends on how fast we can move.'

'How fast we can move from the time I meet him?'

'From that time, yes.' He paused for a few seconds and I think it was because he wanted to get the tone of his voice right. He had to warn me but he didn't want to scare me off. 'From that time you'll be in good hands, but until then – until you make contact with Zhigalin – we're working with diminishing chances.'

Ferris is as bad as Croder sometimes: it's like talking to a bloody schoolmaster. 'For Christ's sake spell it out, will you?'

He thought for a moment. 'I would say that unless you can reach Zhigalin within a couple of hours from now, we won't have any chance left at all. This is the final run.'

The final run, with Croder sitting in London nagging the guts out of the signals people at the console while the monitor sat in front of the board of *Northlight* with scum gathering on his cup of tea while he waited to know if the crooked cross was going to stay there much longer or if he could hit the switches and shift the status for the mission according to what Signals was giving him – *executive has made contact with the objective* or *executive compromised* or *action ends here.*

Compromised: caught, killed or capsule-terminated.

'*Two hours?*'

'Sorry,' Ferris said.

'*But they've got me like a rat in a trap.*'

'You'll have to get out.'

The whole bloody town was down in the Metro and I'd expected that because the streets were still under snow.

Boot full of blood and getting dangerous now: the wound was trying to heal but every time I walked it opened up again and I was worried that it was going to bring attention.

Two of them were on the same train with me, standing jammed in with everyone else and watching my reflection in the steamed-up windows. It had been the only thing to do: they would have run me through those streets for the rest of the day before I finally hit a checkpoint so I'd moved into this phase because it was the last chance and so far it was working all right – I'd broken their chain surveillance mode and forced them closer, close enough for me to recognize them whenever I saw them next, a critical advantage. I'd also lost three of them because I'd gone through a ticket barrier so fast that only these two had time to follow me onto the train. They couldn't cause any fuss; they couldn't do what the militia could do; they were as worried as I was about bringing attention to themselves because their papers were probably check-proof but if they were asked to show them it would hold them up and give me time to get clear.

'Who are you shoving?'

'I'm going to be sick.' That got him out of the way very fast and I made some more progress, nudging through the packed bodies towards the end of the compartment. I estimated that we were halfway between stations and if I could reach the doors first I could hit the platform running and get clear.

'Get off my bloody foot!'

'Sorry, comrade.'

Stink of garlic, garlic and sweat and wet astrakhan, wet rabbitskin, soaked boots and bad breath and tobacco, the tobacco was a real help.

'What's the bloody rush?'

'I'm on the wrong train.'

Swaying together round the bends, lurching forward and lurching back with the flicker of the tube light casting a sickly glow across our faces, a small boy clutching a red plastic windmill and a huge Mongolian with fish-scales like sequins on his longshoreman's jacket fast asleep on his feet, a young woman pressed to the glass panel with no room to move away from the thin furtive-looking man until he went too far and she heaved herself back and brought her hand up and across his face in one beautiful swing, much rough merriment from our good fellow-passengers.

They were starting to move now, one of them looking directly at me instead of in the window, getting a little worried, shoving his way closer as the train began slowing and someone dropped a bottle and the intercom speaker came alive and made some grating noises until the voice sounded: *Proletarskaja . . . the next stop is at Proletarskaja . . . stand clear of the doors!*

A man's weight came against me as the train went on slowing and I turned sideways and let the momentum carry him past me and felt the glass panel behind me and pushed past the upright stanchion and got a curse from a man trying to shield his little girl from the crush, *we're getting off here too, damn it,* a miniature gold Party emblem on his coat. *I'm sorry, comrade, but I'm very late,* and my need is more urgent than yours, my friend, you wouldn't believe.

The brakes came on harder now and I grabbed a rail and got to the doors and saw one of them shoving his way along the packed aisle with his eyes on me through the glass panel, the hard stare of the hunter in a square implacable face as the intercom sounded again and two other men started crowding me at the doors. I let them because I needed them – I needed cover, shields, obstacles, distractions, time and distance and I suppose luck but we never count on that, it can be fatal.

When the train jerked to a halt and the doors opened I forced my way through the widening gap and dropped onto the platform and shoved a path through the crowd, working so hard that someone swung a fist from behind me and sent nerve-light flashing through my head as I pressed on and reached a clear area along the curved wall of the platform where two militiamen were standing so I had to slow, *the last thing I wanted to do,* but only to a fast walk because a lot of people are in a hurry at one o'clock on the Metro, it's the end of the lunch break, pulling the ticket out of my wallet to keep my head down *and longing to run* because the nearest of those bastards wouldn't be far behind me now, not far behind.

A shout came but I didn't look round because I was now on the far side of that critical line that divides the two worlds of the executive during the final phase of a mission, the world where he can still claim a legitimate identity and behave as a lawful citizen and even without reliable papers turn back and somehow cheat his way out of a confrontation with two militiamen and the world where he must keep going and even break into a run and turn his hand to every available device to keep his freedom and survive and complete his mission.

'*Stop!*'

Now I began running and people turned their heads to stare at me as I reached a break in the wall and ducked into the passageway between the platforms and ran harder, ran very hard now with one foot squelching in its boot and the sharp pain of the wound flaring through the nerves – '*Stop!*' – but this time fainter because I'd got it wrong: he'd been shouting at the man behind me because he must have panicked and started running too soon and the militia had noticed it and become interested. That was nice but I didn't slow down because I was still in the crowded warrens of a Metro station and those wouldn't be the only two militiamen on patrol and there's always the odd comrade around who's mindful of his civic responsibilities when you're doing something suspicious and once the fight starts they all pile in and this place would shut down on me like a bloody portcullis, keep running and think about something more pleasant, more pleasant than that.

Then I had to double back because there were two more militiamen at the ticket barrier and I managed to turn before they heard my running footsteps, managed to reach the cover of the tiled wall and slow to a walk, turning again and finding some stairs with people crowding down them with snow dropping off their boots, someone holding a huge bag of onions on his shoulder to keep them out of the way and a man carrying a toilet seat above his head like a halo and two militia – not militia, no, Metro staff – dragging a trolley down the stairs with a crate on it, *bang bang bang, mind your backs there, mind your backs!* Then a crowd of sailors coming down with their whooping laughter sending echoes along the curved ceiling, out of the barracks on a week-end pass with their boots clattering on the stairway and their blue canvas bags swinging above the heads of the crowd as they raced each other to the platform below, it was uphill work for me, I can tell you, uphill work, and when I turned to look down the stairs to see if the man had decided not to stop for the militia, had decided to follow me instead and at all costs, I didn't see him, I only saw the other man, the one who'd been with him on the train, the more professional one if you want to look at it that way who'd stayed at the *other* end of the compartment and gone through the doors and followed me more easily and without attracting attention – or that was perhaps the plan they'd agreed on, one of them setting out to follow me at close range while the other – *this one* – covered the possibility that I would go in the opposite direction past the stationary train – but in any event he was here now and only two or three stairs below me and since we were both hemmed in by the pack of people and I couldn't move any faster in the hope of getting away from him there was no real choice for me in this last hour of the mission when it was paramount, *absolutely paramount* that I should reach the objective and get him out, so I turned right round and let the weight of the crowd force me down against him and then I went for the one area that will kill without a cry and watched his eyes open very wide before I turned again and went on up the stairs, no excuses, this is the trade we're in and this is the way we ply it.

28

PANIC

I T TOOK ME almost an hour to find the right place.

Dark was down now but the streets were still crowded with snow-clearing gangs, and the floodlamps they were running from mobile generators cast a kind of sick daylight among the buildings. They'd brought the lamps in because someone had shoved his spade into a body buried under a drift: an old man had died from exposure and no one had seen him before the snow had covered his corpse.

This was the perfect place, a long alleyway with blank walls at each end, deep under snow but that didn't matter: what I needed was an isolation zone to make absolutely certain.

He hadn't dropped. He couldn't have dropped right away.

The other one must have been stopped by those militia – he hadn't caught up with me by the time I'd walked out of the Metro station. In the normal way I would have moved back to the safehouse without making more than a few visual checks from random cover to make sure I'd lost them, but there was no time to go anywhere now but to the rendezvous Ferris had for me; we were already ten minutes past the deadline at 2:10 pm. There'd been two or three chances to signal him on the way through the streets but I'd resisted them because the moment I telephoned him he would steer me to the rendezvous and it was the objective I was going to meet and I had to be absolutely certain I'd broken the Rinker surveillance.

I'd known he couldn't have dropped in a heap on the stairs

because it would have caused confusion and I would have heard it before I reached the street. I'd counted on that. The crowd on the stairs was so thick that it would have carried him with it on the way down and when he eventually hit the ground he would've been taken for just another drunk until somebody noticed the bluish area.

I do not care.

The alley was quiet after the clanging of the shovels and the drumming of the engines in the open street. Halfway along it I looked ahead and saw no one. I looked back and saw no one. Then I went on.

I tell you I do not care. He would have done the same if it had been necessary. It was his life or a dead mission and a lost summit, what the hell do you expect of me for Christ's sake?

But this was the hand.

The snow was so deep here that it reached almost to the top of the walls on each side. Even the dustbins were buried: I kept barging into them as I clambered my way through. I looked ahead again and saw no one. I looked back and saw no one. I'd broken their chain surveillance when I'd lost three of them in the Metro and from then on there'd been only two and one of them was on the slab now and that left only one, and even if he'd managed to satisfy the militiamen and follow me this far from the Metro he wouldn't have let me into this alley without taking up his position to keep me in sight, because I could climb over these walls if I wanted to and disappear altogether and he would know that. But he wasn't there.

This was the hand, yes, and that makes all the difference you see, it's so very personal, so very intimate, I mean they're not just beasts in the field reared for the slaughter-house any more than we are, they had a girl for the first time and played football and lived like other men until they felt the strange insidious affinity for the shadows, for the devious ways and the serpentine turns of the warren that runs in the dark below the surface of society where we finally choose to make our way through a different kind of life and to a different kind of death. He'd been one of us and this was the hand.

They'd been uneasy about this at Norfolk when I'd been put through my first psychological evaluation. *Until you can bring yourself to face this aspect of the work, Quiller, you'll be a danger to yourself and to those working with you.* Fowler, with his degree in abnormal psychology and his totally blank eyes and his frightened-looking wife. *During your mission it will occasionally be necessary to take life, and we shall expect you to do it only when the need is vital to the mission or to your own survival but with no hesitation, no compunction, no regret.* Fowler, with his cultivated penchant for the telling phrase. *During your missions you must learn to travel light, and leave your conscience behind.*

Another bloody dustbin, this one with the lid off and my foot breaking through something that felt like bones, some kind of carcass, perhaps a dead dog or perhaps only a figment of my own morbidity.

I looked ahead again and saw no one. I looked behind and saw no one. Then I went to find a telephone-box and call Ferris.

'I'm ready to meet the objective.'

Short silence.

'My salutations.' He didn't ask me if I were now certain of a secure environment; he knew I couldn't rendezvous with Zhigalin unless I could go there alone.

He also knew that I had broken a major surveillance chain in not much more than two hours because he'd pushed me to a deadline and it might have meant my taking what the Bureau officially refers to as extraordinary measures. It's sometimes possible for a local director to cover the resulting commotion in both the host country and in London, but we didn't have a consulate in Murmansk to put out a diplomatic smokescreen and London wouldn't make a fuss because the subject had been working for an opposition network: he hadn't been militia or KGB.

'One of them came too close,' I said.

'One of the Rinker people?'

'Yes.'

'And no one is looking for you?'

'Not in that connection. I was clear before anything was noticed.'

'Well done.'

A man of no conscience. Ferris is very sinister beneath the owlish looks and the silken tone. They say that when there's nothing on the telly he strangles mice.

'I'm halfway along the North Harbour Prospekt,' I told him.

'That's convenient.' There was a faint crackling sound on the line and I listened to it with extreme care.

'Ferris? Can you hear–'

'Just looking at a map.' In a moment he said: 'You're within a kilometre.'

That close to the objective.

A man was standing outside the phone kiosk.

'Go to Quay 9,' Ferris told me. 'That's near the end of North Harbour on the east side. There's a seagoing barge tied up there with the serial number K–104 on the bows. There's no security guard: it's waiting for dry dock maintenance.'

The man wasn't looking in at me through the dirty glass panel; he was looking along the street, shrugging himself into his fur coat against the freezing night. I didn't think he was a danger.

'The objective is there,' Ferris told me. 'He's expecting you, and the parole is *Potemkin.* Repeat.'

I went over the quay and the barge numbers and the parole.

'The timing is very critical,' he went on slowly, articulating with care. This was not only the most important briefing for the whole of *Northlight* but also the last, if things went well. 'There will be a dark blue Zhiguli van within sight of the barge and just north of it, facing the shoreline. A courier will be waiting at the wheel. The parole is the same. He will take you both to the airport.'

I looked through the glass at the skyline but it wasn't

possible to see how bad the fog was; since the full dark had come down the fog had been visible only in the floodlit areas. But this was why Ferris had been forced to give me a deadline: he was going to fly us out.

The man was peering into the kiosk now, getting impatient.

'At the airport, you'll be driven straight to a Beriev BE–12 twin-engined domestic aircraft with private markings, standing at the north end of runway Two. The pilot has flown for us twice before in the past five years and was found satisfactory. He is a mercenary. The parole is the same. Your flight time will depend on the weather conditions and on foxing the radar stations along the border, but we expect you to land in Hoybuktmoen, Norway, within roughly an hour from takeoff. I think that's all. Any questions?'

'*Christ,* you worked *fast.*'

'Fane set up most of it.'

Slight reaction in the stomach nerves.

'Have you checked everything thoroughly?'

There was a brief silence and I knew he wasn't going to answer that. 'All right, I know you did *but I don't trust that man.* He–'

'That's paranoia.'

I let the muscles go slack. Paranoia, yes, probably, but that bastard had taken on an execution for Croder and I didn't know where he was, he could be still in Murmansk. I was within a kilometre of the objective and we were triggered for the final run out *and it was Fane who'd set most of it up* and I didn't like it, I could feel the gooseflesh under the coarse sleeves of my coat as the skin shrank and stomach nerves went on crawling just as they'd crawled when I climbed into that van in Kandalaksha and sensed extinction.

'*Do you know what you're asking?*'

The man was rapping at the glass door now and peering in again and I mouthed at him that he was a fucking whoreson and he seemed quite surprised.

'I am asking you to understand,' Ferris was telling me on the line, 'that I came here at your request to get you out if I could. It wasn't convenient, but I came, and now I can in fact get you out, and I'm not going to allow mission-fatigue and a touch of paranoia to stop me. It hasn't occurred to you that you owe me your trust.'

Sweat running down my flanks, the bloody little organism shit-scared to make the final move, take the final chance, teetering on the brink with cold feet and a sickening stomach, typical bloody end-of-mission panic because the nerves had taken enough and they didn't want any more, they wanted peace.

Using Fane as an excuse.

Fane.

A twitch in the stomach nerves every time I thought of him, Pavlov's dog syndrome but this won't do.

He tried to get you killed.

Relax. Let the muscles go, they're in knots again.

Fane. He might still be–

Shuddup.

Fane might–

Shuddup.

Standing here in a bloody phone-box running with sweat and scared to try the final run because it might not work, it might leave me here in this stinking hole with my blood icing in the bullet holes because somewhere along the line that murderous bastard–

Fane–

Shuddup will you for Christ's sake this is just–

Relax. Sweat it out. Relax.

Slow down. Deeper breaths. Slow down.

Easy does it, so forth.

It's like coming up from dark water.

Have you ever panicked? There's only one way out, you've got to do it yourself and it's like coming up from the dark water. You'll know what I mean if it ever happens to you, you'll know.

Panic's a killer.

He hadn't said a thing. He was waiting. It hadn't been as long for him as for me because time slows down when the psyche gets pushed close to the edge of things.

'Do you think that's all it is? Paranoia?'

My voice sounded extraordinarily calm.

'Of course,' Ferris said.

'Sorry.'

'Don't worry, I've been waiting for it. As a matter of fact I was expecting it to happen sooner.'

Perfect handling. This was a model of perfect handling by a local director of an executive in the field suffering from a totally characteristic bout of mission-fatigue at the moment when he felt the final pressure coming on, at the moment when he longed so much to get out and go home that the thought of failing to do that was scaring the guts out of him. Ferris had known it had to come and he'd waited for it and simply held off and let me deal with it alone, which is the only way.

'God knows,' I told him, 'why I got you all the way from Tokyo.'

'Perversity. Any questions?'

'Only one. The objective's likely to be in an unpredictable state of mind. What do I do if he changes it suddenly and decides he ought to stay here in Mother Russia and face the music and all that?'

'Get him out.'

'Regardless?'

'Yes. Get him out.'

'Understood.'

'I shall be here at this number the whole time, until I get the signal that you're down safely in Norway.'

'Fair enough. See you in the Caff.'

I put the receiver on the hook and pushed the glass door open and nearly knocked the silly bastard over.

'I thought you were going to be in there all bloody night!'

'Bollocks.'

I reached the North Harbour soon after four o'clock, an hour and a half later. There were still checkpoints all over the place and I had to make a lot of detours through streets under deep snow, keeping away from the floodlit areas. No one followed me. A dark blue Volga saloon with the KGB insignia on the number plate had passed me twice when I'd had to leave cover and go through a main street but it looked like a routine patrol and I didn't let it worry me. The bout of eleventh-hour nerves was over, and as I walked through the ruts of the harbour road towards the final rendezvous I believed that whatever happened now, Ferris would get me out with the objective.

It was a black-painted hulk with snow thick on its decks and the mooring cables pulling at the rings to the movement of a swell rolling in from the sea. The dark blue Zhiguli van was standing against the wall of a wharf just north of the barge, and I went up to it and exchanged parole and countersign with the driver.

In the distance the headlights of the traffic swept the snow drifts and picked out the dark figures of the work gangs; I couldn't identify individual vehicles from here but some of them would be militia and KGB patrols. None of them turned along the quay in this direction.

It was 04:34 hours when I checked my watch and broke cover and walked across the packed snow to the barge and went aboard. The snow had been packed down between the landing-plank and the open hatch amidships by the passage of feet, and the outlines of boots had frozen into hard grey ice. I didn't call out because there was no need: the briefing had been perfectly clear and there should be only one man on board – the objective.

I went down the companion ladder into the pitch darkness and the acrid stench of coal, and when I reached solid planks I turned and looked for signs of life.

'*Freeze.*'

Light struck across my eyes and I put a hand up to shield them but all I could see in the glare was the blued steel of a gun.

'*Potemkin,*' I said.

'You are the Englishman?'

'Yes.'

The torch-beam was lowered and the gloved hand reversed the gun and handed it to me barrel-first. 'Captain Kirill Alekseyevich Zhigalin, Soviet Navy. I am at your command.'

'Clive Gage.'

I put the gun into my coat. It would have offended him if I'd thrown it into the scuppers.

'Can you understand my humiliation?' He gripped my arm, moving the torch higher to watch my face. 'The *dishonour?*'

'What? Yes of course, but we–'

'Did I fail them in my duty? Did I neglect–'

'Come on Zhigalin, get moving.' I took the torch from him and pushed him towards the companion ladder. 'There's an aircraft waiting for takeoff and the fog's closing in, do you understand?'

His boots clanged their way up the metal rungs. Bloody ideologists, all they could think about was their bloody honour. I switched off the torch and climbed after him to the deck. He was standing there looking across at the shore lights in the distance, a short man in a duffle coat with his hands by his sides as if he'd lost something.

'Here I was born,' he said softly, 'in this land.'

I had to jerk him into motion again and he went on telling me about the "primordial necessity" of mutual loyalty between a man and his country – Christ knows where he was educated but it sounded like a mail-order course. I got him to shut up because he had a voice that carried.

'Get into that van, Zhigalin, and don't talk. This town's crawling with KGB patrols and we're going to be lucky if we get through.' I slammed the rear door after him. 'If anything happens, leave it to me, is that clear?'

'I am at your command, comrade Gage.' An odd kind of whimpering started as I got into the front and shut the door. I think he was actually weeping.

'Airport?' the driver asked me.

'Yes. Have you been over the route?'

[273]

'Of course.' He sounded hurt. 'We're running late, do you know that?'

'Best I could do. What's your name?'

'Antonov.' That's what we all said.

'Are you carrying arms?'

He looked at me as we got into second gear along the frozen ruts. 'I have a gun. Why?'

'If there's any trouble. I don't want you to use it. If you get clear on your own that's your own business but all the time you're with me you don't even show your gun, now is that understood?'

'Whatever you say, Colonel.'

Ferris had given him my executive's operational ranking. 'All right, but don't call me that if we meet anyone.' I watched a pair of blue-tinted headlights turning along the quay from the shore road. 'How long will it take us to reach the aircraft?'

'Not long. Fifteen minutes.' He was staying in second gear; the ruts were sending the front wheels all over the place. The blue-tinted headlights swept across our windscreen and didn't dip. 'Whoreson,' the driver said and lowered the visor.

'Have you a military escort for me?' Zhigalin had stopped crying and was leaning with one hand on the seat-back.

'A *what?*'

'A military escort. That would be correct, and I have no objection.'

'All you've got as an escort to the West, old son, is a shagged-out ferret. Sorry about that.' I didn't expect him to understand but that wouldn't matter because the other vehicle was pulling across the quay right in front of us with its headlights still blazing and we slid to a stop to avoid hitting it.

Two uniformed figures got out and came up to the van with their guns drawn, one on each side and dragging the doors open.

'*KGB! Out! Out! Hands on your heads! Out!*'

29

DOLL

LIZ THREW THE KGB patrol car into reverse across the ruts and then sent it forward in a tight sliding turn to miss the van and straightened up, driving on dipped headlights now.

I could hear a siren somewhere.

Zhigalin had been forced into the front of the car and I was in the rear with the KGB sergeant. He was holding his gun at my head.

Liz got into third gear, sending the car in a series of zig-zags across the treacherous surface. She was in KGB uniform with major's insignia on the shoulders.

'Clive, can you deal with that man?' She said it in English.

Zhigalin sat in the front with his head turned to watch her, not understanding what she'd said.

There were more sirens now from the shore road, and headlights were swinging onto the quay towards us.

I had to take her on trust. There was no other way.

'Clive, you've got to see to that man. It's no good if you—'

There was only a marginal vector available because if I tried dragging the gun-hand downwards I risked taking the shot in the pelvis and if I knocked it aside it would send it in an arc across Liz and Zhigalin so I used a rising wedge-hand to send it straight upwards but there wasn't enough leverage and the first shot ploughed through my scalp and I had to work very fast and connect my left hand with his neck and even then I wasn't in time to stop a second shot smashing into the door pillar before I could impact with the baroreceptors in the carotid artery and shut down his nervous system. The gun dropped across my leg and I kicked it under the front seat and got the window down to clear the air before we started choking on the cordite fumes.

Liz threw a white-faced glance over her shoulder. *'Shit, he had two kids—'*

'He's not dead.'

The car lurched as the wheels lost traction across a patch of ice and the headlight beams swung across the stern of a fishing boat tied up at the quayside. A lot of militia patrol cars were coming past us from the shore road with their code lights flashing and their sirens on, one of them clipping our rear wing as it slewed across the ruts.

'Hit that window, Clive. I don't want anyone seeing in.'

I wound it shut and took a look at the sergeant. He was slumped over across his knees and I dragged him upright because I didn't want him to get the blood back into his brain too soon.

'What about my courier?' I asked Liz. 'The one in the blue van.'

She talked across her shoulder. 'I told him to get the hell out of here on foot if he could. I didn't want him along.'

'How did it happen,' I asked her, 'did they get Fane?' It was difficult to think logically with this amount of action going on but I needed to know things because I didn't want to go into this kind of situation without a rough idea of the score. And that was all that could have happened: somehow they must have got hold of Fane. He'd set up this rendezvous and handed the briefing to Ferris.

'Right.' Liz swung the car at ninety degrees onto the shore road, sending a white bow-wave up from a snow drift. 'They got your courier in the freight-yards in Kandalaksha and grilled him and he blew Fane.' She had to choke something out of her voice. 'It took four days.'

'When did they pick up Fane?'

'Last night when he was getting on a plane for Berlin in Leningrad. They started work on him right away. *Jesus*

Christ–' she was slapping the wheel with the flat of her hands–'*I didn't know it was going to be like this when I–*'

Someone else hit us and she swung the wheel and straightened up along the shore road. There weren't so many code lights flashing now and I jerked a look through the rear window and saw a whole line of patrol cars jockeying along the quay towards the barge. Fane must have held out until only minutes ago.

'Can we make the airport?' I asked Liz. There was some torn metal whining on a rear tyre where we'd just been hit.

'I'm going to try. There was no way you could've got there in that van – we're stopping everything that moves.' She tugged the radiophone off the clip and began talking in fluent Russian. *'This is Major Benedixsen. I have Captain Zhigalin under arrest and I'm proceeding straight to headquarters with him. There is no need for further action. I repeat: I have Captain Zhigalin with me now under close arrest.'*

Zhigalin jerked a look at me across the seat-back.

'Everything's under control,' I told him. 'Don't do anything stupid.' I looked at the nervy green eyes in the driving mirror. 'Liz, how long have you been doubling for the CIA?'

Her eyes flicked upwards to watch mine, and she gave a strange little laugh. 'I've been doubling three years, but not for the CIA. I'm KGB. A defector from the militarist West. I'm working for peace, Clive, and right now the only chance of getting it is the Vienna summit. We've got to make it happen, and this man is the key. You've got to take him across.'

The front wheels hit something in the snow and sent us into a wild slide against a lamp standard before Liz got traction again. The KGB sergeant started moaning and I flicked his earlobe and got his eyes open and said, 'If you make any kind of move I'm going to blow your head off.' I looked back at the mirror but Liz was concentrating on the road again. *Only if we are seen as a fellow nation, with worth to offer the world, with goods to trade, with ideas to exchange and with the future to share on an equal footing, can it also be seen that we are ready to go to the conference tables and join with others in drawing the world back from the abyss of war and mutual annihilation that lies in our path.*

I had seen, in that hotel room, that she'd believed in this, but I didn't realize till now that she'd actually written that pamphlet and slipped it under my door.

'Did Fane give your people the whole set-up?' I asked her.

'No. Just the rendezvous. I got it over the radio twenty minutes back when I was still trying to locate you and get you out.'

And then — oh God, this is going to sound so corny — after two pointless marriages I realized I wanted to spend my life with something much more than a man. I wanted to marry a cause.

She switched on her code lights and got the siren going through the next intersection because a work gang had got half the street closed off. 'Which runway is it, Clive?'

'Runway Two, north end.' I could see the airport tower lights through the haze; then they swung out of sight as we turned into a side street and accelerated past a checkpoint with our codes still flashing. 'Clive,' she called over her shoulder, 'we're still not through yet. They're still working on Fane and if he blows the airport set-up that's going to be it, you know that?'

'Yes.'

'If that happens I'll hear it over the radio but they'll close in right away and from that time on you'll be on your own, okay? There won't be anything more I can do.'

'Understood.' The torn wing was screaming on the tyre again and if it burned through the wall we'd have a blow-out. 'If you can pull up for a minute I'll see to that noise.'

'I can't stop, Clive, we've got to chance it.'

We swung into the airport boulevard and the tyre stopped screaming as the weight shifted on the turn. The sergeant half-fell against me and I pushed him back. 'Remember, you'll get your brains blown out if you try anything.' The gun was under the seat and if he tried to reach it he wouldn't make any progress.

Voices were coming through faintly on the radio and Liz turned the volume up as headlights swung across our bows as we went through the airport gates with the figure of a guard jumping out of the way. Another siren had started up somewhere.

We have a report that Captain Zhigalin has been seized and is under arrest . . . a lot of static as we passed a stationary diesel outside a hangar . . . *confirm the order to call off further action.* . . . Then another voice cut in. *Major Benedixsen, will you repeat your signal that you have* . . . *under arrest and are proceeding* . . . *headquarters.*

She picked up the mike and responded. The windscreen was misting up and she wound her window down; the freezing night air cut against our faces as we gunned up along a taxiway road that had just been cleared of snow.

The radio came in again.

We have a report that an aircraft waiting for permission to take off on runway number two will attempt to cross the frontier into Norway. Patrols in this area will converge immediately . . . The static got very bad and we lost him for five or six seconds. . . . *Twin-engined Beriev civilian machine and the pilot is alone on board. He is to be seized immediately.*

Fane had broken.

The airport authorities are to ensure that this aircraft does not take off.

Somewhere, under a bright light and with the tang of fresh blood on the air, Fane had broken.

The night was filled with sound as sirens began fading in and merged with the whine of jet engines as an aircraft turned into the north end of the runway and a red lamp began flashing from the control tower.

'*Clive, I'm going for it.*'

But the pilot was already listening to the tower's instructions not to take off and he'd know he was blown. We were late for the rendezvous and he wouldn't wait any longer: this side of the frontier he'd be for the firing squad and the frontier was only thirty minutes' flight. *And he'd been briefed to expect a dark blue van.*

I leaned forward. 'Liz, do you know Morse?'

'Sure.'

'Switch off your codes and use your headlights. Spell out *Potemkin*.'

'Like the battleship?'

'Yes.'

She began working the switch. Sand was flying up from the tyres and crackling under the wings. A siren was coming in strongly now and a wash of headlights was filling the car from behind us; then the tyre burst and Liz brought the wheel hard over to counteract the shift in balance, one hand still hitting the headlight switch in a series of jabs. There was no answering light from the aircraft.

'*Clive, are you ready?*'

'*Yes.*'

She used the brakes and we went into a full-circle spin as the burst tyre was wrenched off the wheel and we finished broadside on to the aircraft with the doors wrenching open as Zhigalin dropped on to the snow and began running.

'*Go for it, Clive. Go for it.*'

There was ice and I slipped and went down and got up again and went after the Russian as the door of the Beriev came open and a man stood there with a gun raised in the aiming position and it was then that I began yelling the one word, the one name, *Potemkin* ... *Potemkin* ... until the pilot holstered his gun and crouched at the top of the ladder to grab Zhigalin and haul him inside as I got there and started climbing. The aircraft was lit with the dazzle of the militia and KGB cars as they came crowding in from the perimeter track with their code lights flashing and their sirens wailing and the first shot sounding, a thin crack in the medley of louder sounds as the pilot gunned up and let the brakes off with the red lamp still flashing from the tower.

Another shot came as we started rolling but when I looked out of a window I saw it wasn't for us: the leading patrol cars were sliding to a halt with the doors swinging open and I saw Liz fire again at the KGB sergeant as he tried to go for her. Even as he went down she was turning her gun on the uniformed figures spilling out of the cars and running for the plane with their hands at their holsters until one of them turned and took aim and fired and Liz was rocked back, a small doll-like figure in her grey belted uniform and sable hat with one arm flung into the air before she crumpled and went down onto the snow.

The twin jets screamed on full power for takeoff and drowned out the radio as the pilot put the Beriev down the runway with the red lights still flashing him from the tower. All I could see of him in the glow from the instrument panel was a dark hook-nosed face under a balaclava and one hand steady on the control column. Zhigalin was slumped against the pilot's locker with his head back and his eyes shut.

'Were you hit?'

He answered but I couldn't hear what he said in the screaming of the jets so I went to him and asked him again and he opened his eyes. 'No. I was not hit.' I suppose he was pining for his bloody motherland again.

'You're doing the right thing,' I told him.

'I'm doing the *only* thing.'

Then the runway lights went out and the pilot cursed the tower and I didn't see how he was going to get this thing off the ground because all the headlights showed was a waste of snow with the runway lost in a kaleidoscopic pattern of ruts and drifts and sand without enough definition to keep a straight course and I waited for him to take the power off and slow under the brakes but he wasn't doing that – he was still accelerating because either we were already past the point of rotation and couldn't stay on the ground without smashing into the solid snow-banks south of the airport or all he could see through the windscreen was a firing squad and the only alternative to that was to get airborne if he could.

We were already off the runway because we hit something and the whole plane shuddered and the pilot cursed again and brought the control column back and put a hand out to the undercarriage switch as we nosed up and the rumbling of the wheels died away.

'What happened?' Zhigalin had been flung forward against

the pilot's seat and tried to get up but he had his foot caught in some harness.

'We lost the nose-wheel,' I told him. It had sounded like that. Then the pilot began yelling obscenities as a red flock of tracer bullets came curving up at us and he banked sharply and brought a box of flares off its wall-bracket and scattered them all over Zhigalin.

'Then we won't be able to land,' he told me, 'if the nose-wheel is gone.'

'We'll flop down on the belly.'

'Not if the nose-wheel is damaged. He won't be able to retract it.'

Perfectly right but he wasn't thinking terribly straight because if these tracers found their target we wouldn't need to worry about how to make a landing. Something hit the rear end of the fuselage and I lurched my way back there but couldn't see what had happened unless a bullet had gone clean through. I went back to the cockpit and Zhigalin caught my arm, staring into my face.

'I regret, of course, the death of the submariners. But I had no choice. They were the enemy and they were in our waters.'

Oh Jesus Christ. I like a man to have a conscience but not if he spends the entire time sitting on the pot with it.

I leaned over the pilot.

'Where are you heading?'

He glanced up. *'Why were you so fucking late?'*

'The alarm clock didn't go off.' Some people can't take a little disappointment but I knew what he felt like because this was our last ride by the look of things and I'd got beyond the point of worrying whether we had any hope of getting the objective across and saving the Vienna summit because we were going to finish up like roast pig if one of those tracers hit a fuel tank. 'Are you still going to make the frontier?'

'I'm going to try.'

'What are the chances?'

'We have to get through whatever flak they send up, and they'll be sending up a lot, but we could make it with some luck. But we have to fly close to Pechenga and if they send up a pursuit plane they'll just blow us out of the sky.'

We were heading north-west on the compass and if we turned south even by ten degrees we'd be increasing the distance to the frontier and if we turned north there'd just be ice-floes.

The radio was now audible again with the jets running at altitude but there was a lot of static and we couldn't pick much out and the pilot wasn't answering ... *Warned that in the ... will be attacked and brought....*

The aircraft shuddered again as a brace of tracers made a hit somewhere amidships in close succession and Zhigalin got to his feet and went aft to see what the damage was, dropping something on the floor. I picked it up: it was some kind of ikon he'd been fussing with, that's all very well and you can carry a rabbit's foot with you but don't forget it didn't do the rabbit any good.

Smoke was clouding forward and I saw Zhigalin unclip a fire extinguisher and start pumping it. There was another one on the bulkhead and I broke it out of the clip and went aft with it. It looked as if a tracer had lodged into one of the seats and all we had to deal with was a slow-burn fire. Zhigalin was doing well enough and I went forward again and told the pilot what was happening, but he didn't answer because his head was angled to listen to the radio.

... Repeat that two military machines are now airborne ... forced ... are waiting your response ... a lot of static again ... airborne and moving into an interception course....

'They're up from Pechenga,' the pilot said. 'What's that fire back there?'

'It's under control. So what are our chances now?'

'We don't have any if they attack with an air-to-air missile or even cannon-fire. I'm going north – there's nowhere else.'

'To the sea?'

'There is nowhere else.' He hit a ventilator open to clear the smoke. 'If we make the coast there's a chance of turning west again across Norwegian waters.'

... And upon interception the order will ... we urge you to

respond to this signal. The order will be to attack you without further warning. . . .

I could hear Zhigalin coughing his heart up in the rear of the cabin but there was no flamelight through the smoke. I went into the lavatory and soaked my handkerchief and held it over my face and went back to the cockpit as the pilot put the Beriev into a tight turn for the north.

It was no good at the coast.

The first shot had ripped the skin of the fuselage shell within a foot of where Zhigalin was crouched with his ikon and the air was screaming through the gap and he stumbled past me with his face white but I didn't know where he thought he was going because one of the pursuit planes had us in it's sights and all we were waiting for now was a clean hit from a cannon or an air-to-air missile and we couldn't avoid it.

I leaned over the pilot. 'Is there anything down there we could land on with the nose-wheel gone?'

'Rocks and ice-floes and the sea, yes.'

'Could we–'

Then they hit us with something big and the impact flung me across the cabin and I heard Zhigalin screaming but couldn't see him anywhere because of the smoke. We were angled nose-down in a steep dive and I tried to get off the floor and see if I could find out what had happened to him but the angle was something like forty-five degrees and I couldn't make any headway. Another one hit us and the aircraft shivered to the impact and a lot of stuff came out of the lockers and crashed across the cabin and came crashing back as we went into a tight spiral turn with the nose down and the pilot shouting something I couldn't understand. A fire had started in the rear end of the fuselage and the flames spread, fanned by the air rushing through the ripped shell, and I made another effort to climb aft up the sloping floor to get at an extinguisher and find Zhigalin and drag him back to the cockpit if I could but it was strictly no go because the

[284]

angle was too steep and we were still locked in a lowering spiral and the pilot was shouting again but his voice was half lost in the roaring of the air-rush. All I could do was heave myself round to face the cockpit in case there was anything to see through the windscreen but it was blacked out with the reflection of the pilot's white face in the glow from the instrument panel until bits of something pale began showing up ahead of us across the windscreen and forming a mottled pattern that swirled as we spiralled lower and suddenly flattened as the pilot got the control-column back in a last attempt to put us down on the belly but it didn't work because we were over the sea and black water rose in a wall as we made impact.

30

BROTHER

THE SKELETON DANCED to the tolling of the bell, its bones clinking and its bright eye winking through the dark.

The great steel clamp of the cold crushed my skull.

Smell of blood, fresh blood.

I dropped and screamed and fetched up sharp and opened my eyes and there was the bottomless pit, the vastness of night.

'*What?*'

He was watching me.

'Nothing. I didn't say anything.'

It hadn't been a scream at all, just fright in my throat because in the dream I'd been falling forever.

'Have to keep moving,' Zhigalin said.

'What?'

'Because of the cold.'

'Yes.' I tried to stand up but all we had between us and the cold black water was a rubber raft and you couldn't stand up in it without pitching over the side.

The ice-floes clinked together, making the sound of bones. The one light winked and went out again.

'What light is that?'

'I don't know,' he said.

'*You don't know?*' He should know this coast, he'd sent a hundred men to their death in these waters.

'Perhaps the shore,' he said. I supposed he was ashamed at not knowing what light it was.

The bell tolled with a funeral sound, and I began counting the chimes. The ice bobbed on the water, bringing the skeleton back into my mind, its cackling laughter. Danger there, I knew, but there was nothing to do about it.

Wake up.

There's nothing I—

Wake up.

My eyes came open and found him staring at me.

'*Zhigalin.*'

'Yes?'

'Are you all right?'

'I have no idea.'

The man must be a bloody fool. I shifted my numbed body closer to him and the smell of blood became suddenly raw on the air. I found the torch and switched it on, keeping it low because we didn't want to attract attention. God knew where the plane was, or the pilot. The hunt had moved away hours ago, or we'd been drifting out of sight.

I shielded the torch with my hand.

His leg was half off.

'You caught a bullet,' I told him.

'Rather more than that.'

'I'm going to make a tourniquet.'

I opened my coat and began tearing my shirt at the sleeve. 'Don't move,' I said. It produced an odd spasm of laughter from him.

'Where would I go?'

'Try to think what light that is. I want to know.'

'I think it is the shore.'

'How far away?'

'Perhaps half a kilometre.'

'That close?'

'The fog is thick.'

'Are we drifting?'

'Oh, yes.'

'Which way?'

'To the east, if that is the shore.'

'If that isn't a light on the shore, what would it be?'

I got the sleeve free and twisted it into a cord.

'There are two lighthouses here, at the border. It could be one of them.'

'If we're drifting to the west, we could get picked up.'

'I think we are drifting to the east.'

Another light was moving in the haze, but I couldn't hear the sound of an engine. There was still a degree of after-shock in the organism and the cold was numbing the tissues. It was difficult to know whether we were seeing a light or hallucinating.

I felt for the pressure point in his femoral artery and wrapped the sleeve round the thigh, pulling it tight. He didn't seem to feel anything. We were being slowly frozen alive.

'I gave you my gun,' he said.

'Yes.'

'If they find us while we are still alive, I ask that you will shoot me with my gun.'

'The sea could turn. We could drift the other way, to the west.'

'You still have the gun?'

I could feel it in my coat. 'Yes.'

'Please grant my last request. I wish to avoid the humiliation of an enquiry. They would send me to be shot. I prefer you to do it, as an act of brotherhood.'

In a moment I said, 'Very well. I'll do what you ask, if they pick us up alive.'

Easy enough to say. In the open sea and with these tempera-tures we were going to last another hour at most, if his loss of blood didn't stop the heart before that.

I started tearing at the other sleeve because one wouldn't be enough. Brotherhood. Odd word, but I knew what he meant. You meet interesting people in this trade, and it's when you're in a position to save a life or get your own saved that you know who your friends are. Your brothers.

Her arm thrown up like that in a kind of farewell salute before she'd gone down in the snow, another of those bloody ideologists, when you looked at it, *and finally I discovered, out of anger I guess, a sense of direction, a conviction that there was something I had to do. And I've been doing it ever since, Clive, in my own way, hurling myself at the barricades while everyone else is busy making a detour and maybe getting home sooner. But the barricades are still there, and until I can bring them down. . . .*

Another of those bloody ideologists, but I would wish once more to look into the glistening green of her eyes and feel against this numbed flesh the warmth of the earth mother. *Hi, I'm Liz Benedixsen.* Standing there with her brave little pistol, banging away with it in the name of peace on earth. Saved our lives, at least for a while. Got us airborne. You know where your friends are when it comes to the crunch.

Zhigalin moaned this time as I pulled the second sleeve tighter, kicking with his other leg and opening his mouth and letting the pain out, singing across the dark water as my stomach shrank and I pulled the sleeve tighter again and his song broke to a shriek while the skeleton cackled, clinking its bones.

'Over now,' I told him, and the moaning died in his throat. After a long time he said something.

'What?' I asked him.

'Thank you.'

The light was still moving over there, going in circles, some kind of patrol. I could hear an engine now.

'Zhigalin, what boat's that?' He should know these waters.

'Soviet, since we are drifting east.'

'But if you don't know what that light is, the other one, we could be drifting west, couldn't we?'

'We will hear their voices, when they see us. Then we shall know. But please take my gun. You agreed to do that.'

It's not often, I dare say, that the executive has to kill off the objective at the end of a mission.

He wants Zhigalin taken across, at all costs.

Fane. Finished now. Dead or a madman.

Poor old Croder.

And is that all you know?

That was the last we heard, sir. Ferris got them onto a plane but it went down into the sea.

The red bulb would go out, over the board for *Northlight*.

That's all you know, yes, and all you'll ever know.

The light was sweeping in a circle, and I moved closer to Zhigalin, the idiot ideologist, my brother of the Arctic night. The light's beam cut the sea from the sky, swinging towards us and throwing a back glare against the huge shape of the boat. It was almost on us. I put the gun against my brother's head.

The light hit us like a blow, blinding us, and swung back, steadying. A voice came over a loudhailer.

'Hvem er de?'

Zhigalin touched my wrist. 'Not Soviet,' he said. 'Not Soviet.'

'Dreie til og berede de at redde!'

'No,' I said, 'Norwegian,' and lowered the gun.

STAR BOOKS BESTSELLERS

FICTION

SHATTER	John Farris	£1.50*
REVENGE OF MORIARTY	John Gardner	£2.25
GOLGOTHA	John Gardner	£1.95
BACK OF THE TIGER	Jack Gerson	£1.95
SPECTRE OF MARALINGA	Michael Hughes	£1.95
DEBT OF HONOUR	Adam Kennedy	£1.95
DEATH MAIL	Peter Leslie	£1.95
CONDOR	Thomas Luke	£2.50*
AIRSHIP	Peter MaCalan	£2.50
IKON	Graham Masterton	£2.50*
HAWL	James Peacock	£1.95
DOG SOLDIERS	Robert Stone	£1.95

STAR Books are obtainable from many booksellers and newsagents. If you have any difficulty tick the titles you want and fill in the form below.

Name _____

Address _____

_____

Send to: Star Books Cash Sales, P.O. Box 11, Falmouth, Cornwall, TR10 9EN.

Please send a cheque or postal order to the value of the cover price plus:
UK: 55p for the first book, 22p for the second book and 14p for each additional book ordered to the maximum charge of £1.75.

BFPO and EIRE: 55p for the first book, 22p for the second book, 14p per copy for the next 7 books, thereafter 8p per book.

OVERSEAS: £1.00 for the first book and 25p per copy for each additional book.

While every effort is made to keep prices low, it is sometimes necessary to increase prices at short notice. Star Books reserve the right to show new retail prices on covers which may differ from those advertised in the text or elsewhere.

*NOT FOR SALE IN CANADA

STAR BOOKS BESTSELLERS

FICTION

VOICE OF THE NIGHT	D.R. Koontz	£2.25*
DARKNESS COMES	D.R. Koontz	£2.50*
WHISPERS	D.R. Koontz	£2.25*
NIGHT CHILLS	D.R. Koontz	£2.60*
SHATTERED	D.R. Koontz	£1.80*
PHANTOMS	D.R. Koontz	£1.95*
CHASE	D.R. Koontz	£1.95*
POST OFFICE	Charles Bukowski	£1.80*
DANCEHALL	Bernard F. Conners	£2.25*
GOLD COAST	Elmore Leonard	£1.95*
SPLIT IMAGES	Elmore Leonard	£1.95*
ALL OR NOTHING	Stephen Longstreet	£2.50*
THE BODY	Richard Ben Sapir	£2.50*
HEADHUNTER	Michael Slade	£2.75*
THE LONG AFTERNOON	Ursula Zilinsky	£2.75*
BIRTHRIGHT	Colin Sharp	£1.95*

STAR Books are obtainable from many booksellers and newsagents. If you have any difficulty tick the titles you want and fill in the form below.

Name _____

Address _____

_____

Send to: Star Books Cash Sales, P.O. Box 11, Falmouth, Cornwall, TR10 9EN.

Please send a cheque or postal order to the value of the cover price plus:
UK: 55p for the first book, 22p for the second book and 14p for each additional book ordered to the maximum charge of £1.75.

BFPO and EIRE: 55p for the first book, 22p for the second book, 14p per copy for the next 7 books, thereafter 8p per book.

OVERSEAS: £1.00 for the first book and 25p per copy for each additional book.

While every effort is made to keep prices low, it is sometimes necessary to increase prices at short notice. Star Books reserve the right to show new retail prices on covers which may differ from those advertised in the text or elsewhere.

*NOT FOR SALE IN CANADA

STAR BOOKS BESTSELLERS

FICTION

THE PAINTED LADY	Francoise Sagan	£2.25*
THE STILL STORM	Francoise Sagan	£1.95*
THE UNMADE BED	Francoise Sagan	£1.95*
INCIDENTAL MUSIC	Francoise Sagan	£2.00*
TRADE OFFS	Jane Adams	£2.50*
GARLAND OF WAR	Tessa Barclay	£1.95
A SOWER WENT FORTH	Tessa Barclay	£2.25
THE STONY PLACES	Tessa Barclay	£2.25
HARVEST OF THORNS	Tessa Barclay	£2.25
THE GOOD GROUND	Tessa Barclay	£1.95
THE BREADWINNER	Tessa Barclay	£1.95
SOUTHERN WOMEN	Lois Battle	£2.95
WAR BRIDES	Lois Battle	£2.75
A DARKLING MOON	Ashley Carter	£2.50*
THE OUTLANDERS	Ashley Carter	£2.50*

STAR Books are obtainable from many booksellers and newsagents. If you have any difficulty tick the titles you want and fill in the form below.

Name _____

Address _____

_____

Send to: Star Books Cash Sales, P.O. Box 11, Falmouth, Cornwall, TR10 9EN.

Please send a cheque or postal order to the value of the cover price plus:
UK: 55p for the first book, 22p for the second book and 14p for each additional book ordered to the maximum charge of £1.75.

BFPO and EIRE: 55p for the first book, 22p for the second book, 14p per copy for the next 7 books, thereafter 8p per book.

OVERSEAS: £1.00 for the first book and 25p per copy for each additional book.

While every effort is made to keep prices low, it is sometimes necessary to increase prices at short notice. Star Books reserve the right to show new retail prices on covers which may differ from those advertised in the text or elsewhere.

*NOT FOR SALE IN CANADA

STAR BOOKS BESTSELLERS

FICTION

EMBRACE THE WIND	Ashley Carter	£2.25*
AGAINST ALL GODS	Ashley Carter	£1.95*
THE OFFICERS WIVES	Thomas Fleming	£3.25*
DREAMS OF GLORY	Thomas Fleming	£2.50*
THE CARDINAL SINS	Andrew M. Greeley	£1.95*
THY BROTHERS WIFE	Andrew M. Greeley	£1.95*
LORD OF THE DANCE	Andrew M. Greeley	£2.50*
DEAR STRANGER	Catherine Kidwell	£1.95*
DAYS OF ETERNITY	Gordon Glasco	£2.50*
THE GARMENT	Catherine Cookson	£1.60
HANNAH MASSEY	Catherine Cookson	£1.95
SLINKY JANE	Catherine Cookson	£1.60
LETS KEEP IN TOUCH	Elaine Bissell	£2.50
FALCON CREST	Patrick Mann	£2.25

STAR Books are obtainable from many booksellers and newsagents. If you have any difficulty tick the titles you want and fill in the form below.

Name _____

Address _____

_____

Send to: Star Books Cash Sales, P.O. Box 11, Falmouth, Cornwall, TR10 9EN.

Please send a cheque or postal order to the value of the cover price plus:
UK: 55p for the first book, 22p for the second book and 14p for each additional book ordered to the maximum charge of £1.75.

BFPO and EIRE: 55p for the first book, 22p for the second book, 14p per copy for the next 7 books, thereafter 8p per book.

OVERSEAS: £1.00 for the first book and 25p per copy for each additional book.

While every effort is made to keep prices low, it is sometimes necessary to increase prices at short notice. Star Books reserve the right to show new retail prices on covers which may differ from those advertised in the text or elsewhere.

*NOT FOR SALE IN CANADA